CHOICES

Mary Lee Settle

CHOICES

Published in Large Print by arrangement with
Doubleday, a division of Bantam Doubleday Dell
Publishing Group, Inc.
in the United States and Canada.

Wheeler Large Print Book Series.

Set in 16 pt. Plantin.

Library of Congress Cataloging-in-Publication Data

Settle, Mary Lee.
Choices / Mary Lee Settle.
p. cm.—(Wheeler large print book series)
ISBN 1-56895-266-X (Hardcover)
1. Women social reformers—Southern States—Fiction.
2. Americans—Europe—Fiction. 3. Large type books.
I. Title. II. Series.
[PS3569.E84C477 1995b]
813'.54—dc20 95-42764
CIP

To Southern liberals, past and present,
wherever they may be

Prologue

Italy • April 10, 1993

A Cage of Bone

From weight of flesh and cage of bone
It was I who was set free,
And that other me like a blown weed
Was scattered by the wind.
—"Salome," GEORGE GARRETT

All afternoon Melinda had been wishing she might die in English instead of Italian. She wanted it to happen while Aiken and Maria were there. It was time. She was eighty-two, and frankly, she was tired of their looking troubled when they thought she wasn't noticing. She didn't want them to have to come all the way back to Italy when they were so busy. Except for Tye, there were no two people she loved more or ever had. Her children. Legally.

So almost at the end of one of the bloodiest centuries in history, she sat on her terrace high up a hillside on the island of Santa Corsara, watching the sun glance off the Tyrrhenian Sea, the sea of the Etruscans, off the west coast of Italy. All day the sun had slipped in and out of racing clouds that had brought rain in torrents. It was April, not cruel for her, just violent and childish, if she wanted to think that way.

Tye had teased her about that kind of thinking. He preferred words like "barometric pressure." Melinda smiled at where he always used to sit, over by one of the *putti*. She could almost see the weight of the world lift off his shoulders and fly into the wind. They had had nearly ten years together on the island but even afterward, when she came back, he was always there for her, in the green room, on the terrace, his long body folded down among the roses he loved so. Sometimes when she thought of him, or sensed him near her, she entered an almost unbearable tenderness that had stayed with her always. Tye was a place where everything came together.

She moved with Tye into silence. Down below her, on the stone bench that had been Roger's lookout to sea, the sun touched Maria's white hair; light glanced on the strong dark planes of Aiken's face. Melinda could still feel Maria's cold little hand in hers, when Maria was six, her thick pudding bowl of jet-black hair almost over her huge dark eyes, too large for her small face. She could still see Aiken at eighteen. She and Aiken had danced, when she was fifty-three and he was only eighteen; they danced to Motown, and talked. Aiken was a lithe wild chestnut-colored colt of a boy, with his Afro and his language of dissent and the way he moved his body—a challenge.

Sometimes Melinda felt that her own body was a whole history of dancing. She had always loved it, from the two-step when she was little in the kitchen, to the shimmy and the Charleston, to the dips and whirls, the Ginger and Fred, the Viennese waltz, the palais glide, the boogie, the shag. She hadn't missed any of them, and she could feel them still in her body, her silly body that had grown old and wrinkled and pink as an apple, with stubborn swollen feet that had minds of their own about what they would and would not do.

She thought, Everybody is tiptoeing around everybody else and they don't know I'm dancing. After all, when you are eighty-two, why not? Whirl, dip, Motown; it's only dying, as Tye would have said, not working anymore, like an old watch. It didn't even have the name that Maria kept demanding of Melinda's Italian doctor, as if to give it a name would somehow make it less inevitable. Maria refused to admit that the name was Age. Aiken kept looking at her as if she were going to blow away.

Aiken had turned into a big, solid, handsome man, his body serious, substantial, successful, uxorious—Roger's word, which always made her smile. There was still an echo of Motown left, though. Maria, at sixty, had never lost the sense of discovery that she had had since she was a child.

All the way from the hill beyond them, away in the distance as far as Melinda could see, were acres of olive trees, with misty gray-green spring leaves that took her back to Spain. Tye's roses scented the terrace when the wind was off the sea.

Melinda sat on the wicker chaise longue in the shade of the roof, with her legs out in the sun and her feet bare and an old shoebox from Delman's in her lap, piled with a polyglot of papers, keys, ribbons, pins, medals. Oh, Lord, she asked herself, why in the world have I kept this, any of it? She picked at the key chain with old keys from all the cars she had had, and she thought, My life in one shoebox. That's the way it ought to be, nothing much left over. She smiled.

She leaned back and she was comfortable, and, still smiling—well, grinning, as she did sometimes—she thought, They say you lose your memory when you get to be over eighty. You don't lose memory. You find it, like this shoebox left over from when my father bought me the gold shoes with the high heels across the street from the Plaza. He prided himself that he'd do anything on God's green earth for me. I had fifty-three pairs of shoes. She remembered looking at herself in the window of Bergdorf's and thinking she was the cat's pajamas, the bee's knees.

The way she looked over sixty years later amused and pleased her more. She was wearing a purple T-shirt that said Oklahoma was Indian territory, a blue cotton hat pulled like a cloche around her face because of the afternoon sun. The hat had red words, the friendly islands, on it. She had bought the red shorts at K-mart on her last visit to Aiken and Luella in Atlanta. That was the trip when a supreme white man had made the crack about her, a white woman, being with Aiken and Luella's children, and she shut him up, then and there. "They are my grandchildren," she said, and marched away with all of them, laughing. They had all learned to laugh instead of cry at things like that.

At eight o'clock in the morning, when Melinda had staggered into the kitchen, Maria was already drinking the hell-black Italian coffee they both loved. She looked up and said, "Good God, where did you find that outfit, and what are you doing up?"

"Second answer first—I'm up because I'm better. The swim last night did me good, and it's a nice day and I'm dressed like this because I got too hot yesterday so I rummaged around. Give me some coffee."

"You look disgraceful," Maria told her. She laughed, smelling of coffee, and got up to pour Melinda a cup.

"I'm growing old disgracefully," Melinda said. "Besides, I'm mad and that makes me feel better."

"Mad?" Maria had that look that she had never shed, as if she suspected that she had done something wrong—the look of a caught child.

"I have been in two wars and gone all over the world, ridden a camel, dived in the ocean, crawled into caves, married two times, and I wasted the night on a stupid dream about whether or not I was going to be invited to some party in the West End of Richmond. I could have been with Tye. I am a lot, you know," she said to Maria over the rim of her coffee cup. She had told Maria that for years.

"Sometimes we are together in walking-along-the-street dreams, sometimes he gives me good advice. Sometimes I tell him things." And sometimes, she told herself, between sleeping and waking I feel the touch of his sweater against my cheek or his hand on my shoulder. We did become one flesh. Once, when I was diving, I thought, This is what it is like for us, deep, inevitable. No wonder it only happens once, the love of one's life. I couldn't have stood it more than once.

"Do you ever dream about Roger that way?" Maria picked up the *Herald-Tribune* she had brought the day before and began to read it.

"No. What was it you used to say? He is in my mind but not in my dreams."

Maria looked up from her paper. "Poor Roger."

"No. Not ever poor Roger. You know, the only thing I never got used to was that he hadn't shared our past—not Spain, not England. He was all new. I guess that had its pleasures. I wish you had both known him better, but you were grown and there wasn't much time."

Melinda held her big coffee, warming memory and her hands. Roger had come in 1970, when she thought she was going to be alone for the rest of her life. She was fifty-nine and he was sixty-five, tall and skinny, the kind of man she had been comfortable with all her life. A Southerner, too, who wasn't a bigot. She knew she was going to tell what she had told so often before, especially since Roger had died, but she didn't care. If Maria didn't want to hear it, she did. It comforted her. They thought she didn't remember that she had told them things before, but that wasn't true. She wanted to hear them again, like a favorite story.

"I'll never forget the first time I saw him," she told the hot black coffee. "He was bending down, tying up his beautiful boat to my buoy in the harbor, and I said, 'What are you doing?' and he said, the first thing I ever heard him say, 'I just said to hell with it.' I thought he was talking about the buoy, but he wasn't. He was talking about his whole life."

Maria was deep into the editorial page of the *Herald-Tribune.* Melinda went on, telling the wall of newspaper, "I swear he didn't stop talking after that until he had told me everything he thought was important, as if he hadn't talked for a long time. He hadn't. He had been sailing the Med, from island to island, picking up a one-man crew wherever he stopped and then paying their way back to their islands.

"I wasn't ever in love with Roger," she explained to the paper. "I was more in like with him. He needed somebody to do for, and I needed somebody to nudge. He told me that he had done for people all his life. He did right for his father when he became the architect his father wanted him to, for his mother when he lived at home and took her places when his father was too busy or off hunting, then his wife, whom he had loved since he was a little boy—the girl of his dreams, he called her. He had done all the things you are raised to do right, and then one day he sat on the bank of the James River and there was nobody to do for. They were all gone—his father, his mother, his wife. It was a month after he buried her. His son was a stockbroker in New York, a damned Republican who wore Guccis without socks.

"He said he sat there shivering with fear, sweating bullets, and then, he said, it all lifted, and he realized that for the first time he could do exactly what he wanted to. He never complained. He said he had loved doing for all of them all his life. He wasn't ever a bitter man. But now he was going to do for himself, an aging Huck Finn—buy a boat, follow a hobby, play. That's how he fetched up here. He just stayed. It was a miracle for me. It was a marriage like a smuggler's boat that could go anywhere, shallow draft and light.

"We just went to Rome and got married in the Protestant church there, and came on home. Used to each other, that's important. Used to . . . I felt like he had been around forever, but of course he hadn't. That's why you never really knew him. When he died I was sorry, as if somebody who had been company for a long time had decided to leave. No, it wasn't like Tye, Maria, not like Tye at all—something else, lagniappe."

She thought she might have been asleep for a minute, there on the terrace. The wind had lifted and caressed her hair, and she had thought for a second that it was Tye. She could tell without looking at the watch on her wrist, from the length of the shadows of the house, that it was four o'clock. She lay on the wicker chaise longue, which belonged on a broken-down Southern porch.

Sometimes she thought she could get what the

children used to call vibes from it. It had belonged to her Aunt Maymay, who had left her the villa. The chaise had been the only thing she had brought, years ago, from Kregg's Crossing. Aunt Maymay had lived a marvelous rackety life and done, as her mother had said, everything you couldn't talk about, including getting a dishonorable discharge from the Red Cross in the World War, the first one, for playing around with what she insisted on calling other ranks, which Melinda's father had said was not what Americans said. Melinda remembered her saying be that as it may, she didn't give a damn. That was the first time she had seen her, when she was nine and Aunt Maymay was still plump, a Gibson girl. After that Melinda had followed her secretly through fashion magazines and *Town and Country* as she got older, grander, thinner, and more disapproved of by her family—not because she married money three times, but because she allowed her name and picture to be in print. They said your name appeared in the newspaper on only three occasions: birth, marriage, and death.

Melinda could sense Maymay lying on the chaise longue as a girl, before she broke out of Kregg's Crossing like a filly out of a field, yearning for a lover, which would have been her way in her time of thinking about sex; even fashions in love changed, after all. She would have been in her lacy deshabille with her long auburn hair.

Melinda hadn't cut her hair either, not until she got cooties. It had been thick and blond, Mason hair, her mother said, when she was a girl, and she never did a thing to it—well, a little

Golden Glint, but that didn't really count. It was so long it reached to her waist. It lay in a coil, hidden in a drawer of her bedroom, wrapped in tissue paper, still gleaming. Maria used to take it out and wind it around her own dark head.

For years Melinda had fooled herself that she had changed from that bright girl, that girl with the tiny hopes and dreams and the lovely hair. She smiled. No. She hadn't changed, had just been more awake or less awake, depending on the impulse and the year.

She picked a dirty pompom out of the shoebox. It was soft in her hand. She smiled at it, old and squashed and that rust color that black became when it was old too.

Oh, Lord, when had that been? March 1929—no, February, Valentine's Day, but a warm night. She had hurt Trip's feelings that night because he had found out that she was going out with Gavin Proctor, from Lexington, Kentucky, not a real Kentuckian, just somebody whose father was rich and liked horses. The money had something to do with washing machines—"Really, Melinda," her mother had said, but even she subsided when Gavin drove up in a white Packard roadster with lovely leather seats that smelled of money, and charmed her socks off.

Gavin had asked her to go to the Kentucky Derby with a chaperone and some friends. Trip hadn't been invited and he didn't want her to go. He said, "You don't really know those midwestern people." He was a terrible snob and didn't know it, but he was funny and sweet. When he acted that way she refused to go with him to the fancy-dress party, so he got drunk. He tended to do that. He had the best bootlegger in town. She thought she ought to teach him a lesson. She didn't want him to feel like he owned her.

Her costume was left over from the spring caprice to raise money for little black babies. It was all right then to do artistic things if you did it for the Junior League. She had been Pierrot, in white silk with the black pompoms. The play was called *Aria da Capo.* "Is it Tuesday, Columbine? I'll kiss you if it's Tuesday." That was all that came back to her.

Those were the days of her life when if you weren't asked to the football game or the dance or the party, or if Mrs. Burlington, who ruled the social life of the West End of Richmond with an iron hand, classed you as a B debutante instead of an A debutante, you might as well jump in the James River, and one of the girls had, and Mrs. Burlington said it certainly wasn't her fault. It was well known that the girl came from an unstable family. It had never happened to Melinda because she was, thank God at the time, an A not a B, but it could. One false step and your life was over and you were out in the cold. It was a bloody battlefield.

"Can you believe that?" she said to the tops of the olive trees. There, on the terrace in Italy in 1993, she couldn't believe that all of that had mattered, but it had, and people had died of it—her father, for one. He had been from the Piedmont, where her Grandmother Mason said only plain people lived, and he, they said, had been up and coming, and made a lot of money, not like some who were already down and going, like poor Trip.

She was driving in her new yellow Ford roadster with a rumble seat along Cary Street to the country club, with a skeleton and Columbine—her best friend, Toto—who was necking in the rumble seat with one of the boys dressed up in a clown costume, when she saw the wreck. She parked the car and they all tumbled out, but there was already a woman there, very stern, and she held up both hands and she said, "We don't need help. One is all right, and the other is dead. You children ought to be ashamed of yourselves. He was drunk."

Then the woman said—and this must have been from a dream, not a memory, because nobody would right out say such a thing—"I can help because I am a Christian. You are only friends."

Melinda was still ashamed, there on the terrace, over sixty years later, holding the poor little pompom from her Pierrot costume in her old claw. It had been Trip, all dressed up like a pirate; the black patch was still in place over his eye, and the other one looked at her. The woman had forgotten to close his eye or she didn't want to touch him, so Melinda did it and said the only little Episcopal prayer she could think of.

He lay on the side of the road where the woman and her husband had dragged him out of the car, and thank God he just looked like he was asleep. He didn't even bleed. They said later that if the woman and her husband hadn't moved him, he might have lived. A rib had pierced his dear heart and it was all her fault.

Little old lady, dammit, stupid with tears, frail as one of the red flowers that bobbled in the little afternoon wind, which nudged a bit of paper from the shoebox. She caught it to keep it from flying away. It had been passed to her in the middle of the running of that same Derby, of all times. She told herself she was a vain old fool to save something that didn't mean diddly-squat. Then she remembered that the Derby wasn't the reason she had saved it all those years. It had to do with dawn and rain.

It was odd how the most important moments of one's life, the milestones, whatever you wanted to call them, were unimportant at the time. She hadn't wanted to go to the Derby, not so soon after Trip's death, but her mother had insisted. She had pointed out that after all, he wasn't a relative, so formal mourning was not appropriate. There were rules, even for sorrow.

They had left Richmond on the train, with a young married couple for their chaperons. They had to have chaperons, because if you went without a chaperon you were fast. She didn't mind being called fast—she liked it, frankly—but her mother would have set her little foot down, no matter how much washing-machine money Gavin Proctor had. But he had picked good chaperons, the kind who went to bed early.

She could still hear and smell the train and the night. They ran up and down the aisles saying *shhh* and giggling while the dark green curtains of the Pullman cars moved as if the people trying to sleep were blowing on them as they ran by to the club car. The club car smelled of tobacco smoke and coal and clean starched linen and, that night, of money. Gavin had paid the porter to stay with them all night and keep on serving grapefruit juice, which they were sure would cover the smell of gin. He had a good bootlegger too.

All night until dawn, the train hummed through the dark with that wonderful song of the wheels that meant going somewhere, somewhere, somewhere, rolling along to somewhere that was new. From time to time in the night, the train stopped with a loud hiss of the brakes, and they could see out into the darkness where a few lights were on in the houses. Then the lights slipped slowly, then faster and faster, behind them, and they were in a tunnel of darkness, and the wheels sang, the rhythm that she would remember all her life. Reclining on the terrace in Italy, she could still hear them, crossing to Kentucky in the night, with the lone lost whistle way far ahead.

Just before dawn, she and Gavin stood together at a window. It was raining. He said it was going to be a wet Derby. Through the last of the darkness she saw little round lights, made into stars by the rain, bobbing down a road. When she pointed them out, Gavin said they were trolls going to work in the mines. The color of fog and rain and the first lifting of dawn did make them look like trolls.

Maybe it was the gin, maybe it was lack of sleep, but she saw herself in the window against the darkness and she looked pretty and pert and useless in her little cloche hat with her blond hair escaping just the right way, a few kiss curls. Her face was white, then streaked with rain in the image, and then suddenly streaked with her tears when she leaned her head against her own face in the window and started to cry.

Gavin said, "What on earth is the matter?" and she said she didn't know, maybe it was those men, going to work in the dark. He laughed and said, "They're digging my Packard and your pretty clothes, my dear sweet silly child. Your daddy and mine are in the coal business up to their necks. It's booming, or it was."

She said he was wrong, that her father was a lawyer and washing machines had nothing to do with coal.

"It's investment," he said in that patient voice men used when they thought she was being a dear little fool. That was when he said, "Don't worry about it. Leave that to ugly women. You're much too beautiful to be high-minded," and he laughed. Maybe if he hadn't laughed it wouldn't have been so bad.

She tried to sleep for the few hours left, lying behind the green curtains as the morning rushed by. She had always loved the berth in the Pullman car, with its net to catch underwear and its little lights and its smell of speed and coal and linen, but, still not knowing why, she cried again, and hoped she wouldn't have a hangover and look ugly for the Derby.

It rained cats and dogs and the horses slogged through the mud. She and Gavin were under the roof of the clubhouse. It had been at lunch there that he had quietly asked her to marry him, which was, after all, what you came out for in the first place, and she had surprised herself, as if she were running ahead of her own life.

She had whispered, "Think about this and tell me after a while. Could we wait a few years? There is something I want and I don't know yet what it is. Don't say anything now. Think about it." She leaned over and kissed him on the cheek, but he wouldn't look at her. Then they went to Gavin's family's box, and everybody started to sing "My Old Kentucky Home" and it made her feel a little tickle of tears behind her nose.

It was when the horses were at the first turn that he slipped her the note, of all the bad timing. It said *no,* but when she first looked at it, it said *on,* and she didn't understand. He reached down and turned it in her hand, the answer. *No.* "My father wouldn't stand for anything like that," he whispered under that special horse-race roar of the crowd. "Now you think it over." The horses were at the far turn. She was drowning in noise and rain.

Three months after Trip was buried, she had her coming-out party at the country club. She remembered her dress, white chiffon as light as air, with a big taffeta bow, dagged, they called it, panels that went down in the back to her heels, the latest thing, and a short front above her knees. She wore a crepe-de-chine shimmy under it that moved on her body when she danced, and step-ins of silk and lace, and gossamer stockings, and the gold shoes from Delman's.

Oh, Lord, only three months after Trip, and

she danced the Charleston for him as hard as she could. All she remembered was her dress billowing and the whirling circle of flickering lights, all the colors of the rainbow, and then she didn't remember any more. She sank to the floor, and her mother thought she had fainted. They kept from her the fact that Melinda was the only girl in her season to be carried feet first out of her own coming-out party, passed out cold on the bathtub gin she carried in Trip's flask, which she had asked his mother for to remember him by. It was her first act of rebellion.

The year slowed after October, like a Victrola running down. There was a day that everybody looked back on and called Black Tuesday, when the bottom fell out of the stock market. But they hadn't really felt it at the time, and at first nobody believed anything would change. How could it in a world as solid as a rock, or at least brick and new wormy pine paneling, like the English Tudor house her father had insisted on building in 1927 on land he bought from Grandmother Mason, so they were next door, right across a big lawn that had once been the horse field?

They had gone to England to buy furniture and linen-fold paneling, and one of those uncomfortable box-shaped medieval sofas covered in itchy needlepoint, and a heavy carved chimneypiece, which the architect said they had to have. It was just a mantel, but he called it a chimneypiece. She had a wonderful time on the *Île de France,* and won the Ping Pong tournament, which they called table tennis.

A whole colony of those houses was being built

around a huge one that had been brought lock, stock, and barrel from England and set up again. It had been an abbey; at least, everybody said it had. Instant houses, instant gardens, instant authentic Tudor.

"Well, that's what happens when you marry money," her grandmother said. She was devastatingly polite, as only her generation could be. "He was such a nice respectful boy. I remember him. He used to wait on me at Miller and Rhoades."

The English colony was three years old and the gardens had begun to be lush in that fall, 1929. There was no event that Melinda could put her finger on, at least for her and for all of the people she knew best, except Gavin Proctor, who went back to Lexington at once. She was sent to Oakley Hall, fulfilling another of her father's tense, demanding dreams. She hated it. She looked back on the time, even before October, and it hadn't been, as people said who were fools or forgetful, the best years of her life. She saw herself as a species, not a person, when her pains were small and her longings were shallow.

The event didn't come for her until the summer of 1930. It was a June day, a day she remembered every hour of, even getting up late in the morning after one of those parties, a scavenger hunt. She had crept home at three o'clock, trying not to make noise. She knew every touch in the dark of the linen-fold paneling and the stairs, which ones squeaked and which ones didn't, because she didn't want to wake her father, who hadn't been sleeping well, and she didn't want her mother to smell gin. In the night there was still a light under her parents' bedroom door, and she heard her mother say something and then her father answered, "Mary Cary, I don't *have* a hundred dollars."

Melinda had lain in bed, and even in the night heat of June she couldn't get warm. She had never heard her father mention money in her life. She didn't go to sleep until she heard his Buick going slowly down the gravel path of the driveway.

It was later and the sun was making prisms of her mullioned window, so it must have been eleven o'clock when she heard them downstairs, those special quiet voices, and she remembered the walk down those carved stairs as a walk into a new life, leaving that first part behind forever, in a hot, tousled bed where she had rucked the sheet into a pile, trying to find comfort all night. For years her mother tried to drag her back to that unmade bed, in a panic that became a way of life.

He had gone out in the early morning. He had told her mother that he had a client to see, west of Richmond. Melinda hoped she had thought about him when she heard the car go out of the driveway, but she hadn't. She knew that.

She could see him driving the black Buick along, slowly maybe, with the terrible fear that rode beside him in the car, across the James River before the mist had been burned away by the sun, and she wished she had ever known him well enough to know that he was thinking something beyond what she heard whenever he came into her mind: "Don't you worry about a thing."

From the stairs she had heard her mother say, as if it were important, "But what was he doing way out there in the colored section with a client? He was a corporation lawyer."

A man's voice: ". . . one of those level crossings where they don't have a barrier, way up one of the dirt roads. It seems his car stalled on the tracks."

It was such a quiet remark, and when she heard it, standing there in her pajamas, she ran back up the stairs and hardly knew it until she had locked her door. She leaned against the door and said the Lord's Prayer over and over. It was all she could think of to keep the train from coming, but she could hear it getting closer, and she knew that her father had waited until it was too late for the train even to slow down. He was not a man who could live with the words "I don't *have* a hundred dollars."

The insurance company said it was an accident. Her Uncle Brandon, when he was drunk, said, "Big Brother wanted his girls to live in the style he wasn't accustomed to." The insurance was huge, and the last payment had been paid, and her mother said they would be rich, well, at least well off, with what his law partner said were gilt-edged securities. Melinda had thought for a long time he had said "guilt-edged." It had been the chorus—gilt-edged, safe, money—that she had had to reject from that day on, the obscene sacrifice.

The first thing she had done was refuse to go back to Oakley Hall. Her mother was pleased. "I was always afraid you would come back too smart, the boys don't like it, but your father insisted. Now you can take up the kind of thing we're used to—you can volunteer."

Her mother had moved them bag and baggage back to her Grandmother Mason's, across the big lawn. All winter her mother floated in abandonment, paying attention to nothing but the grief she expected of herself, even when Melinda came home drunk and drove her Ford into the closed garage door. Imogene and her family lived over the garage, and Imogene stuck her head out of the window and whispered, "Go ahead. Wake up the dead. You have the least idea what time it is?"

Imogene had worked for Grandmother Mason since she was fifteen. She had helped raise Melinda, so she didn't tell on her. She just said, "Ought to be ashamed of yourself," still leaning out the window. One of her children was hollering behind her. "Daddy not cold in his grave . . ." But she said that a delivery truck had hit the garage door, she didn't know which one.

It was the first week of September 1931. Melinda was brushing her hair a hundred times when her mother came into her room, the one she had had since she was tiny, with her dolls still sitting there staring, and said, "What is the meaning of this, young lady? Now, what have you been up to behind my back?" She was carrying a letter from the Red Cross saying that Melinda had passed her courses and had been approved to go to Kentucky and help the needy, as she had requested.

She had made her decision the day she found

the useless stock in a Straight Creek coal company that her father had put into the secret drawer of the English desk, along with the goddamn invitation to her coming-out party and her grades at Oakley Hall, which were terrible. A drawer of dreams and failures. She wanted to look back and think she did it because she remembered the miners out of the window of the train, but she didn't, not then, not until much later. Her mother didn't consider apologizing for opening her letter.

She said, "Mother, you told me to volunteer, so I did."

"Oh, dear, I meant something nice in Richmond." Her mother laughed, which she always preferred to arguing. It was usually more effective, a little tinkly laugh that her father had found enchanting. He said so, and she never gave it up. She tinkled that laugh when she was eighty-seven years old.

When the laughter didn't work, her mother finally said, "If that's what you want. Who am I . . . ? After all, the Red Cross is worthy," and her voice ran down both in the memory and when she said it, and she began to cry her tears of last resort—little mother tears, Melinda's grandmother called them. "You have been deceiving me all summer. And here I thought you were playing tennis with nice people!"

"My God," Melinda said to the piece of paper that was still in her hand after all that time. "Every time I entered Richmond I could feel those habits clang shut behind me." She laughed again, for the last time.

She dropped the paper into the wind and the box fell over, and the wind picked up all the papers and junk she had saved, danced them past her along the terrace, into the pool, through the trees, all of it escaping, flying over the heads of Aiken and Maria.

Maria caught a bit of paper that flew toward her. There was one word on it. *No.* It was Melinda's last message to the world, that and the laughter.

When Aiken and Maria ran up to the terrace, catching bits of paper in flight as if they were playing a game, she had gone into silence, in mid-laugh, as she would have wished, just sitting there looking out at the Tyrrhenian Sea, and only her gray hair moved, fingered by the wind.

The first thing that Maria did was close her eyes, hardly knowing she did it. Aiken righted the shoebox and began to put papers back into it. Maria stayed kneeling beside Melinda and held her close and said, "Dear thing, dear old thing," and suddenly she wailed like a child in an empty house.

It was midnight. All over. Aiken and Maria sat at the large round table under the half-roof of the terrace. They hadn't said anything for half an hour. Aiken's big shadow was on the wall of the house, and Maria's was lying out across the terrace floor. When the candles flickered the shadows danced, but they were completely still.

They were drunk. They were not really aware of being drunk. They only knew that they had exhausted everything practical there was to do to keep from mourning: the people to call, the exit of Melinda, feet first, as she always said she would go, into the ambulance, covered until Maria jerked the cover from her quiet face and burst into tears again and said, "Don't do that. She can't see." She cried on Aiken as he guided her back into the house, and the doctor put the cover back and shook his head.

They stood in the kitchen window and watched the ambulance go slowly up the steep drive to the road and heard it long after they couldn't have heard it any longer. Then they turned back into a house that was suddenly empty, too big, too quiet, for the first time since they had known it.

They made dinner as they always had there. Afterward, they put the legal papers, a pile of letters, and the shoebox from Delman's on the table, with the bottles of wine, and set out on a voyage, Maria called it, through what Melinda had called her bits and pieces.

They had made three piles on the table. One was from the shoebox. One was the legal papers from her bedroom drawer—Aunt Maymay's letter, deeds, insurance, and two policies with a note: "You can cash these at once, while my will is being probated. I don't want you to be out of funds." One of them was made out to Aiken, one to Maria. They were for fifty thousand dollars each. Aiken's and Maria's adoption papers were in the legal pile. The third pile was familiar: school junk, letters from them both and their children, and snapshots, some yellow with age.

Maria laughed and held up a photograph. "My New Brutalism phase. You know, rudeness equals honesty. I remember saying to Melinda in the middle of one of our arguments that what she called good manners was only hypocrisy, and she rolled her eyes up in that way she had and said, 'Then God give me enough hypocrisy to get through the day.' She never put me down. She just said things I couldn't forget."

"Oh, don't I know! Some of the bummers she handed me! My God. She saved this. See what I mean?" He held up a pair of broken eyeglasses. They looked like they had been stepped on. "Jakey, old Jakey" was all he said, but he went on holding the glasses.

Maria examined her photograph. She had looked a little like Juliet Greco. She had grown her thick hair long and it hung down like curtains on both sides of a sulky face. She said to herself in the picture, "That was the year she finally took me back to Spain, the year she inherited this house. That's when Tye led me into being an anthropologist. He said it would harness my anger. It was fashionable to be angry then, only of course we didn't know it was a fashion. We just thought that was the way life was at Cambridge. He said, 'Get the Cambridge out of your soul, go to the London School of Economics if you want to change the world. Your mother and I did it the hard way.' I used to hate it when they said they already knew things."

She began to cry again. "Dammit, dammit, dammit. You know what she said this morning? She was reading the *Herald-Tribune,* and she said,

'You know, it's funny. I've always thought *fin de siècle* was another time and another place, where everybody wore mauve and walked slowly and read *The Yellow Book.* Well, here we are again in a *fin de siècle.* I don't like it much. Morals don't change, but they've gotten so noisy. The manners are appalling, the greed is disgusting, and the fury never seems to stop. Oh well, I guess it was always there and I didn't see it.' But then she said she did see it. She said she hadn't reckoned that it still went on and on after you'd spent your life trying to do something about it. Then she said, 'That doesn't mean you don't keep on. What is it? Eternal vigilance?' Then she grinned in that way she had and said, 'I'm sure it was like that right here on this island when the barbarians were at the gates. Roman matrons looking out in the morning and saying it's going to be a nice day. It is, too. I'll sit outside in the sun. I'm not going back to bed. It's boring.' "

They didn't know yet what to do with the pile from the shoebox. There were Melinda's car keys, all labeled, all the way back to a 1930 Model A Ford roadster—1932 Stutz Bearcat, 1936 Ford shooting brake, 1937 SS100 Jaguar, 1961 Ford Thunderbird, 1965 Mustang, 1975 Jaguar. Maria jingled the keys. "She could fix them, every one of them."

There was a pompom that had once been black. There was the note with the word *no* on it. There were several photographs of people they had never heard of. One was a group at a swimming hole; another, a slim boy, shy-looking, wearing a bathing suit with straps over his hunched shoulders. He was hugging his own arms as if he were cold or embarrassed, and in the distance, with her back turned, a girl with blond hair cascading down to her waist, barefoot, in a one-piece bathing suit, walked toward the woods. Written on the back was "Johnny on the first day, 1931. The other person in the picture is me."

"God, what an epitaph, the other person in the picture!" Maria said. She handed it to Aiken. "It must have been a swimming hole or a picnic—look at the falling water."

He tried to see it, but he couldn't; the picture stayed dead in his hand. He said, "I don't know . . . There's so much." He picked up an old faded Red Cross armband. "God, why did she save this? She hated the Red Cross."

"She called it her deed to the house. She always said that she saved bits and pieces so she could tell us about the times they brought back. All these notes, just scribbled to help her remember . . ." Maria picked up scrap after scrap: the word *reddish,* a small tin medal that read *Cristo Rey,* a big button that said HAPPY DAYS ARE HERE AGAIN.

"She played that song every New Year's, just at midnight. She said it had always meant that things would get better." Aiken pinned the button to his shirt and then unpinned it and put it back on the pile.

He picked up an old, dirty, thick linen envelope with the postmark "Richmond, Nov. 5, 1931." It still felt expensive when he ran his fingers over it. It had never been opened. He turned it over. Scribbled on the back, almost too pale to read, he saw "A man that will work just fer coal light and carbide, he ain't got a grain of sense." Aiken turned the envelope over and over.

"I like that. Grain of sense . . ."

"Damn." Maria smoothed a note with her fingers, trying to straighten the creases in it. "It could be saying *on,*" she said. "How will we ever know?" She picked up a card. "Here's one I know. She showed it to me a long time ago. She said it was all there was left. I think she meant more than just the card." It was a soiled, bent pass: *Consell de Sabitat de Guerra. Hom nomena.* The signature had been obliterated by some dark stain.

Maria raised her glass to the light of the candle and said, "I think I can sleep now," and she started to cry again.

So did Aiken. They just sat there and drank the last of the wine and let the tears fall down their faces, and made not a sound.

Aiken carried the legal papers in when he went to bed, and Maria said she would look after the letters and the pictures and maybe make an album herself, but the heap of unknown things they both forgot to pick up. When it was midnight and the house was dark and quiet and the moon drenched it, a little wind picked up the sepia picture of the boy and lifted it over the shrubbery beyond the terrace, and it was lost by the wind in an olive tree.

Book One

Kentucky • 1931–1932

Which Side Are You On?

On the twenty-sixth of September 1931, Melinda was finally ready to go to Kentucky. The roadster was packed. Her mother had stopped crying. Her grandmother had run, at last, out of words.

The seat beside her and the rumble seat were piled high with toilet paper, Milk of Magnesia, Golden Glint, Hinds' Honey and Almond Cream, a little kit from Elizabeth Arden with several colors of lipstick to go with different things, a Whitman's Sampler, plenty of undies, *The Bridge of San Luis Rey,* two books by S. S. Van Dine, a special padded cot her mother had ordered from Hammacher Schlemmer, cod-liver oil, and several sets of linen sheets. Her mother had said, "You might as well be comfortable. You can't tell what you'll find out there. Take Ivory. Servants will be easy to find, with all that unemployment."

There were two boxes of canned goods—anchovies, salmon, asparagus, tiny peas, tomatoes, a Smithfield ham—several bottles of spring water, extra tires, a jack, some inner tubes. There was one box of worn shoes from the Red Cross office and a first-aid kit. At the last minute,

Melinda ran back and got her new backless bathing suit and the pretty little lace-trimmed baby pillow she had carried with her since she was a baby, to Camp Sewell, to Oakley Hall, and all the way to Europe, even though everybody teased her about it.

She had to stop for a last nervous look at herself in the long mirror in her grandmother's room. She wore a gray felt hat she wouldn't have been caught dead in a year before, her hair was pooched out around her face, and the skirt of her gray linen suit, which her mother had insisted on having made in a sort of Red Crossy color, was the absolutely necessary ten inches from the floor. She wore the Red Cross armband she had earned. There was something about being in a sort of uniform, even if her mother had made it up, that made her feel girdled with intent, like soldiers in old newsreels, and her Uncle Brandon coming home from the World War when he was still only nineteen years old and drinking with her father in the dining room of her grandmother's house from a bottle of bourbon.

Uncle Brandon had been gassed and badly wounded in the Argonne Forest. Melinda had sneaked out of bed and huddled against the banister, listening for war, but he didn't say a word about it, even when her father asked him right out if he'd seen many dead bodies.

Melinda had been eight years old then. That evening at dinner somebody outside had let off a firecracker and Uncle Brandon had dropped under the table. Her father said it was shell shock, but her grandmother said nobody from the war in her girlhood behaved like that afterward. Only she said *gul—gulhood.*

Finally being ready to go had taken nearly a year. Melinda had moved through the months after her father's death in a daze, and afterward she couldn't remember where she had been. She had driven through the silent country looking for the crossing where her father had died, her Ford bumping over track after track. Black children stood close together and looked shy and said "No, ma'am" when she asked them if they knew.

Then she looked up the address of the Red Cross in the telephone book and went downtown and volunteered. They asked what she wanted to do and she didn't even know how to answer, so she used the word everybody was using that year, *relief,* but whether it was for herself or others, strangers, she couldn't have said. That was when they told her to sign on for classes in mass feeding and first aid.

When they showed her a list of the places where the Red Cross had been called in, she saw the words *Bell County* and *Harlan County, Kentucky,* and said, "There. That's where I want to go." She had recognized the name from the secret drawer. A place on a map—no reasons and not *noblesse oblige,* as the minister who had christened her said when her mother made her talk to him. He told her she was putting on the armor of God.

Grandmother Mason didn't try to talk her out of going. She did something worse. She took her to dinner at the Jefferson Hotel. She said Melinda was just going to get in the way of people who knew what they were doing. She said that maybe she wouldn't do too much harm, since she had been far too spoiled by her father to stick to anything that didn't suit her. Melinda lost years as her grandmother talked, until she was six years old, saying, "Yes, ma'am."

Then, as they left, her grandmother stood watching the live alligators that were kept in a pool in the lobby and said, "I've done my best. They'll eat you alive out there."

It broke the spell and made Melinda laugh. "Are the alligators a symbol I'm supposed to remember?" she asked.

"Don't be impertinent," her grandmother said, still watching the alligators. "I wouldn't deign to speak in symbols. I don't say one thing when I mean another. Symbols are tacky." They walked slowly down the grand staircase. Neither of them looked at her feet.

Melinda drove out River Road to the west. The country was brown and yellow with drought and fall stubble, and in the distance a grove of maples had turned bright red. She suddenly felt a surge of freedom, like a physical ecstasy; she was her own size in her own skin, just riding along in the car with the top down, going to a place of her own choice, wherever that was.

Well, not a new place the first night. Even though her mother couldn't stand her father's family, she had insisted that Melinda stay the night with Grandmother Kregg, Uncle Brandon, and Boodie.

She had long since learned not to seem too pleased at going to Kregg's Crossing, but she had loved it ever since her father had begun sending her there in the summers because he said she ought to know his side of the family. He was always too busy and too worried to go himself, but her mother said he helped his family out, whatever that meant. It had been a different world. Mornings and afternoons in Richmond were taken up with learning to ride, learning to dance, learning to play tennis, all at the right time and in the right way, but days at Kregg's Crossing were just left to be.

Uncle Brandon was eleven years older and Boodie was five years older, but they didn't treat her like she was a tag-along. They went canoeing on the James and the Gloryann, and Uncle Brandon taught her to turn over in a canoe and breathe under it. All three of them tumbled into the water and came up under the overturned boat. It was bright inside, reflecting the water, and they got the giggles, three heads bobbing in that roofed, tentlike boat. He let her ride the way she liked best, too, with a long stirrup and low hands. "Where do you think the phrase *high-handed* came from?" he joked when he saw how she was being taught in Richmond.

When she phoned to ask them if she could stay the night, Boodie called out faintly, "Why, honey, that's the nicest thing I ever heard in my whole life. We'll put on the big pot and the little one." Melinda had never called her Aunt Boodie because she was only five years older, but sometimes she seemed like a little girl and sometimes like an old maid. The family said that she was fated never to marry.

Melinda's mother said that neither Uncle

Brandon nor Boodie had ever married because they had had to stay at home and look after their mother, who had gone crazy when their father dropped dead, but her father said that that wasn't true, that she was just deeply religious. Everybody knew why Uncle Brandon couldn't marry, but nobody said so, and Boodie had a beau who had been patient for some years. His name was Mr. Percival. He wore gold glasses and worked in the office of the metallurgical plant that had bought the next plantation on the James.

Melinda was coming back into the living room to tell her mother it was all right to stay when she heard her say to her grandmother, "I hadn't known he was sending a monthly check. When they all flounced down here for the funeral, I told them that I couldn't afford it anymore, even with the insurance. I just don't believe that kind of thing helps anybody to stand on their own feet. I told them that of course if they needed anything just to let me know." She was all for other people standing on their own feet. "Well, I just hope he's not on a bender, that's all." Uncle Brandon had been a bender drinker since the war, and her father had had to go and get him out of hotel rooms in Lynchburg and pay for what he broke.

But most of the time Uncle Brandon was the gentlest man she had ever known. Even Grandmother Mason said he had the manners of a saint. When he did, later, talk about the war, he said that he had been wounded severely storming Vimy Ridge, but when he said, "I got my balls shot off in the war," everybody knew he had started in again.

Her mother still called Kregg's Crossing Belmont, even after the house burned to the ground in 1922. She did it when she started talking about how rich the Kregg family had been before the War Between the States, and Grandmother Mason said, as she always did, that all the families west of Richmond were plain people.

Every summer they went for picnics where there were only four great chimneys standing, and a line of stone columns like Melinda had seen in Greece when they went abroad. Boodie would walk through the big grass square and say, "This was the drawing room and this was the kitchen, and that's where Cousin Melinda the toast of the county died who you were named for. I slept right up there," pointing to the sky. Uncle Brandon would call, tender with her, "Sissy, come and have the picnic." Melinda couldn't imagine him storming anything, much less Vimy Ridge and getting a medal, or raging around a hotel room in Lynchburg breaking things.

Her father hadn't even looked like them, or his mother. They said he was the image of his father. She thought about all that in the car, the way people just stayed around year after year and talked about who looked like who and where they got their noses, and they didn't age, they just weathered like apples. Uncle Brandon didn't show in his face a bit of anything that had happened to him.

It wasn't until she got to Kregg's Crossing, after a nearly all-day drive, that she realized that it was her father's birthday and that she was celebrating it in a way he would never have understood, as he hadn't understood Uncle Brandon when he said, that night in the dining room, "I want no part of your schemes, whatever they are." That was when her father said, "I've planned all this for you. I don't understand," and Uncle Brandon murmured, so low she could hardly hear, "You wouldn't. You weren't there."

"Now that's not fair," her father had said. "I was reserved." They were using words in a way she didn't understand then. Reserved was the way your grandmother said you ought to be in public, like walking down the grand staircase at the Jefferson Hotel without looking down, and wearing only clean white underclothes in case you had a wreck, and making your manners with older people before you started having a good time.

The car's rhythm was making her eight and then ten and then eighteen, and then twenty again, all jumbled, and when she heard music she realized she was singing her favorite song, at least the one that month, "Lover Come Back to Me." She had it in the rumble seat with Lawrence Tibbett singing it, and she had played it on her little round Victrola that was shaped like a hatbox until her grandmother had said, "God spare me."

Boodie was waiting at the gate, which still had the old weight on it from before the war. She looked like a wraith in an apple-green voile dress her mother had made for her. It was still low at the waist, as if they'd copied it from last year's *Delineator,* their favorite magazine.

That evening at dinner, Grandmother Kregg

sat at the end of the table in her long black bombazine dress with the high lace around her neck and the family pearls, four strands around her throat, which had belonged to the first Melinda. She had touched them before the blessing and said, "We buried these during the war. We swore then that no matter what happened, how bad things became, we would never sell the family jewels. We didn't even consider it when money was as scarce as hen's teeth after the War, and those people from the North wanted to buy anything that wasn't nailed down, and some that was." She said all that in the small soft voice she had, always sweet, always polite, always considerate, and never yielding one inch.

Uncle Brandon laughed then. He said, "Mother's never forgotten one single piece of property that was sold to a Yankee."

"I should hope not. But some of them became quite nice neighbors," her grandmother said, of people whose children had sold Mont Michelle forty years before. It was now the company office of the metallurgical plant that spewed hot water into the Gloryann River and made black smoke that darkened their days when the wind was in the wrong direction.

Grandmother Kregg asked Uncle Brandon to say the blessing, which they didn't do anymore in Richmond, and then she began to ladle out chicken and dumplings. She tasted it and said, as she always did, to Boodie, "This is the best chicken and dumplings I've ever had in my whole life, darling." Even though Boodie looked frail, she could swing the heads off two chickens at the same time, one in each hand.

They had the silver candelabra on the table because Melinda was company, and the fine lace doilies she remembered from her childhood, which had been patched by Grandmother Kregg but you could hardly see.

When they had finished the baked apple for dessert, Grandmother Kregg suddenly said, "You know that Belmont was burned by the Yankees and they took everything but my pearls." Boodie sighed, and knew it was time to take her to bed. "This little old place wasn't anything but the overseer's house," the old lady explained to Melinda, as if she were a stranger, while Boodie guided her toward the stairs.

Uncle Brandon said, "I wish she'd think of something a little less obvious to go nuts about. She wasn't even born until 1865."

After Grandmother Kregg had gone to bed and they had finished washing up, they sat on the porch as they always had, watching the moonlight in the trees. The swing creaked in rhythm, with Boodie's foot on the floor pushing it. They could still smell the jasmine that late in the year. They talked between big comfortable spaces of silence about the rain, which had been a godsend, and the crops, what there was left of them after the drought. They weren't their own crops anymore. Uncle Brandon couldn't farm because of his lungs. They rented the fields to a farmer, who couldn't pay unless there was rain.

Once in a while one of Uncle Brandon's bird dogs muttered in its sleep, and the other dream-ran. They were Jay Dog and Dan, old scraggy setters. Melinda had known them since they were pups and she was little. Now they were old, and slept and sighed. Brandon remembered to scratch their bellies with his foot.

After a long time Uncle Brandon said, "Mother always said she had two families, your father and Maymay, who had ambition, and Boodie and me to look after her in her old age. She said she'd planned it that way."

Nobody answered him. Boodie kept on swinging. They were quiet together, and then Uncle Brandon said, "I wish you had known your father when he was young. He was like a wonderful uncle to me . . . He would have been forty-six today."

Then he said, as if he were suddenly mad at her, "What are you going out there for? It's a terrible place. I think you're a damned fool. Well, I reckon you ought to. Every stitch you wear and that damned house that broke him all came right off the coal face," and Boodie said, "Now Brandon, it's not her fault . . ."

They were conscious of staying off a subject that seemed too rude for the quiet of the night. They called goodnight, goodnight, goodnight, as if they had forgotten anything unpleasant.

Melinda left the next morning at eight o'clock, after one of those insistent breakfasts that country people call hospitality. When it was over and Uncle Brandon had put her suitcase on the seat beside her, he said goodbye and waited for Boodie. She said, "Go away, Brandy, I want to tell Melinda a secret."

He looked worried. "Now, Boodie . . ."

"No. Honest. Just girl talk." She waited until he had backed out of earshot, still looking worried. She said, "He thinks I'm going to ask for money. I am not, not ever." Then she leaned close to Melinda and whispered in her ear. "Do me a favor, will you? A solemn promise!"

Melinda nodded.

"Do *everything!*" she whispered, and laughed and ran away, waving goodbye.

As Melinda got nearer the Kentucky border, the roads got worse. She could hear the things in the rumble seat shift as she drove slowly around the S-curves of the mountains, blowing *oogah* on her horn as her father had taught her. At least it didn't rain. But it had. The mountain meadows and the trees were green, the first real green she had seen in her whole four hundred miles.

She ran into mud-filled ruts and wondered what she was doing there, on some mountain she had never heard of, going to a place she knew nothing about. She slowly guided the car around the mud and drove in second down into Cumberland Gap. It was running with water from the mountains. She could hear the rush of waterfalls and rapids over the sound of the tired engine. All around her there was the smell of water and green fields deep with grass. There were great red and yellow stands of maples, and the oaks had begun to be haunted by fall color. The place was like a little Eden, lost there in the mountains. She felt as if she had discovered America.

It was evening, too late to try to cross the last mountain. Down in the valley, where a large lawn was made bright green by the twilight and althea massed high like a hedge caught the evening sun, she saw a white two-story house, a big one, with long porches, trimmed with wooden lace upstairs and downstairs, across the front. As she drove nearer, she saw a sign that said MRS. HIGHTOWER. That was all. She parked the car and sat for a minute and realized how exhausted she was, and hoped that Mrs. Hightower would give her a room for the night. The last mountain she had to cross was casting a shadow across the valley. It looked high, forbidding.

The house seemed to grow out of the meadow, with white wings resting across the grass. She could see ducks where the creek from the mountain waterfall had been widened into a pond, and she could hear the waterwheel of the mill creaking when she stopped the Ford. The car wasn't yellow anymore. It was mud-colored; so was she, or at least she felt like it.

The door opened onto the porch as if somebody had been watching for her. A woman who reminded her of her grandmother, only younger, not looking like her at all but with the same slow, deliberate way of walking, came down the brick walk and leaned on the car. She had one of those faces that Melinda expected to be silent and watchful, a carved face, and a thin gray-streaked bun of hair, huge Indian-looking eyes, a body like a slat, a gleaming white apron. Then she smiled and showed a big gold tooth in the front, like a beauty spot.

Her voice was as slow as her walk, deep in her throat, as if she hadn't used it for a while, and when she started she didn't stop. But she talked so slowly that Melinda had moved out of the car and was leaning on the car door with one foot on the running board and the other on the damp grass before she could get a word in edgeways.

The woman said, "I'm Miz Hightower. You're mighty welcome. They ain't nobody here now but me and Hewlett and some hunters. They ain't come back yet. Honey, you look all in. Come on in here and get yourself a bath and I'll fix you some supper."

"Did you know I was coming?" Melinda must have said it aloud, she was so tired and open to dreams.

"Lord God, honey, I never heard tell of ye. I run this place. Red Cross. Well, I'll be." What she would be she didn't say, she just took Melinda's arm and helped her along the nearly sunken brick walk. "Honey, you're stiff as a board. We got hot water."

She went back and grabbed the suitcase that Uncle Brandon had put in the seat beside her, on top of the pile of things her mother thought she would need. "This it?" Melinda nodded. "Now, don't you even think of tryin to carry this. You look all in, a little thing like you drivin around out here where you don't know what. I don't know what your mama and daddy was thinkin about, let you do that. Where you come from?"

"Richmond."

"Jesus love you, you never come all that way in one day. Where'd you stop last night?"

"Outside Lynchburg . . ."

"Well, if that don't beat all"—as if Richmond were Sodom and Lynchburg Gomorrah.

"I reckon you're agoin over there into Bell County, well they sure can use you, Bell and Harlan, I tell you, them places was made for trouble as the sparks fly upward, Job five-seven. Don't worry about your stuff, they won't nobody bother it, unless they's food." Mrs. Hightower was inspecting the pile in the rumble seat. "They's food all right. Hewlett can put the car in the barn. You're too tard. It'll be all right for a little while. Why, I wouldn't hear of you atryin to cross that mountain tonight. Hewlett better go with ye in the mornin. He can git a ride back. They's people over yonder don't like the Red Cross. You just come on in."

It wasn't like a hotel. It wasn't like anything but somebody's big wooden house where the evening breeze was moving twenty or so rocking chairs as if they had ghosts in them, and the swings at both ends creaked back and forth.

"Now the hunters git drunk and they might make noise, but they's all gentlemen from Middlesborough and Chattanooga, you know them kind of men gets drunk and hollers some but they wouldn't bother no woman." Mrs. Hightower's voice trailed behind her.

She helped Melinda up the dark stairs. "Well, I'm mighty glad to see you, I'll tell the world. I ain't seen nuthin but men in I don't know how long. They used to bring their wives set on the porch, that was real nice, but this fall with the trouble, they never done nuthin like that. My, that's a real pretty suit you got on. Ain't it hot, that gray color? I think that would be hot as hell. Now I'm goin to fix you a bath." She opened Melinda's small case. "Oh, now ain't that nice all them nice things? Here's your kimono, my Lord ain't that the prettiest thing? There's a towel behind the door." She was going, still drifting words behind her. "The bathtub's real big. Some Englishman sold it to me when he went broke and left. That was 'twenty-nine."

The room was dark to keep it cool. Dark green blinds sucked in and out of the open window, and the voile curtains breathed. The bedhead was a cat's cradle of brass, and it complained when Melinda sank down into a soft feather mattress to take off her stockings. Her dirty pumps lay on their sides on a rag rug. There was a wooden washstand with a big pitcher and bowl, and a mirror, where she saw herself for the first time since morning. She was pale and dirty and her hat drooped and the blond tendrils she had made escape so nicely in the morning were stuck to her face with sweat and dirt.

There were three pictures. One was of Jesus with a lantern, knocking at a door. The other two were prints and had their names below them. One was Eugene Debs. The other was Nathan Bedford Forrest. Melinda didn't know who either of them was. The patchwork quilt on the bed was a history of Mrs. Hightower's dresses for years, made into a great star in the middle. There didn't seem to be a Mr. Hightower. She couldn't find anything that looked like Mr. Hightower's ties or shirts.

There are times so strange that all you can do is accept them. That was her dream thought as she lay in a bathtub that was so long that her feet wouldn't touch the end and watched a branch with red leaves wave against the bathroom window, letting it lull her nearly to sleep.

Mrs. Hightower heard her coming down the stairs. "Oh there you are, come on in here," she called from the kitchen. "We'll eat in here. I ain't et yet. That's a pretty blouse. I ain't had time nor money to go over to Middlesborough and get me some goods at the store. Set down."

Melinda sat down at the kitchen table. It was covered with red-and-yellow-checked oilcloth. It looked large enough to seat a family of ten.

"Well, that table does hold that many at breakfast when the hunters is here," Mrs. Hightower told her.

Melinda shivered. She was sure she had only thought, not said.

"Oh, don't worry about that, honey, I got the second sight. It's a damned nuisance, let me tell you. The things some people thinks!"

She fed Melinda fried ham and cornbread and grits and corn on the cob, which she took pride in being able to serve so late, later than anybody else in the valley. "The others ain't got nuthin but horse corn this late."

Melinda suddenly felt completely at peace and scared as hell of what she might be thinking in front of Mrs. Hightower.

"Now, don't do that," Mrs. Hightower told her. "I could feel ye shiver. Lord, I wish you could have saw that rain last week. That's the reason it's so green here. Rained like who tied the dog up. Six inches come off that mountain like the flood in the Bible. Don't it smell nice? What are you adoin here?"

"I'm supposed to report to the Red Cross Relief in Pineville." Melinda looked out to where the ducks were waddling across the grass.

"Well, honey, that's a real nice place. You ain't got nuthin to worry about so long as you stay out of Harlan. Let me tell you." She sat down with coffee for each of them. "They's a woman over there that runs the Red Cross, professional, not like the local people. She come from out of state. Ugly as a mud fence. Thinks she's still in the trenches in the World War to hear her tell it. She come over here for Sunday dinner once and she looked like a paddle, one of them paddles the teacher uses. She rules the roost. She keeps lists of people on the books to get food, and she won't let nobody have none who is out on strike instead of unemployed. She's nuthin but a damned scab. There ain't much difference anyhow, let me tell you. Some ain't got work, some bootlegs, some just sets around and talks. She thinks the strikers is Roosian Red, let me tell you a woman don't know the difference between a Roosian Red and a mountain man got his dander up is nuthin but a damn fool.

"That's Harlan County, all run by Sheriff John Henry Blair, and he done deputized enough mine guards over there to start him a regiment, all riding around in them big open cars like Chicago gangsters in the picture show with machine guns trained on them poor little shacks. Most of them ain't nuthin but ex-soldiers couldn't get no jobs is what they tell me. They're supposed to scare people. They done shot up soup kitchens, and shot men and beat men and hung one man with barbed wire and busted in houses drunk and accosted the women, accosted me I'd of shot one and to hell with John Henry Blair the son-of-a-bitch. I had my druthers I'd throw them all out of Harlan and Bell counties back where they come from.

"Now Pineville is different. They're the kind of people you're used to. They'll be real good to you." Mrs. Hightower didn't stop to draw breath; she just trudged on slowly through what she had to say as she changed dishes, gave them more coffee, ran water in the sink. "Nice people there. Real rich, some of them. The others is gone bankrupt. My husband and me and Hewlett, that's my boy, we never had but the one. My womb got twisted up. We lived over there for five years. Mr. Hightower was a foreman up Straight Creek, but they went bankrupt, and then he got him a job on the coal face. He got mashed in the mine over to Everts, a bad mine, run by the Peabody Coal Company, one of them outside interests. Just to get a little cash money, well, he got mashed in the mine by one of them old tree trunks they call kettles just stuck there in the ceiling waitin to come down. People say they are thousands of years old, petrified, but I don't believe that. God made the world in six days one thousand and four years before Jesus and on the seventh day He rested. He last a year all crippled up, my husband, not God"—she laughed at that—"and not one red cent of compensation. Then he died. That's why we're for the union, not this here union, the Mother Jones union. But them coal operators run the UMWA out of Kentucky. This here one is Roosian Red. My husband voted for Eugene Debs ever time he run but I vote Republican, my daddy was a Republican, hit runs in the family.

"So me and Hewlett we come home to my daddy. I was raised right here in this house. I turned it into a hotel. Daddy didn't like it but they wasn't nuthin else to do, all the outside interests come here to eat, but I keep my mouth shut, I mean about conditions. Terrible. But them folks comes in here from outside has to have someplace to get away where it's pretty and good food. Now you stay at the Continental Hotel. That's a good place. Mr. Archibald owns it and he is so old-fashioned he thinks the Bible flood ain't happened yet. They say that in the last election he voted his mine mules, but you know who 'they' is, the biggest liar on earth. But he's a nice man."

"Would you tell me more about Straight Creek?" Melinda got the question in when Mrs. Hightower finally paused for breath. She was shy about asking. She still didn't know how to answer when people asked her what she was doing.

"Oh that place. That's where Mr. Hightower was foreman, Dudley Mine, named after the owner's wife. They went to Florida. You stay out of Straight Creek. The mines is shut down, and the people up there is in real trouble. Mellon or Rockerfeller or one of them bought up most of the Straight Creek mines when they went bust, but they ain't done nuthin with them . . . oh, couple days' work a week maybe." Mrs. Hightower ran her tongue around her gold tooth to see if it was still there. "It sure as hell ain't pretty up to Straight Creek. You just wait. One good thing is, though, the Bell County sheriff don't let none of them thugs into Straight Creek, not yet anyhow." She laughed, longer than Melinda wished she would, and drank her coffee in a big gulp. "You'll be all right," she said, dumping the plates and the cups in the dishpan. "Just stay in the Continental Hotel. Ask anybody where the Red Cross is. They got it in one of the operator's offices. That ought to tell ye somethin."

She leaned against the sink and stared at Melinda. "Lord's love, what in the world did you get yourself into this mess, a pretty girl like you used to nice things? Oh I know, you got to be there, ain't you? My husband used to say you can argy all day long but when you wake up at three o'clock in the mornin a thing is wrong or it's right and you take to drink or do somethin about it one. That's what he said when he voted for Eugene V. Debs. You're one of them gets pulled to where it's at, ain't ye? I bet you never give it a real thought what you was agettin into. Just signed on. They's people like that. You're agoin to be that way all your life, you poor little old thing. Now that can be good or bad, depends on the place and the time and who gits aholt of ye.

"You watch out, you hear me? Them mine guards is nuthin but trash, gun thugs hard by the companies. People is boilin mad out thar. They's a lot of miners in jail they say they murdered or had criminal syndical or somethin like that. All trumped up. The Red Cross won't feed nobody's been blacklisted, that's miners that tried to join the UMWA and them has joined the NMU, that's the Communist one. Them places out there is ripe for Roosian Reds. Hit makes me so goddamn mad I could spit nails." She slammed a cup into the sink so hard she broke it. "Just fly red."

She shifted the plates onto the drainboard and started picking up the broken china. "Hit's all a matter of luck anyhow. Hewlett will ride over thar with ye tomorrow, I won't hear tell of nuthin else. Thar he is now. Hewlett!" she bawled out the door and across the valley. "Move that thar little roadster back to the barn and lock it, you better git that mud off. Not that it will do any good. Here," to Melinda, "gimme the key. Do you crank it?"

"It's a self-starter," Melinda told her when she gave her the key.

Mrs. Hightower bawled out again, "Hit's a self-starter. Don't flood it, and don't strip them gears like you done with that there other one." She walked out to meet him, and the screen door swatted behind her. All Melinda could see was a lone skinny figure away out across the pond, driving a cow with a stick in his hand, his head thrust down and forward like he was used to looking for snakes when he walked.

Sleep came slowly. She was swaddled in the feather bed, and she listened for a long time to the night noises, the drunken laughter on the porch below, the owls' hoot and the crickets' cry. A lightning bug had gotten into the room and it kept lighting up in the dark like Tinker Bell. She slept until Mrs. Hightower banged on the door and yelled, "Breakfast! The hunters is already gone."

The drive across the mountain after the heavy rain was a nightmare of slipping and sliding. Torrents had washed out the hard road in places and she had to cling close to the mountain wall, terrified of the drop on the other side but not daring to show it for fear Hewlett would offer to drive. She had heard him zoom the car into the barn the evening before.

Hewlett said "Yes'm" or "No'm" when she asked a question, trying to get him to talk, and he ventured one fact about his life. That was when he had pulled the car out of a deep flowing rut for about the tenth time. She had long since stopped counting. He wiped himself once again with a towel his mother had given him, but the towel was as dark with mud as he was. He got back in the car and said, "I'm seventeen years old." And he never said another word but "Yes'm" and "No'm."

They drove at last along the bank of the Cumberland River. She could see rags and bits of wood caught high in the trees where it had flooded, and once what looked like a broken privy, a broom, and the leg of a doll. The mountainsides were blazing with color in the sun and she thought of Uncle Brandon, who had told her that the World War was through mud and blood to the green fields beyond. He said it was the motto of some Englishmen. Pineville was the green fields beyond. They drove into the town square.

That first sight of Pineville was like coming home—the white steps of the courthouse, the great trees, the green grass that had been colored by the rain so that it looked like a new spring, the red and yellow maple leaves floating down.

Hewlett pointed across the square to the Continental Hotel. A young man turned around at the hotel desk just as she came in, and said, "You're Melinda Kregg. I know! Welcome to Pineville. You have the nicest room in the hotel," and he grinned. "We saw to that. I'm Bim Slaughter's cousin. He called us. Oh, I'm Sen—Senator Henry Clay Grandy, that's all of it. I'll come get you and take you to my family's house to dinner when you're all settled and you have reported to Nurse Gorgon."

It was wonderful to fall into a net of cousins, a net she was used to. She was tired and didn't get Sen's joke until she was halfway up the stairs. She knew that the nurse who was in charge of Pineville from the national Red Cross was named Gordon. She paused on the way to the second floor. Maybe I heard wrong, she thought, and then she giggled.

The room was a wonder; at least, she thought so. It was only about twenty by fifteen, the size of her bedroom at Grandmother Mason's, but it had four high windows that made it seem like a treehouse looking over the courthouse lawn and the mountain. Its walls were covered with some dark old wallpaper with a faint gold wiggle through it, and the furniture was oak—a chiffo-robe, armoire, a chest of drawers, a narrow bed with a brown chenille cover on it, a washstand with a pitcher and basin covered with red roses. But it was the first place she had ever had that was absolutely her own. The cabin trunk she had sent ahead on the train was sitting in the middle of the room.

She never forgot what she did then, even before she opened the trunk or her suitcase or anything. She put the Victrola on top of the chest of drawers, and she got out Lawrence Tibbett singing "Lover Come Back to Me," kicked off her shoes, lay on the bed, and looked at the blank ceiling and listened to it all the way through before she did another thing.

When she got up and turned off the Victrola, there was a little knock at the door, as if somebody had been standing there waiting for Lawrence Tibbett to finish singing. She called out, "Come in."

A black woman, maybe forty or so, came in, and the first thing she said was, "Don't you holler out 'come in' to every Tom, Dick, and Harry knocks on your door. You hear me? This here is a hotel, not your own house. It ain't safe like you're used to. My name's Loada. Mr. Sen done tole me to look after you. I come to help you unpack."

Like Mrs. Hightower, she never stopped talking the whole time she was helping. "If you got any darnin I can do that, and I can do your washin too. I'll take it home with me and they won't nobody wear it before I bring it back like some that washes and then sashays around in fine clothes before they bring them back to the ladies. I don't use nuthin but Ivory soap ninety-nine and forty-four-hundreds percent pure." She emptied the drawers of the trunk one after another, smoothed the clothes, and said, "Will you look at them things! Lord God help me to live a good life!"

She took Melinda's arm and marched her over to the line of windows in the front. "Over yonder is the Flocoe, that is where the ladies go git their ice cream and sodas, and do their gossipin. Almost next to that is Miss Mabel's and that's where the ladies goes and gits their thread and gloves and stockings and goods and all that."

She pointed out one place after another. "That there is the post office, and right behind it is the entrance to the picture show. They had themselves a union meetin there black and white together and every single one of them men they took their names down and they got blackballed to work in any mine in the state of Kentucky. Right behind that, you can't see it even this high, that is the pretty little house where I worked a long time for them folks, but the bottom dropped out of the coal business and they went to the Florida boom. When my folks left when the bottom dropped out of the coal business and my husband got mashed, roof fell on him in a mine up Straight Creek, they give me this job and I sure am glad to git it, things is terrible here, just terrible. You stay right in this room at night less you go out with Mr. Sen. He'll take care of you. You mind him."

She wasn't a yes-ma'amer like the colored people in Richmond. Imogene had told Melinda about that. She said they talked funny like the rest of the hillbillies and they didn't have one ounce of respect, not like Richmond colored people, but they were friendly as paint instead.

Loada had not stopped talking in a soft running voice Melinda hardly had to listen to, and when she did finish, all of Melinda's things were in place and hung up and in drawers. Melinda only had to change a few things, like her father's picture on the chest of drawers instead of the chifforobe. The last thing Loada said was, "I still got some 'santhimums ain't too wind-blowed. I'm goin to bring them tomorrow so it will be homey. We sure are glad folks like you come to help out."

She was gone before Melinda had a chance to give her a tip, and she thought she ought to ask Sen what she should do about that. It was one of the things that she'd always had whispered to her by her father or her grandmother: "Give a nickel, give a quarter, give half a dollar." All the guidance gone left a faint wind of doubt blowing through the pleasure of her new freedom.

She took her Red Crossy hat and set it straight over her eyes like a uniform cop. She stood for a minute to let a wake of fear pass, then she stepped out on parade to report to Nurse Gordon.

Nurse Gordon seemed bolted to a hard unforgiving chair, with her service stripes from the World War pinned to her white starched uniform, in the temporary Red Cross headquarters in the front of the coal company office. A big sign in painted gold letters on the window read LADY ELLEN COAL COMPANY. All the time Melinda was there, the superintendent that ran it for the English company never spoke to them. He just tipped his hat in both directions, first to Nurse Gordon and then to Melinda, and went on through to the back office. They could hear his telephone ring from time to time, and the faint murmur of his voice.

On that first afternoon, Nurse Gordon looked at Melinda as if she were reading her, her cute little hat and the careful tendrils of blond hair, and her cute little face, and her pretty hands. Then she looked from Melinda's legs to the letter Melinda had handed her. "Hmm." That noise in her throat was the first sound Melinda heard from her. "First aid and mass feeding. Useless. So this is what they sent me," she said, as if Melinda couldn't hear her. She finally looked up. "I can see you're not trained. You're two days late."

She left her standing there for a few minutes, which seemed like hours. Melinda thought she ought to stand at attention, and then she stood on one foot and leaned one leg against the other, and then she stood on both feet, and still Nurse Gordon didn't say another word.

Melinda decided she was waiting for her to speak. "My grandmother called the paper and they said there was bad flooding out here and it was unsafe to cross the mountains until it stopped."

Nurse Gordon laughed. "The Red Cross comes where the floods are, not after they've stopped. You'll be a fine relief worker, I must say. I don't know why they send people like you. Probably volunteered for personal reasons." She sounded as if "personal reasons" were misdemeanors, if not crimes. "You're not the only one they've been stupid about." Who "they" was she didn't bother to say. "What I'm doing here, an RN, I have no idea. Well, ours not to reason why. So I might as well put you to work. Report tomorrow morning at seven o'clock. I'll bet you haven't been up that early in years."

At seven o'clock it was dawn light, and birds called as if they were lonesome for company, and once, far away, Melinda heard a car start and somebody blow a horn. The square was empty until she walked around the courthouse to the headquarters. There was already a long line of women, as patient as trees, waiting for the door to open. Their quiet "Mornins" and "Howdees" seemed as lonesome as the birdcalls.

The first thing Nurse Gordon said was, "Well, at least you're on time." She looked like she had sat there all night. "The place is dreadful," she went on, almost talking to herself. "Can't get any of these poor white trash to help me." She looked out the window at the patient crowd standing outside. "Half of them are not qualified anyway.

Husbands on strike or blacklisted. We only feed the deserving unemployed, don't forget that. Can't feed everybody"—as if she were apologizing for something Melinda hadn't said. "First, I want this floor scrubbed. Now. Pick up the bucket. Use disinfectant."

Later Melinda was aware of Nurse Gordon standing over her, keeping her hard white shoes out of the way of the scrub brush and the puddle that Melinda was trying and failing to control. A voice fell on her from high above. "I can see you've never scrubbed a floor before. Don't use so much water. I forgot to tell you. We at the Red Cross do not, repeat not, talk to reporters. This town is full of them and you just don't know who they represent, some are Russian Reds. Remember that, if you forget everything else . . ." The voice trailed away, the hard white shoes retreated, and she could hear the screech of Nurse Gordon's chair as she attacked it with her seat. She was to hear that maddening screech every time the woman sat down.

Scrubbing the endless floor was Melinda's first job for the Red Cross, while families with dark faces that she could hardly see because their backs were to the sun stared at her through the plate glass window, with LADY ELLEN COAL COMPANY backward in gold letters across their faces. They were the stillest people she had ever seen.

She recognized Sen by his auburn hair, which made a halo. One of the men turned his shadow head and she heard Sen laugh. He pushed open the door.

"Wait outside," Nurse Gordon said, without raising her head from the morning list.

"Oh, come on, Edna!" Sen flirted with her and her face turned red and young and she smiled. "Those men out there say you've got eclatneliddy a-scrubbin the floor and they want to watch. In case you don't learn French up there in Pennsylvania, that's *eclat* and *elite* in mountain language, left over from when the French were here, I reckon." He had turned around and was explaining this to Melinda, who scrubbed harder and was Helen Hayes in *Arrowsmith,* angry and dedicated, but only for a flashing second until he laughed at her, as if he knew exactly what she was thinking. It was uncanny.

"You're the picture show for the morning. One family up at their mine put their baby outside in a Kiddie Koop and these same people came from miles around to see the wild baby in a cage. They don't mean any harm. They're just curious. I'm coming to get you at three o'clock Saturday afternoon. It's Indian summer and we're all going to the swimming hole for a picnic. I want you to meet some people. Now don't look like that, Edna, the girl has to have some fun."

"Fun!" Nurse Gordon said it like a swear word and went back to her list.

Late in the afternoon she finally inspected the walls and the floor and released Melinda from scrubbing. She had smiled only once in the whole day, when she said, "You better get used to smelling of disinfectant instead of perfume. I remember when I started. My pretty hands looked like raw meat." Nurse Gordon didn't act as if she disliked her; it was just that she didn't *anything* her. Melinda tried to think she was young, lonesome, and in love with Sen, but it didn't work.

She fell exhausted into bed in the corner room of the Continental Hotel, almost without seeing it. She had used muscles that not riding, not playing, not Trip's light fantastic had ever touched.

Even with all the hard work, it was one of the happiest weeks she had ever spent, and she knew it at the time, not just looking back. In the evening it was as if she were a cousin visiting in the summer, when things were sweet and everybody was happy in public, and they sat close together on the porch swings and sang and flirted, and Sen played the uke.

One evening they all piled into Melinda's roadster and went up on Pine Mountain to dance, not telling anybody because it was a speakeasy. She wore her gray georgette with the tiny yellow roses appliqued around the neck, and gray silk shoes to match, and she and Sen walked in the mountain wind and looked down on Pineville, a little pool of winking lights away below beside the Cumberland River, and she was aware that the breeze floated her dress too, alight in the moon, and made it almost waltz. He was too shy or too polite to kiss her yet, but she went to bed in the Continental Hotel that night knowing he would.

On Saturday morning when she reported to Nurse Gordon, she got new orders. "Now sit there and take names." Nurse Gordon motioned to a table near the door, with a pile of forms on it. "Names, dates, ages, work status, number of children—take their names, too." Melinda realized that it was her habit to speak without looking up, as if she were too intent on what she was doing to have time. She went back to her desk and the chair screeched. She was reading a book. Later in the morning Melinda saw that it was *The Trail of the Lonesome Pine.* "I'm trying to get some idea of these people," Nurse Gordon said once. "You're to read this as soon as I've finished. Sen lent it to me." It wasn't an explanation. It was an order.

Melinda didn't know whether Nurse Gordon would let her go at three o'clock, so she worked all the day, following her orders, and once in a while a forefinger hit the pages she was trying to fill out while people she could hardly hear gave their names, slowly.

"Not like that, not whole families." Nurse Gordon had stood behind Melinda for a few minutes without her knowing it, until one of the women, Mrs. Haycroft, looked up. She looked scared. Nurse Gordon's voice rose in a litany: *"Number in family ages and if they are unemployed!"* She shouted this and shot at the paper form again with her forefinger. "Every single one! Mrs. Haycroft, those are not all your children and you know it. You have one who is half grown and can work. Your sister has four, and there are ten children here for relief. You ought to know better." She spoke to Melinda as if Mrs. Haycroft had disappeared. "Her brother-in-law is blacklisted at Happy Valley Mine. His family is not eligible, and the rest of these children are God knows who."

"But the children aren't blacklisted, and they're hungry," Melinda muttered at the desktop.

"I would be grateful if you would not talk back to me in front of these people," Nurse Gordon said when she had shut the door on the last of the women in line, so calmly that Melinda knew she was seething with fury, the way she made every word separate, slow, as if Melinda didn't have good sense.

"I see you're going to have to learn a few facts of life, young lady. We've got enough people unemployed without a bunch of no-good Russian Reds won't do a day's work. And if they're going to start faking names like that, I want to see every list before you take them to supply." She went back to reading *The Trail of the Lonesome Pine.*

For the rest of the day Melinda could hear the pages flip, and once Nurse Gordon sniffled as if she were trying not to cry. Melinda couldn't see how she could make so much noise turning a page. She sounded the minutes of the day. Nobody else came into the office. They milled around outside.

At exactly two-forty Nurse Gordon told her to go. She ran around the square to the Continental Hotel. The lobby was full of men. One grabbed her by the arm. "Miss! Are you from Pineville? I'm from the *Louisville Courier-Journal.*" She was about to say something when Sen removed the man's hand from her arm. "The lady doesn't want to talk," he said.

He drove her to where the water fell so gently along the rocks that she could climb them like stairs, and she met ten people who all became her friends at once, it seemed. She thought later, if it had been any other time, they would have been her friends for life. Sen dared everybody to go into the cold October water that rushed down from the mountain into a deep pool, and because it was Sen they all did. But when she dived from the rock because Sen dared her and came up with her hair plastered down her back, another boy, one of those moon-eyed boys who wouldn't dare ask you for a date, said, "You'll catch cold." His name was Johnny Bradford. They sat by Clear Creek and listened to the water while Johnny dried her hair, then braided and unbraided it and didn't say another word.

It was the first time she ever saw Johnny Bradford, not that he was anything to look at, shy as some kind of animal and skinny as a rake. He wore his glasses until he took his turn to slide down the rocks on the big inner tube Sen had brought, but then he was so blind he crashed into the bank. He watched her all afternoon and into the dark when they built a fire and she lay leaning against Sen. Sen whispered to her that they had been at Yale together. "We were roommates at Yale." His mouth was close to her ear, and there seemed to be nobody else around the fire. He already had a crush on her; she knew that.

"We were roommates at Exeter too. His mother's dead and his father is always wandering around Europe. We've been like family to him for a long time. Johnny's all right. He's a braver man than I am. I make him come down to Pineville once in a while. He has some funny ideas, but that's all right. We've been arguing for at least eight years. My mother and father think he hung the moon, but he doesn't talk any of his nonsense in front of them."

She thought it was wonderful that a strong handsome man like Sen, who was such a leader and who glowed when he stood in the sun as if it were shining just for him, would say that some little old skinny boy was braver than he was; it was just like him, being a protector to somebody weaker and shyer. She loved it. She snuggled up to Sen as the night cooled, with her hair down long and the smell and taste of him when he leaned down to kiss her cheek—salt and tobacco and cold spring water. For that minute the days were going to stretch in front of her and it would never be winter and she was half asleep to the sound of their singing, "Lover Come Back to Me" and "The Sweetheart of Sigma Chi" and "If I Had the Wings of an Angel." The songs drifted up toward the dark trees, and the animals watched with their bright reflecting eyes. She heard Sen whisper, "Let her sleep. She's been working like a dog for that damned woman."

She thought it was Johnny Bradford who said, "That Gordon woman is a fascist." It was the first time Melinda had ever heard the word except when people talked about Italy. She heard Sen laugh and say something, but she never heard what it was.

Late at night when she got home she played Lawrence Tibbett singing "Lover Come Back to

Me" on her little round Victrola. She played it again, and then when she started it the third time and was Grace Moore leaning out the window of the Continental Hotel yearning at the dark courthouse, somebody banged on the wall and she cut it off. But she went to sleep with Lawrence Tibbett, who turned into Sen, singing full-throated on the sidewalk below.

It all began to unravel the next morning. She woke to a rumble that she thought at first was rain, but when she looked out the window over the courthouse square, the sun was making dim pools under the bright trees and whole families were standing in the shade. Wagons, trucks, and flivvers were parked all around the square. It was so quiet that she heard one of the mules snort and grumble. She thought at first that because it was Sunday they were going to have a revival.

The crowd seemed to be breathing at the same time, the calm sound of hundreds of people waiting with that awful patience she had already recognized as the mountain fury Mrs. Hightower had talked about. On the steps of the courthouse in front of the columns, a man called out something she couldn't make out. She saw the reporter who had tried to talk to her the day before pausing at one group after another.

From every second-story window, she could see a gun aimed at the courthouse square. In the nearest window across the street, a boy who looked about fourteen held a shotgun balanced on the sill. He was grinning. Farther along, in the windows above the post office, she saw three machine guns, then more rifles. The mine guards in black suits waited as patiently as the people below for something to happen.

Sen was there too. She could see his auburn hair in the sun as he walked from one group of men to another; he seemed to be arguing, his hands waving.

She didn't know whether she was more afraid to go out through the crowd or not to report to Nurse Gordon. Nurse Gordon had told her to go to church and then come to the office. "We have to be seen at church, of course, but there is no Sunday in times of need," she had said.

It was already too late to go to church, and when Melinda tried to make her way through the crowd of men, Sen grabbed her arm and said, "Get back to your room and stay in the hotel today," as if she had done something wrong.

When she went down for Sunday dinner in the dark dining room, with its blinds drawn and its radiators burbling, it was full of men. She was the only woman. The reporter saw her and came over to her table and sat down without being invited.

"Howdedo. I'm Freddie Long, from the *Louisville Courier-Journal.* Where's your boyfriend?" He grinned. "Let's I and you dish the dirt a little bit, how about it?" He didn't wait for an answer. He wore his hat on the back of his head, like reporters in *The Front Page.* She was both too shy and too curious to make any kind of scene or say a word. "Look, sister, what are you doing here? That's all I want to know."

"What is happening—all those people out there?" she asked instead of answering. She nodded toward the window, where the steady hum of the crowd was muted by the drawn blinds.

"Oh, protest meeting," he said, but he didn't explain. "It ain't news. They want human interest, sob-sister stuff. I know you're with the Red Cross." That should have been obvious from the Red Cross band on her arm. She felt efficient and sat straight in her chair. It made him laugh.

"Oh, sister, you've bitten off more than you can chew—you'll find that out. The Red Cross is poison around here with the people who need it, ones joining the union and getting blacklisted. There's no more than two days' work a week anyhow, and they end up earning less than they owe the company store. Unless they make whiskey, they can't make a living. You see kids with shoes and underwear on, their daddy's making whiskey. I know these people. Foreigners come in here and see what they see and I see what I see, like Dayton, Tennessee." He settled back to tell her all about it.

"I covered Dayton. I got to be real good friends with John Scopes. Them outside fellows walked all over him." He looked at her polite, blank face. "Boy, you don't know nuthin. The Monkey Trial. Out-of-state reporters made fools of these people, just told about the lunatic fringe, you know, God-made-the-world-in-seven-days fellows, when all them farmers wanted to find out when they hung around the courthouse was if controlled breeding, you know, like survival of the fittest, could fatten their razorback hogs. Wasn't anything but a ACLU test case, anyhow. Jack Scopes had only stayed in Dayton after school was out because he wanted to take some girl to a Sunday school picnic. He said he just did it to please his daddy. His daddy was an Englishman who had been blackballed in the Pullman strike and raised him on John Stuart Mill, and his mama was one of those hard-rock Presbyterian women. Between those two and the preachers and the outside agitators and the big-city lawyers, he didn't have a chance in hell."

He might as well have been speaking—oh, she didn't know, Greek or something. She watched his mouth move on and on, as she had learned to do when women who were friends of her mother talked too much when she had to be polite.

"This is the same fight, same lawyers, same foreigners, different field," he was saying, "but these folks don't know it yet. They'll learn. That fellow Neal, who was Jack Scopes's Tennessee-registered lawyer, is already here. Go on and eat," he said when the waitress brought her blue-plate special. "Honey, you bring me some real hot coffee," he told the waitress, and she grinned at him and glanced at Melinda as if she were made of poison oak.

He never seemed to stop gabbing, but when Melinda finally was able to get up from the table and excuse herself, she congratulated herself that she hadn't told him anything. She didn't know she had said too much until Nurse Gordon showed her the *Louisville Courier-Journal* two days later and said, "I specifically told you *not* to talk to reporters." She seemed more amused than angry, but she wouldn't let Melinda see the paper.

Sen saved it for her, and it called her a babe in the Kentucky woods.

She didn't see Sen's friend Johnny all through the week, and when she asked, he laughed. Everything that week seemed to tickle him pink because he was in love; even his face was pink. Sen said, "He's running the NMU soup kitchen up on Straight Creek. He's got to stay up there on guard. Those bums you see patrolling the roads shot up one of their soup kitchens last week and killed two men. I wish he wouldn't do it, but you can't argue with a convert."

"Is he Catholic?" she asked.

"No, child, he's a Communist." He went on laughing. "The National Miner's Union is Communist-backed."

"Well, if the people are hungry . . ." she muttered, and hoped he wouldn't hear because she remembered that she had already gotten into trouble with Nurse Gordon about that.

"But you don't need to worry. The Red Cross is on our side. After all, it's our money. Johnny calls us all fascists. We've been arguing ever since the Depression started."

There were small hints of trouble all month, just a click of Nurse Gordon's fingers to get the paper from Melinda's hand when she finished her daily list, and then an almost savage blue pencil through some of the names. Then, on Halloween, when a soft rain made the courthouse square look like it was already in mourning for the souls of the dead and the lights of the Flocoe were smudges in a cold morning mist, Nurse Gordon was standing up when Melinda walked into the headquarters at seven.

"I have warned you for the last time," she said in that awful calm voice she used when she was furious. "The ladies at supply said you were sending over blacklisted children and even the children of men in Harlan County jail for murder. Now this has to stop, or I will release you from your duties and you will be sent out of the state."

Melinda had wondered how long she could last, substituting names. She had lasted more than three weeks, which she thought wasn't bad.

"I ought to have known something was wrong, I mean even more than just your stupid mistakes, when those women started smiling at you and saying good morning when they came in to register. They never did that to me."

It was the beginning of a Saturday she would remember for years, every time there was a dark rain, a whisper of wind skidding wet dead leaves across the pavement. There was the beckoning light of the Flocoe in the distance and she was walking in her raincoat along the courthouse sidewalk with her head down, her rain hat pulled almost over her eyes, when someone stopped her, a hand on her arm.

It was Johnny Bradford. He was too upset to be shy. "Come and have a chocolate soda," he said. "I've got to talk to you. I looked for you at the hotel, and then I waited for you to come out of that place."

He took her arm and began to pull her around the square. His stride was twice the length of hers, and she had to run to catch up. He didn't even notice. "We know what you've been doing. That is brave, no, courageous, more courageous. There's a difference." But he didn't tell her what it was, or who "we" were.

They stood inside the corner door of the Flocoe, dripping water on the tessellated marble floor, turning it shiny. Erma saw them and said, "Can you wait a minute while I go around the corner?" She seemed to know Johnny better than she did Melinda. "I'll be back."

Melinda had watched the Flocoe before while Erma went to the bathroom at the beauty shop around the corner. It was so familiar to everybody that they said, "I'm going around the corner" instead of "I'm going to powder my nose," as she always had in Richmond.

She sat down at a round marble ice-cream table with Johnny Bradford, and he put his head close so that nobody could hear, even though the Flocoe was empty.

"I need your help," he said at once. "I wouldn't ask you, but I am in love with you and I have stayed up all night and I finally decided that since I have trusted you with my affections, I might as well trust you with everything else."

She was too astonished to say that she didn't want to be trusted with anything. She watched the Adam's apple on his thin neck go up and down while he poured out his secrets onto the marble ice-cream table.

Maybe it was because Nurse Gordon had caught her, maybe it was pride at being criticized and called cute little names, maybe it was what Johnny said, maybe it was a way to show her grandmother, who had said she'd never stick to anything in her spoiled life, but she stayed and listened to Johnny as he lost his fidgets and his face began to glow. The glow might have been love; it might have been zeal. Whatever it was, it caught and held her there, and she said she would lend him her car. That was all he asked.

"I can't get food up to my soup kitchen. The roads are being patrolled, and there are hungry people up there. They know you're Red Cross. They won't stop you. After all, the Red Cross is run by the coal operators."

"No, it's not," she told him. "It's run by that nice newspaper editor, Herndon Evans."

He looked at her as if she'd lost all her marbles, but at least he didn't call her anything cute. "That man has been spreading false information to every newspaper in the country," he said instead.

They nearly quarreled right then. She argued, "He has not. He's just told their side."

"That's what I said." He looked at her as if she hadn't heard him. Then he sighed. "So much of life is a question of semantics," he told her.

Since she didn't know what he was talking about, she didn't answer.

They met early on Sunday morning outside the Continental Hotel. It had finally stopped raining. He guided her to an old warehouse on Pine Street, and he got out. She still had the canvas car roof and the side curtains up, and he told her to leave them. He and a woman took the rumble seat out and carried it into the warehouse. Melinda didn't say a word.

She felt like a packhorse being loaded, and the

thought made her giggle. When she did, Johnny looked up at her, annoyed. Then he smiled. He really smiled, nicely. "I'm sorry, I haven't heard girls giggle for a long time," he said.

Mrs. Haycroft was one of the women loading the rumble seat. "Call me Eulalie," she said, and grinned. "Looky here, honey, I didn't never mean to git you into trouble with ole Miz Starch. Them youngins is living with usn. We're all at my mother-in-law's up to Straight Creek. We're the only ones got our own place up on the side of the hill. We still call it the farm, but they ain't much left. The rest was in company shacks and they got throwed out." She stopped with a large bag of flour in her arms like a baby. "If you ever need a place to stay, we always got room for one more." It was the old mountain hospitality. "You hear me?" she added, and dumped the flour into the empty space where the rumble seat had been.

"Now you'll have to go up the creek by yourself. I'm not going to endanger you by being seen riding with you." Johnny began to stammer what he had to say, so softly that she thought he was telling her a secret, but he wasn't; it was just that he was so near it made him tongue-tied.

The rain began again, a fine mist on the windshield. "Uh, they see me in the car with you, they'll know what you're doing. Now you cross the tracks and go about ten miles up the river, and then you turn left into Straight Creek. There'll be a young boy with red hair there at the corner to signal you in. Give him a ride on your running board. That will be Eulalie's boy, Truxton." His face was losing its shy twitches and uneasy grins.

He seemed years older, she thought, and really quite nice-looking.

On the day after Halloween, the town of Pineville, still asleep early on Sunday morning, was lovely and funny to Melinda, even in the mist and half-dark. Festoons of wet toilet paper hung in the trees, and on the front porches, forlorn jack-o'-lanterns sat, their carved mouths and eyes blackened by guttered candles. Somebody had put a wheelbarrow on a porch roof, and there was confetti in the street.

The evergreens were still dripping from the dew and mist. In the air she smelled earth, and old leaves and wood smoke from the chimneys in the kitchens, where Sunday breakfast was being cooked. There was only the lonesome sound of the movement of air and her own engine, and the windshield misting up so that she had to turn on the windshield wipers, and the slight breathing of the canvas car roof as she picked up speed just across the railroad tracks from the town.

She passed by a little board-and-batten church, and then another, and then one with a sign that said THE CHURCH OF JESUS CHRIST ONLY, where there were trucks and wagons and flivvers and people singing inside. The air was dim with mist. Instead of the cars patrolling the roads full of the black-suited men with their iron faces and their guns, there was nobody. She felt like a ghost, twenty years old and nothing but a ghost on what her grandmother called All Souls Day, instead of All Saints like the younger Episcopalians.

She wouldn't have been afraid of the men, not with the Red Cross armband, which she knew would be her passport. Sen called the men mine guards, but Johnny called them gun thugs, which made Sen laugh. "My best friend I grew up with and played on the football team with is one of them. He's a swell fellow. He just couldn't find another job." But she was afraid of the silence, the gray air, the mist, the ghostly singing that faded into nothing as she drove past.

Truxton was a long, lanky, redheaded fifteen-year-old with the face of a child still. He waved from the roadside, and he jumped up on her running board as if it were a game. But he didn't say anything, just pointed up the muddy road to the left.

She drove up the narrow hollow lost between the mountains. Everything that Johnny had told her in the Flocoe was true. It was, as he had said, another country. Frail unpainted empty shacks perched above the ground on stilts. A half-starved dog ran out from under one of them and she nearly hit it.

She slowed down and passed houses, outhouses, tents made of old quilts, shacks of piano crates, and a few real tents. On one she read a painted sign that said, YOUR DOGS EAT BETTER THAN OUR KIDS. The sign, the quilts, the tents, the sagging porches, wavered through the isinglass of the car windows, as if what she saw, and not the isinglass, were scarred with use and weather. Her windshield wipers seemed to be trying to wipe it all away. Truxton waved at people who came out slowly to see the strange car. They stood beside the mud road in front of the shelters. Not one of them wore shoes. She half closed her eyes to peer through the wavering mist, afraid that a child would dart out ahead of her.

Here and there, where a few families had not been evicted, men sat on the porches. On one, a tiny old woman fanned herself in a rocking chair, not because it was hot but because she always had and always would. Melinda knew the habit. It was her grandmother's, with her ostrich-feather fan that spoke its own imperious language.

She drove so slowly she might as well have been walking up the creek. She dodged rain-filled ruts. There were already skeletons of trees, blown naked by the wind, and water in the ruts, water running along the sides of the stony dirt road. As she drove on there were more and more people, completely silent, just watching as if she weren't quite real, couldn't hear, couldn't see.

Truxton finally signaled up a steep dirt track where water ran between flat rocks. He guided her up the mountainside into a yard as hard as bone. Rickety wooden steps climbed farther uphill to the house above them, a long, one-story log cabin that had spread-out wings of board and batten and a long porch, mountain color. The only movement was a thin snake of smoke that wound into the sky from a huge mud-and-stone chimney.

Truxton ran around the car, opened the door for her, and took her arm to help her out—good manners for ladies. "This here's Grandma's, Miss Kregg. My name is Truxton Haycroft." He spoke as if he weren't quite used yet to his voice being so low.

She wanted to cling to the kitchen door so she wouldn't have to go any farther. A man got up from a huge pine table that had been scrubbed white through the years. He had one leg. The other one was a pegleg, like the scary man in *Treasure Island* had. She was afraid. "Now you set down right here," he said in a low voice not much used. "We would of got ye some coffee, only we ain't got no coffee. I'll git ye some well water."

A low rumble came from the corner of the room. "You'll do nuthin of the kind, Houghton Junior. Git Miss Kregg some sassafras tea. We got plenty. Don't you go awhinin like them poor whites downhill ain't got nuthin. You set over here by me so I can hear ye."

"I'm sorry, Ma," he said, as if he weren't at least sixty years old.

The largest woman Melinda had ever seen had made the corner into her domain. A Crosley radio with a square antenna sat on a table beside her. Her great body and legs were covered with a crocheted red wool throw, and astonishingly little bare feet peeked out from under it, as if the toes were watching Melinda on their own. The woman wasn't fat. She was massive. Her arms were leg size, but not soft. When she moved one of them to order Melinda to come closer, the gesture was to be obeyed.

"Now you set right down here and tell me why you're out here in Bell County. Ain't you got nuthin better to do?"

Melinda was struck dumb. She simply sat on

the cane chair where she had been put and said nothing.

"What's the matter, girl? Cat got your tongue? I'm Grandma Haycroft. I heared what you done, come all the way from Richmond, Virginia. That's a real fer piece for a little old thing like you. You got a yaller car," she informed Melinda.

The man brought her an old china cup of sassafras tea. Then he limped back and sat down at the table.

"Go on. Drink it. Sassafras and sorghum. Good for your stomick," Grandma Haycroft said, and then silence settled on them and on the room. Melinda could hear someone talking away on the other side of the wall, and once a baby cried. That was all. She waited for someone to speak again. They sat as if it didn't matter whether anybody spoke or not. She had never felt such silence. There was only the creak of cane chairs, loud when somebody shifted.

The walls of the room had been faced with plaster; here and there a log peeked through. The floor was covered with rush mats and rag rugs. All around the walls were streamers of dried green beans, onions, corn, herbs, pumpkin slivers, draped so that Melinda thought at first the room was decorated for Halloween. A white electric stove with a side oven, the largest she had ever seen, almost new, dominated the wall beside the stone chimney.

Finally Grandma Haycroft was ready to speak. "Me and Essie put up two hundred bottles of corn and tomatoes, and okra, and let me see now, we strang about two hundred foot of green beans.

Wouldn't you say two hundred foot get your har out of your eyes, and don't you dare start in playin that fiddle while I'm atalkin to a lady." This was to Truxton, who had taken a fiddle down from its hook on the wall and was looking at it with some longing. "That thar fiddle come over the mountain with Mr. Haycroft's great-grandpa. Truxton knows how to play hit. He taught hisself. I jest don't want to hear it right now."

She pointed to festoons of dried leaves. "Them's yarbs. Now let me see. Sassafras, sour sobs, wild garlic, fennel. That thar is sang. Hit's good for your blood and lady's trouble and I don't know what-all. That thar is jimsonweed, make your eyes purty. Of course you can't see a thing when you use it, but the boys can see you. We make our own cornmeal and our own whiskey. We don't hold with nuthin store-bought. Hit's got poison in it to save money. This here town used to be called Sugar Hollow for sugar maples. Now they call it Number Eight. They ain't no more sugar maples, and that ain't no name for no town.

"If they thow you out down there at the Continental Hotel, you come right on up here, and you live with us. We got plenty of room. Them trash downhill didn't grow enough in them truck gardens they put in to stuff a chicken, I tole them. I tole them they was agoin to starve in the winter like them grasshoppers. I tole them we would loan them more ground to plant on while the strikes was on, but they wouldn't pay me no attention. Strike. That's all they give a hoot in hell about . . ."

"Now Ma, I'm on strike too," Houghton Junior said to the bib of his overalls.

"You ain't nuthin of the kind. You got mashed in the mine. He got mashed in the mine. He sees everthin backwards. He's on the compensation. I seen to that. I marched right down there to Mr. Terry. I've knowed him since he was knee high, whipped him once when he thowed a rock at a girl. Them folks are Quakers. They don't believe in sayin nuthin in church jest set thar like a bump on a log. I said now look here G. W., we'd still be upside that mountain amindin our own business if your pappy hadn't of come in here with store-bought stuff and big promises. Now you do your duty by my boy got mashed in the mine. You people are supposed to be Quakers, well, let me see what Quakers do when a boy gits mashed in the mine. Of course nowadays, can't even git to G. W. most of the time. He don't know what to do. He jest sets down there in Pineville and leaves everythin to his superintendent so he won't have to come up here see how bad things are. Well, at least he didn't sell out like most of them wildcatters on Straight Creek, sell out or kicked out when the bottom dropped out of the coal business.

"Now let's see, that started round about 1927. At first they wasn't much warnin, just like a faulty ceiling, you don't know until hit's agoin to come down. Them things can breathe and talk fer a long time before they fall. I could have tole them in Washington, that Mr. Hoover and all them others, watch the coal business. When the bottom drops out of the coal business, hard times will spread right out from the coal face, you listen to me."

She moved herself a little in her huge chair, and when she saw Melinda looking at it, she said, "This here chair belonged to my great-grandpa. He settled this farm. He come here to fight in the Indian wars, and they give him the land. We got his uniform. Hit's red with gold braid. He was some kind of officer. He married a Boatwright. The folks who was out here fit for the king. A lot of folks, well the few that was out here, did that. They didn't want no more trouble with the Cherokee, now her sister was scalped with her whole family." Whose sister she didn't bother to say. "They was jest settin thar of an evenin when the Cherokee come. My great-grandpa tole my pa they found them still asettin in front of their cabin in the cool of the evenin right down thar where the company store is now. Just settin thar without their hair on. They'd been eatin chestnuts, and my great-grandpa tole my pa they had to warsh the chestnuts out of their mouths when they berried them. We was all berried uphill from here, still are, you can't even go up thar except for berryin and Decoration Day since the company leased all that land from my pa. He made a mistake.

"My great-grandpa was a little skinny man when he come out here and then he got so fat he got this here chair carved so he could set at his desk. Been in the family. Houghton Junior, go tell your pa we got company."

When he had left, she announced, "Now my other boy, Eulalie's husband, he was funny when he come back from the war. He was all right when he come home and then hit got worse as he got older, so he went out in the woods and shot hisself with a shotgun."

Melinda could hear Houghton Junior's pegleg retreating behind the door, deeper and deeper into the house, peg, foot, peg, foot, fading like the hymn in the roadside church, then gone.

Grandma Haycroft's voice rolled on like a river, as rhythmic and timeless as the clock that ticked on the wall above her head. "Ever stick of furniture was made right here on the place," she said, ignoring the electric stove. "We don't hold with no company store furniture you sell your soul fer."

She chomped her gums like an old horse. "Them gun thugs tried to throw my little granddaughter-in-law Rose outin their company shack. So I went down thar. I walked right in. They was astandin around with shotguns takin the Lord's name in vain. I said to them I said, I said you git out of this youngin's house ascarin her and her kids she don't know whar her husband is at and she done tole you that. They was drunk and staggerin and stormin around that little old house ain't fitten fer a hog no-how, and I said to them I just said right out hell's far and molasses if you ain't got no warrant you better git out I don't care if you are the company law I'll git the real law on ye. I never done nuthin to the one doin the most damage. I just stood on his foot and he stopped. I weigh three hundred and twenty-four pounds. One of them fellahs was Lem Fleener's boy. He shot that fellah down to the soup house last summer and they never done a thing to him.

"Been a miner caught even talkin to another one that Sheriff Blair that son-of-a-bitch would of had him in jail before you could say Jack Robinson whoever that was, some coal operator. That little youngin my granddaughter-in-law wasn't nuthin but a scared kid, her no more than seventeen years old and half naked with three kids already. I said to her, Rose, you listen to me. I ain't akeerin what your Houghton the Third has went and done I want you and them kids to come right up to our house. They're right here.

"Later we stood on the porch out thar and watched them thugs thow everthin we wasn't able to move right quick right out on the dirt road. They picked up Houghton the Third for criminal syndical. Have you ever heared the like of that? He wasn't doin nuthin but standin out in the woods with some fellahs drinkin a little busthead moonshine. So he was in the county jail down there in Pineville but I marched right down to the company store and I said I'm agoin to use your telephone and they wasn't nobody to stop me, not then and not now let me tell you, and I called up and I said now lookee here G. W. you better know what's agoin on up here and Houghton the Third was out of that jail in the time it took G. W. to walk down Jefferson Street."

The voice mingled with the slight breathing of the fire in the stove, and the tick of the clock, and the rocking of the chair. Melinda was almost asleep when she heard the car.

"Go see who that thar is," Grandma told

Truxton, who had laid his head down on the kitchen table. He picked up a shotgun from the corner and ambled over to the window that looked out over the hollow. "Hit ain't nobody but Ma and Johnny," he said, and ambled back and put the gun in the corner.

"Well, git on out thar and help them unload. Now git."

Melinda heard the slow drag of footsteps and the sound of the pegleg long before Houghton Junior opened the door. Grandpa Haycroft came slowly into the kitchen, a man in a dream, softly moving, softly speaking. He shuffled over until he was standing close to Melinda, and he peered at her. "Howdedo, ma'am?" He made a slight bow, almost courtly. He had a fine white beard down to his waist, and he wore an old-fashioned frock coat. "I'm sorry I wudn't here to welcome ye, ma'am, but I couldn't find my coat," he said. He turned around and spoke to Grandma Haycroft as if she too were a visitor. "Howdedo, ma'am?"

Her great wide face softened, and she smiled at him as if she were a young girl again. "Houghton Junior, set yore pappy down," she said gently.

As Melinda ran past him to the door to help Eulalie, who was staggering under a load of clothes, Grandpa Haycroft smiled. "Why, here's another purty girl," he said. He tried to get up to shake hands with Melinda, which was difficult, since he couldn't get up without help and Melinda had taken the pile of clothes into her arms.

Behind them, Grandma Haycroft called,

"They ain't but one purty girl, Mr. Haycroft, now you set down. Truxton, set your grandpa down. Hit ain't his grandpa hit's his great-grandpa, Junior's his grandpa. His pa's dead . . . ." The voice returned to a litany of family relations which reminded Melinda that Abraham begat Isaac and Isaac begat Jacob.

There were sixteen people around the pine table for dinner. Houghton Junior said the blessing, and Mrs. Haycroft explained right through it.

"Mr. Haycroft said the blessin from the day he got home from our war and we got married. I was fifteen and he was handsome as paint, a beautiful man but half starved walked all the way from Appomattox in nuthin but what he stood up in, but we always had the land. If you want to be safe from them folks get yourself a little piece of property they can't throw ye offn but two years ago he would start into rantin like he was still in the war ever time he bowed his head in prayer, so Junior started to say the blessin instead."

"Amen," Houghton Junior mumbled, but Melinda hadn't heard a word.

Johnny Bradford had sunk into being part of things as if he too were kin. Mrs. Haycroft looked around the table, scanning it to be sure everybody was there, until she came to him. "Johnny's stayin with usn since the soup kitchen down to Three Mile got shot up. He's as much my boy as if he had of sucked my titty. I love a fellah got guts when he don't have to. They're atryin to starve the miners out. Hit's gettin worse. Swear to God them folks would be better off if they was borned into slavery. At least if them fellahs had to buy them they'd look after them like they do their mine mules. They wouldn't dare to look here for Johnny, not with me here. They know I shoot. I done it before. Mr. Haycroft used to, but he can't see good no more," she explained, as if he weren't there at the table and listening.

They ate cornbread and a bite of ham apiece, and drank buttermilk. Melinda managed to smile at the children, who seemed to be all sizes but with the same solemn stares. They were polite and quiet. One of them, a little girl of three or four, reached for another piece of cornbread, and her mother, Rose, slapped her hand and she started to cry. "You had your share," Rose told her. "Now quit that."

Grandma Haycroft complained to Eulalie as the little girl began to run down into sighs and sniffles. "If we had of knowed that we was goin to have company ye could have killed a chicken and cooked some of them green beans . . ."

After Eulalie had told Rose it was her turn to wash up, she followed Melinda and Johnny out onto the porch. They stood at the log rail and looked far below, down the hollow. Behind them Rose pumped water into the huge old iron sink. The sound of Truxton's fiddle kept time with the fall of the water. Eulalie smiled. "He played for the dances when we had the dances. He's purty good, ain't he?"

She whispered before the others straggled out after them, "Grandma don't know the milkhouse and the smokehouse are both empty, and they ain't much left in the cellar. Well, she knows but she don't admit it or she forgets it, somethin like that. We put up a lot but with this crowd hit's nearly gone in November when it ought to have done us till the first spring crop."

When Melinda and Johnny left, the family lined the log porch rail, waving and calling, "You come back, you hear, you come back anytime."

They drove down the hill. The minor wail of the fiddle became part of the wind in the trees. At the tipple, Johnny told Melinda to stop. "We're going to take a little walk," he said. He motioned her out into the mud of the road.

Johnny held her arm as if she were going to run away. Above them the half-fallen tipple ran in a jagged rusted metal line all the way up the mountainside, like some parody of a carnival ride. A sheet of tin had loosened in the weather on the powerhouse roof, and it kept banging in the wind, as steady as a clock.

They walked from the tipple past the closed company store with its Coca-Cola sign on the wall and its pay window so covered with dust that she could see only ghosts of counters and empty shelves inside. There were faded places in the unpainted board and batten of the outside wall. Johnny told her that the miners had torn the tin advertising signs off to patch their houses before they got evicted. Only the Coca-Cola and Bull Durham signs had survived.

He took her from tent to tent, quilt shelter to quilt shelter, through the cold afternoon, as slowly as if they were walking through a park. He was secure there. There was a sense with him that he knew he was in a place he ought to be. It wasn't love that made his face relax and made him seem somehow taller, in control; it was a strange calm security.

"Thirty years ago, this was all Haycroft's farm," he said, and waved his arm. "They sold it for five dollars an acre. It was the most paper money any of them had ever seen, and most of the land was hill scrub they couldn't pasture a goat on. Now the railroad tracks take up most of the level ground, and the miners and their families have to grow their patches up behind the houses on the hillside. See up there?" He pointed to where dead cornstalks leaned along the mountainside above the roofs of the shacks. "Houghton Junior leased the mineral rights to what they didn't sell to the company. He didn't know what he was doing. Oh, even old Grandpa Haycroft thought it was fine. They got the electricity from the company, still have it free, and they got themselves an electric stove and a washing machine and a Victrola and a Crosley radio, and all the things they thought would see them right through to heaven, and then Houghton Junior had his accident, the bottom fell out of the coal business, the radio went dead, and the Victrola records wore out, and there was only one day's work a week, and then the mine shut down altogether. Only the stove works—thank God, they feed so many. The company owns some other mines where some of these men went to work, but when they went on strike the last time they got blackballed, and now look at them."

Johnny seemed to know everybody. They

stopped and passed the time of afternoon. The whole town of people was waiting, still, except for six or seven little girls who were playing and singing a song Melinda never forgot, "Catching Julie." They sang under the high mountain, their thin voices escaping like smoke in the vast cold afternoon: "The needle's eye, it doth supply, the thread that runs so truly; many a beau have I let go, because I wanted Julie"—a play song brought in colonial times from places they no longer knew existed.

Two of them made an arch with their thin arms, and the others danced through it until the word *Julie,* and then their arms came down and they trapped Julie, who went and stood behind first one girl, then the other, until they formed a tug-of-war. They looked like wild children out of the woods. Their feet were bare and red. One of them was so beautiful Melinda turned her head away. Her face was slim, her profile that of an English lady, her thick hair the color of corn.

When they saw Melinda, they stopped their song and gathered around and felt her coat and reached up and touched the escaped curls, and stared at her as if she, not they, were the wild one. They did not smile. The beautiful one said, "Jesus Christ, look at them stockings and shoes. Ain't they purty?" A woman called from the nearest tent front, "You quit that takin the Lord's name in vain or I'll warsh yore mouth out with soap."

"We ain't got no soap," the little girl said to Melinda. "She ain't my ma, I ain't got no ma and pa. I'm a wood's colt, but I don't keer. My

Uncle Samuel named after the prophet is a scab. My name is Essie, that's short for somethin but I forget what. I been to school." She took Melinda's hand. She was so dirty that Melinda wanted to withdraw it, but Johnny was watching her and she didn't want him to think badly of her.

"You want to be friends with me?" Essie said, looking up at her as if she were awarding her a prize.

"Sure thing," Melinda said, and they walked together for the rest of the walk, with Essie holding her hand. When the other girls got up the nerve to come nearer, Essie said, "Y'all git on home. This is my friend."

Melinda had never seen people so thin, except very rich women of a certain age, like her Aunt Maymay. A girl that Johnny said was twenty, like her, had no teeth and the bent body of an old woman. Four children, the youngest just beginning to stand, clung to the woman's dress, all she was wearing in the November wind. She didn't seem to notice.

Melinda saw no shoes on any of the children. When she tried to ask about underwear, some woman, she didn't know who, said, "Lady, don't ye come up here askin charity questions. We ain't got no *underwear.* Who do you think you're atalkin to?"

She was ashamed of her clothes, ashamed of being there, ashamed that it all existed. She wanted to go back to where things weren't like this and she didn't know it and didn't want to know it, and she hated Johnny Bradford for putting her through it. She didn't speak to him all the way to her car, and she turned it without saying goodbye. She could see him in the rearview mirror, just standing there staring at the car, his arms folded across his chest the way she had first seen him, and his whole body shimmering beyond her tears.

When a man in a black suit and a black broad-brimmed hat tried to stop her on the paved road, she sailed by and waved at him, willfully misunderstanding the signal.

She sat at the window of her room at the Continental Hotel for a long time, alone, not seeing, just staring. She didn't cry. She just felt cold. She lay down for a minute on her bed and slept, but her dream woke her up when a ragged company of children with Grandma Haycroft were being entertained for tea by her mother and her grandmother in the parlor in Richmond. Her mother whispered, "Tell them to go to the bathroom outside," and she woke up again in her room at the Continental Hotel in Pineville, Kentucky. It was dark outside.

It had been only a slip, a sigh of a dream anyway, but she remembered her mother's voice, and she thought her mother had called her and waked her. When she looked at her watch, she saw that she was an hour late calling home for Sunday evening. Grandmother Mason had said, the last thing, "Don't be late calling. You know what she's like. I don't want to have to listen to her complaining."

She went down into the lobby, where a crowd of men were having another one of those meetings that seemed to turn into the sound and smell of smoking and drinking and laughing and punching each other. They parted to let her through a babble of remarks. She asked to use the telephone in Mr. Archibald's office.

It took a long time to get Central and even longer to get Richmond, and her mother picked up the receiver before the telephone had stopped the first ring and called out, "Are you all right? What happened?"

Melinda slipped into her language of half-truth, coloring things as easily as breathing. She had been doing it, after all, for most of her short life. "I went to Sunday dinner with some people who have a place near Pineville. I just got back." She answered a long, long question. "Oh yes, a Yale boy. Bim's cousin, Sen. I told you about him. His daddy owns several mines, and he is going to be a lawyer. He just graduated last spring, he's clerking in the best law office in town. That's the way they become lawyers in Kentucky . . ." And she fell into the gossip that she knew would make her mother do what she wanted her to. It always had. "A very nice family. There are lots of nice people here, lots of parties, boys from Princeton and girls from Sweet Briar, and everything. It's a pretty little town, I told you about that," and she listened again until her mother's voice had eased below shrillness. It was time.

"Now listen, Mother, there *is* a little something I want you to do. All the nice people here are doing it, and I want to be part of that. I want you to get those two big old trunks out of the attic and fill them with all the clothes we don't wear anymore—your old clothes, Grandmother's, and anything that is left of Daddy's." She heard her mother gasp. "Mother, he'd want you to do that. You know how much he cared about the mine here."

Her mother said something, and she answered, "Well, he did to me. Lots of times. It's already getting cold here, and people are going barefooted. So you send *everything*. Get Imogene and Marshall to help you tomorrow, and call the depot to come get the trunks right away. I forgot a lot of things I need, too. So don't leave anything of mine out—shoes, stockings, evening clothes, my best step-ins, everything, and don't forget those two awful dresses I had to wear when I was a bridesmaid, and oh yes, you know I left most of my pretty things and there are so many parties here, so send them too, like you did the cabin trunk, on the train to Pineville. Send all the trunks tomorrow, special delivery. I absolutely need them by Thursday."

She did cross her fingers at this downright lie to her mother. She listened for a long time, and then said, yelled rather, so her mother would hear her and get it right, "No! *Please,* Mother, don't send the things through the Red Cross in Richmond. They'll be weeks getting here, and they might even decide to send them someplace else. I need everything right away. It's very important. It isn't at all like we thought it was here."

She searched for something to say that her mother would consider urgent enough to make her move. "There's a special party this Friday, and I have to have an evening dress that is warm enough and my evening coat with the ermine on it that I forgot . . . and there's a fancy-dress party and two dinner parties. I need *everything*. Be sure to get them on the train tomorrow so they'll be here in time. Imogene knows where everything is. I know how expensive it is, but Mother, it's *parties* and *charity!*"

Melinda could hear her mother's catch of breath. "Listen, Mother, there's only one phone here, and several people are waiting to use it. I'm fine. I'm happy, and everybody here is nice. Nice people. Yes, ma'am. Our kind of people, of course. First thing tomorrow morning. Promise. Yes." She finally got the promise; the urgency went out of her mother's voice. It became fainter, and trailed on and on until the receiver was damp against Melinda's ear. She didn't dare look around because she sensed that somebody was standing in the office door exuding impatience. Finally she was able to hang up.

"Well, well, well." She knew it was the reporter from the *Louisville Courier-Journal* before she turned.

"How long have you been listening?" She was furious and didn't quite know why, except that he was there and grinning. She could smell corn liquor on him. She wanted to hit somebody or cry.

"So the little lady has just found out there ain't no Santa Claus." He laughed.

She pushed past him and said, "It's none of your beeswax. I'm not supposed to talk to you." She could have bitten her tongue, because she remembered too late that Nurse Gordon had told her that that too was a secret.

She didn't want to think of what she had seen, not on a new crisp Monday morning. She told herself she was doing something, even if it was secret. She walked through the dark to pick up the lists and take them to the Red Cross feeding center, where Nurse Gordon was finally letting her do the first cooking for mass feeding.

She loved the great vats that the volunteer ladies kept so spotless. She could see her face distorted like a clown when she moved them, heaving them up against her stomach with both hands. She grinned at her funny face. She had already found a way to feed any child who came to the station by putting it on another family's list. It was easy. She always used new families that came from upriver that nobody in Pineville knew.

She had taken the meat from the refrigerator and begun to slice it into the one-inch-square pieces that provided minimum protein when the door behind her opened. It was Nurse Gordon, standing there at six-thirty in the morning.

"You are to put that meat back in the icebox and come with me to the office," she said, without any "Good morning." She simply turned and marched away again. Melinda wiped her hands, put the meat back, and followed her around the corner and into the courthouse square. She was walking so fast that Melinda had to run after her like a dog. She watched the blue cape swish into the office, and the door slammed behind it.

By the time she got inside, Nurse Gordon was sitting at her desk as if she had not moved or hurried. Her voice was so quiet it was scary. "You are to take off that armband and never wear it again. You are obviously not to be trusted. I will call your mother long-distance and tell her you are coming home."

"What have I done?" Melinda was for a minute genuinely surprised.

"You have used your position in the Red Cross to move food for striking miners."

"I forgot to take the band off my arm." It was all Melinda could think of to say.

"How dare you contradict me? You are not wanted here." Nurse Gordon stopped herself from saying any more and dismissed Melinda by putting her head down and pretending to read *The Trail of the Lonesome Pine,* which Melinda knew she had already finished. Her hands were shaking the pages.

Melinda had a terrible need to giggle but stopped herself in time. She took off her armband and laid it on top of the book. Nurse Gordon brushed it aside. It lay there between them. The silence became embarrassing.

Melinda picked up the armband and put it in her pocket. Nurse Gordon never looked up. Then she took her coat and her galoshes and the umbrella she kept at the office and started to the door.

"You have forgotten your coffee mug" were the last words Nurse Gordon ever said to her.

After that, Nurse Gordon treated her as if she didn't exist, even in the Flocoe when they met.

Melinda was able to cry only when she got to her room and realized that she had failed at her first job, the first useful thing she had ever done in the world.

At noon someone knocked on her door. It was Sen. "I'd like to kill him," he said, trying to take her in his arms. She stopped him, and held the door open so nobody would think she had a man in her room, which was expressly forbidden. Nurse Gordon had said so.

"Why?" was all she could think to say.

"A sweet, well-brought-up girl like you, out there with that bunch of rednecks . . ."

"Don't you tell me whom I can go to dinner with. I can go to Sunday dinner with anybody I want to." She didn't know why she was so furious. "I just don't want things hidden from me."

He leaned against the door. "Come on out of there and I'll buy you a soda at the Flocoe." He realized that he had to reason with her. "You just don't know the whole story. Those people are outside agitators, honey, don't you see? Some of them have been shot already. You've got to stay away from them. That's what I couldn't tell you about Johnny. He's a radical anarchist—"

"He is not. He's a Communist. An anarchist is not a Communist. Anyway, what does all that nonsense have to do with children going barefoot in November? Answer me that if you're so smart."

She was beginning to crumble and she tried to

stop herself, but it was too late. "What you don't know is, I've already been kicked out of the Red Cross, and she's going to call my mother, and I'm going to have to go home . . ." The word *home* lasted all the way into Sen's arms. She was crying, and he held her the way he had intended all along.

"She can't do that if we tell her not to. Who does she think runs this place? I won't let her call your mother," he said. "Don't you worry your pretty head. I won't let you leave."

She buried her nose in his nice safe tweed jacket.

"A girl like you." The voice over her head reminded her of Gavin Proctor and the train to Louisville and the miners in the predawn and the smell of gin and the sound of rain. She almost missed what Sen was saying. ". . . taking you up there with that bunch of white trash and New York Jews, a girl like you . . ."

She pushed him away. "I can't breathe," she told him, and she tried to smile politely. She went on crying a little, as sorry as he was that it had happened to her, and even sorrier that he had said what he had. She told him she just didn't feel like going to the Flocoe, and he understood and went away after she had promised to eat something and take a little nap. As he left, he said he was going right over there and have a word with Nurse Gorgon, and that at least made her smile.

But when the door closed, a space of sorrow opened in the dear room that she had made into her own. She sat all night leaning her arms on the wide windowsill, and she watched the courthouse and the Flocoe as the lights came on and then went out, and the people went into the picture show and came out again, and those lights went out, and it was midnight and not a soul stirred, and she was alone in the world until the first dawn came, and she grew up.

At least, that was the way she remembered it. Ever after that she had a rule. Sometimes she heard it in Mrs. Hightower's slow, deep voice: "My husband used to say you can argy all day long, but when you wake up at three o'clock in the mornin a thing is wrong or it's right, and either you take to drink or do somethin about it."

So Melinda remembered saying aloud to herself and the empty town, "Listen here. You don't do anything until you've thought about it at three o'clock in the morning. Then you don't lie to yourself. A thing is right or it's wrong, that's all. It hasn't anything to do with politics or God or anything outside."

She couldn't think of anybody to tell what she had decided to do. She just had to do it and didn't want to do it. She never wanted to see all that ugliness again. Once, sometime in the night, she put her head down on the windowsill and cried, "I don't want to do this. I want to go home."

The trunks arrived on Thursday morning. They sat, with all their labels from England, France, the *Île de France,* Baden-Baden, forlorn on the station platform in the rain. A thick special-delivery letter from Melinda's mother had arrived with them, but she put it in her pocket to read later. She called the headquarters of the NMU warehouse and asked for Johnny to come with a truck. He had told her the night before that Thursday was a good day if the trunks came, because a committee of famous people, Theodore Dreiser and John Dos Passos and all, was coming from New York City to investigate the coalfields, and the coal operators had withdrawn all the deputies in Bell and Harlan counties so they wouldn't see them.

She certainly knew about those people. Toto, her best friend in Richmond, had read every dirty book she could get her hands on and had told her about them. She had read *An American Tragedy* and *Forty-Second Parallel.* Toto said *An American Tragedy* was better, only she had to wade through about a thousand pages to get to the good part. She said they both were all about people going the limit.

Both Toto and Melinda knew better than to go the limit, because if you did that, you sullied your reputation and gave away the pearl of great price and nobody would want to marry you after that, not the kind you were brought up to marry, anyway. The other thing they knew was that if you put a penny in a Mason jar every time you did it the first year you were married and took a penny out every time afterward, you would never empty the jar. That was a proven fact about sex.

So she didn't say anything when Johnny said she was as ignorant as a rock. She put it down to excitement. He told her that Theodore Dreiser had written the Great American Novel, and then he said that Dos Passos was writing another Great American Novel and he had read the first part, which was all about the left wing and capitalism. Melinda wondered where the going-the-limit part fit into that, but she had already learned to keep her mouth shut and listen when Johnny talked.

Johnny had been stopping by the hotel every evening since Monday, when he heard what had happened. He sat on the stone parapet of the porch and discussed things with her—his doubts, his hopes. He called it discussion, but she didn't say much. Half the time she didn't know what he was talking about.

Once he confessed that he was in the League, but they wouldn't let him be a full member because he was still too bourgeois and needed to prove he was worthy. She thought he meant the Junior League and she was about to tell him he was wrong, that was only for girls, but he must have read her face, which he said was as open as a plate. "No, Melinda, the Young Communist League," he told her in a whisper. "Not even Theodore Dreiser can get into the party yet. They decided he has too many bourgeois habits, even though he was desperately poor when he was a boy. He isn't anymore, so he has to prove himself too."

To Melinda, it sounded like Mrs. Burlington had taken over the Communist Party and was making the rules, A- and B-class Roosian Reds. She giggled, and it made Johnny mad.

She and Johnny and Eulalie managed to heave the three trunks into the truck after she had looked to see if there was anything she needed that wasn't part of what she intended to do, and then she remembered Straight Creek and her full armoire at the Continental Hotel and shut all three trunks and said, "Let's go up Straight Creek." Johnny kept glancing at her, pink in the face the way boys always looked when they had a crush, all the way up the creek until they got to the Haycrofts' farm.

The Haycrofts helped to open the trunks and lay the clothes out to air along the porch railing. Everybody oohed and aahed. Rose said, "Don't touch a thing. We have to be fair to all. Quit that, Althea," and she slapped one of her daughters on the hand.

Melinda's whole life and her mother's and father's and her grandmother's, all the years past, were laid out in a line on the Haycrofts' log porch rail. Essie came running up when she saw Melinda and just stopped and stared. She got closer and closer, like a shy animal, until she was standing in front of the trunk where Melinda's white crepe-de-chine shimmy that she had worn to her coming-out party lay on top of a pile of silk underwear.

Essie looked for a long time, and then she said, "Jesus Christ, look at thim purty thangs." Rose shooed her away, but like a hound dog she only went out of hand-slap distance and kept on staring.

Melinda took the lace step-ins and the shimmy to Essie and gave them to her.

"Kin I keep thim?" Essie started to sniffle.

"They belong to you now. You go on inside and wash yourself . . ." Melinda glanced at Eulalie to see if it was all right, and Eulalie nodded.

"Hit's all right. Grandma Haycroft likes her."

"They're not a dress, they're underwear," Melinda called after Essie, and Rose laughed. "She don't know nuthin."

When Melinda got back to the hotel, dirty and tired, the lobby was in a turmoil of reporters and miners and men who were standing around as if they were important. It looked like every man in town had found a way into the Continental Hotel. Some woman was yelling at a big man she called Baby Jones, and everybody was talking and nobody was listening.

Ever after the famous, taut, unreal days when the committee was in Kentucky, Melinda was able to recognize a certain walk. She called it a famous walk: fast, purposeful, like a busy dog with a bone, making shoals of the people they walked through. She saw a tall man wearing a billed cap and a bow tie who looked to her like a Holy Roller preacher trying to look like a senator. Another one had a head like an elegant egg. It was easy to see that they were the most important of the strangers. There were four or maybe five of them.

She couldn't quite tell, but she noticed that

the mayor was holding forth with the tall one in the cap and bow tie, so she supposed that he must be the great Theodore Dreiser, which meant that the one who looked like an egg was Mr. Dos Passos.

She finally managed to push her way through the lobby. There was no hot water. The nearest bathroom, which she had thought of as almost her own all the time she had lived at the hotel, was occupied. She lay on the bed for a long time that evening, waiting to go into the bathroom and have a long hot bath to get rid of Straight Creek. Then there was a knock at the door and it was Johnny.

"Have you seen them yet?" He was so excited that he stammered. She told him she had, but he had to let her sleep.

She never got the chance. Somebody came into the room next door and slammed the door so hard that it shook her bed. He was ranting and raving at somebody as if he were crazy or drunk, something about "I'm the leader of this committee, and if you don't do what I say I'll go straight back to New York. Now let me tell you—" He kept pounding a table. It went on for two hours, and the men seemed to make friends again and were right back where they started, with him as what they called the moderator. They decided that they could set up a place in the writing room of the hotel where the miners and their wives could give evidence. It was what they had been going to do all along.

Finally there was silence. She heard the door open and shut. She went out into the hall to try the bathroom again, and just then the man who looked like the Holy Roller preacher came out of the room where all the yelling had been. It was Theodore Dreiser who had been making all the fuss. She knew that the minute he opened his mouth.

"Well, little lady," he said. "Right next door, eh? Now, isn't that friendly? Do you know who I am?"

She said she did and he put his big hand right over her breast. "We'll talk later, you and me," he said. "Right now I've got to go down and rescue some coal miners."

"We will not," she called after him; she had never been so disgusted. But he didn't even hear her.

When she went down to get some late supper, the dining room was full of reporters going back and forth from the writing room, where the committee had set up a long table, and the doorway was crowded with what seemed like everybody in Pineville. She heard Mr. Dreiser's voice yell, "Where's Sheriff Blair? I sent him a telegram to meet me here," and the low voice of one of the locals: "He don't come like a damned dog. He said you come up thar to Harlan ifn you want to see him. He said tell you he's right thar where he belongs, and he ain't going to go one step for no outside agitator."

Everybody around the man laughed. She saw Johnny's head, but he didn't look around. He was just standing there, rapt.

Just then Sen grabbed her arm. "You get right back upstairs and lock your door," he whispered.

"I'll get Loada to bring you something to eat. You're to stay in your room, do you understand me?" He sounded like a safe echo of her father, the same low voice of protection.

Later she wondered if anybody in the world would understand that the biggest decision of her life so far had been not to go to a football game between Pineville High School and Harlan High School. It sounded, in memory, ridiculous. Sen said so at the time, but it didn't do any good. She had waked at three o'clock in the morning.

She and Johnny drove slowly up the river toward Harlan, with horns honking and high school students piled into cars and trucks, and one, all dressed up like a Confederate soldier, galloping a farm horse back and forth along the slow line. It was a beautiful fall Friday, football weather, football colors in the sweaters and the pennants and the last of the leaves and the shining hair of the girls and the boys' bow ties. They rode by yelling "Rah, rah, sis-boom-bah," or just yelling without any words at all.

It was a joy she had always been part of, and she felt left out of things for the first time in her life. Tears rose in her throat, but she managed to swallow.

Everybody seemed so happy. There wasn't a miner in sight, just argyle sweaters, and Fords and Packards and Chandlers, and a red Stutz Bearcat, all filled with people who waved when they passed them. Johnny had said to go slow and let them by so they wouldn't get caught up in the crowd at the football game and not be able to get away.

The Harlan "hearings," set up as though they were official, were in a dim room over a store, almost drowned out by the band passing around the courthouse square and the whistles and the rah-rah-rahs. All the color was outside. Inside there were only the gray room, the drab bodies, the clothes washed too many times in an attempt to dress up for the occasion.

Men and women, their voices low, told on and on about murder and about getting evicted from their houses and about living in tents and being shot at and insulted and blackballed so they couldn't get a job anywhere in Kentucky if they were union men, even UMWA, while all the time the band outside played Sousa marches.

Eulalie Haycroft sat beside Melinda, and when the voices were so low they could hardly hear them, she whispered, "God in heaven, honey, you ought to see what's happened to the clothes. They're just astruttin, and I mean astruttin . . . You're a-comin tonight, ain't ye?"

"What's happening tonight?" Melinda whispered. She was planning to meet Sen and at least go to the party.

"Why, honey, you got to be thar. Hit's at the Wallins Creek Baptist Church. All them writer fellers are a-comin, and everbody that's union has to be thar. We need you."

Melinda, who couldn't remember anyone ever telling her she was needed, nodded and tried to make the party up on Pine Mountain retreat from her mind, but it wouldn't.

In the darkness and the cold, she drove Johnny to the church. They could see, in a ring around the place, the men in their black suits and their black Stetson hats, with their guns, but nobody seemed to pay attention. The word was around that once the writers had been there, the whole world would know about them and they would be safe. Anyway, it seemed as if the gun thugs had their orders only to scare and not to shoot anybody.

Melinda felt a cold shiver of fear and thought, Somebody is walking over my grave. She pulled her fox collar way up so it half hid her face.

One of the men in black was taking names, using a flashlight to shine a beam on men's faces as they went in the door of the little church, but nobody showed a light in her face. Inside, it all looked like it was just another church meeting. Kerosene wall lamps with shiny tin plates behind them made bright circles. People's faces flickered as the door kept opening, letting in the November wind.

The place smelled of varnished wood, kerosene, and bodies. She and Johnny were packed close together on one of the wooden benches near the back, and when Eulalie got there she made some man she called Ezra move and give her his seat, beside Melinda. She seemed to want to protect her. Johnny sat on the other side, but he was so intent on the speakers that even when somebody fell against her, drunk, he didn't notice. Eulalie did, and told the man to go to hell.

Melinda felt smothered by the smell, the dark,

the close bodies, the whisper and shuffle of people, the calls to newcomers, and finally a silence as the committee marched down the aisle of the church with that famous stride.

Johnny whispered, "That's Aunt Molly Jackson, and the woman beside her is Tania O'Reilly, the new political education leader sent from New York. She's just wonderful. She can speak Russian and she lived there when her father was an engineer on the Dnieperpetrovsky dam. She came back really dedicated. She's already a member of the Party, and she's only twenty-one. God, she's my age. I have so far to go."

The woman wore no makeup at all. Her dark thick hair, pulled back into what Melinda thought of as a Spanish knot, gleamed in the kerosene light. She had a perfect profile, and her eyes glittered—dark eyes, with black lashes. Johnny whispered, "She's Irish from Boston, and she graduated with honors from Vassar, and she—oh, you'll see. Learn from her." Melinda caught the sound of mild disapproval in his voice for the first time since she had known him.

Melinda had been told to learn from people like this woman before: the honor girls at camp, the girls with their hard calves, the noble girls, the tennis players, the girls with their feared certainty, who had always made her feel knock-kneed and pigeon-toed. While she was looking at Tania and thinking, Her name is no more Tania than mine is, their eyes met. Tania seemed to be looking for somebody. Then she stared at Johnny, of all people, skinny Johnny, and Melinda read something that she had seen a thousand times before—pure jealousy, the same old thing.

The meeting began with Aunt Molly Jackson singing her Hungry Miner Blues song. Melinda thought too late of taking down the words. She only got one line on the back of her mother's envelope, and then she realized that she hadn't yet read the letter.

Aunt Molly Jackson had a faint minor voice, half heard and half forgotten, when she sang. Then she bore witness, which was right for the church, and it didn't seem political. She told about being a midwife, and how many babies had died, and what people had to eat, and people shouted "Yes, yes," and "Amen" as if they were in a real night meeting.

The New York writers sat there looking as if they were at the picture show, and Melinda wanted to kick Theodore Dreiser in the behind. He was beginning to look bored, as if he had done his duty just by turning up.

"They call us rednecks," somebody was saying from the platform. "That's because we're so damned hungry and skinny ye can see the sun right through us, yes, livin off nuthin but Bull Dog gravy and beans when we can get them and not enough pay to take home, yes, and havin to buy at the company store and not a damn bit of compensation when we get hurt, yes, and don't y'all fool yourselves ever last one of us miners will be blacklisted for being here. You just watch and wait. Them gun thugs will be up these hollers athrowin everbody out of their house they ain't already done. I tell you we can't do nuthin but strike!" There was a roar. "I'd sooner starve astrikin than aworkin if I had my druthers." He sat down.

Tania O'Reilly told in a calm and dedicated voice how the workers in Russia owned the state, how nobody went hungry and nobody got fired, how it was the wave of the future.

When the voices and the singing finally stopped and Melinda and Johnny got outside, the night was brilliant with stars. It had grown colder. Somebody had painted "Communis Get Out of Kentucky from a Good American" in blue paint on the side of Melinda's yellow roadster.

They went in a caravan of cars down the river to Pineville. Johnny insisted on going with her. He said he would get a ride back to Straight Creek, and she was too tired and furious to ask how. She couldn't find a word to say halfway down the river toward Pineville, and when she finally did say something, she asked a question. "What is Bull Dog gravy?"

Johnny said, "They make it with grease, flour, and water. It fills you up, but that's all."

She made him wait outside with her until the light went on in the room beside hers and then went out again. She didn't tell him why. They were parked in the shadow of a tree, so that when Sen come out onto the porch with some of his friends, they didn't see her. They were laughing.

Some of the committee people were still standing around the reception desk, looking at small white cards, when she went in. There was one in her own box. It read

Good for One Day Trip
Kentucky-Tennessee Line
Overlooking Historic Cumberland Gap
Pineville Transportation Company
Incorporeal
Resplendent Lincolns, Fords, Packards,
Special Service for New York Writers

Finally she was mad enough.

She could hear a poker game going on in the writing room. She sat there in the lobby by herself and waited until the strangers had gone to bed. She knew that Mr. Archibald was in the poker game. She could hear his voice and see the sleeve of his canvas jacket. Sen had told her that Mr. Archibald dressed in two uniforms, a white linen suit in the summer, puttees and an old canvas jacket with a red collar from October on, so he could pick up his gun anytime he wanted to and go hunting. He wore a wide-brimmed Stetson hat summer and winter. People said he even ate in it, and Mrs. Archibald had long since given up. His old setter followed him and lay down beside him with a sigh that everybody said sounded like Mrs. Archibald.

Johnny told her the joke about his registering all his mine mules to vote in the last election, the one when they elected Sheriff Blair. Johnny said Blair was the kind of man mules would vote for. It was the only joke she ever heard him make.

When the lobby was finally clear, she walked into the poker game. "Mr. Archibald," she said, "I believe you own this hotel."

"Why, yes, little lady, anything wrong?" He

was a large, fat man with eyes that twinkled as if he were running for office every time he talked to somebody.

"It has become necessary for me to speak to you," she said, and she stood there, feeling solid, compact, and very like her Grandmother Mason.

"Deal me out," he told the other men, who were so surprised that they forgot to take the cigars out of their mouths in front of a lady.

She closed the door to his office behind her, and she stood almost against it. She was as surprised as he was by what she said.

"Mr. Archibald, I came to this town innocently, to help people who I heard were in trouble. My daddy owned some stock in a mine up Straight Creek that went bankrupt. My uncle told me that in the boom, every stitch I wore came right off the coal face. I didn't even know what a coal face was before. I am not a Communist or a socialist or a Russian Red or any of those things that people are being called here. The car my daddy gave me has been painted with a big blue sign that says, 'Communis Get Out of Kentucky from a Good American.' I have been hollered at and teased and run out of the Red Cross, and had a smart-aleck card left in my mailbox.

"Now, let me make myself entirely clear. I came here to help children eat. There are children up Straight Creek who are hungry because their daddies are on strike or are blacklisted. It is not their fault. I intend to go up there tomorrow and help feed them. I am going because the National Miner's Union soup kitchen is the only one open.

I got kicked out of the Red Cross for doing this, and I do not intend to be run out of this state for doing something right. I know you are a coal operator and I know you own this hotel. I would like to stay here, in my room, as long as I can stay in Kentucky. I am not taking sides. I am mad as hell at seeing children used as ammunition. My room here is the only place I have to go where I don't hear either side and where I can be by myself with my own things. I am sick to death of both sides of the argument. Now I want your solemn promise that I will not be bothered and run after and . . ."

She had to stop. The tears were very close to her voice, and they were not of sorrow but of pure anger.

Mr. Archibald didn't say anything for a while. He just looked at her, and then he smiled. "Now it's my turn, young lady, and you listen to me. I would rather die and go straight to hell than have the unions in my mine, but I don't use youngins. I don't like what's going on here any better than you do. I'd like to go to bed or to Florida until the damn thing is all over. You are to stay in your room as long as you want to, and I will see that nobody bothers you, not in my hotel. If there is any trouble, you come right to me, you hear me? Nice girl like you. Now can I go back to my game? I was winning." He patted her on the back as he went by, not like Mr. Dreiser but like somebody's father. "I'm going to call up Sheriff Blair and tell him to call off his dogs. You needn't to worry one bit about driving up there. Nobody will bother you if I say so."

"I don't want special treatment," she told his back. He turned around.

"Don't be a damned fool. How do you think we would look if a nice girl from the West End of Richmond got shot on the road to one of our mines? My Lord," he was saying as he disappeared into the writing room again, "out of the mouths of babes and sucklings." The last words she heard were, "Deal me in."

She did manage not to cry until she got to her room and the door was closed behind her. She didn't even see Loada. She only felt Loada's hands rubbing her back as she sobbed, face down on the bed.

"I heared that. I heared every word. I made it my business. Now you got some nice hot water in your pitcher, and you git up and warsh yourself. They ain't nobody going to bother you, honey, Loada will see to that. You're union, and we looks after ourn. Now I'm goin to bring you a somethin to eat. You're skinny as a rake."

When Melinda shook her head against her baby pillow, Loada went on rubbing and talking. "Don't you shake no 'no' at me. You got to keep your strenth up. Now don't you get yourself all sick and hongry, all you got to do. I got to leave. These outside fellers come down here are makin one godawful mess. Lock your door behind me. I don't trust none of them strangers. You be sure it's me when I come back and knock, you hear me? My boy Armstrong is wipin the paint off your nice little car with kerosene."

When she was gone, Melinda got up and washed her face. Loada came back with one of the large hotel trays, and she found that it was easier to eat a bowl of vegetable soup and four hot biscuits and drink a glass of milk than she could ever have imagined.

That was the longest night she had ever spent. Drunks ranged up and down the hall outside her room, one of them yelling, "You red Commu-nisses can't see me but I can see you," and next door voices went on and on and on in the night. When, finally, at six o'clock in the morning, she gave up trying to sleep and decided to have a bath before the crowd wanted the bathroom, she saw that a line of toothpicks had been leaned upright against Theodore Dreiser's door.

On her way to the soup kitchen, she drove up the dark November road through wisps of mist from the river. The kitchen had been set up in the old Elks Club, long since abandoned. She could see a pale light from the window stretching out across the dark road. There was no other light at all.

Inside, Eulalie was firing up the iron cookstove. All she said when she saw Melinda was, "This damn thing must of come out of the Ark." Two young women were whitewashing the walls. Eulalie looked around her. "Don't hit look fine? We got company comin so we figured to make hit look nice."

It was then that Melinda saw that the two women were wearing clothes she had brought, one a Harris tweed suit of her mother's that she had grown tired of, the other one of Melinda's bridesmaid's dresses with a sweater over it that had belonged to her grandmother. They were both wearing her father's shoes.

Eulalie saw her looking at them. "You got such little feet we saved all your shoes for the youngins," she said as she heaved a large corrugated washtub onto the stove. She began to peel potatoes and throw them into it.

Melinda turned her coat inside out to keep the whitewash from flicking onto it and laid it in the corner. She picked up a knife and began to peel. Eulalie looked at what she was doing with some admiration. "Lord God, I would of bet you never peeled a potato in your whole life, and look at you go."

"The Red Cross taught me," Melinda told her, and they both laughed, and the laughter spread to the two women who were whitewashing the wall. When Tania O'Reilly stomped in in "Russian" boots, which Melinda recognized as just like the ones Toto had bought at Bonwit's, it was like a party.

"Who the devil dressed everybody up like a bunch of clowns?" were her first words. "I've passed a man in a dress suit, and some woman in purple velvet lounging pajamas, and two little girls with fancy underwear over their dresses. These people are supposed to look poor for the committee. They're bringing photographers!"

The women laughed harder.

"It's a damned disgrace," Tania went on. "How can I make people up here politically aware when you just joke around?" She was nearly in tears. "After all the planning. No, dammit, I told you you can't!" This was to Essie, who had come in behind her and was pulling at her coat.

She slapped at Essie's hand, and Essie ran to Melinda and buried her face in Melinda's stomach and wailed, "That goddamned old bitch won't let me be in the play!" She was wearing the shimmy and the step-ins over her dress; they had turned almost the same color, gray lace flowers, gray crepe de chine.

Melinda knelt down and began to wipe the tears and snot from her face. "Essie, honey, you're supposed to wear the underclothes under your dress to keep you warm. Later we'll see if we can find you a coat."

Essie stopped wailing, and she said politely, "No, thank you, ma'am. I ain't saw nuthin as purty as these here flowers and this here lace in my whole life and I sure ain't going to hide them under no dress or no coat. That Yankee woman come down here was mean to me. She said I didn't look right. How the holy hell do she know? She don't know nuthin, and she won't let me be in her goddamn play."

"Don't use the Lord's name in vain," Eulalie said to the stew.

"What play? Why can't she?" Melinda asked Tania over Essie's head.

"Her uncle is a scab, and we don't let the children that live in scab houses in the class, and they shouldn't be fed in here, but I can't do a thing with these women. They just don't understand." Disgusted, Tania left with a parting shot. "I hope you calm yourselves down when the committee gets here."

Her words drifted behind her as she stomped back out into the road, with Essie after her, yelling, "Tania's mad and I'm glad, and I know what will please her, bottle of wine to make her shine, and a handsome boy to tease her . . ." Melinda's gold shoes from Delman's flapped around her bare feet.

Eulalie was throwing onions and fatback into the washtub. "Them Communist ladies won't let no kids in the education if their daddy or uncle is working. They say hit's the only way to stop scabbing. She ain't got no daddy, and her uncle has one day's work a week up to Pittston. Don't nobody blame him. He's got seven kids, four of them hissen. We got to have more potatoes."

"It's just like the Red Cross, only backward," Melinda said, and she went on peeling until the daylight came to Straight Creek.

They sang together whatever songs they all knew—"The bear went over the mountain," and "Little Corey," and "If I had the wings of an angel," and "It was sad when that great ship went down." But the best one was "Life is like a mountain railroad," and she never forgot two of the verses she learned that morning. They sang it over and over, louder and louder as the whitewash brushes flew and the potato peels jumped:

You will often find obstruction, look for
 storms of wind and rain;
on a fill or curve or trestle, they will almost
 ditch your train.
Put your trust alone in Jesus, never falter,
 never fail;

keep your hand upon the throttle and your
eye upon the rail.

When they came to the last verse, Melinda thought it ought to be heard in heaven:

As you roll across the trestle spanning
Jordan's swelling tide,
you behold the Union Depot, into which
your train will glide.
There you'll meet the Superintendent,
God the Father, God the Son,
with the hearty joyous plaudit, "Weary
pilgrim, welcome home."

The soup kitchen was like a carnival. There was the huge stew with fatback, and there was a whole case of Coca-Cola for the first people who got there. Melinda showed Eulalie how to make coffee in Mrs. Haycroft's apple-butter kettle, which was big enough to bathe a child in and had been used that way, Eulalie said, not once but many times.

When Melinda was sent to get more carrots and green beans from the Haycroft cellar, she felt as if she were driving through her whole life. There was her coming-out dress, already coal-dust-streaked but whirling around on a fourteen-year-old girl with long wild hair.

An old man sat on the steps of the closed company store in her father's best suit, which he had worn to funerals and to church. Her mother had always hated it. The man beside him wore the canvas coat from Abercrombie's with the red corduroy collar that her father had always taken to shoot grouse with Uncle Brandon, and the boy beside them wore the pink hunting coat he had been so proud of and worked so hard for. They were just sitting there in the gray morning, which seemed to make the clothes brighter as twilight brings out the color of flowers, doing nothing, not even talking.

Later in the morning the committee drove up in cars that looked like the cars the gun thugs used, open so the members could be seen. People ran from all over the hollow to get close and stare. The committee stopped and had their pictures taken in front of the soup kitchen, but they didn't let any of the local women in the pictures, because they were too dressed up.

Melinda heard one of the women on the committee say, "Don't they know this is a serious business?"

Eulalie heard her and took her aside, close to where Melinda stood in the corner by the stove, unnoticed by any of them. "Listen to me, ma'am," she almost whispered, "this here mornin is the first time I've heard anybody laugh up this creek in a long time. See that there woman in the purple velvet pajamas? Her husband was mashed in the mine and died without no compensation. See that girl in the purty underwear?" She pointed at Essie, who was darting in and out among the crowd, delighted with the party. "Her mother run off to Louisville, and she ain't got no father. You know why? He got hung with barbed wire up on the mountain last summer by gun thugs because he went on strike and was what they called gatherin. He wasn't doing nuthin but standin around with some fellers."

The woman didn't say a word. Eulalie went off to stir the third washtub of stew. She muttered to Melinda, "I don't like none of this. They done took those people only to the worst places. I'd like to see them go up thar and talk to my mother-in-law. They took two of our fellers up to Chicago to show them off and them fellers up there said they wasn't no God and no Jesus, and they come back and said to all of us, you shut up and let them feed you and organize the strike, but don't pay no attention to what they say." She grinned at the stew. "Hit don't matter none if they're ignorant as rocks." Melinda knew then where Johnny had gotten the phrase.

Eulalie sighed and stirred. "Oh well, they're what's to hand. I just wish my boy Truxton hadn't of picked up all that comrade talk. You'd think he invented it, but there you are, he's only fifteen, and he ain't had nuthin so excitin happen in his whole life. But his grandma done tole him if they come up thar atalkin about they wasn't no Jesus and no God she for one would shoot them her own self. You don't talk that way in Harlan and Bell counties, but I can't say the same for them western counties over to Lexington and Louisville—they're different kind of people."

Melinda didn't see Johnny all day, until he came into the soup kitchen late in the afternoon. When she asked him why anybody would set toothpicks up against Theodore Dreiser's door, Johnny said he didn't want her to know about things like that, and then he was so angry that he let it out. He said it was a damned joke started by Sen. The boys knew that Mr. Dreiser had brought a woman down with him who wasn't even on the committee, and they waited until they saw her go into his bedroom about eleven o'clock. So they leaned toothpicks up against the closed door, and when they saw the toothpicks still there at six-thirty in the morning, they got the Bell County sheriff to arrest Mr. Dreiser for adultery, which was a felony in Kentucky.

"Sen thought he was playing a big joke. Don't they know who Theodore Dreiser is?"

Two days after the committee left, every miner who had been to any of the meetings was evicted, and when Melinda went up the river road in the morning, she could see their belongings, beds and clothes and calendars and quilts and even cookstoves, out in the rain.

A week later when she drove up the Straight Creek road before dawn, there was a huge globe of light. Smoke was rising straight up where the soup kitchen had been. The people stood around in the cold as if the fire would warm them. At three o'clock in the morning the soup kitchen had been dynamited. The one-room building was open to the sky. The wooden walls were snaggled from the fire, and the whitewash was streaked with black. All Eulalie said was, "We got plenty of warshtubs, and Ma's app'e-butter kettle didn't git hurt."

Grandma Haycroft told Melinda to drive her down to the company store because it was too cold to walk all that way. She beat on the door until the one clerk left let her in. Melinda stood in the empty store, where the pickle barrels were cobwebbed and the cloth bolts on the shelves were covered with dust, and Grandma Haycroft's voice echoed in the big empty room when she called Central.

She yelled, "I'm atellin you what we're agoin to do up here. We're asettin up a tent in my yard so these people can eat. Now, you listen to me, G. W., don't you let them fellows set one foot on my piece of property, you understand?" Then she laughed at something Mr. Terry said, and they settled down to a long telephone gossip about how bad things were, with Grandma Haycroft yelling into the phone as if she were calling to him across the hollow. They both were enjoying it. They had known each other for over sixty years. Grandma Haycroft finally said, "Merry Christmas to you too," and hung up.

Johnny said he was going to have to go into hiding so he could go on with his work. He was calling Tania "we" by then. He said she knew how to do things and lie low. They were running a series of meetings for the strike that had been called for the first of January.

There were shootings by drunken thugs into houses in the night. The cars were still open in the cold so that people could see the men in black, as straight-backed as store-window dummies, dull-eyed, with their guns sticking out the sides. They cruised slowly back and forth, up and down the hollows, looking neither left nor right.

Melinda didn't see Johnny for several weeks,

and she didn't see Sen because he was mad at her. Johnny had told her that if she went home to Richmond for Christmas they would never let her back in the county again, so she tried to find a way to explain to her mother, and then just gave up. She said she couldn't come and that was that. It was too cold for lies and excuses. Her hands hurt, even in the mittens her mother sent.

Her room was piled high with presents her mother and Toto and lots of others had sent, but she couldn't look at them without feeling homesick. She wanted to get on the train and forget that there were such things as coal and communism and Kentucky.

Her mother had decided to treat her as if she were at the South Pole with Admiral Byrd, who, she pointed out delicately, was a distant cousin. The bedroll designed for arctic weather had arrived from Abercrombie's. The camp stove for high wind was already in service at the tent kitchen. The rubber bathtub from Abercrombie's had not yet arrived, and her mother kept calling to check.

Melinda was saving the huge box of canned fruit, whiskey cake, plum pudding, marmalade, Skookam apples, caviar, Stilton, water biscuits, coffee, Westphalian ham, a whole smoked turkey, and chocolate for the Haycrofts' Christmas. Loada had put a wisp of tinsel in one window of her room. It looked more and more like a rat's tail as the days before Christmas got more oppressive. Loada had even hung a piece of mistletoe at Melinda's door, but Melinda knew that nobody would ever catch her under it and kiss her again.

When Melinda couldn't stand the room anymore, she sat in the Flocoe and was as lonesome as she had ever been in her life. She walked along the street and watched people who wouldn't speak to her putting up their Christmas trees in the warm glow of their houses. Once she passed a house where she had been to a party when she was still in the Red Cross, and a Christmas party was going on. She could see Sen and a friend laughing at something together.

On Christmas Eve, Sen came to her door and said he and his parents didn't want her to be by herself at Christmas. She was so grateful she nearly died right there in front of him. He smiled a lovely Christmas smile and caught her in the doorway under the mistletoe and gave her a lovely kiss. Everything was suddenly all right. She promised to be at his house for Christmas dinner as soon as she had finished up at Straight Creek. They had decided to give Christmas dinner at noon up in the Haycrofts' big kitchen.

She was just sitting there, happy again, watching the little lights come on in the stores that were still open for Christmas Eve, when somebody knocked on her door. It was Johnny. He had two books in his hand.

"I brought you a Christmas present," he said. "I sent off for them. I didn't wrap them up because I couldn't find any paper, and besides, that is just bourgeois sensibility." He wasn't making any sound of crying, but tears were flooding down his face and pouring onto his coat collar.

Melinda led him to the bed and sat him down

and started to help him with his coat. He said, "Pull your blinds down. I don't want anybody to see me here. That's why I came down after dark on Houghton Junior's horse and left it outside of town at the first coal camp."

She pulled the blinds down and sat back beside him and waited. "Here." He thrust the books at her. "Read these." They were *Forty-Second Parallel* and *An American Tragedy*.

He wouldn't say any more, just sat there with the tears sliding down his face. She tried not to look at him, and started to thumb through the first book, *Forty-Second Parallel.* It was drawing her in, even if the writing seemed funny, when he said beside her, "Goddamn, they've shot Truxton. He was passing out strike leaflets in the street, two streets over from here, when they came by in one of those cars and just shot him and left him for dead in the street, with leaflets settling all round him. They were lying over him like a shroud when Tania and I got there. Do you know what she said? She said we would have to stay there and be seen by the miners. She said it wouldn't be dangerous, since the thugs had already shot somebody. She just said *somebody.* And then she whispered, Well, if this doesn't get them out on strike, nothing will. They were just using him. Oh please, God, everything I believed slipped off like a coat. I hate both sides. I hate them, I hate them both. A plague on both their houses. I had to go and tell Eulalie, and she just stood there."

Melinda started to cry too. She put her arm around him and drew him close to her so he could keep on crying on her shoulder and be comforted. It was all she knew to do. He was crying out his sorrow and belief and growing up in her arms, and she knew about that, the loss, the blank time when you see how it is and you can't go back behind it.

"But don't . . ." He had stopped crying enough to talk. "Don't think I don't still know what is right."

"I'm sure you do," she said politely, completely unclear about what she ought to do to help. So she let him lean there against her until she could feel the warmth coming back to his thin shoulders. He had begun to sob at last, and it was better than the awful silence of his grief. She stroked his hair and said "Shh . . ." and hoped nobody was passing in the hall who might hear them and tell her to get the man out of her room.

"You don't even know anything," he mumbled, out of some thought he hadn't said.

She held him close and said "Never mind," and "Never mind" again, and the warmth grew between them, as if there were one person made of both of them. It wasn't ecstatic, and it hurt her a little, not much, and he sobbed all the way through it, and when he lay beside her, he said, "We'll get married as soon as this strike is over."

At least, she told herself after he had gone, she hadn't said anything. The last thing he said to her was, "We thought Truxton of all people would be all right. Everybody liked him, and the whole county is afraid of old Mrs. Haycroft. Most of the gun thugs had gone home for Christmas anyway.

Truxton was only fifteen, but he didn't have much to look forward to, did he? Down there in the dark for the rest of his life, or unemployed." She remembered the fiddle, but didn't remind Johnny when he was trying so hard to comfort himself.

"I won't see you again until the strike starts. It will be safer then—at least, everybody says it will. I'm hiding up in Harlan County. Nobody knows." He was standing right under the mistletoe, but he didn't look up. His voice had taken on the old joy again. "I'm organizing. We're all fine. Uh, I love you." He was gone.

She went to the mirror and smoothed her half-fallen hair. She cried a little then, and put "Lover Come Back to Me" on her Victrola, and lay down and looked at the ceiling as if it had something to tell her. Then she laughed.

"Oh dear Lord," she told the ceiling, "I must have looked a sight in my garter belt and my bare legs and my step-ins flapping down one leg. Well, at least I didn't lose my virginity the way I was always warned about and Toto and I said it was our pearl of great price, and I haven't sold it for a good marriage the way I was trained to do, and I haven't sold it for ten dollars like the other kind of whore. I've given it to a boy for Christmas."

She fell asleep in her clothes, and then it was the gray dawn of Christmas morning. A little snow floated outside her window onto the courthouse lawn and through the bare trees. She got out the new box of linen thank-you notes with her initials that her mother had sent with a note: "For all those parties. Don't forget to thank."

She had to write twice, in her best copperplate, which the headmistress of Oakley Hall had insisted on so her girls wouldn't write in common Palmer Method. The first time she wrote "armed gun thugs" and had to tear up the note. The second time satisfied her.

December 25, 1931

My dear Mrs. Grandy,

It was so kind of you to ask me for Christmas dinner. I am sorry I can't come. A family I know in the country has had a tragic loss, and they will need me to help them all day. Their fifteen-year-old boy was shot yesterday in Pineville by company guards. Please forgive any inconvenience I may have caused by not telling you sooner.

Yours Sincerely,
Melinda Mason Kregg

She dropped the note into the mail slot in the door of the Grandys' house, and she was gone before anybody looked up. Sen and his little sisters and their parents were opening presents in their dressing gowns. She could see them through the window in the half-dark of early morning. The candles had all been lit on their tree. The angels made of gold paper glittered, and the Star of Bethlehem at the top reflected the big wood fire they had built in the hearth. She could smell coffee.

Truxton was laid out on the kitchen table in a wooden coffin. It was open. They had put a handkerchief over his chin because, one of the men whispered, it had been shot to pieces. He looked peaceful and neat and clean. His red hair was damp and slicked down on both sides of his face, with a perfect part in the middle. The fiddle lay beside him in the coffin. Somebody had put a round paper doily behind his head like a halo. He was wearing Melinda's father's morning clothes.

She made three batches of coffee in the apple-butter kettle while the silent people filed by, into the kitchen and out again. She had never heard such silence, except that a sob now and then was lost in the cold air.

In the afternoon they carried Truxton up the mountain, where men had worked all night in the frozen ground to dig him a grave. Around them as they stood high on the mountainside, wooden crosses leaned. A few stones had writing that had been almost obliterated by time. One had a lamb, home-carved. The trees were skeletal, and the sky was white with snow. Straight Creek looked like it had been drawn with a black pencil far below them. Several mine guards were leaning against the wall of the company store. They looked, from the mountain, like dolls.

The lay Baptist preacher, who was a coal miner during the rest of the week, didn't say much. He said, "Better love hath no man but that he give his life for his friends." Then he prayed and rubbed his hands together to keep them warm, and his words made smoke in the cold air. Up among the trees Melinda caught a glimpse of

Johnny, hiding behind a tree. He hadn't been able to stay away from the funeral.

On January 1, 1932, the National Miner's Union strike started in the Harlan coalfields. Over five thousand miners were out, but the figure came from the *Daily Worker* and people said it was deceptive. Many of them were already either unemployed or on the blacklist anyway. The streets of Pineville were dead with cold, empty, as if the whole town were under some kind of siege.

On the third of January, early in the morning, Melinda woke up with a cold and the curse. She felt awful, but she knew she had to go up to the tent kitchen. Eulalie had just begun to talk again, and she clung to Melinda's arm every time she appeared. She only talked when the two of them were in the tent, long before anybody else came, and then she couldn't stop. Melinda knew every year of "my boy Truxton's" life from the day of his birth, which Eulalie repeated over and over: June the fourteenth, 1916.

"That was the year before his daddy went to the World War. They told him he was going to Paris and we all thought it was Paris, Kentucky." It went on, fact after fact, without a tear, just a low voice, mourning.

So there was no chance Melinda could stay in bed. She took aspirin, and she packed a box of sanitary napkins in her bag, and a pile of handkerchiefs because her nose was running like a faucet, and she went to the warehouse to get supplies.

There was nobody in the street. It was a typical Sunday morning. They had changed the name of the warehouse to the National Miner's Union headquarters and had put a big banner across the front that said WORKERS OF THE WORLD UNITE. It flapped in the winter wind. Somebody had tried to pull it down in the night, but they had only managed one corner.

Inside, it was warm. Eight people, including Tania, were having a conference. There were four other women, all strangers. They looked up when she came in, as if they were telling secrets or having a club meeting and didn't want her. She did get a good morning from one of the women, older than the others.

Melinda crept over to the pile of canned goods, rice, and coffee and started to load the space in her car where the rumble seat had been. Every time she opened and shut the door, Tania looked up, annoyed.

She was gathering the last of the supplies when she heard banging on the door. She was on her way to open it when the sheriff and three deputies and the district attorney broke it in and nearly knocked her over. They were all armed with shotguns, and the sheriff had a revolver he was waving around as if it were a baton.

"All right, ladies and gentlemen, get over there and put your hands up," the sheriff yelled. "You are all under arrest for criminal syndicalism, which is a felony in the state of Kentucky."

Tania started up and shouted, "We have a right—" but she didn't get any further.

"Young ladies," the district attorney said with

a smile, in one of those quiet voices that lawyers used. He loved to talk. Everybody said so. Once he had given a whole speech on the courthouse steps in his red flannel BVDs. "You have your rights and we have ours, all under the same laws. You have a right to come to Kentucky and stir up trouble with peaceful people, and we have the right to throw you in jail until you are ready to leave this county and go back where you came from."

They were prodded out into the cold street by the deputies. A small crowd had already gathered, completely silent. The sheriff led the way across the street as if he were leading a parade. Melinda looked back, worried about her car. She remembered that she had left her keys in it, but she had a spare set.

One of the deputies was up a ladder and had succeeded in tearing down the banner. Another one was coming out of the broken door with a pile of leaflets and newspapers in his hands. "There go my knitting instructions," said the woman who had smiled at her, who was now walking beside her. "Seditious literature. Oh well, I've still got my knitting. I keep it in my pocket for times like these. Knitting calms the soul."

A third deputy had gotten into Melinda's car and was driving it around the corner into the courthouse square. She grabbed the sheriff's sleeve and shouted, "Stop him! He's stealing my car."

He said, "You be quiet, young lady. That car is contraband. We got orders for contraband."

"I'm going to tell Mr. Archibald!" she shouted again, shaking his sleeve.

"Well, now, you do that. But it won't be easy. Mr. Archibald went to Florida yesterday."

Melinda never forgot how quickly she felt like a prisoner, heavy and hopeless. The deputies marched all nine of them across the street and into the county jail, and herded them up concrete stairs that hadn't been swept. The men were locked in the men's cell, the women in the women's cell, a big room with dirty windows that looked out of the back toward the Cumberland River and out the front toward Pine Mountain. There were two lines of double metal cots, an upper and a lower, that sang when anybody lay down. Several whores and a woman who had shot her husband were lying on the cots under harsh wool blankets marked U.S. ARMY.

The walk up the dirty stairs had even quieted Tania, until the sheriff had locked them inside and gone. Then she smiled.

"They've done it! The stupid bourgeois fools have done it. Jailed us! Jailed women! Sing! Sing as loud as you can." They started to sing the "Internationale" while they tested mattresses, and found their places as if it were Camp Sewell instead of jail and they were those damned honor girls Melinda had always felt so shy with. They left her the corner upper bunk, overlooking the river, and ignored her while they sat on the beds, trying them out and making the metal sing in time with their own voices.

At least she was high enough to see over the tops of the houses and the trees. She saw her car, far away, like a toy, surrounded by men in black suits. She watched them run back across the road and stoop behind the near corner of an old barn. There was a fireball that had been the car, and then a faint boom.

The woman who liked to knit came over and stood beside her. "That was your little car, wasn't it?"

"My daddy gave it to me three years ago for my birthday." Melinda was too stunned to be anything but calm.

"What on earth are you doing here?" The woman reached up and touched Melinda's hand. "Poor child. You've never seen hatred before, have you?"

The fireball had already dwindled. The men walked up the county road. Melinda could see some of the shape of the car still, black inside a small, bright fire. "I was just picking up some supplies for the soup kitchen."

"Their excuse is that it's contraband, I suppose." They watched the fire.

Tania strolled over. She explained Melinda to the strange motherly woman, whose hair hung down one side in a wisp that her hairpins hadn't caught: "She's just a bourgeois reactionary full of guilt." Melinda realized that Johnny had talked about her, and she thought, I'll never speak to him again as long as I live. Tania dismissed Melinda with one word: "A liberal."

There was a second explosion, way in the distance.

"Oh dear, what this time?" The woman was casual, as if she were used to destruction. Then she smiled. She had a lovely smile that lit her face and her eyes. "Those girls are so solemn, aren't they?" she said to Melinda as Tania walked away. "By the way, my name is Grace. Grace Church Van Winkle, like Rip." She settled into the cot below Melinda and got out her knitting. "Fortunately, I've made this scarf about twenty times, so I don't need my seditious instructions," and she began to knit.

Melinda watched until the car was only a black heap, then lay back in the upper bunk and got out *Forty-Second Parallel* and a handkerchief to blow her running nose and hide the fact that she was crying.

"What are you reading?" Grace asked. Melinda showed her the book.

"Oh, I like that. I like the people in it. Don't you think that that is the most important thing about a novel, that you care what happens to the people in it?" Melinda could hear the squeak and sprong of the metal as she settled herself below.

Melinda had a hard time keeping her mind on what she was reading. Her nose ran, she had cramps, and the others made too much noise. It grew into a terrible winter parody of summer camp. Most of the political people seemed to be at home, and certainly the whores were. Only the woman who had killed her husband lay on her bed, and Melinda thought she was going to die of grief right in front of their eyes. She just turned her face to the wall and wouldn't eat or look or speak.

The sky outside the window changed color: sun, then mist, snow, then a bright clear winter blue over the white ground, then snow again. The woman jailer came to the cell bars and bawled, "Anyone ministratin?" and Melinda had to raise her hand, ashamed in front of the others, but one of the whores said, "Me too, honey, thank the Lord."

The jailor passed two piles of rags through the bars. "Y'all put these here in that there trashcan over by the commode. When hit gits full, we warsh it. My name is Violet. Holler if ye need more."

Melinda went back to her cot with her arms full of rags of old Turkish towels.

Grace smiled. "It's domestic, isn't it? A nightmare of domesticity." It was as if she had taken the words from Melinda's mind.

There was bread and margarine and coffee in the morning, and a dry sandwich at noon, and cabbage soup with a piece of fatback and some potatoes at night. Violet never announced a meal without bawling.

Finally Melinda said, "She just doesn't know any better, yelling like that," and Grace looked at her.

"Don't be a snob," she told her. "You still have to watch that. Violet shouts because she shouts, not because she's working class. Her sister is probably as quiet as a kitten. Don't look like that. You look like a pup that's peed on the rug."

Melinda saw that Grace knew how to make herself comfortable, all the little tricks—plugging the drafts in the window, piling some of the extra blankets under her, holding her wrists in warm water to stop shivering in the early morning. She did that before any of the rest of them were out of bed.

When she saw Melinda watching her, Grace said, "Oh yes, my dear, I have been in jail before. Let me see—Lawrence, the Scottsboro boys. The unemployment marches. I've gone to all the demonstrations since my children grew up and left home. They don't tell anybody. My eldest son and my husband voted for Herbert Hoover, so we don't talk politics at the table. I don't think it's an aid to digestion. Now you want to know if I'm a Communist. No. I'm just a Democrat, the only one in the family, and I don't toe the party line when it doesn't suit me. The Communists can be cold-blooded and terrible. But they seem to be the only people doing anything in this poor sick country of ours. Of course"—she turned the scarf and began to purl—"they're doing it for the wrong reasons. They batten on despair. But right now that's not my business. At least they are there. Nobody thinks to get rid of the despair. I think sometimes with me it's an act of despair too. I asked an old man in the picket line at Lawrence when he had become a Communist and he said, 'Oh, not until I was fifty. It was not a youthful error with me.' I liked that answer. I'm forty-six, and my boys are ashamed of me." She turned the scarf again and began to knit. "There are never very many of us, so we have to make a lot of noise, like children in the dark."

She turned the scarf once more and said nothing for a minute, and Melinda saw that she had begun to purl with a new color, red this time, after an inch-wide band of yellow. "Don't pay any attention to me, I'm talking nonsense. Jail is very depressing, don't you think? We're all scared, as if all the things we took for granted to protect us are swept away. I feel that way too, I always do. There, I've said enough. Get on with your book. I'll bet you wish you'd stuffed S. S. Van Dine in your reticule instead of that."

Melinda grinned for the first time since the jail door had closed. But she was finding the book easier and easier to read, and when she looked out the window at the winter skeletons of trees, she thought she could see them better, incised against the sky.

They began to get used to the smell in the big gray room: menstrual blood and overflow from the toilet and the bodies of the ones who had started to sweat from fever, and then chill as their colds got worse and their temperatures rose at night and heated their dirty clothes. Grace unplugged the basin with her knitting needle, but it was too small to do any good for the toilet. The smell clung to the hair in Melinda's nose, and in her clothes. Once she had to vomit in front of the others.

In the time of going to sleep and the time of beginning to wake, the voices went on through the passing of days. She didn't know how many. Sometimes the voice was hers, telling Grace why she was there, the first time she had told anybody. "I couldn't stand everybody asking me why," she said, and she explained about three o'clock in the morning, and Grace said she knew.

One afternoon Violet came to the bars and bawled *"Kregg!"* like a top sergeant. "You're wanted. Five minutes," she said to somebody behind her, and as Melinda got up and put her book away, she heard Violet stumping down the stairs. The last thing Melinda wanted was company.

It was Sen. "I've been in Louisville with my cousins for ten days, or I'd have gotten you out sooner. What the devil are you doing in here?" he said, not caring who heard him, and in a chorus the women from the strike called, "What are you doing out there?"

Melinda didn't know what they meant until Grace told her later.

"I've got a court order to get you out of here, but you have to promise to leave the county in two days. I'm sorry about that—"

"What about the others? They haven't done anything wrong."

"Now, I can't argue with you right now. They will get the same treatment. They can get out if they promise to keep the peace and leave the county." He either didn't notice or was pretending that he didn't see the others, who had gathered close to Melinda as he talked.

Grace said, "We can't leave the county. We have work to do," in that tender voice that packed such a wallop when she talked to Melinda about the way things were.

"If they can't come out, then I can't come out," Melinda said. She had to admit later to herself that she was sorry the minute she said it. She hid her face in her handkerchief, because she was afraid she was going to make a fool of herself.

She stood at the bars until his footsteps had

faded all the way out of the door below. Someone had her arm around her and she thought it was Grace, but it wasn't. It was Tania.

On a gray bare day when a sound made her look out of the window, she saw below her a massive line of people, stretched all the way to the river. She called to the others, and they gathered at the window, their arms around one another. The people had no banners, no slogans; they carried nothing. They simply came downriver with the slow mountain walk, in what seemed like a never-ending line, dignified in the winter cold, until they had gathered around the jail.

"My God." Even Tania was impressed. "There must be five thousand people."

"Let our people out!" somebody shouted, and the rest began to yell, "Let them out, let them out," like a football chant. Someone got up on a car hood and bellowed, "We don't jail no women in Kentucky!" The woman who was in jail for murdering her husband looked up and didn't say a word.

Then the wailing minor voice of a woman began a song. "Which side are you on? Which side are you on?" The words Melinda never forgot were "Are you goin to be a union man or a thug for J. H. Blair?" For years people wanted to know who J. H. Blair was, and she seemed to be the only person in the world who remembered him.

The woman finished her song and called out to the crowd. "I wrote that thar on the back of a calendar because I didn't have no paper. Come on, you sing. Which side are you on?" From above, Melinda could see Eulalie in the coat with the fox fur she had given her for Christmas, her head lifted up and her mouth open like a baby bird's as she sang.

After the march, the streets below were emptier. The world outside seemed to have forgotten them again. Then, in the night, Violet came and shook her awake. "You come with me. Git your things." She whispered for once. "That's an order."

Melinda gathered her books and her bag. Grace touched her arm. "I think you're getting out," she whispered. "Goodbye, my dear girl." They hugged each other, and Melinda found that she was afraid, or shy maybe, of leaving the room where she had spent three weeks. Grace wrapped the finished red-and-yellow scarf around her neck. "Here. You're not over your cold yet. Keep this up around your throat." It hung down almost to the hem of her dirty skirt.

Grace sensed Melinda's strange sorrow when she hugged her. "Poor child," she said, "you can't go back to innocence. It's the most comfortable of crimes . . . Every time you go to one of those pretty houses, you will see all this holding the bricks and mortar together. Every time you see a lump of coal, you'll see a man. I do, and I hate it."

Melinda was afraid to let go of Grace. She whispered, "What can I bring you?"

"Oh, just some more wool, four-ply, it's cold in Cambridge. Crimson and white. My youngest son is at Harvard. Oh, I've told you that so many times. Don't forget to write, and remember, you have my address in New York, and there's room for you when you need to come." She didn't say *if*; she said *when.*

"Come on," Violet said, "I got to git some sleep."

Tania, across the room, had sprung up like a mother hen. "What are you doing to her? Where are you taking her? You have no right to interrogate her without a lawyer present. You have no right—"

Melinda heard Sen's voice from the dark corridor. "I'm a lawyer. Melinda." He reached through the bars and grabbed her hand tight. "You've got to come out. I have the court order. They shot Johnny, and they left him out beside the railroad track with a hole in his stomach for three hours while he nearly bled to death, and all he asks for is you."

"God, the newspapers will use this! A Yale man!" Melinda heard Tania call after her as she followed Sen down the dark stairs.

He left words behind him for her to pick up. "He was walking along the railroad track up at Easy Creek, and two of the mine guards came by on one of those hand-pumped railroad cars. You've seen them. It takes two fellows to pump them," he said, as if that were important. "They saw Johnny and they shot him in the stomach and left him there. They figured he had been there for about three hours when they found him. Maybe the cold helped him stay alive." Who "they" was he didn't say. "They brought him into the hospital here at Pineville. They were afraid to take him to Harlan Hospital, there's stronger feeling against these fellows up there." He stopped and turned on the stairs and explained, like a man in a dream, "You have to go straight to court. They are waiting for you. Then I'll take you to the hotel so you can get cleaned up. You can't go to the hospital like that. Loada is waiting for you. I went and woke her up."

The court hearing in the night shadows was cut and dried, and they all sounded bored, their voices coming out of the darkness. Nobody had bothered to turn on more than one naked light. The empty courtroom still smelled of whitewash and tobacco juice. Sen posted a bond for her, and there was something about being bound over to keep the peace, and that was it.

Loada was waiting in her room. "Mr. Sen tole me you was gettin out, so I come. This never would have happened ifn Mr. Archibald hadn't of gone to Florida. Git thim clothes off, you're dirty as a pig. You sure smell like the people. Hole still. Let me see your hair."

Suddenly she was gone, down the corridor. "Mr. Sen! Mr. Sen! She cain't go over to the hospital like that. Her hair is full of cooties. All that hair . . . Love of the Lamb, hit's goin to take all day to dry. She can't go noplace with wet hair and the croup." She stuck her head back in the door. "Now, you keep your door shut. I'm goin to get some Packer's Tar Soap and a fine comb. You wait right thar, you hear me?" She picked up the clothes as Melinda shed them. "I'm takin these here with me. They are perfectly good. I'm goin to take them home and get them clean.

They'll be good as new." She looked at Melinda as if she were going to ask her a question, but she didn't. She didn't say another word.

When she came back, Melinda was standing at the chifforobe mirror, staring. She had put a sheet around herself. She had cut her hair off in bundles an inch from her head, and it lay in front of her in a great blond coil.

"Now what in the world made you go and do a thing like that for?" Loada picked up the coil.

"It will dry quicker." Melinda sounded as if she didn't care at all.

In half an hour Loada had scrubbed what was left of Melinda's hair with a hard brush and soap that smelled like tar from the road, rubbed it dry, gone over her scalp with a fine-tooth comb, and found clean clothes for Melinda to wear. Melinda hadn't said anything. She did pick up the baby pillow with the lace around the pillowslip, and she clung to it and didn't ask herself why.

Johnny lay on a narrow army cot in a small, very narrow room filled with snowy light. His head lay on a hard hospital pillow. His eyes were closed. There was too much dying. Too much dying for her when she was too young. She bent down close to him. She thought for a second that there had been some mistake, that he was a stranger. He seemed to be so much smaller than she remembered, lying in the cold light, his face paper white and drawn back as if he were trying to grin. She lifted his head gently and put the baby pillow under it. It was all she could think to do.

The hall outside Johnny's room was as familiar

as the jail cell by the time he died, three days later. He didn't struggle. Sometimes he groaned, and she would run in then and put her face close to his to see if he was going to speak. Sen came to relieve her on watch as soon as he finished work, and she went home to her room and slept as if she were nearly as dead as Johnny. He died at two o'clock in the morning, and Sen didn't tell her until she got to the hospital.

She remembered only too well the embarrassment of funeral arrangements after the death of her father, but this funeral was stripped down to nothing. Johnny's father was the only family he had, and he was in Europe. He cabled Sen and told him to take charge.

The strike committee in New York called long-distance and said they would pay for the funeral if Sen would send the body—Johnny was no longer a person—to New York so it could lie in state in the union hall. "After all," one of them yelled at Sen over the phone, "it's our fallen comrade."

"Oh, go to hell," Sen said and hung up.

It was evening when he knocked on Melinda's door. The twilight was getting later. It had already started looking as if spring were going to come again and the sun would come back and the buds and it would be all right.

"Come on, Melinda, we're going to bury Johnny. Don't say a word. I couldn't even get a preacher—more than their damn jobs are worth."

The cemetery at Pineville was on a steep hill like the one where they had buried Truxton, as if the bottom land were reserved for the living and the dead could watch over them. The steep road up the hill, around it, and down again was shaped like a giant horseshoe. The hearse could just get up it to the top, where they stopped and looked out over the valley. They had passed marble monument after marble monument, some together in families, some alone, all white in the deep twilight.

Sen said, "Those people filed an injunction for Johnny's body. I wasn't going to let them bury Johnny up there in New York when they don't give a damn about him. He couldn't be down there low on the hill with all the people he disapproved of, who ruined the land and the people. He thought I didn't care." He was muttering to himself. "Dammit, the river is dirty and the game is gone and the coveys are dying. The coveys are dying. The—" And he started to sob as only a man sobs, deep and loud. It echoed in the bare trees. His mother put her arm around him; his father stood and stared out over the darkening valley.

So they stood, four mourners, high on the hill. The undertaker and his helper put Johnny underground as it finally got dark. Melinda could just see the flash of the shovels in the light from a porch over across the cemetery wall. Sen had his head down, and she thought he might be praying. She could only be silent, there in the dark with the snow beginning again, falling on the new raw earth.

Two days later, when she changed trains at Corbin, the reporter from the *Louisville Courier-*

Journal stopped at her seat. "Well, hello, little lady, you've bobbed your hair! It looks cute." He sat on the arm of her seat. "I got pulled out of Harlan. The owners of the *Courier-Journal* have too much money invested down there. I heard one of those outside agitator fellows got shot."

"Goddamn you," Melinda said, without looking up at him. "He had a name." She could almost hear Eulalie say, "Don't use the Lord's name in vain."

In the spring, the rubber bathtub her mother had ordered for Christmas from Abercrombie's finally came to the address Melinda had left, in care of Mrs. Haycroft. The children blew it up and floated around Straight Creek in it until it snagged on a rock and was left there, forgotten, lodged against the weeds on the bank.

Book Two

Spain • 1937

The Visitors to War

When Melinda went door-to-door in the West End of Richmond to ask people to vote for Franklin Delano Roosevelt, her mother said, "If your father were alive, this would kill him," and went to bed with a sick headache. She sipped hydrochloric acid over crushed ice and said over and over through thin blue lips to a watercolor of flowering fruit trees by Wallace Nutting, "I don't know what I've done wrong." She said she could stand the boyish bob; she even swallowed the dishonorable discharge from the Red Cross, because she said she had worked with "those people" during the World War and some of them were—"Well, you know."

But she told Melinda that she should have looked after her car. "After all, it was one of your father's last gifts to you." She only used the word *gift* instead of *present* when she wanted to stress that gifts were more serious than presents and were bought at some sacrifice.

When Grandmother Mason couldn't stand it any longer, she bought Melinda a red Stutz Bearcat and said it was a late birthday present.

"Present," she underlined, "not gift, for heaven's sake, Mary Cary."

When the disreputable Aunt Maymay was mentioned, it was not in front of Melinda. Once, coming into the hallway, she did hear her mother say, "Do you think it is the Kregg or the Brandon blood?"

But her grandmother answered, "Certainly not. It's Mason blood, if anything. After all, *I* marched in a suffragette parade right through the middle of downtown Richmond."

Her mother said, "That's not fair. Now you know Morris didn't want me to."

Melinda slammed the door loudly enough for them to change the subject.

After the election, and after, as her mother and grandmother said, That Man even kept them from getting their own money out of the bank for several days, there was nothing left to do. Melinda got engaged twice, broke them off and made her mother cry, worried her grandmother, who said she was running around like a loose marble, stayed awake at night, and felt like an empty paper sack.

She couldn't even go to Kregg's Crossing. It didn't exist anymore, except as a place in her mind. Where it had been, a paper mill was being built. Melinda passed it once. They had thrown down the columns of the old house, and there was a bulldozer where she and Boodie and Uncle Brandon had picnicked.

Uncle Brandon had a pension as a disabled veteran, and when Melinda's father died, they found that he had been sending his mother money every month, but Melinda's mother stopped it. She said that people ought to stand on their own feet, and that they need only ask when they needed anything, but Uncle Brandon always said, "I have my pension," and wouldn't let Boodie say a word. Their mother wouldn't let them take anything from Maymay. She held forth about it at the dinner table. She said Maymay's money was tainted with sin because she had been married several times.

So one day in the winter of 1933, because he wouldn't ask anybody and his mother was sick, Uncle Brandon went to Lynchburg and pawned his overcoat and his gold watch and bought the medicine the doctor was giving her. They were gold tablets and they were expensive. He came back to Kregg's Crossing in a light snow and laughed it off. He said he'd lost his overcoat in the bus station. Because he had been gassed in the war, he caught pneumonia and was dead in one week.

Boodie muddled along like a lost child for the few months between his death and her mother's. When Melinda drove her mother to the second funeral, her mother said, "Now we'll have Boodie on our hands," and Melinda didn't say a word.

Two months later to the day, Boodie and Mr. Percival were married. Melinda was her maid of honor. It was the third wedding she had been in in a year, and her mother pointed out that she was always a bridesmaid, never a blushing bride until Melinda wanted to scream, and Grandmother Mason said, "For God's sake, let the child make up her mind."

Boodie sold what she called those damned family pearls. It was the first time Melinda had ever heard her say a swear word. She bought herself everything that wasn't nailed down at Miller and Rhoads. She made Melinda go with her and pick out clothes, china, new linen that she ran her hands over, smiling to herself. Boodie, as her mother pointed out, didn't wait until they were cold in their graves. She sold the old family place to the paper company. She even refused to stay with Melinda and her mother and grandmother when she came to Richmond to shop. She stayed at the Jefferson Hotel. She and Mr. Percival lived for a month in the house, and when Mr. Percival was transferred to Louisiana, Boodie sold everything and bought new antiques, except for a sewing table and her mother's tester bed.

It was the only thing that happened in two years that gave Melinda real, guiltless pleasure, that and Grace's seldom letters to remind her that she existed. Grace's voice began to come back to her, as if she had been half asleep for a year and the waking up was hard. "No," Grace had told her when she said she "had a little money," the acceptable phrase. "You have a lot of money. The gulf is not between the rich and the poor but between three hundred dollars a month and nothing. That gulf is uncrossable." When her mother found out that Melinda was not using any of the income her father had left her, she went to bed with another sick headache and said that Grandmother Mason's money was no better.

One day, at last, Melinda wrote to Grace. She

was ready. She told her that she had persuaded her mother to allow her to go to Katherine Gibbs and learn to be a secretary and study languages if she could stay with Mrs. Van Winkle. Katie Gibbs was what nice girls did when they graduated from finishing school and hadn't married yet. She had told her mother that Grace had three boys who had been to Harvard and that she lived in a big apartment on the corner of Fifth Avenue and Sixty-third Street, so she was nice.

Grace laughed when she heard how Melinda had presented her, but she didn't let on. After all, she did live on Fifth Avenue, and she did go to St. Barts, and she did lead two lives, one for her husband and children, whom she was fond of, and one for herself.

Grace was so happy to see Melinda that she began to treat her as if they were still in jail, and Melinda accepted it and was comforted. She fell into a pattern in the New York of the fall of 1934. She went to Katie Gibbs all day—shorthand, typing, French, business Spanish from a tutor. Sometimes at night she went to "21," sometimes the Stork Club, sometimes Union Square, and sometimes she filled in as an extra girl, almost a daughter, when Grace gave dinner parties for her husband's friends.

Grace had the ability to let conversation that would have set her teeth on edge at any other time pour over her in the big dining room that glowed with silver and crystal and the soft surface of English china. The only thing she wouldn't allow was any remark against Jews, and when one of her boys called out to his brother from the shower, "No, I'm not at Kirkland House—I mean Kikeland House," forgetting that he was not still at Harvard, she rushed in and dragged him out of the shower, and while he yelled, "Mother, I'm naked," Melinda heard her yell back, "Nevernevernever in this house use those words again. Do you hear what I say?" And the boy said "Yes, ma'am" to a woman Melinda hadn't really known existed, not on Fifth Avenue, anyway.

She grew to love New York; it was a wonderful time. New York in the fall was the most beautiful place on earth, the sky bright blue by day and a pillar of pink glow by night. The seats in the taxis smelled of good leather. It was a black-and-white year: the streets agleam with rain, the separation between busy day and formal evening, silk underwear again, silk stockings, chiffon, and model clothes, because after Katie Gibbs she worked as a secretary at *Harper's Bazaar* and could get them. She listened to the sophisticated, sleepless, soft jazz of 1935, stayed up until dawn with Spivy singing "Going on a binge with a dinge."

In 1936, the war in Spain broke out. Grace and Melinda gathered clothes for the Republicans and took them down to the warehouse run by the International Labor Party, filling the back of the Stutz Bearcat like the Ford had been in Kentucky.

Melinda had graduated to editorial assistant, which meant only that she moved to a different office, the layout studio. She typed captions and columns to go with the pasteup printing on the layouts. It was early September. She was typing

Diana Vreeland's "Why Don't You" column, which had to be done very carefully, and she was halfway through a sentence before she knew what it was saying. She had typed "wear bare knees and knee-length socks" when she stopped and read the rest of the sentence. It ended, "as Unity Mitford does when she takes tea with Hitler at the Carlton in Munich?"

She left the paper in the typewriter. She opened her right-hand desk drawer and took out the makeup bag she used when she didn't have time to go back to Grace's between work and cocktails. She found her little pile of clean handkerchiefs, her daily diary, her small copy of *Webster's Dictionary*. She put them all in her big handbag, which could hold a change of clothes. She walked into the art director's office and quit.

At the beginning of 1937, Melinda decided to volunteer to go to Spain. She said gathering people's old clothes wasn't enough. Grace didn't want her to, but she said, "I had a three-o'clock-in-the-morning," and there was nothing Grace could say to that.

The volunteers were being organized by the Communist Party, but they made it clear that because of the Popular Front they would take any qualified people who were not members of the party, even New Deal Democrats, socialists, liberals, anarchists, and Trotskyites.

When Melinda walked into the recruiting office, there was Tania. When she saw Melinda, she seemed to be glad to see her. But she said, "I'm truly sorry, Melinda." Melinda had long since learned to watch people who said *truly* in front of *sorry*. They were just about to slaughter you.

Tania went on. "We have to be extremely careful. You are just not politically responsible, and we can't turn you loose in Spain. If you had trained as a nurse it might have been different, but as it is . . ."

"Isn't there anything I can do?" Melinda heard herself almost begging.

Tania pretended to go through a list. "Let's see. You are not a nurse. We need motor mechanics, truck drivers—men's jobs, I'm afraid," and she smiled that smile that said, You haven't got as much hope as a snowball in hell.

One of the young girls who had volunteered as a nurse followed Melinda out of the office and put her arm around her shoulder. "So much for the Popular Front. Right? I'm no Communist either, and I'm going. I have to." She was a pretty, dark girl who spoke with an accent Melinda could hardly understand. They went across the street and had coffee together at a drugstore counter.

A whole life story poured out with the coffee. "I have to. We're Jewish. My aunt and my cousins just got out of Germany. People don't know how bad it is there. We have little cousins sleeping in our dresser drawers."

Melinda said she knew, she had to go too. But she didn't say any more. They exchanged phone numbers, and never saw each other again. But the girl had said a magic word—Brooklyn, a place where people understood if you had to go to Spain.

Melinda started living on her trust money. She

looked in the classified section of the Brooklyn phone book and found a motor mechanics and long-distance truck driving course, jobs in six months. That of course wasn't true, not during the Depression, but she signed on, the only woman. The men treated her like a soft-boiled egg.

She spent her days at the motor mechanics school and her nights, at El Morocco. When she would sneak in, Grace would get up and make her cocoa and say, "If you try to keep up this pace, you'll kill yourself. You are like somebody on a swinging bridge over a canyon—you can't go forward and you can't go back."

When they graduated, the men gave her a repair kit that they had all pitched in to buy. It was red. It had a set of wrenches, an adjustable wrench, a set of screwdrivers, a set of feeler gauges, needle-nose pliers, regular pliers, a spark-plug cleaner, a crank, a dozen sets of spark-plug points, and a long tube for siphoning gas, which they put in as a joke.

She took her certificate to Tania. Tania just glanced at it and said, "We don't take women drivers." Then she put down her pencil, which she was using like a baton, and said, "I'm truly sorry about this, Melinda. I had no idea you would go off on some wild goose chase like that. People like you would just clutter up Spain. Don't you *know* that? You are such a—" Then she used the word she so obviously despised. "—liberal." She added, trying to soften what she had said, "I'm sorry. I really am sorry," and, trying to find a more acceptable reason, added, "We only have a certain amount of money . . ."

Melinda jumped at that. "If it's money, I've saved some. I can pay my own way."

Tania was furious. "You don't understand a goddamn thing, do you?" She picked up the pencil again and twirled it.

There was a young man there that morning, and he followed her out of the office like the young nurse had. "I heard all that. Come on and have some coffee." She felt condemned to spend the Spanish Civil War in the drugstore opposite the recruiting office.

"Listen, do what I'm going to do," he said. "If you have any money, go to England. They have a medical aid office there and they don't give a damn about your politics. These American Communists are like Irish Catholics, they are more puritan than the Puritans." She was crying, and he was making her laugh at the same time.

"You're not a Communist?" she finally asked him.

"Good God, no, I'm from Boston." He said that he had escaped the puritanism of Boston Common and he wasn't about to replace it with political puritanism. He told her his name was Endicott Newton but that he was condemned to be called Fig, that he was a poof. She didn't know what that meant. "A pansy." He was patient with her. Then he asked her to lunch at the Plaza.

Grace saw her off on the *Île de France* and kept drawing Fig aside to tell him to look after her. She hugged Melinda, told her to be sure to write as often as she could, and finally said she was proud of her and handed her a soft parcel. Melinda knew before she opened it that it was a scarf with the colors of the Spanish Republic, red and yellow and deep blue. Scarves were all Grace ever made, and only when she was scared. This time Melinda knew that both the fear and the scarf were for her.

The *Île de France* was the same ship she had sailed on with her family in 1927, but it might as well have been completely strange to her. The companionways were smaller, the so-called lounge was tiny, and there were women nursing babies. Canadians and English boys huddled together in their own circles. There were American boys from all over the country, and a bevy of nurses, who looked formal in their capes and blue hats. They could admit that they were going to Spain. They had humanitarian passports. Most of them looked tired, drawn, and older than Melinda had expected.

By the first evening, some spell that had hung over them all was broken. They burst out of their huddles and their silence. They became young again. The only ones over twenty-two were Melinda and Fig, who were twenty-six and felt, for a little while, staid and responsible.

The bartender was a French socialist and believed in the Front Populaire, so he kept the bar open as long as anybody wanted to argue, and said over and over that he would go too but he had five children. He said it in French, and only Fig understood him.

One night two of the boys, both eighteen, got into a brawl over one of the nurses, who was so disgusted that she went to bed; but they kept right on, liking the brawl better than the nurse. They called each other every dirty name Melinda knew and a lot she hadn't yet learned, but nobody used a fist until one of them called the other a "reactionary deviationist." Then the fight really started and they had to be parted, while the bartender kept calling, "Front Populaire! Front Populaire!"

Melinda and Fig landed at Southampton, and their new friends watched from the deck and shouted to them. From the dock the boat rose like a great apartment house. It towered above them, and they couldn't hear the shouts, only see arms waving in the mist.

In London, they got rooms at a hotel near the British Museum. In the afternoons an aging string trio played while ladies from the country in tweed suits sat and drank tea so silently that Melinda wanted to yell and charge up and down the lobby, but she and Fig got the giggles instead.

They went together to a square way down by the House of Commons where the Spanish Relief had an office in the Trade Unions Council building. When they walked up the stairs and through a heavy door, a young woman looked up from a littered desk.

"I'm Penelope Cranwell. I'm the dogsbody. Everybody calls me Penny," she said, and reached up to shake hands. She said she always shook hands with Americans. They expected it. "Thank you for coming." She had one of those soft upper-class voices that can be heard for miles.

"Now. Questions. Sorry about that. What can

you do?" she asked Melinda. "We can't send totally untrained people, you understand."

Melinda said, "I've been getting ready for years, like Jacob working for Rachel," and realized that neither Fig nor Penny had the least idea what she was talking about. She laid all her certificates on the table—three courses, in Red Cross first aid, motor mechanics, mass feeding. She added while Penny was looking at them, "I speak French slowly, and a little business Spanish. I think I ought to tell you, I do have some money of my own."

"How nice for you," was all Penny said while she studied the little pile of certificates. "Katherine Gibbs, what's that?"

"It's a business school." Melinda was a little ashamed. "All you learn there is typing and shorthand and—" She didn't get any further.

"She can type!" Penny told the ceiling. "Thanks be to God. They need a typist who speaks Spanish in a new hospital they are setting up in Albastro, wherever that is. Can you really drive a truck? How absolutely divine. Reggie, come here. She can drive a truck and type!"

Fig was worried. He was afraid he would be left out, so he said, "We are prepared to buy an ambulance to take—"

"Marvelous. We need a Fordson for the new hospital. They're the best." Penny looked worried. "But they cost about five hundred pounds."

Melinda didn't say a word. She hadn't known they were going to buy an ambulance, so she tried to do figures in her head, and didn't succeed.

"Oh damn, I'm supposed to ask you one more question. They insist. We are trying to weed out loonies. Oh dear, this is embarrassing, nobody can answer it—why do you want to go to Spain?"

Melinda just stared at her, and all that came out was, "Well, we're on the right side, and . . ."

She couldn't say any more. How could she tell a stranger that she wanted to be a member of the right side when she couldn't even define the right side? How could she say she just knew what it was at three o'clock in the morning? She was afraid of sounding like one of the loonies they were trying to weed out. "Democratically elected government" sounded pompous, and she was afraid she would drive Fig into giggles. How could she tell a stranger that Grace had been right when she told her that she would never be satisfied with innocence again, and that she wouldn't like it?

Finally some more words came. "I can use my training there if they need it." It was the only limp thing she could say.

Penny smiled. "That's all we need. Now both of you go to the Army and Navy Store and get kitted out. And for God's sake, don't forget to take oceans of typewriter ribbons for a Corona portable. We can let you have one nobody knows how to use. When you come back I'll have all the papers for humanitarian aid, and if you get into trouble at the border, call the office in Barcelona. We have instructions for you to take the road through Carcassonne and Perpignan. We have telephone numbers there. You have to speak French. Oh damn, they've already moved the office to a villa in Valencia. It means more driving. Sorry."

Everything was a game in their last few days before war. They went to the theater; they went to the Cafe Royale, where Fig tried to recognize people. They took walks through Hyde Park. "*Morituri te salutamus,*" Fig said when they had drinks at the Cavendish, which he insisted on. She didn't know what he meant, and she was damned if she was going to ask.

They went to the Army and Navy Store. The salesman, who looked like he had kitted people for the Boer War, told them that ladies and gentlemen going to Spain preferred leather coats, leather jackets, and high boots. When they were both dressed, Fig said they looked like members of Hitler's Brown Shirts, and then he twirled in front of the mirror and said, "Don't you think I look marvelous, sort of Four Feathersy?" and shocked the salesman.

After they had found the typewriter ribbons, Fig said, "Now we're going to think about our tum-tums. An army travels on its stomach."

They went to Fortnum and Mason, in Jermyn Street, and bought coffee and tea and asked for crackers, and the salesman there, who was dressed up as if he were on his way to a wedding, said it was the wrong time of year. Fig explained later that the bastard knew they didn't want Christmas crackers, but he had to put them down a little because they were ignorant, innocent Americans who couldn't speak English. At the time he said in his most Boston, "Will you show us what biscuits you have in sealed tins? And we want caviar and smoked salmon and a case of Gentleman's Relish."

Two men in morning coats filled the floor of a taxi with two wheels of Stilton, two of Cheshire cheese, two smoked turkeys—"Like the Ark," Fig said, "everything in twos"—two Westphalian hams, a case of brandied peaches, a case of caviar, a case of smoked salmon, and a case of Gentleman's Relish, which Fig said he adored. There was almost too much food to force into their Fordson ambulance after it had been packed at the headquarters in London. Penny stood in the cold street with her clipboard, checking off supplies. It still wasn't like war. It was more like the Red Cross classes where somebody volunteered to be the wounded.

They took turns driving to Dover, thanking God aloud that the road was nearly empty. The ambulance had a left-hand drive, and they were both afraid of going into the ditch and overcorrecting right into traffic. Fig tried to get comfortable and complained that manly wartime cars were all edges and he had never tried to rest against leather that had corners sticking into him.

The ambulance was what Penny called chock-a-block with supplies, including ether canisters, so they had to crawl while English cars tooted behind them. It was stripped down from comfort to its essential use, iron-colored, without even a red cross painted on it. Penny told them that the red crosses had had to be taken off because the Germans and the Italians dive-bombed them. The steering was so high that when it was

Melinda's turn to drive, she sat on a cushion that she had bought at the Army and Navy Store.

Penny had told them over tea at Gunther's how to say *camarada,* which everybody was called, whether they were Communists or not. It was part of the third language, the language of the Popular Front. She said they mustn't say *señor* or *señora* anymore, or even *adiós,* except to older people in the villages, who thought the new language was blasphemous nonsense even though they were all on the side of the Republic. They said it was *desvergonzado,* shameless, an insult.

When Fig asked Penny how she knew so much Spanish, she said, a little embarrassed, "I was wounded at Madrid, well, really Casa de Campo, so I can't go back. My ambulance was hit." She had been friends with them for three days and she hadn't said a word about being in Spain.

Fig had been in France so often that he had a map of restaurants in his head, some so obscure that they had only two tables, some very grand. He and Melinda stopped at all of them. Fig moaned about liking good food and said that his lovely thin body was going to blow up like a balloon when he was older if he didn't stop eating.

They avoided Paris, as they had been told to do. They went through Blois because Fig said she simply had to see it, and then to Vouvray, where he bought a case of white wine, and made a detour to Bordeaux, where he found room for just one more case of red. He said he loathed Spanish wine.

They stayed in Carcassonne and walked

around the Roman walls. The last place they stopped was just before the border beyond Perpignan, at a little shed on the side of the mountain road. "You'll be surprised," Fig said when he climbed out of the ambulance and stretched. "The best omelets in France."

Then they were at the border. The border guard said, *"Viva la República,"* grinned, and clenched his fist. They drove through the high passes of the Pyrenees toward Figueres, where, at the castle that served as the headquarters of the International Brigades, they found friends from the *Île de France,* who were complaining about the smell of piss and rotten food.

Melinda and Fig were lucky. They had humanitarian passports. Most of the boys they had come with had had to climb the high passes in their city shoes, with guides who had been smugglers and knew ways across the border that nobody had ever been able to seal. Some of them had died in the olive fields, in the clothes they had worn from Manhattan and Toronto and Cleveland.

In Figueres they found a restaurant, and once again everybody in the world was twenty-two or eighteen or in between, and they spoke so many languages that they had fallen into signs and clenched fists and hugs to explain what they meant. They sang the "Marseillaise" and the "Internationale" in German and Polish and Italian. They never seemed to stop singing. "The right eats and the left sings," Fig grumbled when he saw the food.

All the way down the coast road to Valencia

there were signs that they were in another country, not just Spain but war. The fields bloomed as if they were trying to cover over what was happening, but the roads rumbled with brute-colored cars, and when they drove near a railroad track the train was slow and full of men who leaned out the windows and called *"Viva la República!"* and kissed the air at Melinda.

Open pickups crowded with soldiers, ambulances, and huge grinding trucks were a steady stream going to war and coming from it. Along the sides of the roads, people trudged as if they had been born trudging and would trudge forever, without any expression, even of despair. The restaurants Melinda and Fig stopped at were stripped down to dim light, dirty tables, bread and nameless meat. "Hopeless." Fig shook his head.

Melinda drove into Valencia because she had been there before, but it was a different city. There were the Rolls-Royces she remembered, fine cars, old wrecks, ambulances, and buses in a never-ending argument. Valencia had been a rich and arrogant town. Now the fancy cars were painted with signs: UGT, "Visca POUM," *"Viva la República."* The red flags of the Communists, the red and black of the anarchists, and the red, yellow, and blue of the Republic floated above the city and at the windows. When traffic moved at all, it moved fast and wildly. The cars were driven by boys who once had stood along the pavements under the trees and watched them pass, and most of their owners were either dead or in Portugal. Fig said so.

Melinda was floating in fatigue from the long drive. How different it was from the pictures of war she had carried with her. She had been expecting troops like the ones she had seen in the movies of the World War when she was little, and the voice of Uncle Brandon, telling not of it but around it, as if war were a mystery.

All the walls were covered with gaudy posters. Militia girls swung along the street wearing their ammunition belts across their breasts like jewels, their caps jaunty on glossy hair that had once been covered with *mantillas*, when they were allowed to go into the street in twos for the *paseo*.

The streets were also full of soldiers, and here and there as they were slowed to walking pace by the traffic, with Fig trying and failing in the new darkness, to read the map they had been given, snatches of singing came through the open windows. The Emilio Castelar was a carnival of war, a ballet of uniforms and rifles and girls and men and boys fifteen or sixteen years old. It was the time of the *paseo*, which war had not stopped. They drove toward evening in Valencia through the boy and girl soldiers strolling, and leaning with one foot against the walls of the houses, and lounging at the tables in the outdoor cafes. They could not know yet that the *paseo* also meant being shot by the Fascists.

Melinda and Fig finally found the villa that British Aid used for its headquarters. Melinda sat in the car, as Penny had told her to in London. "Don't under any circumstances leave the ambulance unguarded. The POUM steal from the Communists, and the anarchists steal from the

POUM." Lying there half asleep, she grinned at Penny's voice. What the Poom was she had no idea, and she was too shy about her own ignorance to ask.

Darkness had fallen above the trees. She laid her head against the thin leather seatback and nearly slept to the sound of distant singing.

"Now it's your turn, dearie," Fig said, and slid into the seat beside her. "You won't believe what you're going to see and hear."

The office of the British Medical Unit looked like the drawing room of somebody who had lost all his money. There were tattered easy chairs and a beautiful carved desk against the wall covered with papers and maps, some of which had spilled over onto the floor as if somebody had been looking for something and had gotten impatient. The posters around the walls were there to brighten the place rather than extol the virtues of the militia, the Brigades, or the farmers, or warn against whores and syphilis.

A man and a woman sat there looking the kind of tired that elegant people did, the ones she had seen in first class on the *Île de France.* They were having drinks because it was the right time, war or no war.

The woman, who had a strong Italian accent, said, "*Camarada,* do sit down and join us. Your friend did, so he can just wait for you. Poor darling, you look exhausted."

The man unwound himself from the chair and took her hand. "Jolly good, *camarada,*" he said in the Spanish way. "I think it's marvelous your coming like this. Frightfully sorry you have to leave tonight, but the convoys go at night, don't you know. Anyway, we have chits for you to use for food, and a map of where you are to go. It's called Albastro. It's a convent."

"You've said all that, *camarada,*" came from deep in one of the chairs, where the woman had subsided.

He said, annoyed, "I know, darling, but if both of them know it is a bit safer." He went over to the desk and scrambled among the papers. "Here you are—petrol chit, meal chit, billet chit for the day, if the convoy has to wait on the road for night. It could take several days. Oh, petrol chit. No. I've given you that. Oh dear, just you wait, this damned war is the worst bloody shambles in Europe. Have a drink."

They finally introduced themselves. Penny had told Melinda that they were both peers, but they called her *camarada* and they were dressed in beautifully fitting dark blue boiler suits. When the man saw her looking at them he said, "It's too bad you won't have time to get yourself well-made *monos.* Everybody wears them, or really whatever they want to. Nobody goes into the street in a jacket and tie. You can get shot. Spanish brandy, Fundador, really not bad, want a splash?" Melinda thought he meant a bath, which would have been wonderful after all the driving, but he squirted some soda water into the brandy when she nodded yes.

"It will be an all-night drive. Sorry about that. The convoy leaves at eleven, so you will have time for food. And a wash. Here's a chit for the hotel where most of the British medicals stay.

You'll be taken care of there. Take some food with you for the road."

Melinda said nothing about the hampers from Fortnum's.

"Oh, darling, what else do we have to tell her?" He turned to the Italian peeress.

"I think we told him everything. Oh God, the passes!" She floated up from the chair. "Here you are, darling, all ready for you, too awful of me to forget and almost let you be shot. Oh, and remember in the convoy to keep twenty meters behind the *camión* in front of you. That's almost like yards to you." She was kind about the information. "That way, if the convoy is dive machine-gunned, you have a better chance. I drove that route for a year. It's absolutely bloody."

She showed Melinda the passes. "Here, you sign here, most of the guards on the road can't read so we put lots of lovely seals on them. Here, after *hom nomena,* and tell your friend to sign his. That's important. They do know where the names are supposed to go, and if they aren't there I suppose they'll shoot you or jail you or something." She subsided into the torn easy chair again. "Now, darling, you had better beetle off to the hotel and have a wash and some food. There isn't any here. You've got simply hours. It's only down the street, and they have somebody at the door day and night to look after the *camiones* that belong to us."

When Melinda climbed back into the ambulance, Fig woke up long enough to say, "Noel Coward at war, can you believe it?" They sat in the ambulance together and read their passes under the carriage lamp, which made the leaves above them electric green. *Consell de Sanitat de Guerra.* They drove on to the front of the hotel, where a long line of ambulances and trucks were parked. The one in front of them looked like it had been in a war. Fig said so.

Several drivers were draped across the bar. They made room for them, and one of them, older than the others, said, "Jolly good. Have a drink but not too much. This stuff is lethal. *Salud.*"

Melinda and Fig asked for rooms and washed up. They ate lots of *tapas,* some shrimp and beans and rice, and tomatoes and peppers. The bar looked neglected. Nothing was shiny. If, later, Melinda had had to define what the buildings of war looked like, she would have remembered the bar with so little light, dim on the glasses, dim on the bottles behind the bar, a slanted world with strips of paper across the windows, and said, "Nothing was shiny, and they were all so young."

Scotty was a bandy-legged little Glaswegian with a lined face as if, as young as he was—and he said at once that he was nineteen—he had spent too many years in the sun. "Ach, it's a bloody fucking war, no like a proper war at all," he told them, very conversational and easy. "You ought not to be here. It's sheer bloody ignorance. And what do they call you?"

When he heard Melinda's voice, he said, "Ooo, it's like the flicks, that Southern tone—speak more. We'll call you Miss Jasmine, and you, my dear, are Fig."

"I always have been, alas. My worst enemy

is that bloody biscuit." Bloody biscuit. Fig was already speaking the language, and Melinda realized that if she were to be understood at all, she had better learn. "Bloody." She tried it out to her glass.

"Listen to the wee girl. Bloooooody, Miss Jasmine."

They told their ages, as if the way they looked had to be explained somehow: eighteen, nineteen, twenty. There was an adulthood about them, as if they knew things they weren't saying.

"He's twenty-nine—we call him Pop. An old bugger, aren't you, Pop?" someone called from along the bar to a man who was nearly asleep in his drink. Pop said, "Look you, comrade, I have been in more unemployment marches than you have been in fancy houses," and he wanted to fight and said he was a good Communist and everybody else was a bloody Fascist and didn't know what the bloody hell they were doing in Spain.

From all across the length of the bar came a medley of insults: "Belt up, you bloody Pop," "Stow it," "Knock it off." Melinda decided that the English had more ways of saying shut up than she had ever known. It should, she thought, tell her something about them.

"Here is Auld Boy." Scotty introduced the man who had advised them about the drink. He had come to lounge over the bar beside them. He had one of those choked-at-the-age-of-five English voices.

"You know, you really shouldn't be here, my

dear," he said. "It's not what you thought it would be. It's not, oh, not at all."

It was getting late, and Pop was still muttering into his drink. "Bloody Trotskyite pooms."

Scotty patted him on the back, and said, "Pop, don't get in a bloody snit. You know the rules, no politics."

"What is a poom?" Melinda asked Old Boy.

"Partido Obrero de Unificación Marxista," somebody chanted.

"It's not bleeding politics, it's the bleeding truth." Pop sobbed, and nobody paid any attention except Old Boy, who whispered to Melinda and Fig, "There are as many bleeding initials in this war as there are bleeding *chóferes* at this bar."

"They all seem to be quite drunk." Fig was worried. "Can they drive?"

Old Boy laughed. "You'll be surprised. All right, children," he called. "It's nearly eleven. Wash your faces, comb your hair. Don't forget to brush your teeth and make peepee—we're off in fifteen minutes."

In one minute the bar was empty except for Pop. "All right, Ooold Booy." Pop strung it out like a comic saying, "Tennis, anyone?"

"Knock it off, Pop, don't be such a fucking Bolshie," Old Boy told him, and then apologized to Melinda for his language.

Scotty came back from the gents and called, "Time, gentlemen, please. Belt up, Pop, my darling."

Fig said, "Oh God, we're supposed to join some kind of convoy and they didn't tell us where."

"That's typical of this bloody mess. We're the convoy." Scotty, who had sung more and drunk more than anyone, was suddenly sober and in charge. "Remember, you two, wee Miss Jasmine and wee Fig, you remember this. Blackout lights, and if your ambulance doesn't have them, put tape over the headlamps with a one-inch gap. That's all you get. Keep the sma' taillight in front of you in your sight at all times, and stay twenty meters behind the *camión* in front. Oh, I forgot. You stop when we stop. We do it to change *chóferes* and make potty, as Auld Boy here says."

Old Boy grinned slightly at something only he could see. He paid no attention. But he added, "One sleeps, the other drives. Can you really drive a *camión?*" he asked Melinda.

"I can if somebody will tell me what it is," Melinda said.

"She can drive anything," Fig had to brag.

"Marvelous, we certainly need you. These things are put together with string and sealing wax. It's a lorry, my dear," Old Boy said in what Melinda thought was a kind and lordly way, and she didn't know any more than she had before until they were motioned into the street between two enormous trucks.

Scotty was already taping the headlights. "You'll be fine." He leaned in the window. "It's a braw bricht moonlicht nicht with a bloody shit of an *avión* bomber's moon."

They did leave at eleven. They heard Old Boy's voice far ahead call, "Girls, girls, keep to the crocodile," and the grumble of engines starting all the way along the convoy. The roar grew louder and louder, the growl of gears all the way into the distance.

Melinda and Fig followed tiny taillights along an empty road in a long line—it must have been a mile long. They were tired, half drunk, and cold. They agreed that it was all ridiculous and wonderful.

"There is nothing more satisfying," Fig said, "than knowing you are on the right side." Crawling through the dark on the right side in the right direction for the right reason, they knew they were damn right, as Fig put it several times, both to keep his spirits up and because he had a habit of repeating himself.

They were driving slowly through the emptiest land Melinda had ever seen, under the huge bright moon, the *avión* moon, and it bathed a fawn-colored pelt of emptiness as they drove toward the mountains, as if they were not on the land at all but swimming along under Scotty's braw bricht moon. Melinda slept until Fig waked her two hours later and said, "We've stopped. They're changing over and peeing on the side of the road." The land on both sides of the road seemed completely bare of any cover.

"Well, I can't pee out in the open under this bloody shit of a moon!" She was weak and tired and as grumpy as a child.

"I think you'd better learn, my dear," Old Boy's voice came from the cab window. "We've had to stop for a while. One of the *camiones* is ill."

"What if there are snakes?" She was almost crying.

Old Boy called, "They've all gone beddy-byes."

"Oh, for God's sake," Fig grumbled. "Haven't you ever been to camp? Get on with it. There's nothing out there but lions."

"I hated camp and everything it stood for." She grumbled off and squatted behind the ambulance, not caring anymore. It was so late and everybody was annoyed.

For an hour the *chóferes* tried to get the truck going again. Melinda wandered up to see what was the matter. Old Boy swore, "No bloody extra contacts left. This one's been filed until it won't spark."

She went back to their ambulance, rummaged under the seat, and brought back a set of new points. Everyone crowded around her and said, "Have you got any more?"

"No," she lied, learning fast. "Just an extra one for our ambulance."

"How do you know about contacts?" Scotty called after her. She didn't answer.

By Melinda's watch, it was five o'clock in the morning when they limped and groaned up the steep hill of Cuenca. The town square was still dark; the church rose up like a huge stone ghost. One bar was open, down in a street tucked under the square, and the proprietor was waiting for them.

Old Boy went around to the drivers. "You know where to stash your *camiones.*" When he got to Fig, who was driving, he said, "Now, what we do here is find a narrow street where the ambulance won't be noticed. We stay here until nightfall. There's a hotel up the street toward the hilltop, but it won't open until later, so find your place and come on to the bar." He pointed down the steps to the lower street.

Most of the drivers had gathered at the town fountain, a Renaissance marble trough on a wall of the square, and were filling cans with water to cool their engines and their canteens. They were drinking and arguing, but so softly that they sounded like a hum of bees.

Melinda went off just to be by herself for a minute before she joined the others. She wanted air. She wanted to think. She wanted to ask herself all the questions she had refused to answer. There in the stretched exhaustion after the crawl across the night land under the moon, she wanted to know where she was and why she was in a place where even the dawn wind felt strange in her face.

The small town was beginning to color with the dawn. She went through an arch and found a stone parapet. Beyond it the hill dropped straight down, and the road they had come by looked like a tiny track far below her. She could just see the outline of some sort of building beyond the road in the valley, which was so narrow it was like a gorge; there was a stone cross in an empty niche above the door, so she supposed the building was a convent.

When she went back, Scotty was still standing in the middle of the square, looking around. There wasn't a vehicle in sight. He said to nobody in particular, "In' it bloody cruel?" Then he saw

Melinda and took her arm and said, "You come and get yourself warm."

Old Boy was sitting with Fig. Melinda and Scotty pulled up chairs, and she put her head down on the scarred wooden table that smelled of spilled wine and tried to shut out their voices so she could sleep.

"How is she?" she heard Old Boy ask Fig. "Is she all right?"

"Of course she is," she heard Fig say. "She's as tough as a nut."

"I am not," she muttered so that nobody could hear.

"We had two girl drivers like that at Jarama," Scotty whispered. "They both bought it."

"Shh, Scotty, she'll hear." Old Boy was whispering, as if it were all right for men to buy it, but not for women. It was the last thing she remembered until Fig woke her and said they could go to the hotel and get baths.

"Oh my God, really? With soap and towels?" She stretched, half awake.

"Soap and towels—well, maybe soap and towels," Old Boy promised.

They found the hotel and went to sleep so quickly they didn't think of baths until it was evening.

When they were already in the ambulance, ready to go again in the dark, Old Boy put his head in the cab window. "You're in luck," he said. "I have a guide for you. He's looking for a ride to Albastro."

He was a tall, slim man with a shock of hair and a gentle face that made him look like a fifteenth-century miniature painting in the Victoria and Albert Museum. Fig pointed it out when they were introduced, as formally as if he and Melinda were not crowded into an ambulance cab with the young man, who smelled terrible.

"People tell me that," he said comfortably. "My name is Tandy. I am not what I seem, thank God. I am a student of Arabic influences on Spanish architecture of the twelfth century," he began, and he didn't shut up. Melinda fell asleep with her head on his shoulder. She woke up when it was her turn to drive and he was saying, "I was traveling with a friend in Catalunya when this damned thing began. Well, there was nothing else to do, was there?"

Tandy told them there wasn't any hospital in Albastro yet. They were going to open one, and it was going to be a bloody shambles.

"The drill is first to get rid of fleas, rats, sheep shit, people shit, dog shit, and old hay . . ."

The dawn was a streak above them, then a faint light. The hills began to take on color. They drove through an ancient landscape of rocks and pines. Melinda could see faint bundles of soldiers asleep beside the road.

Tandy, who was half awake, said, "There must have been a fight. Patrols, I guess."

Melinda said, "They're asleep as if nothing had happened."

He said, "No, they are dead. The dead wagon will be along. See their bare feet? We scrounge the shoes and the blankets and the guns when a man is killed. We have so little—just men and men and more men." He began to doze.

It was in the hour of that cold dawn, with the two men asleep beside her, that she crossed a barrier she would never be able to recross. It was being at war instead of going to war, and it was like nothing she could ever have known. But Uncle Brandon had known, and he had drunk in hotel rooms before he died, and she knew why for the first time. Her mind was tumbling through past and present when Tandy woke up, just at the right time for his turn. He explained that he could do that and she had better learn.

The pine woods smelled wonderful in the morning. She looked over the hillside at the flat fields beyond, to where a line of old trees moved slightly in the wind.

"That's the front," Tandy told her before she asked. "About five miles to the west across the fields. It's jolly hard to find, let me tell you. It's quiet now, only snipers and a few fights when people want to sleep in the same barn, or when our chaps see a Moor on horseback and then they shoot the horse so they can eat."

They turned away from the convoy onto a long, blank, straight side road that seemed to stretch into the distance as if it would never end. Away to the east were the mountains they had crossed, or clouds. They passed ruins of farmhouses, all isolated, and once the ruin of a convent, high on a hill. On both sides of the road the first grain crops were beginning to turn, and some of the fields were red with poppies.

Where there were meadows a few sheep were grazing, and once two cows, all of them guarded by shepherds with rifles. "They don't want us to steal them—commandeer, excuse me." Tandy laughed. The morning had cheered all three of them. Fig stopped complaining and stretched and pointed out wildflowers and blooming gorse.

"Oh my God, look!" Tandy called, as if he were seeing a lover in the distance. "Pure Moorish castle and town, right on the twelfth-century border. Oh, loves, there is a God!"

Melinda saw a pile of what looked like bare rocks in the distance, but as they drove nearer the rocks turned into houses, the church spire rose up at the top of the first hill, and behind it, so high on the next rise that it commanded the valley, were the bare ruins of a castle.

"Albastro. I knew it. *Albastro* means 'perfume flask' in Arabic, so this must have been a place where somebody important had a harem. They were always on hills—no, not as high as the fortress castle. Oh dear." He was struck dumb as they drove past the first of the houses. One faced the square with the church across from it, and through a Moorish arch—Tandy, who had found his voice again, said it was a Moorish arch—they saw *camiones* and some ambulances clutched up in front of a convent with a huge, nearly black oak door that was studded with brass nails so large and still so bright from years of polish that Melinda could see them in the distance. There were niches in the walls where statues had been removed.

They heard somebody yell, "Move those bloody *camiones*. Don't you know what a fucking target you are?" The engines began to grumble as the trucks moved into the side streets, so that

Fig could drive straight up to the door. "Move, for God's sake," the man called.

"Can't," Fig yelled, very cheerful. "We have to unload goodies from London!"

He opened the rear door. Melinda stayed for a minute in the cab, too surprised to move. There was a small grove of pine trees, and under the trees people seemed to be crisscrossing each other's paths without direction. She thought of the way people moved getting ready for picnic. From that distance she couldn't tell men from women, and it didn't matter. They were all dressed in overalls, some of them like the *mono* she had seen in Valencia. Someone flung open the great door to the convent and they began to form a line, moving bundles, stretchers, one with a toilet, some with huge cartons marked BANDAGES, in an ant line into the building.

Fruit trees in the convent garden were wild and untended and vines flowed out along the ground. Heather and some kind of thorn bush had grown up as high as small trees. The first color that Melinda thought of was of sand; then there was the green—green vines, green lichen, the green of neglect and abandonment. Some of the villagers had begun to help. A hungry dog watched with its tail between its legs.

When Melinda tried to get out of the cab, she nearly fell, her legs were so stiff.

"Ooops. Watch it!" A woman in overalls grabbed her and then held out her hand. She had a hard handshake and a healthy wide face, but there were dark circles under her eyes, and she hadn't washed for a while. Her sleeves were rolled up. She had large, useful forearms. "Hello, Tandy, I wondered when you would turn up," she called. "This place is dreadful, only one well, no electricity. But they are fixing that and trying to dig another well. The villagers are helping this time."

She motioned to the tile roof. Several soldiers in leather jackets swarmed over it while a man with a red-and-black shawl around his black peasant pants lay full length on the tiles, reaching down out of sight for something. Melinda wondered at the leather jackets. Later she found that the survivors took them from the dead, so that the more leather jackets there were, the fewer live men.

"You are the Americans. Jolly good," the woman finally said. "Have you brought some Dettol? I can't tell you how badly we need Dettol. God, this place is awful. We had to take an old body out and bury it—the local people wouldn't come in here to do it. They were afraid. It must have been a year old. We've only found one, repeat, *one* loo in the whole *town.* It was so clogged up that nobody would touch it, and then Dr. Wimpy thrust his hand right down in it, and so now we have a loo, thank God. He's a hero, but nobody will go near him. He's gone to find a spring or a creek to wash in. What those nuns did, I don't know. Lined up and prayed, I suppose. Sisters, come. Here are the supplies. Find the Dettol! You two, find a place to kip down for an hour. Then I will put you to work." The woman never did tell Melinda who she was, but she heard everyone call her Sister McCall.

Tandy called from the door, "Come! Come quickly. You have to see!"

He took Melinda's arm and began to show her around as if she were his guest. Beyond the heavy great door was a vaulted stone corridor, and at one side a cell. Beyond the corridor an open cloister lay in the sun. There was a long refectory to the right of the cloister, where some of the men were already setting up cots. The windows were high, so that Melinda could see the road they had come by only by standing on her toes.

"They didn't want the girls to see out, whether they were nuns or harem girls." Tandy laughed, delighted.

On the other side of the cloister were cells, and at the end opposite the entry arch was a small chapel and a room that must have been the mother superior's because it was more comfortable than the others. It had a huge stone fireplace that Tandy said had Roman carving.

But the cloister itself quieted even Tandy. He touched the white arches like a blind man learning, and he sighed. "Alabaster columns . . . ," he breathed like an incantation. He rubbed dirt and dead vines back with his foot to expose a bit of the paving. "These are *azulejos,* tiles from Portugal, very late," he said, disapproving. "At least sixteenth century." They looked gray with dust, but there were footprints where the others had come in to take out the body.

Sister McCall yelled out, "Tandy, stop that and come and get to work."

"Nobody wants to know anything." Tandy sighed. "Ignorant sods."

When they came out of the door, the ambulance was crawling with people. Sister McCall thrust a clipboard into Melinda's hands and told her to tick off things. "Put your typewriter and your gear in the little cell to the right of the main door. You're the dogsbody in charge of equipment." She had forgotten that she had told them to rest.

Melinda stood there ticking off bandages, splints, ether, morphine, Dettol, as they were called out. There was a cheer, and then suddenly everyone went as silent as stone. She looked up and Fig was looking, quite horrified, at the ground. There in the middle of the courtyard, isolated from the cots, cartons, oxygen tanks, and linen that had not yet been taken in, sat the cases of wine and the treasures from Fortnum's.

"Don't touch them," Sister McCall said, almost reverently. "How absolutely marvelous of you. How did you know?

"I will take charge of it," she announced. "We'll get this place cleaned up, and then we'll have a feast."

She came over to Fig and Melinda, who were trying not to look embarrassed. "You are dears. We've been eating mule meat for months, and we haven't seen a decent cheese. I sound like Ben Gunn, don't I?" She hugged Melinda and then solemnly shook hands with Fig. Melinda thought Sister McCall was going to cry.

Melinda made lists and lists of lists. Her small cell was piled high with equipment. She got out colored pencils she had bought in London, thinking they might come in handy, cut a side off one of the empty cartons, and made lines, blue, red, black, green. Then she headed the columns EQUIPMENT, WOUNDS, IN, OUT. She found a nail that had held a crucifix for so long that the stone wall had a lighter patch in the shape of a cross, and hung up the sign. She stood back. She was already learning that it was a makeshift war. She was not satisfied. She printed at the bottom of the chart PLEASE ENTER ALL EQUIPMENT USED AND FOR WHAT PURPOSE. Then she was satisfied at last and didn't know what else to do.

She asked herself one question. "What would Grandmother do? Not Kregg, Grandmother Mason." She straightened her dungarees and went to find Sister McCall.

"Clean out the cloister." She gave the order as if she had not nearly cried over the cheese.

Melinda stood in the corner of the cloister and waited to decide where to begin. There was nobody to ask. The vines had escaped their columns and gone mad, as if they had been searching for water, blinding the arches, running along the ground, twisting around each other in a deadening embrace. One was in wild bloom, a defiant red. Another drooped like a Victorian immortelle over the wellhead in the center.

She heard a rustling sound, as if the nuns were still pacing along the arcades in their starched habits, and then a rat ran out from the tangle of vines like wild hair on the floor. She didn't let herself scream. She went back to her cell and found her Swiss knife and her shears, then put on her knee-length boots with her dungarees inside, so that no rats could run up her legs. She went back into the cloister and began to clip vines and pile them up. She clipped them back to their alabaster containers, crudely carved into urns in front of the graceful whirled columns.

She found a broom then, like a witch's broom. The cloister was a still center in the midst of all the activity. She turned around at a sound, thinking it was a rat, and raised her broom to scare it away, but it was two young Chinese men, scrubbed very clean. "We found," one of them said; "a fine spring. Plenty of water. I am Sung Lee, and this is Sung Woo."

He spoke an English purer than any she had ever heard. "We are *camilleros,* stretcher-bearers," he explained. "We have come to help you. We are from the London School of Economics."

Tandy wasn't able to stay away from the cloister. He said so when he came back, and added that he was going to help. Then he forgot and stood by one of the columns and chanted, "*Albastro.* Scent bottle of alabaster." He let his hand drift down its spiral carving. "Look at these columns. Pure Moorish, the twisted graceful carving and then at the top, the capitals put on later, Christian, by somebody who was having it on with religion. They are jokes. Look, Melinda." He was calling to her, but she hardly paid attention. "Just look! You see, the devils and the monsters and the imps showing their asses to the nuns swanning around below in the cloister."

Sung Lee, who was making a pile of vines and dead leaves to clear more of the floor, said, "For God's sake, belt up and get to work, Tandy."

Tandy said, "Nobody loves me or appreciates my great knowledge."

He finally started scrubbing, but it didn't stop the lecture. He argued with himself, like two professors, that the floor tiles could have been Seljuk, whatever that was, instead of Portuguese. He said he couldn't make up his mind. As they all scrubbed on their hands and knees, a bright picture came out from under the dirt, chicken shit, rat turds, dried frog snivel, dead blossoms, and long vines. Tandy grumbled, scrubbed, and commented, "Look at that. Definitely Seljuk," and from another corner of the cloister, Sung Woo called, "How the bloody hell do you know so bloody much?"

"I read Persian. It was the court language of the Seljuks," Tandy explained across the cloister floor. "You inscrutable nit."

They scrubbed the cloister until it was clean and calm. The floor tiles were bright with designs of flowers. The afternoon sun filtered in through vines too high to reach, their tendrils making shadows on the floor. Melinda and her helpers piled stalks, some the size of small trees, in one corner of the cloister, and wood for a fire in the fireplace, which was big enough to walk into. It was built up like a table and it had a huge spit.

By night the convent had become a hospital. Cots were regimented in the cells. A refectory and kitchen had been set up. The mother superior's room was an operating room, and Sister McCall said she would commandeer the fireplace to boil water as soon as the feast was over.

By eight o'clock everyone was slumped on the

empty cots and on the floor of the cloister, leaning against the walls, making shadows in front of the fire as they moved. Melinda was so tired that everything was brighter and louder and quieter at the same time, and the reflection of the fire jumped and gleamed on their faces. She sat with her back against the wall and tried to take them all in, the people she was going to work with. There were Sung Lee and Sung Woo, and a Polish doctor with a fine baritone voice who sang sad songs they couldn't understand. There was Dr. Wimpy, who had washed and was neater than anyone else, but he still had to sit a little apart from the others. There were several Spanish Republican *practicantes.* Tandy, who had sloped down beside her and was whispering, told her that they were medical students. He said that the friend he had been walking through Catalunya with at the beginning of the war had come from University Hospital in his last year and was a *practicante,* really a doctor, front line.

Several Spanish girls sat with their caps on the sides of their heads, their Republican scarves around their necks, and their black hair gleaming. Tandy called them *chicas,* nurses' aides.

There were three more Americans, one a nurse who knew some people Melinda had traveled over with. She sat down on Melinda's other side and whispered that she had just been posted from Albacete. She had been at Guadalajara, and she said that all but two of the Canadians who had come with Melinda and Fig were dead. They had been shipped straight to the front without any training, and they had just been mown down in a line between the trees in an olive grove, with their feet sticking up in their city shoes. She had stood at their funeral, all of them in a line, the way they fell. Somebody had taken their shoes and their bare feet stuck out the ends of the coffins. Guadalajara had been a great victory.

One of the Spaniards was playing a guitar and singing a flamenco song that sounded to Melinda like she was hearing it from far away. It was so peaceful that she was nearly asleep. The whole cloister was scented with woodsmoke and wine, Stilton and ham, and tomatoes somebody had scrounged, and then for a minute she really was asleep, or must have been, because she thought she was with Uncle Brandon and Boodie when they went camping in the mountains and Uncle Brandon told her about the twin stars made by the eyes of the animals reflecting the fire.

But they weren't animals. Silent, proud, thin children from the village and the caves, where a lot of them had been living since their houses had been shelled, watched from the doorway while the strangers ate and sang. Their eyes glittered in the firelight. They didn't say a word, and they didn't ask for anything. One by one, dark figures began to get up and guide them in to the fire, to share the food. It was dead quiet, and everybody was shy.

Melinda saw the shadow of an older girl, taller and completely still, an etched figure in the doorway, with the bright moonlight behind her. She went over to her and took her arm.

The girl whispered that her name was Concepción. She was the daughter of the mayor, who was a socialist. Her mother, she explained, was a Republican but still said her prayers, and her aunt was bedridden and had gone mute because she was too old for war.

All of this was told in a rushing whisper, in a kind of English. "We study together, my aunt and I. She speaks only to me, nobody else, not even my mother. I am the age of fifteen, and I am pleased to work at the hospital, please."

When Melinda offered her some Carr's biscuits and cheese, she refused politely. Then, after a while, she took one.

Gradually they were growing into the village. Flowers in the cloister began to bloom again. A huge rose bent from the weight of its blossoms. Down the hill from the side windows of the refectory, the second planting of grain was bright green and in certain lights completely red with poppies. The war seemed to have stopped someplace else, except for a few men who had been caught by snipers, and three appendicitises, and one syphilis. They just went on, finding jobs to do, day after day through May and June.

Sister McCall hired Concepción because she was one of the few who could write her name and speak a little English. She learned quickly, so quickly that Sister McCall said she would make a fine nurse, and in two months she was in charge of an empty ward that had been the chapel. Cot after cot lay ready under the saints and the demons that watched with their stone eyes.

But the rest of the time Concepción followed

Melinda, the only lady who wasn't so tall that she made Concepción feel like a child when she wasn't a child anymore. She was almost old enough to marry, except that all of the men had gone to the war. She and Melinda taught each other their languages on long walks through the village and around the roads of spring, where the poppies and the wildflowers, yellow and purple, and the bright gorse caught the sun. Concepción called Albastro a town, not a village, because it had been a real city long ago, and because there was water in a tap at the nunnery and at the small hotel, where in peacetime people from Madrid had come to be in the country for a few days.

Sister McCall had been wrong. There was more than one toilet. The hotel had one, just like the nunnery, and the priest's house, which had been turned into an annex for convalescents, and Concepción's house, the house of the mayor. Its façade was like a high stone wall, with windows set so that the rooms must have been at every level, grown like a cave system. A wide stone bench in front of it looked onto the square.

Melinda and Concepción walked the country roads under heavy clouds and a blue sky that was as huge as the sky over the ocean. They talked about themselves and the distant hills. Gradually, as Concepción's English got better, Melinda learned what had happened in Albastro when the war came. There were bullet holes in the church wall, and there were still skeletons of dead cats, a dog, and even a goat, which nobody had ever moved, on the slight slope down from the retaining wall, eight feet thick, that held the church up above the town like a lighthouse or a fortress. Finally Concepción allowed her to understand that that was where the Falangists had been beaten and then shot. The largest landowner had already gone to Salamanca to join Franco, and had sent his family to Portugal.

There had been only four Falangists: the priest, the postmaster, the town clerk, and Juan Alfonso, whose mother had named him for the deposed king and who, Concepción said, "made wind," which Melinda finally figured out meant "put on airs." She told Concepción not to say "made wind" because that meant something else, and they giggled.

"He was not harmful," Concepción said, "just silly, but he went into the church with the others where they had arms hidden, and when the revolt of the *generales* happened they made the church into a fortress and sniped at the villagers, who only had their hunting guns, and bullets were so expensive that they were only used to bring home meat. Never shoot unless you are sure," she informed Melinda. "The Falangists yelled out that we were Republicans and Reds and Jews and liberals and Freemasons. We only had one Communist, and he was a drunk who was always talking and laughing to himself and nobody paid any attention to him.

"The nuns were barricaded here at the convent. We could hear them crying, but nobody bothered them. The mother superior was very popular in the town, and she had many relatives here. *Pop pop pop*— nobody dared go within range. So they stood behind the houses and shouted out *'Viva la República,'* and the ones inside shouted *'Arriba España'* and *'Arriba muerto.'* I thought it was very silly, but then," she added shyly, "I shouted, too.

"Then our militia came, and I was looking out the window even though my mother and my aunt said get away from there, and I saw one of the militia—we didn't know them, they came from someplace else—one of the Reds, that's what they called all of them, sneak up to a window that had been broken by one of my uncles with his rabbit gun, and he heaved two grenades inside and blew a big hole in the wall with fire and a huge noise. But the men inside were not killed, so they dragged them out, and there was a noise in the square like animals coming in from the fields at night, only louder, and my mother grabbed me and hid my eyes and I could feel her heart thumping, but she struggled with me and wouldn't let me see, and my aunt, who wasn't mute then, kept saying prayers and so did my mother.

"I did see that they were all bloody when they lined them up against the wall there and shot them. Isn't it sad to be shot because you put on airs? It was all his mother's fault for giving Juan that silly name, my mother said.

"Then the militia went away, and nobody dared go near the place where they had been shot. Some of the women said they could still hear them in the night, moaning and crying, but my aunt said it was the night wind. It took a long time for the rain to clean the wall.

"We thought it was all over, and we were even

able to go out to the harvest, when the *señoritos* came in their blue shirts, the Falangists, strutting and riding horses and looking down on everybody. They came with a *camión* to rescue the nuns from being raped and killed by the Reds, who hadn't paid any attention to them except to make them take off their bird hats and put on some lipstick while they cried. That was all.

"The nuns put their white bird hats back on, and when they left, they looked like they were about to fly away. A lot of them waved to us. It wasn't their fault, and the nunnery had been popular in the town because ladies from Madrid came there for retreat and *señoritas* came with their fine clothes and brought money and the hotel was usually full of their *novios* and their fathers and their husbands."

That was all Melinda could learn from Concepción for several weeks. In the evening they sat on the stone bench under her aunt's window because her aunt was bedridden and liked to hear them sing, but Concepción never in the whole time invited Melinda inside the house, even though her mother came out and said, *"Mi casa es su casa."* In the twilight they sang "Night and Day" and "Stardust." Their voices drifted past the half-ruined church at the top of the hill, past the wall where the Falangists had been shot, and whispered through the fields as night came.

Melinda finally asked, although she sensed that it was rude, where Concepción's father was. She only meant to find out where he was stationed in the militia. But Concepción began to cry, and led her by the hand to the same church wall.

"Here, in the same place," she said, "was where the *señoritos* shot my father, because they said he was a Red mayor, and they shot the drunk who was a Communist, and there wasn't anybody else to shoot, but the men who were made to watch said my father stood quietly and refused to confess to the Falangist priest, but just before, he bowed his head and crossed himself. That was a comfort to my mother. But it was the drunk, old Manuel—we called him Risitaboca—who acted like a real hero in the movies. He spread his arms out and he shouted, *'Viva la República!'* just as they shot him. He was drunk, but even so he was brave."

Weeks passed and they waited for war. The hospital was perfect. Sister McCall said so. There were a hundred beds. The four local *chicas* were trained, and three of them were being taught to read and sign their names. One of them, sixteen-year-old Manuela, was brash and sassy and acted as if she had been let out of jail. Her mother still came to the door of the convent to see if she was all right. Carmela was so timid that Sister McCall almost fired her, but when one of the soldiers was brought in with a head wound from sniping, it was Carmela who, without being told to, stayed with him, holding his hand until he died. Teresa was forgettable. She had that talent. Everybody said so. It took weeks to remember her name, but she could already write and she was tidy, and she seemed to be learning the lingua franca of the hospital. One of the phrases that Melinda was to remember all her life was "Basta, basta, for God's sake," and the other, "Tu *bloody* coño."

She found her own jobs to do. One was revising and improving her lists, to be ready when the time came. It seemed like some sort of exercise in disaster, sitting out in the cloister in the shade of the vines, making a grid and then writing at the head of it, "Head injuries, abdominal, intestinal, leg wounds, shoulder wounds," and then a second chart that read, "Morphine, plaster, Dettol, bandages, splints, shoulder and leg." There were a hundred other objects on the list, and by hand she made a hundred copies of both of them, for a hundred days. Sister told her to, and when Melinda had done it, she said, "That will be your job when the time comes. Enter every wound, every day by date, and then check the stores to see what we are short of—every day, don't forget." Time stretched into an every day that was never going to come.

Melinda found an old building full of trash that had once been an almshouse for pilgrims. When she went through the broken door, it was so dark inside that she stumbled over a pile of metal. Then she shone her flashlight around the walls and up to the ceiling. The walls were gold and the ceiling was deep blue, vaulted and painted with gold stars. It looked like it had been newly painted, but Concepción said it had been that way ever since anybody could remember.

Melinda had found her place to set up a motor pool. The ambulances were in terrible shape. Some of the Diamond T *camiones* were so old that people said they had been used at the front in the World War. The vehicles, as Melinda insisted on calling them, using the language of her motor mechanics course, had all been in several battles.

The *chóferes* had been scrounging whatever they could take from broken-down cars and *camiones* and ambulances that had been abandoned beside the roads every time they passed on their way to do the errands Sister made up to keep morale high when so little was happening. There were already piles of rejected engines, tires, dead batteries, old seats, and stretchers that had been dumped outside in the sun and rain. Melinda got Tandy to help her clean the almshouse and sort the spare parts that she thought she might be able to repair.

She gathered sparks, cleaned and tested them, and filed sets of points until they gave out. She tried to recharge batteries, which spat acid onto her overalls until she had only one pair that she always wore, which she didn't even dare wash in the little stream the Chinese *camilleros* had found for fear it would come apart from the acid holes. She cut and beveled fan belts out of useless tires, blew fuel lines, emptied fuel pans, cleaned engines, scraped rust, adjusted brakes, and fussed at the *chóferes* for stripping gears. She lay awake at night figuring out how to beat nails into rivets. She felt sometimes as if she were in charge of the war she hadn't seen.

Gradually the word got out that she could fix things, everything from flashlights to a tooth that had fallen out of a plate one of the nurses was wearing. She wondered to herself who the hell had repaired the British Empire. The English didn't seem to be able to do anything, but the local blacksmith helped her, and Tandy, of all people, turned out to be a natural.

He lectured about the ceiling as he worked. "Obviously fifteenth-century post-Caliphate, but the squinches are copied from the Moors." Melinda didn't ask what squinches were. She knew it would take some time to answer, and she wanted to think and be quiet.

Melinda taught the *chóferes* what to scrounge. She made her own list and gave it to the two Chinese, who were being sent with Fig to Valencia, to the villa. "Get them wherever you can, but get them, please." She and Fig had grown apart with the weeks, and she was sorry and resolved to do something about it when they came back. It was just that he didn't know anything about engines.

They came back with everything she had ordered, including battery acid, spark plugs, motor oil, and two perfect carburetors. She didn't ask where these things had come from. That wasn't, in the circumstances, polite. Everybody had learned that.

Fig brought her a lipstick and said, "Isn't war bloody boring?" and they were friends again.

She hadn't heard a word about politics while they had been so busy getting the place in order, but when they began to get on each other's nerves, they divided into Communist and socialist and Republican and just plain humanitarian, which Sister McCall talked about as if it too were a political party, until Dr. Wimpy called a meeting and said, "Stop. This is bad for morale. You sound like people who don't have enough to do. Now, I have had an order to be at the ready from tomorrow on."

The cloister was completely still. Melinda suddenly thought, All those words I wrote are going to turn into real wounds, and how can I bear it?

There had been rumors for several weeks, but rumors at that time were like the hint of rains that never came, until nobody paid any attention and they went out into the fields to help with the harvest until their backs ached and they could sleep.

When the first of July came at last, there were four clean, running *camiones* and two repaired ambulances as well as the one Melinda and Fig had brought. She knew them all.

At dawn on the morning of the second of July, the order to move came. It was quiet, quick, efficient, the way they had been trained. It still felt like an exercise.

Melinda went from driver to driver of the *camiones*. "Don't let her run low on water. She needs more oil than the others. I've put some under the seat. Don't flood her. She floods easily." Then she came to the ambulance that she and Fig had brought. "This one is okay," she said, an understatement that she was proud of having learned from the English.

Fig was driving, and the two Chinese were with him in the cab. He was chalk white, and the two Chinese were asleep. She reached up into the cab and hugged him. "Jesus," was all Fig said. It sounded like a prayer.

She came to the second ambulance and stood beside it, worried, and stroked its side as if it were a horse. "I don't know," she said to Tandy, who was driving. He had two *camilleros* with him. One was called Mogie. He was from the East End of London. The other was from Birmingham and had made friends with Fig.

"I'll take care of her," Tandy said, meaning something else.

"The springs—I've tried to fix them, but the job needed a lift, and I couldn't." She turned away. The dawn wind pulled at her hair, and tears came to her eyes because the springs weren't quite right.

She and Concepción watched them go in a long line down the hill as far as the horizon, along the dirt road through yellow fields. The great clouds made shadows as they passed. They seemed to toss the *camiones* and the ambulances like galleons at sea.

They were gone to a place the other side of Madrid. The town was empty and forgotten. Melinda and Manuela—who insisted on being called Libertad—Carmela, Teresa, and Concepción all sat together on the stone bench at the time when, in peacetime or lull-time, there would have been the *paseo*, and watched the empty road stretch out down the hill and through the empty plains of La Mancha in the distance, until the twilight dimmed it and then the darkness hid it. It was the dark of the moon, and the stars were so bright they were deep in the sky.

It became, in the days they waited without news, a habit. The girls told Melinda about having to wear sleeves, and about how the priest hadn't wanted them to learn to read but Concepción had done it anyway. Her aunt taught her to read, and her father taught her English. She said that her aunt had fought with the priest about the girls learning to read. She said they fought all the time, but then she seemed to realize that she had said too much and shut up. There wasn't a word said. The girls didn't look at each other.

Carmela and Teresa had obeyed the priest and their mothers, and Manuela didn't care, so they were just beginning to learn, and everybody was helping them—too many people sometimes, and they got mixed up. They told her about how reading a Liberal paper had been a mortal sin before the war but was not anymore.

The *practicante* who had been left in charge had a crush on Teresa and had asked her mother if he could be her *novio.* Two boys of fifteen had run away from the Jesuit school in Madrid. They were being trained as *chóferes* but had not been allowed to drive on duty yet, so they teased the *chicas* and played tricks on them.

All they had were rumors: that a battle somewhere else was a success, that there were a lot of casualties, that the Escorial was overflowing with wounded. Sometimes they were sure, when the wind was right, that they could hear faint guns miles away, but it could have been thunder, and the glow in the distance at nightfall, summer lightning. The sounds, the glow, the rumors of a great victory, all were faint, far away from the bench where they sat.

It was Teresa who saw it first, a faint dark moving dot on the horizon, just at twilight. They watched with her and it grew larger, and then the noise came ahead of it—a motorcycle, a dispatch rider. The motorcycle had a shape, then a rider, then a face, and then he handed the *practicante* a dispatch and fell off his motorbike in a faint. He had lost blood from a wound in his shoulder.

From twilight into darkness the line of *camiones* and ambulances and commandeered cars never seemed to end. They crawled up the narrow road, growling under the dim moon, and in the last of the light a gauntlet of Stukas screamed down for the last few miles of the retreat from the Escorial. The women could see them plunge like hawks and hear them scream in the distance until the true darkness came.

They ran to see that cots were ready, but the *practicantes* said there would be more casualties than they were prepared for. So the villagers filled the cloister with mattresses, iron bedsteads, bright brass beds, carved wooden headboards, beds covered with all the colors from all the winters of crocheting and quilting, with small paths in between, so that it looked like a refugee camp instead of a hospital.

Melinda knew that night forever as always new and as ancient as the light and the darkness. Out of the window of the refectory she could see them still coming, the tiny blue lights, the shadows darker than the darkness, moving at snail's pace, and then the screams of the Stukas away in the distance, as terrifying as ancient war screams, the convoy lit for a flash with a red glow, then later—they were so far away, still on the dangerous main road—the sound of the machine guns, rattles of rainstorms, and then darkness again.

Faces in the dim lamplight all looked dirty. The nurses walked by as fast as they could but looked ready to drop down and sleep on the bloody floors, which the *chicas* tried all through the night to keep clean.

Sister McCall never stopped, even though she sent her nurses to bed in shifts of two hours. She had changed color in the weeks she had been gone. The light had gone out of her hair and left it thinner and brackish. She was gaunt, dirt was ground into her face no matter how much she washed it, and in the faint lamplight she looked gray, like a ghost.

It went on for two days. The staff gave up their beds to the wounded, and they slept where they could when they could. One of the nurses slipped on the bloody floor and broke her leg. It had been like that, Tandy said, for days at the Escorial. He couldn't remember a whole night's sleep. Once he had had to sneak off because he had to sleep, and he had found a little bed up some stairs. Later he was told it was Philip II's bed. He said it was like any other bed, except his feet hung over the end.

In the few minutes that Tandy could speak, in passing while they worked, he told Melinda about what had happened. It had been the first battle of the International Brigades since Jarama, and they had been pinned down in a village called

Brunete that nobody would have heard of if there hadn't been so much death.

Once he began to cry, and she made him go out of the cloister and walk with her down the once again empty road. He couldn't stop talking. It was to himself. He brought back the swarms of Stukas, the heavy Heinkels, the flattening of the men by the Condor Legion from Germany. The rolling country had looked flat on the maps, and wasn't. The men and the ambulances struggled through deep arroyos. The temperature was over a hundred degrees. The artillery of the mercenaries pounded them from the far hills.

The men who came back said they couldn't find the enemy half the time, they were just fish in a barrel: "We weren't human to them—some kind of game. That scream of the Stukas, as far back as the Escorial."

Tandy said that the stink was horrible in the heat, and at night they had to work by lanterns with gasoline in them because they had run out of kerosene, and one night one of them exploded and burned some wounded men, who were by that time two to a bed. There had been over three thousand of them. The road to Madrid, from which they got supplies, was under attack from the Stukas, and refugees from Nuevo de Canadá and Brunete and tiny villages without names they could find out lay by the road with their dead animals, flotsam of the battle, shoveled aside so the *camiones* and the ambulances could move.

Tandy said the awful thing was that you got used to it. The refugees were just bundles of rags lying beside the road, stinking to high heaven.

He said he never knew how high heaven was until he knew that stink.

They hadn't been able to get supplies anymore. They had run out of bandages, they had run out of anesthetic, they had run out of time, out of everything but fatigue and working, and once in a while the faint singing of the men who lay there. They threw the limbs into the convent garden until they could be taken away, and the rats came before they could move them, and the flies gathered. They had to burn the dead in the field below the Escorial, but in the daytime, so the fire wouldn't draw the planes. When the bodies were gone, there was just a pile of ashes and oozing black tar around the pyres.

They had one German pilot, who said that the Germans were there as an "exercise in war." That was what he called it. He spoke almost perfect English, and he said, "Spain is for us our Sandhurst." He was nineteen years old, and as he was walking wounded, he helped with the stretchers as well as he could with one arm strapped to him. He had been hit in the shoulder by a bullet from one of the few fighter planes they had, the little snub-nosed Chatos from Russia.

When they stripped the dead Moors, they found that they, all Muslims, had been told that if they wore the little metal disks that read "Cristo Rey" as amulets, they wouldn't be hurt.

"Muslims with 'Cristo Rey,' socialists of fifteen who cried for their mothers and the Virgin Mary in more languages than I ever knew existed." Tandy sat down on a rock and just stared out at the fields. The sun of noon was hot on their heads.

For two days Melinda was afraid to ask about Fig. She kept her graphs of wounds and sent her *camiones* off, patched up as well as she could. She had a new helper. It was Scotty, who told her he was one of the few survivors of the convoy she and Fig had joined what seemed years ago instead of a few months.

They operated in the chapel in twenty-four-hour shifts for three days. The *chóferes* helped the *camilleros* take out the limbs and the dead. The smell of rotted meat and gangrene and blood and Dettol lifted into the hot day with the scent of flowers. The nurses and the *practicantes* ran to take blood from the newly dead and pump it into the veins of the dying. Some of the dying survived.

Finally, when she and Tandy were sitting on a rock in the sun that they had named the Dragon, she made herself ask about Fig. He and Sung Lee and Sung Woo were dead. They had been hit when they were traveling toward the front in the ambulance that she and Fig had brought. Tandy didn't say Fig's name. He just said, "It was a direct hit. They couldn't have felt a thing." It was the formula, part of the lie of war.

Melinda felt like her soul was dry. There were no tears. There was only a shivering she couldn't control, and she thought she might have had too much sun while she and Tandy sat on the stone. The handwriting on her charts grew untidy. Sister McCall told her so. Everybody spoke in passing. Nobody seemed to sit down.

She knelt by dying boys from Brooklyn and

California and Arkansas and took down their whispered names and the things they wanted to say when she wrote to their families and their girls. Some of them remembered to will their boots, and one boy held her hand so tightly that it ached. All his energy seemed to go into his grip. After he had died, she had to pry her hand loose. He had said something about "tell somebody I'm sorry," but it was too faint, so she wrote to his next of kin, a brother, and said he had died a hero's death. And that it was so quick he didn't suffer.

It was the fifth night, and nobody had slept except for catnaps when and where they could, some in the cabs of the *camiones,* some on the blood-soaked stretchers. Melinda heard Sister McCall yelling just beyond the arch to the open cloister, and when she ran toward her, Sister was standing there having a tug-of-war over a half-torn blanket with one of the Spanish *chóferes,* who was doubling as a gravedigger.

"No!" she was shouting. "You can't bury these, you can't wrap the dead in blankets. We need them. It gets cold at night and half these patients are in shock, and you can't have them."

He was shouting back in Spanish. They stood against the dark cloister full of men lying there quietly, some asleep.

"And the shoes, damn you, don't you dare bury shoes! If they are wearable, clean them and put them in the pile and the shoemaker says he will fix them."

The cloister was completely quiet. The men

who could still hear at four o'clock in the morning were listening.

Dr. Wimpy ran out of the operating room and grabbed them both by the arm, so that they dropped the blanket between them. It fluttered down to the tile floor, which was no longer bright with flowers but gray, the way it had been the day they took over the convent.

"Vergüenza, camarada," Dr. Wimpy whispered to the *chófer*. And then to Sister McCall, "Shame, Sister. We are all beyond fatigue, but you cannot let go."

She had sunk back to the low wall of the open courtyard. He put his hand on her head and stroked her ruined hair. "Listen, Sister, I will see that no blankets are buried and no shoes, do you hear me?" An almost imperceptible nod. "You do hear me," and then to the *chófer*, *"Comprende, camarada?"* The *chófer* nodded and hung his head. He was one of the trainees from the Jesuit school.

"All rifles, all shoes, all blankets, are to be saved. *Armas, zapatos,* what the bleeding hell is the word for blanket?"

Sister McCall whispered, "Maybe *sarape.*"

"Now, Sister, you sit there for a minute and pull yourself together. I came out to get you because Sister Drayton has collapsed and you are the only one who can assist. Come as soon as you can." He walked away, back into the chapel.

She just sat there with her head in her hands, and tears dripped through her fingers and made the tiles bright again in the shaft of light from the lantern that Melinda carried.

"Can I do anything?" Melinda touched Sister McCall's shoulder, but Sister McCall flinched at the touch.

"What the hell can you do but make lists and fix *camiones* and type? We need nurses," she whispered, and the whisper was a harsh faint wail.

"I have an advanced Red Cross first-aid certificate," Melinda told her.

Sister McCall jumped up, furious. "Why the goddam fuck didn't you tell me? You are to go out there and test all the bandages, especially the tourniquets. List any patient who has begun to stink. That's gangrene. They were all clean when we left the Escorial, but after the drive over the mountain and after the last strafing, we have to keep checking. Go." Then she held Melinda's arm and said, "I'm sorry I was rude. I . . ." They hugged each other, and Sister McCall walked away toward the chapel.

The whole cloister was crowded; the floors near the balustrades were lined with men leaning against the walls. Some of the ragged soldiers had thrown out their arms in their abandoned sleep. Melinda walked along the narrow crooked path between the cots and beds and started at the far corner, with her writing board, checking the tourniquets, checking the bandages and changing them, checking the smell for gangrene and marking those patients down on her board. It was the first time she had ever touched anyone who was torn and bloody; there had only been clean volunteers to be wounded at the Red Cross classes.

She hardly noticed when the sun rose. Men

began to wake and blink their eyes, and the dead of the night stared at the new morning sun.

When Sister McCall finally told Melinda she could take an hour, she walked along the road toward the church. The breeze was coming from that direction, and she wanted it to clean her. But when she turned the corner behind the church, she heard someone sobbing. It was Fig's friend from Birmingham. She held him in her arms and cried with him, and neither of them had to say anything.

The first week in August was calm and regimented again. Sister had recovered her starch. There was the smell of the flowers, the heat on the bright tiles at noon, the inevitable Dettol, the clean sheets. There were mornings and afternoons again. The lists were finally finished, the supplies sent for, clothes boiled to be used again, uniforms, aprons, blood-soaked sheets and bandages, all saved. The convalescents tried on the shoes that had been collected and left their own in a hierarchy of wear.

There were only a few patients left, and they became that terrible thing, friends, as if affection were food and blankets, some balm of haunted love to wrap around them, even the ones who swore softly and continuously, even the ones who were unconscious. From their youth's certainty that they were never going to die, they had all crossed over into a land, a time, beyond the arroyo of innocence.

The mortally wounded had died, and they were

buried in the village cemetery, even though it had to be a mass grave. There were sixty-three men of twenty countries, most of them Spanish boys, none more than twenty-three years old, some as young as fourteen.

One had had his eyes put out by the Moors at Brunete, but he had lived two weeks. He mewed like a kitten and called his mother until the men around him made him shut up.

The convalescents had been sent in the ambulances to the coast, to the convalescent hospitals. Melinda had gone to each ambulance and tested it and given her warnings, so much that the *chóferes* teased her and said, "Yes, ma'am," imitating her voice, "I'll be careful, Mother."

Melinda went back to her cars, her hiding place, a privacy of oil and the smell of machines instead of the memory of the smell of death. There were still deaths, but they were quieter ones, and she had time again to listen and to write their letters, those in English, quietly, and to hold their hands quietly and murmur quietly, lovingly, as she thought she would like to know that love, even substitute love, was near when she died, too.

"The first rule of this order," Sister McCall had said, as if she were a prioress, not a head nurse, "is never let a boy die alone."

Finally there were only a few cases left. A boy called Mort, from Toledo—the one in Ohio, he kept telling them—was dying and didn't know it. From time to time there were refugees who had been strafed on the roads.

One was a woman who was carried in by her

husband. A little girl followed them, carrying a baby she didn't seem to realize was dead. The first person the husband saw was Melinda, fixing an engine.

He said in English, "I beg your pardon, sir. My wife is ill—"

"Come on." She jumped up to guide them, and then she touched the hair of the little girl, who looked about five, and took the dead baby from her arms. She cradled it too, so that the little girl wouldn't know.

"I'll take care of her. Does she know English?"

"Yes," the man said as he watched his wife's still face. Her whole chest was covered with blood. "I am a professor at Madrid University. We speak both English and French at home." Tears came down his face, and he didn't notice them. He said, "I was trying to—"

Melinda stopped him. "Don't talk now. You are exhausted. I'll take your little girl to the kitchen. Go on in and ask for Sister McCall." It was what she always said when she was the first to see refugees struggling up the long road. He was one of so many who had come through that they had set up a soup kitchen with whatever they could organize to feed them.

Melinda delivered the man and his wife to Sister McCall and the dead baby to one of the nurses. She led the little girl to the soup kitchen and sat with her while she ate some soup, trying not to watch her hands tremble and spill. She didn't ask what had happened. There was a politeness about that which everybody learned quickly, except the doctors and nurses, who had to ask. She just kept the little girl's hand in hers and waited until the father came out to claim her. He didn't look at Melinda; he just took the little girl's hand and they walked away.

Sister McCall told her that they had been strafed on the way from Madrid to the safety of the mountains. The wife died a few hours later, and the man went on, with the little girl. Melinda watched them walk down the road. It was again as empty as if nothing had ever happened. She sat where she had sat to watch for the *camiones* before it had all started. The man and the child grew smaller and smaller. She promised herself that she would tell the first *camión* to leave the motor pool to pick them up, but she forgot. There were so many, and there was so much to do.

So she worked hard on the *camiones,* and the ambulances, and even the old Diamond Ts. She had found some instructions in one of them. The only problem was that she was so short and the Diamond T engines were so high that she had to hoist herself up to her waist, with arms that were getting stronger by the day, and drape herself over the fender with her feet hanging down into air, so she could get to the bottom of things.

She was there fitting one of her makeshift fan belts, ass-over-tip down in an engine, when she heard somebody say, "*Niño,* if you can fix engines, mine's on the blink. I've tried, but I'm really bad at that sort of thing." All it was was a voice, right over her behind, and she didn't dare move for fear of backing into him.

"All right, young man, if you can fix it, I'll be in trying to scrounge some food."

Whoever it was had begun to walk away when she managed to tip back up, but he hadn't gone far enough. When she turned, so did he, and then he said, "Good God."

She just stood there. He looked embarrassed, so she said, as politely as she could to make him feel better, that she would see if she could find what had gone on the blink. She had already learned that embarrassment was the most profound emotion of the English.

But then he made her so mad she wanted to hit him, not only embarrass him, but she didn't tell him that. He said, "Is there someone else you are helping—one of the *chóferes,* one of the, uh—"

"Men," she said. "No. They're all English and don't know enough about cars to keep oil in the engines and the carburetors clean." She tried to saunter, with her hands in her pockets, as slowly as she could, to the ambulance he had driven almost to its death at the medieval gate of the motor pool. She took a dirty glove out of her pocket and unscrewed the radiator cap. Steam hissed out.

"My God, you limeys," she said. "You've let the bloody engine boil down. You don't know a bloody cog from a bloody camshaft."

"I'm delighted that you are learning English, whoever you are." He was shirty, a new word she had learned, and she later found that he could get shirtier than anyone she had ever known, at least at first.

"How many bones are in the human body?" he demanded. "Miss whoever you are, I'm not a *chófer.* I'm a *practicante.* You'll find me inside.

I haven't eaten in two days, except some bloody awful grapes I stole that gave me the shits."

He started to walk off, and then he turned again. She knew she was seeing him, really seeing him, through and around him. It was something like when she saw all the way through words in a book into new memory, or once in a while when she listened to music, but she couldn't for the life of her remember what music, only being all the way there, wherever it was.

She put all this into straggling thought later, when she was alone. But at the time she just stood there, in front of the medieval gate of the motor pool, as dirty as a grease monkey, her hands in her pockets, and stared at the beginning of something.

He still looked mad as hell. He was about six feet tall. She measured it by how far she had to look up at him, furiously aware that she was too damned short to saunter, and that he was beginning to grin. He had a pale, thin face and thick dark brown hair and deep blue eyes. His whole body seemed taut. He seemed to be swaying against the sun, and she saw for the first time how exhausted he was.

"The kitchen is that way." She pointed downhill to the old monastery barn, where they had moved the kitchen to make more room for the wounded, and when he turned to go, she called after him in a little burst of panic, "My name is Melinda Kregg. I'm an American."

"My name is Tye Dunston, and I'm not." She still couldn't see his face well enough, but she heard a grin in his voice. "I'm a third-year medical student at University Hospital, but I was on—"

"A walking tour of the Pyrenees!" She was so happy, suddenly she laughed. For a second the death around her had paused and nobody was alone. They were all connected by the frail but safe cords of the kinship of friends. "You're Tandy's friend. He told me about you."

"You're Melinda, Miss Jasmine from America. He told me too."

They laughed for no reason on earth that she could remember.

From that time, eleven o'clock in the morning of the third of August, they were together—at first tentatively, but they admitted later that each knew where the other was most of the time, and when they didn't know, they searched until they bumped into each other, carefully.

It was calm. They had an illusion, which they lost from time to time, that they didn't need to be impatient. They let themselves drift into taking for granted, as well as they could when there was war, that the other was going to stay for a little while. It was a way of blotting out the shortness of everything from food to life, to being at the mercy of orders that could take them away from each other.

Tye said that they were organizing time, not stealing it. Time was, he said, at least in the first two weeks of August, just lying there, more every day.

One early afternoon, Melinda was trying to finish what she had to do and then find Tye. She walked into the heavenly shade of the arched hallway, and from the dark, in the distance across the cloister, she saw Sister Grafton kneeling by Mort, the boy from Toledo. She smiled. Sister Grafton was one of her favorites, a friend, a companion in homesickness for New York.

Sister Grafton was CP, she told everybody, from Montreal. She had gone to New York to train as a nurse at Bellevue. "Some *belle vue!*" she said. Everybody liked her. She said the Party had told her to go with the British, since they weren't organized by the Party. The Party, the Party. They teased Sister Grafton and called her the Party girl.

Melinda heard Mort say to Sister Grafton that he had to admit he was a Catholic and that he wanted a priest, even though he believed in the Republican cause. He begged her to understand that. It was the first hint they had that he knew he was going to die.

He said this to Sister Grafton in so thin a voice that she had to go down on her knees beside him to hear, and Melinda, who had stopped still so she wouldn't interrupt, stood there with the lice-infested overalls that passed for uniforms that she was taking to one of the village women to boil. She could feel lice from the clothes begin to crawl up her arms. Sister Grafton was leaning close.

Then Melinda heard her say, "You must forget all that and join the Communist Party before you die. You can't die with that on your conscience. They sent you here from New York—"

"Hell, Sister, they didn't do nothin but buy me a ticket. That don't mean I have to kiss the bus driver." It was an old tired answer in the perpetual argument, but he was dying, and it was only a whispered echo.

Melinda dropped the clothes on the tiles, grabbed Sister Grafton by the shoulders, and pulled her up to her feet—not easy, because Sister Grafton was a lot taller. She marched her out of the cloister. Sister Grafton was too surprised to balk.

Melinda said slowly when they were out of earshot of the patients, "Don't you ever, ever let me hear you saying anything like that to a dying man again. He's only beginning to realize, and you have no right to stuff your goddamn politics down his throat. Now you go try and find a goddamn Catholic before I goddamn report you. I'm not going to tell Sister McCall, but one more time and I will. Now I'm going back to comfort Mort, and you can take the goddamn lice-ridden uniforms that I dropped on the floor."

"Who the hell are you to talk?" Sister Grafton fought to get away. "You're just here for personal reasons."

"I've been told this before. One day, if you are lucky, you will find that they are the only reasons worth more than a tinker's dam." It had been a phrase of her grandmother's; she had never known quite what it meant.

She brushed the lice from her arms and went back to Mort and held his hand and told him all the jokes she could think of, but softly, and then he asked her to sing "Night and Day" for him. He told her he had heard her singing it with Concepción when she taught her English, and that he waited for them to sing every evening. It had drifted like a sigh, he said, all the way to his bed from the bench where he knew they sat, as if the night carried it. She sang it, like a lullaby.

He whispered, "I think I ought to tell you, I lied. I'm only sixteen. I volunteered when I was fifteen, but I'm tall for my age. I'm going to go back to school when I get home and go to college and be a doctor. Melinda, can't you get me a priest?"

Melinda found Concepción, who said, "When there's no priest, anybody can take his confession, but I think it ought to be a man. We do this for many of the Spanish boys, but we don't tell. We thought you foreigners might not understand. I'll get Teresa's *novio*. After all, the absolution is in Latin, and everybody knows that. It isn't, oh, *prohibido ahora.* The government made a new law, private, *privado, nada más.*" Melinda thought she said "not a Mass."

Melinda had found out about what was worth more than a tinker's dam, and at three o'clock in the morning, as usual for her. She awakened as if she had been called. But she hadn't been called, not by anybody in the hospital. She lay there, stunned by knowing. She felt herself in a vast web of love, personal grief, personal hopes, all the personal ties of the war—women mourning their men and their sons, girls mourning their *novios,* not 'suffering humanity,' which meant nothing, but all the single hurts and griefs of war, all the lonely, scared, homesick men, all the children numb with fear.

She was part of it. She knew the women who came through on the way to the mountains, most of them only caught in the way, innocent of war, carrying the last of their belongings, and she touched them, for them and for herself, to remind them all of something she couldn't name.

When she told Tye about Mort, he said, "Everybody is trying to steal this war." She didn't know what he meant, but she couldn't ask—not yet, anyway. He didn't say anything else for a long time.

Every evening that they could, they walked their own *paseo* down the long empty road at six o'clock, after Concepción's lesson. The *paseo* had become daily, like the blessings and the boredom of habits and summer, the days of waiting and the times when they helped with the second harvest. She showed Tye the valley that she, Fig, and Tandy had discovered as if it were her home and she wanted him to approve of it—pride in the shade tree, pride in the olive grove. They climbed the Dragon and sat on top. They wandered in the ruined convent and looked up at pale stars. They took the winding roads and picked the wildflowers that were left in early August.

They talked. They talked and talked and talked. There was nothing they held back, as if they wanted to register with each other their separate lives, in case. But that was never said by either of them. It was a courtship, an old-fashioned courtship in the midst of all the trouble.

The hospital had become so quiet again that it seemed to turn back into a convent. Two of the village women had babies there, by husbands who had come back on leave and then gone away again. Dr. Wimpy had finally persuaded them that they were safer there, where it was at least relatively sterile, than in their own beds. There were several cases of influenza, mostly from lowered resistance due to the diet and the fatigue.

There was an outburst of amoebic dysentery, which made Sister McCall furious. She said it was everybody's fault because they didn't follow orders. She had found two of the *chóferes* bathing in the creek, naked and spitting water at each other. The nakedness she didn't notice, but she yelled, "Don't put that water in your mouths! What the fuck am I going to do with you?"

On the seventeenth of August, Melinda and Tye took some bread, wine, olives, and some cheese that Concepción's mother had given Melinda and climbed up to the ruined castle to have a picnic. They looked down through the arrow slits into the valley and began to argue about whether the V of the window should point out toward the view, for a better scan of the valley below, or in, for more protection. They argued to hold off what they knew was happening.

They made love, lying on the drift of hay that one of the farmers had left stored there for his two cows. It smelled sweet and had kept its warmth from the day's sun for them as the night began to lower into coolness, as it did every night. They lay side by side and looked at the moon, which was rising so slowly that it seemed to slow their hearts.

"It's only been two weeks since we met, and it's been a lifetime," Tye told the moon. "Tandy thought we would never get together. We're going to marry—you know that, don't you?"

Melinda began to cry and buried her face in his dirty shirt.

He said, "Sit up, and don't whinge."

So she did, and he took her by the shoulders. He shook her a little. "If I'm to have a life at all after this goddamn shambles, I want somebody who *knows.*" He shouted the word, and a mouse or a rabbit ran from the hay. "I want somebody who will help me and who I can talk to, which is worth all the lovemaking anybody ever invented. Now shut that up, do you hear me?"

Melinda stopped crying and tried to keep a smile from spreading all over her face and ruining the moment.

"I want to guide you, if you will let me, so you won't be destroyed by this." He shook her again, and then he touched her hair. "I love your hair. Oh, darling, you've got nits again." It was the first time he had ever called her darling.

"Cooties. So have you."

"I'll never teach you English." He hugged her again. "Nits."

"Cooties," she said to his chest.

She sat there until he let her go, and when he looked at her, he caught her grin and they both fell back into the hay and laughed all the way to the moon. From below, Tye said, when they picked their way back down the hill in the moonlight, they must have sounded like two donkeys, which set them off again. They even forgot the *avión* moon and let themselves enjoy the light.

The first air raid, a single plane, came at four o'clock in the morning, just at first dawn. It was a Heinkel from the German Condor Legion. The Condor Legion and the Italians had fields within striking distance for the first time. A bomb knocked the corner of the church down, and the pilot machine-gunned the two cows that were left. He missed the convent. The next day orders came from the villa in Valencia that they were to move.

They worked day and night, flap on again. They waited for the dark of the moon. Concepción followed Melinda like a stray lamb. Melinda let her be with her while she fixed engines and replaced spark plugs and charged batteries, and she taught Concepción a torrent of English, some of it obscene. Every evening Concepción insisted that they sit on the bench in front of her house and speak English and sing. She said it comforted her aunt.

They set out finally in late August, toward a place called Alcañiz. Melinda felt as if she were being pulled from Albastro like a plant that had taken root there. She and Concepción clung to each other and made promises they knew they couldn't keep, while Tandy and Tye waited in the cab of the loaded ambulance. She saw Concepción sit down on the bench where they had watched the empty road for so long, and she knew that the girl would sit there as the long caravan disappeared into darkness and the blackout lights became like fireflies in the distance.

They were told that the first hundred kilometers would be the most dangerous, and that as soon as they drove into the first dawn, they should stop and take cover, then drive on again at noon, at least twenty meters apart. In the hours of noon, even the Condor Legion and the Italian *pavas* took their siesta, as if the planes themselves had caught the Spanish habit and the pilots had to wait.

Twenty *camiones* and the three ambulances that were left made up the long snake, dark shadows in the dark road. Tye drove. When Melinda said she would spell him, he said no. She found out why a few miles down the road to Cuenca. He turned aside and went south. As nearly as she could see in the dark, the road was nothing but a goat track. All he said was, "Dear me, we seem to have taken a wrong road," and Tandy laughed.

In the morning they had bypassed Cuenca and were south of the main road. Everything had changed. The fields were gone, the pastures, the wheat, and they were in a pine forest in the morning dew. They slept to the sound of a little river, and they had a picnic under the pine trees, with their feet in the water. Tye said it was called the Río Turia.

Across the river a high crag hovered over a village, making the spire of the church seem delicate and small. Men moved slowly along the river road in their donkey carts with great wooden wheels that cried and creaked. Here and there among them, women and children carried loads of grass and wheat.

All the way along the valley of the Turia, they drove past a steady line of refugees, the ever-present refugees, who walked a different way, not as people go to work in their own places but as if the earth were a treadmill. Some carried children.

"They know something," Tye said. "I've seen it ever since we got here, haven't you, Tandy? They are like animals that turn their tails to the wind before anybody knows there is a storm coming."

Melinda felt the tears spring.

"You have to get used to it," Tye told her. "You will see thousands now, all going north. A river of people flowing north."

The mountains came nearer, first as a line, then in an argument about whether the white rim was clouds or mountains, then as the white of perpetual snow when they had to drive near Teruel. They saw Teruel from the south, a long, low line of hills, and Tye said it was the Nationalist line.

"If there is a line," Tandy said. "We can't ever find them. They are artillery and shadows, and we are old guns and men."

Beyond Teruel they began to climb up toward the mountains. The dirt road was yellow with summer dust. Gorse bushes and trees lined the road and gave little patches of shade and protection. Tye drove fast, and then, a few miles north of Teruel, he stopped by a spring surrounded by huge rocks and said, "Now look south at Nationalist Spain."

Above them an old *finca* seemed deserted, but when they climbed up to it, they found it full of Republican soldiers having their siesta in the cool shade of the stone walls.

"Saracen," Tandy said, but only Melinda heard him. He had long since given up expecting anyone to listen.

The soldiers were a machine-gun company, stationed across the dirt road, where a stone lookout rose into the sky. Ruined huts were left over from some ancient village, or a village hit a few weeks before. Not even Tandy could tell. The soldiers insisted on giving Tye and Tandy and Melinda wine. It was in a goatskin, and they drenched themselves trying to drink it like Spaniards. The soldiers bragged about their well and said that the farmers gave them food, as if they had learned to take quick pride in where they were, to protect them from the fact of it—within six miles of Teruel, not yet in artillery range.

When Melinda stood on the top of the mountain at the lookout, she seemed to be on another border of Spain. South and west of her the grain fields, the pine forests, and rugged rocks stretched away to the long line of hills. But when she looked north she saw olive groves and snow-capped mountains, so far in the distance they looked not like facts, but thoughts.

Tandy, beside her, pointed to the mountains. "Look what they had to climb over from France to get here, all those city boys in their cardboard shoe soles."

At noon they started again for Alcañiz. A small *finca* by the side of the road had several Republican *camiones* and one commandeered Rolls-Royce parked in front of it. "Whoops," Tandy said, "brass," only he pronounced it *brahss*, and it made Melinda laugh.

All round the *finca* were olive groves, and she insisted on stopping and walking up to one of the trees. She lay down under it, and it looked like the rough brown hide of an elephant, safe, an old tree that had been pollarded until it had stairsteps of lopped branches with heavy new growth.

When she went back to the ambulance, after she had stayed away long enough to let Tye and Tandy pee in peace, Tandy said, "Where are the olives?"

"I didn't think of that," she told him.

Tye spoke over her head. "We checked back there at the *finca*. It's a headquarters. There is a big rumor of a push north of the line at the Belchite-Saragossa road. Ergo Alcañiz. Ergo more rumors. It's a good choice. Could even be a base hospital."

Tandy had talked to one of the soldiers, idle talk, rumor talk. The words floated over Melinda's head. She was still under the olive tree.

She said, "I was thinking of the men, all those men who were killed at Jarama, trying to hide behind the olive trees for shelter."

They drove for a while without a word.

Tandy said one, "I still cannot see how a small blond American and a tall drink of water can begin to look like each other so soon. Your faces are mirrors of each other." Nobody said a word again until they were down into the valley of the Alfambra.

The valley was full of Republican soldiers. They had taken over the turn-of-the-century train station at Villalba. When Tye stopped to find out what was going on, he was told that the train still came, once in a while.

"Something is happening," he said when he came back to the ambulance. "I can't find out what it is."

"But they all seem so relaxed." Melinda watched them, peaceful under the trees.

Tandy said, "Soldiers do that, whether it is an hour or some days or some weeks. They learn to collapse and sleep and tell themselves the lie that whatever it is, is over, at least for a little while."

But some of the refugees on the platforms had waited for days by a makeshift shunting yard at Villalba, where the southbound trains that had once gone all the way to Valencia shunted to turn north again.

All the way from Villalba to Alfambra, the peaceful valley was full of soldiers of the Republic. Tandy said that someone had designed the train shed at Alfambra at the time of the New Modernism, early in the century. Melinda could see the soldiers asleep, in that loose-flung way of children and the dead. The neo-Moorish arches cast shadows across their faces. Some soldiers were under the trees gambling; some were grouped around a commissar, learning the alphabet; some wandered toward the village, tired of siesta.

They were camped in the tiny *fincas,* the cow sheds, the olive groves; they sprawled under the trees as the shade grew longer. In the distance—Melinda remembered it for years as always in the distance—a few were singing the songs that she would never forget, the repetitions, the flamenco rhythm: "Ay Carmela," and the phrase *"Franco se va a paseo . . ."*

Tye turned east into the mountains, where the road was again a goat track that wound up and around, so that the mountains were dizzying, as sharp as spears. They drove down into narrow hollows and up again into the mountains, past huge rocks looming against the sky, gorse, and scrub. Near the tiny villages in the gulleys there were terraces all the way up the hills, where the olive trees stood in rows, most of them so old that their boles made elephant-colored mounds, thick and stolid.

They smelled sulfur, heavy and pungent in the air that had been so pure. "What the hell?" Tye said, and Melinda said, "It's a coal mine."

"Don't be daft," Tandy told her.

But when they came down into a crooked hollow, it was a coal mine. "The shift is changing," Melinda said when she saw the line of men coming out of the mine entrance.

"How do you know that?" Tye asked her.

She shook her head and began to cry.

"Oh my God, what do we do with her?" Tye said over her head, but he stopped the ambulance in the last deep cut and let her cry against him.

"Maybe it's her period," Tandy said, being helpful.

"Oh, shut up, Tandy," she said to Tye's chest.

Soldiers were coming their way, some still running along the *barranco*. Some had slowed to a walk. "What's happening?" Tandy called.

"Big push at Belchite and all along the front north. There isn't any front," an English voice came back. "We were told to wait in reserve, and we're looking for a place beyond the river. They've flooded the Ebro from upstream. Some of the men have been drowned." He leaned his head on the sill of the cab window. "Let me rest a minute."

The soldiers had been bivouacked in narrow *barrancos* too close to the river. The file of men, some of them Americans, gathered around the ambulance.

"Take this letter!"

"Where are you from?"

"'Ere's my 'ome address."

"The river road is flooded," one of the Americans, a Southern boy with a voice as slow as his walk, called out. He was resting his rifle on his head with one hand and eating an apple he had organized somewhere along the road.

"Where are you from?" Melinda called out, and when he said, "I'm from Georgia," she thought of Confederate soldiers moseying along other roads with their rifles balanced on their heads.

Melinda handed the soldiers bits of paper torn from her notebook, and her lap was full of messages by the time they started again. Tye turned back into the scarred hills behind the Ebro and went cross-country. It took them until the evening of the twenty-fourth of August to get to Alcañiz.

They could see the castle on top of the hill almost in the center of the town from the last height before they went downhill. Melinda took out Fig's field glasses and handed them to Tye. He scanned the widening valley of the river. In the distance were two great cones of hills, one letting smoke slide into the evening's pink clouds.

"Volcanoes," Tye told them.

"Slag heaps," Melinda said.

"There they are," he said after a while. They drove down the hill to where the *camiones* and ambulances filled the courtyard. He pointed to a large *finca* on the edge of the town, where tents had been put up. The cow barn was being cleaned out, with a lot of complaining. An operating room had been set up in the parlor, where family pictures were still on the mantel. They showed the parents and six children of various ages, one boy, in Falangist uniform, and five girls, four in First Communion dresses, all white flounces and simpers. Little bourgeois brides of Christ, someone said, and someone else laughed.

They worked by the evening light and the light of lanterns that smelled of gasoline. There were already long lines of wounded on trolleys, waiting after triage in the shadow of the courtyard. Blood had pooled under the trolleys. The smell of blood mingled with the feces of the dead and of the gangrene, which was forever unmistakable, the high smell of rotten meat.

"It's a shambles," Sister McCall said as she passed. "Melinda, go and clear the big bedroom on the first floor—get some cots and some mattresses in there. We need a quarantine ward. Then get everybody's name and address. There are a lot of Americans here, and British. Don't forget type of wounds, and what equipment is used." She spoke as if Melinda hadn't done the same thing when the wounded came in from Brunete.

"The line, if there is one, is about fifty miles away," she said. "The field hospitals are already so full that—" She stopped what she was saying. "Wait a minute, Melinda. Men have sand caked into their pores from the wind. As soon as you've taken this lot of names and checked the dying, start washing faces. That first, the bedroom second." She didn't say a word about the ambulance's leaving the convoy. Some of the *camiones* had been caught in the flooding.

When Tye asked why they had picked the *finca* and its outbuildings instead of the castle and convent on the hill, one of the *chóferes* told him, "New orders. They are bombing all the convents so we can't use them."

All night Melinda washed faces with the last of the soap Fig had insisted she buy at the Army and Navy Store. Night rolled into morning again, and nobody had slept since they had come to Alcañiz. She found time to go into the bedroom at last.

Morning came, the sun splashed through the window with its torn curtains. The bed had been slept in by people with boots. The sheets were embroidered, gray, and torn. On the carved dresser she found a thick coil of black hair that had been left on top of a black lace *mantilla* that nobody had scrounged yet, as if the woman had been interrupted on her way to Mass, her false hair a little vanity she would confess and wear again.

A sepia enlargement of the woman and her husband hung over the carved double bed, both of them heavy, solid, uxorious. Nobody had dared or bothered to find out whether they had been shot or had escaped. There was something obscene and private about the hair, the *mantilla* it lay on, the photograph of the son in his Falangist uniform, the emptiness. A medallion in the first drawer Melinda emptied onto the floor said "Cristo Rey," like the medallions that had been found on the Muslim troops, but this one was silver, not tin. The second drawer held large abandoned underwear, all embroidered; the third, nightshirts; the fourth, a doll, a First Communion dress, and the photograph of a daughter who had died, with a black mourning band across the glass.

Melinda put the *mantilla* in her pocket, gathered the rest for the bonfire, and prepared to clean the drawers, the walls, the bed, the rug covered with red roses, the potty, with the ever-present Dettol.

Day was night again, and she washed new faces and took new addresses and checked beside them for the dying and the dead. A wild electrical storm in the night lit up the vast sky so brightly that they could see each other for that second as if it were day, and after the lightning they all carried the shape of dark faces, a negative image. The crashes of thunder mixed with the sullen sound of distant artillery.

They moved forty-three men and three women in the dark blue *monos* of the Republican army into the cow barn and laid them on beds of straw that smelled sweet after all the stink. But by midmorning the whole stable yard, and the mud that had once been a kitchen garden, was a pigsty of pools of water and blood that had been dampened again by the storm, then covered with the wounded, whom Melinda and the *chicas* tried to shield from flies and the sun. The sun made the place stink again of the sweet rotten scent of death and hot cow manure and silage. It clung to the hair in Melinda's nostrils.

Day turned into night and night to day and day to night again, and the shadows of the arches from the dim, moving lights in the little courtyard passed across the patiently waiting faces as the *camilleros* moved the stretchers in and back out.

The Americans fixed the generator that they found in the dairy barn. Sidestepping the wounded, who had been put two by two in the milking stalls, they worked on it. But its electricity had to be concentrated in the operating room. The doctors and the nurses and Tye and Tandy had to walk slowly to keep from slipping on the bloody floor. There had not yet been time to begin to clean it up. Operations went on for twelve, then twenty-four, then forty-eight hours, and once in a while one of the doctors or the nurses from the parlor would be helped out to sleep on one of the stretchers for an hour or so and then jogged awake again.

Every time the door to the parlor opened, Melinda could hear them inside, singing to keep themselves awake: "Ilkley Moor Bar T'at," and "The Music Goes Round and Round," and "Night and Day." Tandy kept running in and out to check with Melinda about the dying. His job was to race to the newly dead and drain their blood before it stopped flowing.

One of the wounded started to scream when planes came over on the third dawn. His company had been strafed and bombed in a *barranco* where they had thought it was safe to rest, and he was one of only two that had survived.

"Goddamn, shut the hell up," a slow Southern voice called once, but he screamed until Dr. Wimpy came out and gave him a shot.

"This bastard is using up morphine. We're nearly out," he said to himself as the boy quieted down, and then he saw Melinda. "We're losing a quarter of our patients from the wrong blood. There's no time to test. Have you given blood? The Americans and the British are wearing their blood types, but most of the Spanish soldiers aren't." He stopped and was completely quiet in the midst of all the movement and muttering and rolling of stretchers on their trolleys. The dawn was streaking the distant snow-covered mountains with red slashes.

"You know," he reflected, "it does bear out the statistic. The blood of over three quarters of humans is O-positive. Have you given blood?" he asked again, forgetting.

"Twice," Melinda said.

"Are you dizzy?"

She wanted to giggle and say, "No, I'm Daisy," from a joke Fig had told, but she answered a simple no with a hard-won straight face. It was strange how laughter bubbled up from time to time, as if it had to have its release.

He watched her. "Are you feeling weak at all? I say, you American girls can all drive. Rather well, I think. Jolly good." He was staggering around the point, partly from fatigue and partly for manners. "Do you think you could go to Benicasim in my car and get some morphine and bandages? And for God's sake, antiseptic. And canned blood if they have it. Nobody else can be spared. You will be careful with my car, won't you?"

He had started leading her to his car before she said, "Of course."

"Jolly good, *camarada,*" he said, half asleep.

It was a 1937 Hispano-Suiza with a Sanatair sign scrawled on its broken windshield.

"Windscreen's a bit iffy, but it's a jolly good car. We organized it. Left over from an Italian colonel, poor fellow."

The car had been red. A layer of signs—anarchist red and black, Communist hammer and sickle, VIVA LA REPÚBLICA, and initials—covered a camouflage of gray paint that had begun to flake.

"You will be careful with it, won't you?" Dr. Wimpy said again, as if he longed to drive it away himself and go to sleep someplace quiet. "Oh, you'd better get your gear. You'll have to spend the night. I'll get you a chit."

When he came back, Melinda was lugging a

knapsack, two five-gallon cans, her repair kit, and a long rubber tube and putting them in the tattered back seat on what had been fine black leather.

"Good God," he said, "what's that for?"

"Gas siphon. Never travel without it." Melinda opened the luggage compartment, checking for tools. "Somebody's organized all the tools—the jack, the spare, everything."

"You mean you really know how to syphon petrol?" he wondered aloud.

"Of course," she told him. "This car only gets about eight miles to the gallon. I have to go over a hundred miles, and there are only twenty gallons in the tank. So I've taken another ten in these cans." She thought she ought to explain. "I'll organize more whenever I can."

"Well, I'll be buggered," he said as she got into the car. "Oh, by the way, bring back oranges, thousands and thousands of oranges!"

She did not see a car, a cart, a living thing, all the way up the mountain, just granite spears of black rock, gorse, and trees that grew at a sharp angle to the mountainside. Thirty miles into the mountains, she drove into deep forest. The trees were so thick that mist from the night rain was rising from the sweet-smelling forest floor, even at ten o'clock. It had taken her three hours to get there, easing the car over almost nonexistent roads, cart tracks deep with mud.

At the summit she came to a road that had been made by the centuries and the animals into an avenue that went as straight as a Roman road into the mist under a cathedral canopy of virgin oak trees. She let the engine die. There was not a sound. She was in the eye of the war, the silent place like the eye of a hurricane. In the road in front of her a doe and her fawn moved slowly, munching the weeds along the roadside. She put her head down on the steering wheel to rest for a minute.

The sun woke her two hours later, when it pierced straight down between the trees. It was noon. She took water from her canteen and threw some in her face, and drove with the water dripping onto her overalls across the flat top of the mountain.

There was not an abandoned car, not a wrecked car, not a car at all. It was almost time to use the gas in the cans when she saw below her in the distance a cluster of *camiones,* partly hidden by trees in the valley of the Rambla de Severa. They looked abandoned, but they were abandoned to siesta. *Chóferes* slept on the ground beside the river.

"Jesus, if it's no wee Miss Jasmine!" Scotty came walking up with his bandy-legged, cock-of-the-walk strut. "Now look what you've got to drive. All the luck. Come here, you wee bastards, and look at a real car." They gathered around the mud-covered, paint-flaked Hispano-Suiza as if it were a jewel. They touched it and then stood back, and then one shyly said, "May we see under the bonnet?"

"If you'll fill it up with petrol," Melinda told them. She had learned to drive a hard bargain.

"You never came over that bloody thing," Scotty said, pointing up at the mountain, when they settled back to rest under the trees. "I wouldn't take a *camión* on it."

"That car will do anything," she told him, as proudly as if it were her own.

"She came over El Maestrazgo," he yelled to the others, who gathered around again to stare at her.

"Wasn't it the way to Benicasim from Alcañiz?" she asked.

"There's no road," somebody said. "The Spanish comrades tell us the place is haunted."

Scotty said they were on their way to Tortosa with supplies for the front. And then he said, "Here, let me show you on the map." He drew a torn, filthy map out of his pocket. "Never let the bloody thing out of my sight. You leave one of these maps in the lorry for two minutes and—*phoop!*"

Melinda lay down on the grass for an extra few precious minutes, then sat up and pored over the map with him. The sun slid toward the west.

"I've got to leave." She traced the route he showed her with a finger.

She got back to Alcañiz the next evening, clean, fed, cosseted. She had swum in the ocean, and floated there and let the war and dirt slide away from her. She had heard news, fragmented as it was, of Quinto, of the shrine at Boro, where some Americans, new ones, had been killed because they did not think the Crusaders of Cristo Rey would put a machine-gun nest inside. She had washed her hair and eaten, and strutted a little because she had come from nearer the front than the nurses and the doctors at the convalescent centers.

She drove the orange-laden car into the courtyard. It was piled high; oranges rolled onto the ground when she stopped. She saw Tye leaning against one of the pocked stone arches, nearly asleep. She knew he would be furious that she had been sent, so she crept under his arm and laid her head against his chest, where his apron was bloodstained.

"Umm," he whispered. "You smell nice." Then he pushed her away and stared at her. *"You smell nice!* Where the devil have you been?"

"Want an orange?" was all she said.

The walking wounded, the nurses, the *chóferes,* the *camilleros,* were clustered around the car, throwing oranges behind them for anyone too far away to grab one. They took oranges to the men who couldn't get up, to the doctors and the nurses in the operating parlor. Oranges were spread all around the hospital, and the fresh scent of oranges being peeled almost covered the smells they had grown used to.

It was late October. The road was deep in mud and rain and empty again at last. The battles had not ended; they had died in the rain. The hospital was almost empty, and the nurses were able to move into the upstairs bedrooms and glory in sleeping on the thick feather beds. It was another of the pauses in the war. Belchite had been captured, but Fuentes de Ebro had not. Tye said that was a disaster.

On one of the few days when the sun shone, they walked up to the empty convent-castle on top of the hill. Far away they could see the little river that ran into the Ebro. The convent had been shelled. It had become, in a few months, an ancient ruin, as if war were a thing that speeded time, and left the jagged walls, the little round windows, the Moorish arches intact but leading only to heaven.

It was in the middle of the cloister where tree branches lay dead on the weeds that Tye said that they should go on leave and get married while they could, before another push came. "I want you to see my Spain before it is destroyed."

The way to Tye's Spain was easy. They hitched rides on the *camiones* to Tortosa. Then, from the north bank of the Ebro to the French border, they were in Republican Spain. They crossed the brute mountains and had glimpses of the sea. Outside Barcelona, at the crossroads that Tye said led to Vic and the base hospital that had been opened there, they waited to hitch a ride in rain that was turning to snow.

In the mountains to the north they rode a hay cart. The world was white with snow on the floor of a deep evergreen forest. All they could hear was snow falling from the branches and the snorting of the horse, which blew clouds into the cold air. The day was fresh and clean, and there was no bombing, no war. At Manresa, they ate eggs for the first time in months.

The women of the mountains looked alike to Melinda: solid, their hair still dark and thick at fifty, their faces grown into a kind of beauty that she had seen only in the very young. Tye spoke to them in a different language that she couldn't understand, harsh-sounding after the soft Castillian Spanish.

At Montserrat, they bought coats and mountain boots that smelled of sheep. They stood warm against the wind and watched the snow swirling around the dark jagged teeth of the mountain. The monks of Montserrat went by in their thick habits and their sheepskin boots, bent forward against the wind, which seemed to come from everywhere. In the little village that had grown up through the years below the shrine, the women gossiped and talked about who would marry and how they felt. Tye said those were the words of a peace he thought he would not remember—food, copulation, and the state of the stomach.

On the way to Cardona, they half lay, half sat on the hay in the back of a large open *camión.* Tye talked to the driver, who said that the farmers hid their sheep in the *barrancos* to keep the Moors from stealing them. Tye whispered to Melinda that all people south of the mountains, both Franco's army and the army of the Republic, were Moors to the driver.

So, by *camión,* by cart, by hay wain, they rode into a peace that both of them had forgotten. It was almost frightening, ephemeral, as if it would disappear if they slept too soundly. In the early evening, at the time of the *paseo,* they rode the last few miles up the valley toward Cardona. The castle in the distance was honey-colored in the evening sun, and the salt mountain glittered, surrounded by snow.

Cardona seemed shrunk in the cold below the flying domination of the castle. But when they walked under the town arch into the plaza, the houses around it were five stories tall. Tye led Melinda under arches, along steep alleys where the buildings were an arm's length apart, through the deepening twilight, into a street of shops with their windows lit so that it looked like a fiesta—but it was only evening, far from the blackouts of war. Women and old men strolled from shop to shop, complaining about supplies that looked to Tye and Melinda like the riches of India—real meat, real cheese, real eggs, and even, smuggled by their relatives over the French border, which they hardly recognized, at least where the mountain goat paths crossed, fruit, wine, and brandy from France.

It was dark when Tye led Melinda through a narrow passage with a low roof. At the far end, a small light on a stone sconce guided them.

"Listen." He was whispering. "If ever at any time you are in trouble, knock on this door. These are my friends. Their name is Zuda. Tandy says it's Arabic for *well,* but not in front of them! Most of them have gone to war, but their mother hasn't, and neither have their wives." They stepped out into dim light and down deeply worn stone steps.

Tye turned her around and said, "Now look, before I knock. I have been staying here since I was fourteen—twelve summers. I came here first with Tandy, and then his family took him off to the South of France for his hols. We were both fourteen, and my mother allowed Tandy and me to come alone, without one of those dreadful earnest guides she used to pick up at Fabian Society meetings, who were all zeal, sandals, bad breath, bad French, and knapsacks. You have no idea what dreadful snobs English schoolboys can be.

"This is my favorite house—that is why I brought you here. Señora Zuda is my Catalan mother. She has seven sons, and she took me in when I didn't know I needed to be taken in. Tandy and I were here when the war began, and we never went back to England."

The house's stone walls grew out of the living stone of the hill, and Melinda knew what people meant when they said "living stone"; she had felt it in the passage, damp and cold and alive, a whole town that had grown up out of rock, helped by the masons and the carpenters as long ago as Christ.

Tye knocked on the dark wood door, whose iron studs had grown smooth and shiny with age. The door opened, and a tall, heavy woman with a mass of gray hair piled high, not for looks but to get it out of the way, stood there, not saying a word. She looked as solid as a tree trunk, and even her dress, the rusty black of perpetual mourning, had molded to her body a long time ago. She stood in the half-light from a fireplace they couldn't see, and the leap of the flames made her still face move.

The woman and Tye waited for each other. Her great Byzantine eyes were as blue as the sky between heavy clouds. A huge grin wiped out the sternness of her face. She threw herself into his arms and said over and over, *"Tallo, Tallo, mi Tallo!"* then a scramble of words that Melinda couldn't follow, except that she caught *muerte,* and *coño.*

The house had at some time been the corner of a large convent. Too long ago for anyone to remember or care, the high-vaulted corridors and cells had been chopped up into rooms. Melinda and Tye walked into what had been a refectory, with a huge fireplace that cast light and heat all around the walls, where dried mushrooms and onions and garlic and herbs hung from the rafters. The whitewash of centuries had made the walls curve softly to the ceiling, white with beams so black they looked as if they were carved of iron. There wasn't much furniture, but a tile floor shone in the light with pictured riots and tangles of vines, flowers, and faces, like the tiles at Albastro.

Melinda was left there, standing and staring, while Tye and Señora Zuda held each other and talked over each other's words. She caught one name after another, and then Tye said, *"Mi novia."* She knew what that meant, and smiled.

Señora Zuda let Tye go and moved over to Melinda and hugged her. Her arms felt like branches, heavy with muscle, but her hands were delicate, and she touched softly. She kept on asking questions over her shoulder, so rapidly that Melinda just stood there, getting warm from the fire and her arms.

"It seems," Tye said at last, "that we are going to have a wedding right here in this room, since we are *moros* and can't be married in the church, and it won't be the kind of wedding Señora would like for one of her sons, but she is going to do her best and we have nothing to say about it. She asked if we have made a marriage contract, and if we have an *abogado,* and if you have the permission of your mother, and I lied about all of it.

"She says of course we can't be married by a priest. There are only two, and one of them is a *cabrón.* She doesn't know why they haven't shot him, but he has a brother in the town who is a Republican and he stays at his house. The other is the mayor of Seu de Cols, in the next valley. Her son, the youngest, will go to Seu de Cols and bring back the mayor, who can marry us tomorrow evening as the mayor and bless us as the priest, even though he can't marry us as a priest but only as a mayor. She says you can't marry in a sheepskin coat and trousers, so she will see that you are dressed, and I, when supper is over, am to go to the *posada* on the corner of the plaza, because it is not seemly for us to stay in the same house tonight. Besides, it is bad luck."

Señora Zuda let go of Melinda and began to measure her carefully, her hands on her hips. When she had made up her mind, she said, in Spanish English, "*Cena,* it will be *cena,* nine o'clock. You take Melinda to the *paseo,* that is what the *novio* does at this time of the evening. When you come back, it will all be ready. There is a fire in the stove at the *posada.* Put her close to it. She is cold. Tallo, a delicate girl like this, *Dios.*"

They walked out into the dark and along the

street. As soon as they rounded the corner toward the church, Melinda began to ask questions. "What else did she tell you? Why did she call you Tallo? Tell me everything, right now."

"She told me that four of her sons are dead, two at Jarama and two at Madrid. She has three left, but now that I am back, she has four." He looked away and wouldn't let her see his face. "They call me Tallo because I am tall and thin, like a blade of grass. I have hunted and walked the mountains with all of them. They called me Tallo the first time I came here, and I have come back ever since." He leaned his head against the stone wall of one of the arches. She left him alone until he was ready to move.

Something drew him back into smiling. "She told me that of course all but the youngest are in the Republican army, and the youngest is carrying on the business until he is old enough."

"What business?"

"Smuggling," he said. "Where do you think the peaches and the wine came from? Look up at the mountains. All seven of her sons and her husband, until he was killed in a fall, knew every goat path. To them, there is no border. She says they have brought hundreds of men over the mountains to fight with the International Brigades.

"Now, she told me that you had to sit in the corner here so the men won't think you are a whore, but to hell with that." He had pushed open the door of the *posada*. They walked into a bar that was a womb of heat. It smelled of damp sheepskins, sausages, hot peppers, and wine. A little dog ran up to Tye's feet, growled, yapped, sniffed, and began to wag his tail. Some of the small gnarled old men in the bar shouted "Tallo!" and gathered around and slapped and pushed and hugged him.

"This is my *novia,*" he said, when they stood back and began staring at Melinda. They made comments to each other, to Tye, looking her over with the judging looks of men about to buy animals. Tye answered every question. Then there was a roar, and they took her by the shoulders and propelled her to the bar and handed her a skin of wine. She lifted it and managed to hit her open mouth while they all cheered.

Tye said they kept saying, "She is very little and very pretty and she came all the way from America and she can repair a *camión* engine like a man. Wonders and miracles!"

For the rest of her life, Melinda remembered days of joy or of disaster obliquely—what things looked like, what they smelled like, what the weather was, not how sweet or how sorrowful, but pierced into her memory with every detail intact, she remembered always where she was. It was that way with her wedding. As in weddings all over the world, and as in disasters, the principals had decision taken out of their hands.

She remembered the firelight, the cold, the snow, the smell of food, the *mantilla* that Señora Zuda had found for her by the time she and Tye got back from the *posada.* The *mantilla* was the señora's own; the skirt belonged to one of her daughters-in-law, the white blouse to another. Its huge sleeves, with intricate embroidery, had been made over long winter evenings, for hope. The rushing of the women and the constant complaint from Señora Zuda, Melinda remembered in Spanish: *"Tan poco tiempo."*

The wedding itself was as ancient as the white curved walls, the leaping fire, the threadbare clothes, and the exhausted eyes of the mayor from Seu de Cols, who had tramped over one of the low passes to get there. She remembered the great eyes of Señora Zuda, who stood behind the mayor and nodded when Melinda was supposed to answer with "Sí," since she didn't understand a word.

The feast that came afterward was full of wine and chestnuts and apples, a roast pig, and yams cooked in the embers. Every time afterward that Melinda smelled chestnuts being roasted on the streets in Paris or London, she was back in the room in Cardona for a second, with the fire leaping, and the color of all their best clothes, and the priest's voice in Catalán, and then, what surprised her, a round of applause when she and Tye kissed, as shyly as if they didn't know each other very well.

When they were escorted to Tye's room at the *posada,* they found that the women of the Zuda family had been in and replaced the sheets with their own embroidered linen. They had spread across the pillows two-hundred-year-old night-shirts that had been used in every family wedding as a good-luck charm, so that the new wife would conceive on the first night. They lay folded side by side, freshly laundered and smelling of some kind of scented geranium.

The wedding guests marched Tye and Melinda to the *posada,* through the dark passage, down the street of high shuttered houses, past the ancient church, under the stone arch, and into the plaza, with its winter-stunted trees in rows, waiting for spring. For most of the night they could be heard in the bar-restaurant below, singing, laughing, holding a fiesta for Tye, the foreign son.

Melinda and Tye made love, then lay together like spoons and drowsed. Daylight came. The snow had stopped, and the sun, just over the mountains to the east, colored the castle that they could see high above them out the *posada* window.

Tye sat up in the old nightshirt and put his bare legs over the side of the bed. He put his elbows on his knees and his head in his hands.

"There is something I haven't told you," he muttered, so quietly that Melinda moved over so that her legs were cosied up to him and she was curled around into his lap. It didn't work. She kept trying to find a soft place. "God, you're bony," she complained, and grabbed a pillow and put it in his lap.

He stroked her hair, and then his hand was still on her cheek. He couldn't say what it was.

"I don't care. Don't you know that? After all . . ." She was about to say that she knew about English public-school boys and that they grew out of it, when he said, "I didn't dare tell you because of your politics."

"I'm just a New Deal Democrat." She nuzzled closer to him.

"Well, so many of you Americans are socialists and Communists and anarchists and libertarians and all that nonsense."

"What are you trying to tell me?" She finally took his arm. "All right, your mother's a Fascist, your brother is a Conservative MP who speaks out for Franco. Come on."

"It's worse than that." He was still muttering. "My mother is a Fabian League socialist. My father was an old-fashioned Liberal from Cambridge. He was a landowner in Wiltshire until he died and left the country house to my mother, and that was where I spent my hols when I was in England. He died last year, and I couldn't even get home to his funeral."

There was more. She knew it and waited. But it wouldn't come. Instead he said, "My mother wears tweed skirts and does Alexander training and is a vegetarian from time to time, until we all revolt. She is quite literally one of the nicest women I have ever known."

It wasn't what he meant to say. She could tell from his voice, trailing to a stop.

Then he took a deep breath. "My brother is a baronet and a very nice queen of England, so I am next in line. Oh, God, that's over. I hope you don't mind."

"Mother will be pleased," she said, and then she made her own confession. "I wrote her and told her I had found the person I wanted to marry, and I didn't show you the letter she sent back because you wouldn't have understood. The

West End of Richmond is very . . ." She searched for a word. "Primitive, like a tribe. Her opening words were, 'If your dear father weren't dead this would kill him'—but she always says that. The letter went down from there. She told me that Imogene—that's our maid—stood in the garden and cried because I wasn't going to come home and marry one of those nice Carr boys. They are supposed by all the mothers to be catches because they own an eighteenth-century house on the James River, but the girls all know better. One of them is a drunk, and the other is one of those drips who gropes. Mother always makes up little Imogene stories when she doesn't want to admit something herself. I never believe them, because Imogene is as tough as nails, and she and my grandmother have known each other for so long that they look alike, even if one is black and the other is white, and neither one of them has been surprised at anything I have done since I was nineteen."

"I wrote to my mother and I told her that I had seen the girl I wanted to marry, if she would have me and if I could get her cleaned up. Anyway, that's not very old," Tye said, and turfed her out of his lap and got up and stretched.

"What?"

"That house in Richmond, in Virginia." He looked long and lanky with his bare legs sticking out below the nightshirt. She thought she would love him forever, just like that.

"Don't say that in Richmond," she told his back.

"I'm going to shave." He went to the ewer and

basin in the corner. It was covered with huge flowers. "I've forgotten what hot water feels like when you shave. Ouch," he said and put his hand to his cheek. "The Zudas' house is a thousand years old, and our house in Wiltshire was rebuilt in 1655. That's why it has such bloody awful windows." He wiped the blood from his cheek and smeared it on the bed.

"What on earth are you doing? Those are Señora Zuda's best sheets." Melinda tried to stop him.

"Now you be still a minute. I want to tell you something." He tried to hold her, but she had already twisted away. "Now listen, darling. There may be revolutions and there may be democracies, but women in the country will always examine the sheets after a wedding night, and they will always dress in their best clothes on All Saints Day. They may learn to read, but this whole generation of women Señora Zuda's age will go to the priest and confess afterward. These are ceremonies, and they don't mean anything and they mean a lot. Now go and slosh your face and don't be silly, and get dressed. I have to take you somewhere. It's important."

Late in the morning he made her climb up toward the castle in the cold. Above their heads, a small lookout tower was like a stone eagle's nest against the deep blue sky. The road was rutted and muddy from the *camiones* that had torn their way up the five-hundred-foot hill to the castle. They slipped and slid and held each other until they got to the first gate, and after that the road was paved with small dark Moorish stones.

Soldiers lounged around the walls and offered them wine. They let them wander through the ruined courtyards, under the arches that led nowhere, past the iron bars that no longer kept anything out.

The tenth-century church was intact, and dark. There was only opaque light from high alabaster windows that had survived time and bombing. Inside, three wooden floors had been built. They could see what looked like the shadows of hundreds of prisoners, moving as if they were under water instead of in half-darkness. There was only a quiet murmur of voices. One of the soldiers said they were rebel prisoners, and laughed.

Melinda and Tye walked away across a courtyard hand in hand. Then they lingered at one of the Moorish gates. Then they stopped. Tye seemed to have forgotten why they had come. He retreated into guiding her through the ruins. He said that the main castle was supposed to have been built by his favorite king of any country and any time. "He was known as Wilfred the Hairy, and he made Cardona into a refuge, no questions asked, when the Moors retook Barcelona. He welcomed thieves and rebels and men who had run off with other men's wives."

In the open court, broken, pointed arches stood around what was left of a cloister. There was nothing else but a tomb of someone unknown, covered with lichen and so old that it had tipped to the side.

They strolled under the heavy arched entrance to the inner courtyard, which led into ruined space. A huge stone wheel leaned against the wall. A water trough for animals held brackish rainwater. The courtyard was full of boys in the *monos* of the Republican army.

They climbed up stone stairs and steep ramps, higher and higher, until they were in what had been a convent garden. In the middle was a square well with a trellised wellhead; whatever plant had grown there was long since gone. Soldiers, or rather boys, *jóvenes* from the village, sprawled on the grass. "*Que tal, Tallo?,*" they all called, and stared at Melinda and smiled.

Tye and Melinda had climbed to just below the highest point of the castle. A tower rose above them, uglier than the rest, its door iron-studded, its walls massive. Tye said it had been built in the second century by the Romans. It was a lookout, maybe for a castle that had long since been buried under the one that had survived.

The tower looked like it had grown without the help of men's hands, rough stone on rough stone. Its wooden door was almost petrified. Its lock was huge. A small grille made of bronze was pierced with tiny holes. Tye pushed open the door and they were in the dark.

The *jóvenes* followed them and called out, excited, to Tye. He told Melinda what they said: that the Fascists of the town had been imprisoned there and had been shot when the anarchist militia came. Not many, only three or four, two landowners and of course the priest. The priest wasn't shot, he was thrown over the tower wall, and they said he flew through the air for nearly a minute before he landed on the rocks below.

He was a drunkard and he tried to seduce the girls. At least, that's what people said.

"That isn't true, probably," Tye said. "They always say that about the priest. They seem to like the idea of tossing them to heaven."

"I hate this place," Melinda told him. "I want air. This place is evil. I want to go."

"Not yet." He held her arm. "There's something I have to show you." He led her to an iron ladder that ran to the top of the tower and called up into the sky. Melinda understood only the word *arriba.*

A young soldier leaned his head over the side of the tower high above them, *"Sí, camarada, sí. Bienvenido. Ay,* Tallo! *Que tal?"* He held out his hand, and Tye began to climb.

"Wait a minute. I'm not going up there." Melinda grabbed his foot to hold him back.

"Yes, you are. You follow me."

"No."

He came back down the ladder. The soldier was laughing. Now a line of children's heads were watching them like Baroque *diablillos.*

"All right," Tye told her, and took both her arms. "You have to do this. There is a reason."

"Then I will go first, and you can be behind me if I fall, and the children will help me up the last of the ladder, and to hell with you!" She was finding that embarrassment in front of the *jóvenes* was worse than her fear.

She began to climb, looking straight at the stones of the wall in front of her, neither up nor down, just stone after stone after stone after rung after rung, until one of the *jóvenes* took her hand.

She was on top of the world. The snow-peaked mountains surrounded them. The town was a doll town far below, and she looked straight at the Pyrenees, peak behind peak, growing faint in the distance. She forgot to be scared. She forgot Tye until he came up and stood beside her and held her shoulders. Far below, the roads to the north wavered like small black lines drawn by a child through the snow patches and what green had not yet left the fields. The black evergreen forests stretched around the lower mountains, and the salt mound glistened like a small jewel.

"This is what the Condor Legion sees when they strafe and bomb us," Tye said. "The arrogance of the air. To them it is a game, a practice. And the Capronis of the Italians—that's what they see, ants and targets. Count Ciano said that bombs bursting were like flowers. *Les fleurs du mal. Les fleurs de sang.* I'm overeducated." He grinned. "Most English public-school boys are, but they get rid of it as soon as they can. I didn't molt, like so many."

The *jóvenes* were standing around watching Tallo hold his new little wife and murmur the nothings they hoped to murmur sometime to their *novias,* when they were old enough.

"I'm scared to climb down again."

"Oh, bravery is only doing things anyway. Everybody is scared, and hungry, and losing the war, and I would rather be here than anyplace else in the world." Tye pointed north. "That is the real reason we came up here. You see that road? Memorize it. Keep that road north in your mind like the lines in your hand. Keep it." He pointed to where a black pencil line curved through the snow and disappeared into the trees in the distance.

He was grasping her too hard. "Listen." He wouldn't let her go. "I cut through all that ghastly red tape and got you up here to marry you to show you this. Now just listen to me. We're going to lose. We don't have enough guns, we don't have enough tanks, the Republic is goddamn being squeezed to death between the Communists and the Fascists."

"Don't talk like that, Tye!" She shook herself loose.

"I saw it at Jarama, and at the university, and at Belchite," he went on, softly, so that it sounded like love talk to the *jóvenes,* who had lain down to listen, not understanding a word. "Men who could hardly stand on their feet were fighting without sleep because there were too few guns. When a man fell, the man behind him picked up his gun. Tandy and I were carrying a stretcher when a boy, a Polish boy, fell down beside us. We thought he had been shot. He hadn't. He had simply fallen asleep, in the midst of all that blood and stink and death, an eighteen-year-old boy flung out there in the rubble of a street, asleep. We moved him out of the way of the *camiones* and the ambulances. I saw him later. He looked—can you believe this?—refreshed."

He grabbed her so hard it hurt. She tried to twist away. "Listen to me. We have to pay for every bandage that comes from Russia, and the Communists tell the people that Russia is their only friend. The French won't open the border and let anything in—" He was talking to himself.

"Stop it. Tye, just stop it." She was pounding at his chest, and the *jóvenes* laughed.

He held her tighter. "You have to listen. I have been here two years. This is a Spanish civil war, not a romantic ideal. We are all visitors. We can leave. Most of the volunteers are as innocent as we have been. We are so bloody ignorant. Some friends of mine in Barcelona were shot because they were in the POUM, just the wrong goddamn initials. Everybody is trying to steal the war."

Melinda stopped trying to get away from him. It was so unlike Tye to talk like that, that she waited for something more, not just depression but reason.

Tye's voice went on. "I saw people happier in the years of the Republic than in all the years I have come here. I wish you could have seen it. It was gay and exciting and everybody talked all the time, and there were plays and fiestas, not those solemn purgatorial religious processions there had been before. Everybody was a poet. There were strikes and arguments and hatreds, but there was affection, and there were . . . Oh Jesus, do you know that I was told they shot Lorca twice in the ass before they killed him because he was homosexual? And they hunted out intellectuals and screamed *'Arriba muerto,'* and let the Moors have the Republican women in the villages. I could hear their screams sometimes at Jarama and at Brunete, away in the distance, and the *ullalah* of the Moors. I will hear it forever, even when the sound of the guns is long gone. I can't stand what I am seeing . . . ."

His face had gone white, and he stood frozen, to keep from crying. She could hardly hear him when he added, "But even if you know they haven't a chance, you help anyway. You do things anyway."

He pulled away from the past, and his voice was harsh. "Now look again. Memorize the road. That is the road to the border." He turned her body away from him. She looked out over Cardona.

"The road. You see the farmhouse about eleven o'clock? Do you have a birth certificate?"

She nodded. The wind had risen and blew their hair, and she nestled closer. The *jóvenes* were so pleased to see that they had patched up whatever lovers' quarrel they had had that they began to sing. It was a sweet song, not one from war but one that they had learned when they were little—a love song, she was sure, that floated out and joined the wind.

When they got down the ladder, Melinda said they sounded so sweet. Tye laughed. "No. No. They are singing the Spanish words to 'The Lovers of Teruel.' Every schoolchild knows them. It is a revolutionary song, but a revolution against grownups. The grown-up song tells about two lovers who died of grief because they couldn't marry and who were buried together. The children sing, 'Here's to the lovers of Teruel. He was a fool and she as well.' "

"Why do you want my birth certificate? I have

a passport," she remembered to ask as they climbed back down the hill.

"I have to send our marriage certificate and your birth certificate to Valencia to get you a British passport. You lost your citizenship when you joined a foreign force. It's American law. I got a friend in Valencia to look into all of this. You will need a British passport with a diplomatic visa for France to get you over the border."

"I'm not going anyplace," she said. "Don't talk like this, Tye. It scares me."

When Melinda looked back at the castle, the highest tower looked like a small windmill. They talked in fragments which they made into words at the tip of what they were thinking, and they held hands.

"Both sides hate us, so we must be doing something right. We're in the way." She muttered, but he heard her.

"How the devil do you know that?" He turned her toward him. "You know, darling, you seem either to know things or not to know things. There's nothing in between."

"Come on!" She grabbed his hand and pulled him along. "I'm hungry, and I want three or four sweet buns from the bakery and some real coffee, and I want to sit in that wonderful room with all the squiggles."

"That's the only modernist building in Cardona." He followed her.

"Stop telling me things. You sound like Tandy." She ran away, careful to run lightly over the ice-slick path.

Book Three

Catalunya • 1938

Whetstones

The winter followed them south. People said that it was the worst winter in twenty years. The water froze in the washing bowls; the ruts froze in the roads. The traces of summer blood froze, and bodies left in the fields froze into statues of death. They tried to think of Christmas and what they could do for the children in Alcañiz, but it was hard to think.

Everybody in the hospital who could walk went to the country to gather firewood, and the cold and the exercise made the faces of the walking wounded young and pink again. The smoke of chestnut wood and fir climbed over the *finca* and scented the cold air. Melinda and Tye had no time together. They couldn't even sleep together. There was no place. Once they went to the small hotel in the town, but the bombers came over on the way to Tortosa and the Ebro bridges and kept them awake all night.

On December fourteenth, General Líster, with only his Spanish troops, all the men they had seen lounging under the late summer trees at Alfambra and Villalba and the villages on the way to Alcañiz, were gone, drawn into the vortex of

Teruel. The government had decided it needed a Spanish victory, without the Internationals, and the army took Teruel. Spirits lifted, as if a spring breeze had slipped through the ice of winter.

There were Christmas fiestas in the villages, where the International Brigades gave out the chocolate they had saved. At the hospital they cut the frozen feet off young Spanish boys who had been caught in the cold of Teruel.

Tye drove back and forth from the front-line hospital on the hill north of Teruel, where the machine-gun corps that had given them the wine had been. Their lookout was a blackened ruin. He said that Teruel in the distance was an etched black line of jagged stones against the white snow.

Villalba was destroyed. Alfambra, where they had talked to the men, was destroyed. Bodies lay all along the road where Melinda and Tye and Tandy had driven, and the snow covered it all as if the world were ashamed.

Winter is a silent time. The blind hate the snow, because they cannot hear the footsteps they depend on to recognize their friends. There were no footsteps, only the wrecked *camiones*, the icy roads, the constant to-and-fro of the convoys, which sometimes slid on the ice and pitched over the steep hills. In some of them the gasoline ignited, and they burned into metal skeletons in the white world.

Melinda made a list of the roads. She clung to the idea that she could take a *camión* as soon as the spring thaw came and rescue spare parts. She was sure, but she didn't tell Tye, or anyone.

There was no panic. Politics forgotten again,

there was a growing closeness, a tenderness with each other, as if they were very old, or very young. They tended to touch each other as they passed in the courtyard, in the bedrooms that had once again become wards, so the staff slept where they could.

The wedding had been a luxury. Melinda kept the notes of the dead and the wounded and a list of the material used, the material needed, a list that got longer and longer. She had started writing by hand, because there was no paper and the typewriter tore toilet paper, which was all she could find to use, and she had to steal that. Sister McCall got the same obsession with toilet paper that she had had with Dettol, but nobody complained. They just touched her too as they passed.

Melinda looked back on the terrible winter that turned into a terrible spring as the tenderest time of her life, a kindness. Nobody blamed anybody, and they drew together against outsiders.

Nobody talked about politics or ideals except the visitors, who came in famous droves and were supposed to lift their spirits by being there. Then they left and things went back to the normal waiting and waiting and waiting for more of the lost to straggle in.

At one point the ragged, hungry men who had fought to a standstill and had finally been relieved, when they could be found, were being taken by cattle car, without food, in rags, back from the huge area of battle south of the Ebro.

Tye went with them as a *practicante.* He said he had things to do in Valencia, and when Melinda kissed him goodbye, she said, "I wish you wouldn't be so bloody secretive."

"Sec-*reet-* ive," Tye said.

"It sounds like somebody peeing," she called after him, and he grinned goodbye and raised his fist. It had become a habit with all of them, the raised fist. *"Viva la República, viva el Frente Popular,* shit," Tye always finished.

When Tye came back, he told her that the train had been stopped and they had been ordered to pile out into a field where Earl Browder, the head of the American Communist Party, was waiting to talk to them. Browder said that he had heard that there was low morale. The men looked at each other and grinned, some of them; some of them looked at the frozen ground.

"Those of you who are disturbing elements will be sent home if your morale does not improve," Browder had yelled into the icy air. Tye told Melinda that the men had all cheered and catcalled, and some of them had shouted, "Get some in, civvy," and others, "Please, sir, can I be a disturbing element?"

"They began to sing, but it was not the 'Internationale,' it was the World War song that the English had taught them all, 'I want to go home, I want to go home . . . oh my, I'm too young to die, I want to go home!' When they had finished, they cheered again."

"What did Earl Browder do?" Melinda asked.

"God, I don't know. I wandered off. It was ludicrous."

The rebels took Teruel back, and it cost Spain more than sixty thousand men. Melinda tried to remember that each number had been a man, that the piles of bodies that grew outside the hospital when the ground was too cold to dig their mass graves had been people, men and women, that she had known and even comforted. Then, for her and for the rest, a scab of indifference grew over the wounds of winter as the spring came. There was no other way to survive, day after day, step after step, dull and heavy. They cursed the dead sometimes for dying after they had wasted all the bottled blood and splints and time on them.

There was nothing left that was personal. People didn't steal from each other, exactly; they scrounged and organized anything that was left around. Melinda had long since lost her sheepskin coat and was wearing one that Tye had brought back that on her was as long as a greatcoat. She had better sense than to ask where he had gotten it. She had lost all of her eating utensils, which the English called "irons," except for a large spoon, which did for cutting, eating, stirring the beans and mule meat.

In early spring, masses of tanks and planes and bullets and guns were sent to Franco by Hitler and by Mussolini, and the democracies did nothing.

Teruel fell. Belchite fell. Soldiers walked the roads toward the northeast, to the Ebro, without talking, without singing. They slogged, one foot in front of the other.

Orders came to evacuate the *finca* three days before General Líster retired to make a stand at Alcañiz. They drove out at night, without lights, in a line of *camiones* and ambulances. Scotty was there, and he said the whole thing had been a fucking balls-up of the worst bleeding order, a short cock, mother of a fuck-up. Tye liked Scotty. He said he liked the rich swearing and the Gorbals bite of his Scottish accent. It made him laugh. So he rode with Scotty in the convoy.

They started at dusk. The column was over a mile long, fifty feet only between the *camiones* and the ambulances. It moved slowly because of the wounded and the stark terror of the dirt roads, which by late March had already been either baked dry by the spring sun or turned into deep mire by the local rains. A shepherd rode in front of the convoy on a burro to guide them.

Melinda drove a Fordson van, with two of the nurses in the cab. One of them, Sister Maureen, a young girl from Dublin, spent her time either muttering, "This bloody fucking benighted country with its bloody hills and its fucking rocks and its naked earth," or saying the first day of a novena. She said she did it for all of them, and she said, "Thank God I'm a Catholic, how do you bloody Prots stand this?" and went on either swearing at the landscape or murmuring the novena until Nurse Lily, from Liverpool, told her to knock it off.

All night they could hear sounds that were either guns or thunder in the distance. When the convoy stopped and dawn came, they were in the hills above the Ebro. After they started again, one after another the signals for air raid began at the head *camión* and rippled through the convoy, so that every fifteen minutes or so they had to stop, run to the ditches or the gorse, and lie flat, with their heads on their folded arms so their chests were raised a little from the ground.

The first time the signal came rolling toward them, a series of small-caliber shots that they had been told to listen for, Melinda plunged into a gorse bush, which scratched her, and she wriggled behind its frail and thorny barrier as a black plane, she didn't know what kind, screamed out of the sky toward the convoy. One of the walking wounded who had tried to scratch into the rocky ground beside her vomited steadily into the dust.

She was three people. She watched herself thinking that she was completely cool, and was surprised on examination that she was not afraid. Then the two of them watched her body shake as if she had suddenly gotten a chill in the warm morning. She looked with some interest at the goosebumps on her arms.

The ground was strewn with the jettisoned equipment of the refugees and the soldiers who had passed along the road; there was a tin marmalade can sitting in front of her, with a knife beside it. She watched and heard herself say, "I mustn't forget to pick that up when this is over," and then, distracted from her body and mind, she looked up along the convoy.

Black vultures of planes screamed and rattled machine-gun fire along the sides of the *camiones* and the ambulances. Her own van was so far back in the convoy that the Stukas, still screaming down to level off, missed it. She heard human screams, weak under the screams of the planes. They were far away, and they had little to do with her. Only a minute had passed since the first plane's dive, and it had seemed as slow and deliberate as disaster. Every thought, every move, stood out separately, and she thought, How can they stand it?

The single shot that was the all-clear sounded. She helped the wounded man beside her back into the van. He kept apologizing for having vomited. It went on until they drove down out of the stark heathered hills and were at last by the river. They drew to rest under the trees in an olive grove. The kitchen staff made some black stuff they called by different names, all disgusting, and the nurses laid the wounded who couldn't walk under the trees to try to sleep.

All day the Italian Capronis and the German Stukas screamed in the distance, so that they couldn't move again until twilight. The sun had turned the distant snow-covered ridges pink and gold, and there was time for Melinda to let herself love what she saw. She had not let herself think of Tye for the whole day; she had lived in minutes, immediate and isolated.

Tortosa had been hit so many times from the air it was almost flat. Incongruous domestic life hung in the air in the crushed buildings and sliced houses—a bed with the covers thrown back on the ledge of a bedroom, a towel in half a bathroom. Where the refugees and the soldiers had passed, canteens and packs and pots and pans and broken dolls were strewn along the roads. Once, when Melinda lay face-down in the garden of a ruined house where the land flattened out into the Ebro, she saw just in front of her eyes another knife, a good knife, and remembered that she had forgotten to pick up the other one. She reached out and grabbed it before anybody else could see it. Then she watched a flowering shrub cringe in the noise and bombing wind.

It was blessed black night when they finally crossed the Ebro on the shaky pontoon bridge the engineers had made, had seen destroyed while they lay against the ground, and then had gotten up and built again. The convoy, when it could move at all, had picked up men along the roads, men so exhausted that they couldn't speak but who clung to the sides of the *camiones* and the ambulances. Their fellow soldiers who could still walk helped them onto the slowly moving machines.

Somebody heard a baby crying, still alive and unhurt, whose mother had been killed and lay like bloody meat on the roadside. One of the soldiers who had rested jumped down and ran to the baby, raced back to catch up with the van, and thrust the baby inside. Sister Lily held her, a girl about three months old, all the way to Vilateresa, the Catalán villa they had been assigned as a hospital.

It took them all night. They had to cross the long pontoon bridge one at a time, slowly. It was midnight when the first *camiones* drew up to Vilateresa, and early dawn by the time the last parked under the trees. Melinda was so far back in the column that it was light enough for her to see the soldier who thrust his head in the window.

"Unload your wounded and then drive your

vehicle under the trees. What supplies have you brought?"

Sister Lily laughed. "Oh, for God's sake, Terry, you're acting like a soldier. Here, take this baby. She has peed all over me. We have lashings of toilet paper, kitchen supplies, splints, and a vast need to go potty."

They had lost only two ambulances and three *camiones* in the dive-bombing.

When Melinda and Sister Lily walked into the dark, cool hall, Tandy was standing with Tye and Scotty in front of a huge glossy mural with paint so slick it glistened in the half-dark. He was holding tight to Scotty's arm.

"Good grief," Tandy whispered, appalled beyond the common obscenities. "You could skate on it."

It was signed by one of the leading Falangist poster and mural painters, a painter of ideal portraits of the Falangist leader Jose Antonio which they had seen shining, still new and bright, on the ruined walls of towns that the Republic had taken for a short time: Belchite, Quinto, Mora de Ebro. The main figure, at the right of the mural and gazing straight at them with disconcerting attention, was a larger-than-life-size female, suitably half draped, vaguely what Tandy called Greekish, a goddess without arms but with a large muscular body and aggressive breasts. A tendril of drapery hid her genitals. Someone had written very carefully, in best copperplate, across the drapery, *"Fascista, Coño."*

Tandy turned away. "God, it looks like it's been painted with shit."

Sister Lily was fascinated. "I think it's lovely," she said. "Don't you think it looks real? Like a photograph? I don't know why they had to write on it. Isn't it lovely, isn't it a shame?" she said to Melinda and Tye, who were simply holding on to each other. When she couldn't get their attention, she glared at Tandy. "Where do you bloody get off, anyway?"

Behind the goddess rose some sort of masculine figure, not a god but an idealized torso with a face in half profile, chin lifted toward the future, which seemed to be just beyond the extreme left of the mural, out of sight. He was half naked, but he waved a blue shirt that he had taken off or was about to put on or let loose.

Tandy couldn't resist a chance to educate. "Now look at that. That's the difference between naked and nude, right there in front of your stupid eyes. It's obscene." The figure was draped in red-and-black flags with falanges of gold, and the flags of Spain and Castile and the Carlists. An unfelt wind was part of the future beyond the left of the painting. It made a healthy stream of flags, hair, half profile, all the way across the hall.

The hall and the downstairs rooms had ceilings fourteen feet high, great rafters nearly black with age, and carved wooden grilles on the windows, set in walls that were six feet thick. "This part is old." Tandy still held on to Scotty. "Saracen. Look at the dentils."

"You're bloody daft." Scotty pulled his arm away and went to start unloading. Tandy stood there, forlorn.

It was the most comfortable place they had

been. The rooms were all large, the walls white, and the darkness and the thick walls made the place cool. It had been reconstructed as a traditional Catalán villa so carefully that it was hard to tell old from new. It had electricity, washing machines, seven indoor bathrooms, its own generator, carved, stained copies of old wooden shutters, a medieval crucifix huge on one wall, and a refrigerator that could have held an ox.

"Oh, moneymoneymoney." Irish Sister Maureen danced around the kitchen. "I'm going to light the stove. An Aga, I can't believe it."

Tandy was bringing in wood. "Well, all it says to me is that the owner was a Fascist, a snob about English gadgets, and is probably living right now in the West End of London, pretending to be a Spanish grandee." He had offered to get the wood for Sister Maureen and was following her around the large kitchen to tease her, which was his way of beginning to court her.

She smiled, hearing the words behind the words, and said affectionately, "Fuck off, Tandy. I'll put a kettle on. I've saved some tea for us."

Already Sister McCall had begun to order the setting-up of beds, the scrubbing of an operating room. All through the day she went on while people slept where they fell, mostly under the huge old trees weighted with branches and new leaves. A large lawn that turned into forest surrounded the house behind a long stone wall and hid the *camiones*. *Chóferes* slept on the cab seats; *camilleros* slept on their newly washed stretchers, still stained but clean again. They could hear Sister McCall's voice when they turned over and half woke.

By evening the villa was a hospital. They set up a refectory in the dining room, where a gaudy *torero* and life-size *picadores* on horseback marched around the walls.

One of the *chóferes,* from Glasgow, who was snerging around the grounds, found an underground crypt and took an ax and opened it. The Spanish *chóferes* said it was a family grave and they would be haunted. It was not. It was Aladdin's cave. "Look! Look! A bloody paranoid loot for a siege that didn't happen!" the *chófer* from Glasgow yelled, and they all woke and came running.

There were cans of food all the way to the crypt roof. The place was about twenty feet by twenty feet and had once been a wine cellar. Only a little wine was left, but the owner had been very fond of brandy. There were sardines in cans; there were great wheels of cheese and dried eggs and dried milk, and cured hams and dried fruit and grains, and smoked beef and chocolate, and a six-foot-square shelf of canned vegetables. There was English tea and South American coffee. Somebody murmured that it was like being in church. Then they were totally silent as treasure after treasure came out of the cave.

That night they had a feast. Everybody got a tin of sardines and some chocolate and bread and ham and one helping of vegetables and one cup of coffee. Then Sister McCall shut the door again and put a guard on it so she could mete out the supplies slowly. She said the crypt was provident.

Sister McCall was the life of the party. She talked too fast, laughed too hard, and bragged that they could take a full complement of wounded already, in one day. She said it twice more. Melinda saw Tye and Dr. Wimpy glance at each other, and Tye got up and whispered to him.

Dr. Wimpy stood and raised his brandy glass. "Sister McCall, I think that we should drink to the wonderful work that has been done today."

She stood too and drained her glass. One of the *camilleros* beside her glanced up at Dr. Wimpy and filled it again.

"Now, Sister McCall, you and I should drink to our staff, and to the wonderful *chicas* who have left their homes and what is left of their families to come with us."

Sister McCall said, "Hear hear!" and drained her glass. Dr. Wimpy hardly touched his to his lips. The *camillero* filled hers again.

"Now to the motor pool. Now to the *chóferes.*" Nobody moved except Dr. Wimpy and Sister McCall.

"Now, only one more toast. Everybody fill up."

They all stood. *"Viva la República!"*

Sister McCall shouted, *"Ole!,"* drained her glass, and passed out on the floor.

They carried her to an upstairs bedroom and laid her on the bed. "I had to do that," Dr. Wimpy said to the others. "She was running on empty."

Nothing happened. May turned to June, and still nothing happened. They waited. Two of the

Aussies planted a garden with seeds they had scrounged from a local farmer. Lettuce grew; tomato plants began to straggle, and they staked them up. Cucumber plants climbed a tree. "If one of you buggers takes one cucumber, we'll bloody do you, mates," the Aussies said, defending the garden as if it were their child.

Lovers too snatched time and tried to make it last. Tandy and Sister Maureen had retired from the others and were glimpsed behind the trees, lying on the grass bank of the little river that ran behind the huge grounds—half a mile away but still within the walls—and ended at a waterfall with a deep pond. Everyone at the hospital went to bathe in it, soaking off the winter, the scabies, and the nits.

Correspondents turned up, looking for stories to cover a war when there was no battle to write about, and offered them chocolate. Nobody said anything worth printing.

Melinda and Tye found a place to have their siesta together, in the room that had been made into a VIP bedroom. It was understood that it was their place when nobody was visiting and informing them about the war.

"Our first home," Melinda said, giggling. She was lying naked so the breeze could cool her through the dark slatted windows. "I could do without him staring at us." Tye got up and took the large oil portrait of King Alfonso from above the fireplace and set his face to the wall.

In the evening, at the time that would have been the *paseo*, they all strolled around the grounds, up and down the graveled paths, which were showing weeds that never would have been allowed in peacetime. Roses trailed along the ground.

Their faces began to get color again. The sores that they had battled all winter, sores from lack of food and from dirt, began to heal. The gauntness of the winter began to disappear.

Down the back road, beyond the stone wall, a stream of traffic moved into July, from bright red poppies beside the road, and unknown yellow flowers, and sweet grass, to dry dust and heavy-leaved gray-green olive trees. Within the magic compound, the old trees had long since drawn up the water level, and water still trickled down from the mountains, so the little river still flowed and the waterfall still danced. Soldiers who stopped by on their way to headquarters farther down the road toward the Ebro were brown and healthy from constant maneuvers outside the small Catalán villages, and indulging in their favorite off-duty sport, narking and complaining.

Tye and Melinda strolled with the others along the borders deep in flowers and tried to make themselves forget for a little while where they were.

"Something is going to happen. I know it." Tye had long since learned to separate rumor, which was rife, from possibility. "I hear that the French have opened the border, and that the Republican army is being resupplied. But I don't know. How can we know? There's a feeling of joy, and I don't know where it comes from. It's like a whisper from 1936, before all the death. I don't know."

"Why do you keep saying 'I don't know'?" Melinda looked up at him, and she saw that his eyes were glistening. Not with tears, though. He was looking ahead along the gravel path, but he wasn't seeing anything.

"Hope," he told the long line of pollarded trees. "You know, some people say that the last gift from Pandora's box was a curse."

"I hate that." Melinda was fierce with him because she was afraid in some unsaid way too.

Her English passport had come, with its diplomatic and humanitarian visas and another visa which seemed to be very flowery.

"He did a good job, didn't he?" Tye said. "The more stamps, the more impressive. Thank God for public schools."

"I feel like we are taking advantage—"

He stopped her then, and made her sit down on one of the self-consciously primitive stone benches under a large oak tree.

"Now, don't think I haven't thought about this, and worried about it, and finally faced it. If I could get something like this for every Republican Spaniard, to save them from their future, I would do it. But since I can't, I have pulled every string, used every handle that I can, to see that you are safe. Any man would do it." He sounded as if he were trying and failing to convince himself. He watched the ground, his arms on his knees. "I went to school with the third secretary. He's the only one left at the embassy in Valencia. The rest keep going home for consultation—they're trying to get out of the bombing, but Freddie stayed. He's always been silly and brave, expects it of himself. Now I want you to strap this next to your body. Now tell me again what your directions are."

They had done it over and over since the retreat had begun in late February. It had become a game.

"All right." She laughed. "Señora López at 33 San Miguel in Figueres, and I will know it by the old mural of Christ on the corner of the building. Hers is the balcony with the birdcage. There are stairs up to her apartment over a shop, and the stairs have white tiles with yellow flowers on the rises. I leave a mark on the fourth step so we won't compromise Señora López in case the rebels take the town."

"What kind of a mark?"

"A little moonface."

"Then?"

"I go west to Besalú, because the main road to the border will be clogged with refugees, and I look for Señor Díaz, who owns a wine shop and bar beside a square behind the church. It is down steps, and its terrace looks out over the river and the old bridge."

"He will be good to you, and he won't be afraid to take a message, and he will remember it. We have been friends for ten years." Tye had said all this over and over, but it seemed to comfort him.

"Then I go to Cardona, to Señora Zuda—"

"And let her son take you over the border at Puigcerdà."

"You won't ever let me finish. You just tell me over and over."

"I love you, you silly git," he said, still watching the trees as if they were going to march away.

The next day the idyll ended. They were ordered to a cave three miles from Mora la Nova. It was ten miles nearer the river and a thousand miles from the comfort of the villa. They made wards on two levels of the cave, one a room that was nearly fifty feet high and a second, on a ledge behind it, that was twenty feet high and caught the cold breathing of the deep corridors that disappeared into darkness.

On the night of July the twenty-third, Melinda finally, after all the work, stood alone for a minute in the black night at the entrance to the cave. She leaned against the rock wall, where vines were soft against her cheek. She was so tired she thought she was going to die. People had died that way, boys too young, men too old—they just lay down and died in the middle of things.

The night was noisy, but it was a rhythmic noise beyond the olive grove outside the cave, where the land was terraced down to the road. On the road below her, she could see, when she got used to the dark, the shadows of the *autochir*, the reception tents, and the triage tents, and she thought, What words cover. Oh my God. She sighed at the night and the time.

Rumors flew, and everybody was too tired to pay attention. There was only the steady movement of people on the low road just beyond the olive grove, and once in a while the complaint of a goat or a sheep and the barking of a dog. The refugees were flowing north again.

Away on the high road, beyond a cherry orchard and a vineyard, she could hear the *camiones* and, for the first time in months, men singing, *jóvenes* who had come to war with little suitcases, which they had had to throw away. There were *jóvenes* who had not yet shaved and whose faces were still sexless, and they sang, "We are going across the Ebro, ay Carmela." She listened, and then, nearly asleep on her feet, crawled into the cab of one of the *camiones* and tried to sleep. But there was no sleep, only dozing.

At about three o'clock in the morning she heard gunfire in the distance, just a small patter of gunfire, like a few drops of rain before a storm. The *camiones* never stopped, nor the marching along the high road. The refugees from Mora la Nova never stopped flowing north, all night long until the first dawn, when the first casualties were brought to the cave hospital.

It was the beginning of what they called later the battle of the Ebro, the bloodiest battle since Verdun. But they were not aware of big or small, or day or night. The cave was full of men—Republican troops and Moors and conscripts from the rebel territory, who were shaking with fear because they thought the Republicans would shoot them. "No, we are your brothers," the *camilleros* and the *chóferes* and the nurses told them, in whatever language they could find to try to make them understand.

Melinda worked with the *chicas* to clean them up. The rebel conscripts were as young as the

Republicans' own *jóvenes.* While Melinda was washing one of the boys, she thought how in peace men had a chance to get older and older and in war they got younger and younger, and suddenly she felt like vomiting. She was surprised that she did. But there was nothing to bring up; she hadn't eaten for too long.

Inside the cave the nurses' shadows grew like the shadow monsters that the early people, like the artists at Altamira, must have seen thrown huge onto the cave ceiling by their fires. Men came back who had crossed the wide Ebro in little boats, had run between strafings across the pontoon bridges that the engineers kept rebuilding and rebuilding as they were destroyed. But no ambulance could get across. They brought the wounded in the hot morning by donkey or on their own backs down to the south bank of the river, and the local fishermen and boaters rowed them across, as slowly and carefully as if they were not being attacked. Every time Tandy made it to the cave he kept talking about the little boats. He made it sound like some sort of peacetime picnic.

Somebody yelled, "This kid speaks nothing. Tandy, see if you can get to him." A thin Moroccan boy was cringing against the wall. He had a wound in his shoulder, and he was holding his hand over his genitals while the blood ran down his arm. Tandy ran through the half-dark and murmured "fuck" as he barked his shin on one of the iron beds.

He stood in front of the boy, bowed, held his palm to his heart and to his forehead, and said,

"Salaam aleikum." The boy stood up, made the same gesture, and answered, "Aleikum salaam." Then Tandy put his arm around the boy and spoke in Arabic.

After a minute he grinned. "He'll come with you now. The rebels told him that the Republicans would cut his balls off if they caught him. He has whip marks, new ones, on his back. That's discipline for the Moroccan mercenaries. This boy has probably never been out of his village before. Oh, by the way, this is the Cristo Rey he wears as an amulet against being wounded or killed. They told him it never failed." He motioned to the boy and spoke in Arabic again, and when the boy nodded, he put the medal in his pocket and said, "What a bloody silly war this is."

The Republicans had taken the first ten or eleven miles of territory south of the Ebro, which was, Tye said, not tomb enough nor continent to hide the slain, but then somebody told him to belt up. They had taken it in five days and they had won the war, for those five days. Even the air held ecstasy, and they knew that it had been right to keep their hopes.

Then the equipment began to slow like a river in summer, and dry up. The pact was back in force, and war materiel lay on the French side of the border. The soldiers stayed in Gandesa and the hills around it and held their small, quick gains for two months against the worst attacks of the war.

The German government sent more planes; the Italian government sent more tanks, more men, more guns. The Republican soldiers were pinned down around Gandesa while the rebels rearmed and got ready to sweep them away like dust in the way of their banners.

"Oh, shit," Tye said in the night when he told Melinda that Tandy had been killed at Gandesa. He held her close under one of the olive trees. "I've got to get you out of here . . ." He had brought back the Cristo Rey and put it in her hand.

In the first week of September, Tye went across the Ebro by boat as usual. It was the only time, he said, that he enjoyed, just the water flowing and once in a while blessed silence and the smell of night and vines. He went back to his forward post as a *practicante,* as he had over and over during the weeks of August, while the vineyards that were their protection were destroyed and the olive trees were blasted into stumps and the sharp rocks of the escarpments they were holding grew hell-hot in the sun. There was no place to dig in. The soldiers cursed the rock hills by numbers, not by the old names they had had for centuries.

Tye left at midnight, and Melinda was too busy to say goodbye. It had happened often, but he found her and kissed what he called her dear dirty face, and he was gone into the night, where they had to hide from the moon.

He didn't come back. Nobody could tell her if they had seen him. They began to avoid her, and she stopped asking and just waited, aware sometimes, when she didn't keep herself on the run with work, that waiting was a hollow thing.

On the twenty-third of September, Negrín, the

Republican prime minister, finally withdrew the survivors of the International Brigades to shame the democracies into stopping the hemorrhaging of Spain. The *chóferes* who came back from Barcelona said they had never seen so many people crying as when the ragged men straightened up and marched down the Rambla, knee-deep in fields of thrown flowers. It was the last gasp of joy or sorrow or any other thing except the prayer that it would all be over.

The medical unit was ordered to move farther north, to a castle with a moat full of rats. Near the village of Vallverd, they were assigned to a farmhouse. The farmer and his wife and their nine children moved into the barn. All the children were under fifteen. The eldest, sixteen, was with the army. Nobody talked very much. The excitement of the months before drained out of their faces and their minds.

At the farmhouse, most of the wounded were civilians who had been strafed along the roads north, toward France. The strafing never let up during the daylight hours. Some of the wounded said they could see the pilots' faces. They were not evil. A woman discussed this with Melinda, who was trying to get a name, which the woman was afraid to give.

"They didn't look very interested. We were just in their way."

Melinda's deadened senses made her efficient, and she could listen and mark down, bandage and comfort, and not think about it. Compassion was automatic. At night, when she could snatch a few hours' sleep in the hayloft of the barn, she told the raw wooden rafters that she would know if Tye were dead.

In three days they were ordered to move again, to a half-bombed schoolhouse that had not been finished before the war began. There was something more poignant about that building than any of the others they had made into hospitals. The others were old and had been there through centuries, but the schoolhouse was new, a frail Republican symbol. The proud whitewash was streaked with rain and dirt. The desks had long since gone for firewood.

They were moved again, nearer the border. On the way through the twisted mountain roads, rain-slick and growing colder and colder until the rain turned to snow and sleet, they stopped at the large American hospital at Vic, and Melinda ate decent food for the first time in weeks and begged five ten-gallon cans of gasoline from a *chófer* she knew. He threw in an extra tire. She had calculated how much gas she would need to get to Cardona if they were told to move again.

They were no longer going anyplace but north. They joined the refugee trains. She and her own group of walking wounded, and the fourteen-year-old *camillero*, Jose, who had been assigned to her, hid the gasoline under a pile of spare parts and blankets that they had picked up along the road.

On the day before Christmas, they met for the last time, in an abandoned railway tunnel, which they sheltered in for the night and the next day from a storm. Even though it was noon, it was dark in the tunnel. It smelled of burning gasoline from the lamps, which had to stay lit all day, and the Primus stove, on which the nurses were still trying to sterilize instruments. They worked by rote and cursed the wet wind and the drops of icy water that fell from the condensation on the tunnel ceiling.

Refugees had joined them, and at night the blankets they clung to looked like a vast bright quilt in the lamplight. They slept together, close, as if other bodies would protect them and keep them warm. The nurses made a path between them, and in the night children flung out their arms as they slept. Melinda and the others stepped over them carefully.

There were only ten people from the hospital staff of ninety—what was left of the *chóferes,* the *camilleros,* the nurses, the *practicantes.* Some were dead, they didn't know who; some had been separated from the core, led by Dr. Wimpy.

Then Dr. Wimpy made the nurses come away from the stretchers they used for cots. He stood there for a minute. He was, as usual, immaculate, his uniform clean, his face shaved. But his eyes were sunk in his face, and he had sores around his mouth that would not heal. A drop of icewater fell on Melinda's head, and she brushed it away. It was hard to remember things, and her stomach hurt. She wondered if she were pregnant.

She made herself pay attention to what Dr. Wimpy was saying. He had finally made himself speak, and most of what he said they already knew.

"Franco has started his last move across the Segre. No. That's not what I ought to say. Hitler has started his move across the Segre from the west, and has reinforced the army moving up from the south across the Ebro. You must know this. Now. We have decided to disband. The nurses will go with the badly wounded. The *chóferes* and the *chicas* and the dogsbodies who know their first aid will take the walking wounded, who can help them.

"We will take the wounded, as many as we can, in the vehicles we have left. The others we have arranged to leave in what village houses are standing. We will go north slowly to the French border and regroup on the French side. There are several ways into France, and those of us who have medical visas will have no trouble. Try to take as many Spaniards with you as want to go. Some of our people can never go back to their villages—there is nothing there.

"Teresa will go in my car, with four wounded and a *chófer.* We cannot leave her to the Moors. She has no home, and her *novio* is dead. My wife and I have decided to adopt her and let her train as a nurse, a theater sister, when we get back. She is a natural-born nurse." There was a little spatter of applause, a faint echo of exhausted hands.

"On the way, you must look after the wounded from the strafing. I am told that there are already people clogging the roads for seventy or eighty miles. You will only be able to go at walking pace. Pick up whoever can cling to your vehicles. The last rations we have—bully beef, hardtack, and tins of beans and milk—will be divided equally among you. Make it last—share it, but make it last. Avoid Barcelona. That is all. Sister McCall will give you the assignments that we have worked out."

He turned away, and then turned back. "Oh." He was still for a long time, and Melinda heard him mutter, "Hard. It's so hard." Then he called out, "We have learned to work together and loved each other and our fellow men. Take that with you. And the gates of hell shall not prevail against us."

His voice broke and he stopped. He thrust his way through the crying men and women, and he looked at Melinda with some surprise. "I can't believe I said that," he whispered in wonder at himself. "You see, my father is a Plymouth Brother. We loathe each other."

The van had to be abandoned. Not even Melinda could make it go. Then a miracle: she found an abandoned car on the side of the road beyond the railroad, where so many had passed and jettisoned so much. It was an English Ford shooting brake, a station wagon, with wooden sides and leather seats, with scars and tears on the leather of the back seats where dogs had pawed them, impatient to be out of the car. At least she liked to think of it, for a restful minute, that way.

She opened the hood to see what was wrong. It had only run dry of oil and out of gas. She smiled, for the only time during the evacuation, and thanked God for people who abandoned machines when they ceased to work. For a minute she wondered where it had come from. She could see it on some estate, given like discarded clothes to the Cause. After all, Tye had said, there are Liberal landowners in England. Then he had laughed. The tears rushed into her eyes, but, annoyed, she brushed them and the thought they had brought away.

The car would hold at least eight humans. It was another list in her head—eight humans, one driver, English right-hand drive. She liked that. It would mean that she could watch down the treacherous icy mountain roads if she had to drive where Tye had told her to go.

By the time she had driven a mile, she had filled the car. There were three walking wounded, Jose, five refugees, all women with children in their laps—ten refugees, she thought, correcting the list in her head. The sleet turned to rain again, the rain to sleet, the sleet to snow, and the little group in Melinda's Ford grew as close as lovers, or, she thought, as kings on the mountain, repelling boarders from the mass of slowly trudging people, black against the snow. They moved slowly up the hill roads as far as she could see. She drove at walking pace. There was no other way. Women and children with their animals walked almost against the sides of the car, to get its shelter from the cold.

By noon the snow was heavy in the fields, but the people trod it down in the road. The line of figures behind her in her rearview mirror disappeared in snowfall. Something ahead stopped the column, as wide as the road—soldiers and old people and women and children, all simply facing north and walking. The incident, whatever it was, caused a ripple of stopping along the column.

Melinda switched off the engine to save fuel. She refused to think that they might be hit by the strafing planes that screamed and whistled through the snow overhead.

Then there was silence. The planes had gone back to their airfields while they could still land, and men and women huddled close against the car and put their hands on the warm hood.

One woman pounded on the door, and Melinda told Jose to say there was no more room. The woman fell to the ground. People formed a circle and were trying to shelter her. Melinda got out to see if she could help.

The woman lay in the snow, which made the blanket they held over her head white. Someone had put her blanket over her. Melinda called back to Jose, "Get some blankets from the back. She is having a baby."

The baby came easily; the woman groaned for the last time and then smiled. "Born in Spain. He was born in Spain."

One of the walking wounded, a young boy, said he knew where they were and he would head for the mountains, maybe Montserrat. The woman hoisted herself and her baby into his seat. She said the baby was her fourth and all the rest were dead, but she didn't say any more. She just gazed at the child as if a miracle had happened. Then she nursed it and went to sleep.

Cars and bodies littered the roadside as the darkness came, and Melinda decided that they had to rest while they were safe for a little while from the *aviones*. But before she slept, she took her siphon and drained the tanks of abandoned cars and filled one of the cans she had been given in Vic.

It was nearly dawn before she could sleep. The whole world seemed to have grown completely silent, except for the breaking of branches in the pine forest where she had parked the car.

They lit a fire and shared what little food there was, and the men melted snowwater to warm the engine and to fill the four canteens they had picked up by the road. Melinda simply sat, watching the dawn come, too numb to think of anything except silly splatterings of memory from a thousand years ago. She was jumping her horse, and he was flying over a fence, and then she woke and dawn was breaking over the Pyrenees and already in the distance there was the drone of the *aviones*.

They gave the front seat to the new mother and to an old woman who had trudged across the meadow beyond the pine wood and simply climbed into the cab and refused to move. She had grown very small with age, and her little seagull eyes stared straight ahead at the road.

People gathered close to the car and walked along beside it as if it were some kind of home or campfire. They had found barns to rest in, and a farmer and his wife had taken some of them in by the fire and fed them. Melinda was sure it had been pork.

Nobody spoke for hours on end. They walked, and when the planes came they scattered under the screaming into the gorse and the ditches. Jose insisted that they take back roads to Figueres, and even on those there were people, but not so many, not that steady, road-wide ribbon of people.

It took two more days to drive the thirty miles left to Figueres. There were bodies by the roadside and in the fields, left with the rest of the jettisoned treasures. Melinda picked up a snapshot of a dog, a silly-looking dog that had probably already been eaten and mourned.

Outside Figueres, they slept on a hill away from a meadow crowded with people. Jose had found a goat path and driven the car up under an outcrop of rock for shelter. The people in the car had been together for nearly two weeks. In that vast anonymity, they had begun to like and even dislike each other. Melinda could speak so little to them that she could only watch their arguments, their friendships, and their ever-present manners. The young mother, whose name was Ana María, had named her son Buenaventura, after the Republic, and Francisco, after her favorite saint, and Juan, after his father, whom she had not heard from for five months. She had told all this to Jose as they gossiped around their fire. They had all told about themselves, as if they were trying to establish the dignity of belonging somewhere.

On the hillside, the fire turned blue in the rising sun. They had gathered around to eat what was left of the bully beef, a spoonful for each person, a sip of water, when one of the women called out from the car. She had tried to rouse the old woman, but the old woman was dead, had just drifted off. The men lifted her out of the cab. They buried her at dawn in a shallow trench in the hard rocky ground and covered her with rocks. Melinda gave the baby the old woman's blanket.

In the meadow beyond them, crowds of wanderers had made nomad homes around their fires and were huddling there before they had to move again—thousands of them, all in the same kinds of small groups as what Melinda thought of as her own. All across the gorse bushes brightly colored clothes were hanging to dry, the women still domestic in their flight, trying to keep their families clean. A man held his son's bare feet to the fire and rubbed them gently, as if he were thinking of something else. The boy, who looked about ten, was still drowsing. It was a moment of peace, too early for the *aviones.*

The snow sparkled under the bright sun and the crisp blue sky of winter. Some of the little groups began to sing in the distance, and the sound drifted toward Melinda. It was the first time she had heard singing since the exodus had begun. They were beyond fear for a little while, and only glad of the morning.

Figueres was a solid mass of people, from a mile outside the town into the streets—the end of a three-mile queue of soldiers and refugees who waited to go across the border into France. Jose said he would go into town and see what he could find to eat. Word had drifted from group to group that the Quakers had set up a soup kitchen. The women and children and the walking wounded followed him to stretch their legs and find food.

Melinda knew she had to stay by the car to protect it until they came back. The small clutches of people in the meadow, huddled by the last of the fires, which sent thin smoke toward the sky, were polite and dignified. They moved slowly. As far away as Melinda could see, some of the women were gathering the clothes, which were stiff with cold. But they, like herself, were survivors, and if she left the car, she knew that they would do what she would do—steal it.

She watched her friends thread their way through the crowded meadow. Ana María had insisted on taking the baby, which she would not let out of her arms. The other five women and their half-grown children had made their own familiar village as they moved north, and they walked together.

Melinda watched until they disappeared into the mass that clogged the road to the town center. Figueres had already been bombed over and over. The snaggled buildings she had grown so used to were familiar. There were still the narrow streets in the distance, dark with bodies, dark with ruins, under the bright winter sun and the indifferent blue sky.

She stood there, letting the sun warm her, not hoping, not despairing, just breathing and aware of being alive—no past, no future; a moment in the sun.

At first she was not aware of the hand that had taken hers. Then she began to feel the warmth. She looked down. It was a child. She thought it was a girl, but she wasn't quite sure. Like so many of the others, it had eyes that were enormous from lack of food. The black hair was cut close to the child's head. Somebody had been taking care to keep it clean and neat. The face had been washed. The skin was still pink from the scrubbing. She thought it had been washed in snow. A man's anorak that came down to the child's ankles and a man's sweater worn under it were clean. There were even laced-up shoes, when so many of the other children were barefoot in the snow. They were peasant *botines,* with thick socks under them.

The child said nothing, did not smile, did not stop looking at Melinda. A lost child, Melinda thought quickly, and she waved toward the crowds in the meadow. "Papá?" she asked. "Mamá?" she asked. The child didn't make a sound—no words, no crying. Melinda walked close to the fire, and she did not let go. She had chained herself to Melinda with one small hand.

The *aviones* came over, some so low that Melinda could see the faces of the pilots, faces of boys obeying orders, almost bored. Away in the distance, the castle where so many of the International Brigades had first reported was taking hit after hit, but the sound was far away. She could see the geysers of smoke and rock.

The planes were bombing and strafing the town, the crowds of people in the streets. Even so far away there were screams. Smoke rose over Figueres. Melinda and the strange child waited under an overhang of rock. Some of the crowds from the meadow huddled with them.

Only Jose came back. The others had taken shelter in an open *refugio.* There had been a direct hit. Melinda found herself crying at last. There was one thing she had to do, and she told Jose that she had to do it: leave a message for Tye. He had told her to. Jose could see that there was no use arguing; she seemed frantic, and it was the first time he had seen her that way.

The child would not let go of her hand to stay with Jose, but hung on tighter and tighter, even when Jose tried to pull the hand away. The expression never changed. He said the *niño* or *niña* had been shocked to dumbness. Melinda had to take her with her.

The *rambla* in the middle of Figueres was a charnel house. Most of the people who had gathered there had been killed. Melinda had heard of blood flowing in the gutters, but she had not seen it before. It made so little difference to her that later she was shocked at herself.

People huddled in doorways, as if they could go no farther. Some of the wounded had been carried into a cafe and laid on the floor. They were calling for water, their mothers. The child's hand gripped tighter, and Melinda turned into the side street she had been looking for. She kept repeating to herself, Tiles on the stairs with yellow flowers, a mural of Christ, a birdcage on the balcony, as if any bird or any cage could survive what was happening to Figueres. She and the child stepped over people who were either dead or so exhausted they had slept through the bombing. She kept telling herself, Thirty minutes. Thirty minutes. It was the time between raids. The targets were as used to it as any other time, dawn, twilight.

She found the house. The street was completely empty, like a sudden pause in the shifting of a storm. There were the stairs, as polished as Tye had said they would be, but the balcony had been hit, and there was no birdcage and no Señora López. Her apartment was empty. Food was still on the table, but had been there long enough for the mice and rats to have eaten into the cheese and the bread. Melinda and the child grabbed what was left and ate it.

Melinda had kept one of her colored pencils for the charts and had guarded it all the way from the Ebro. She had checked her pocket over and over, in a small panic, which nobody noticed, to be sure she hadn't forgotten it, or dropped it, or lost it. On the fourth step from the bottom of the flowered stair, down in the corner, she drew a tiny round face with crossed eyes and pointed ears, the kind a child would draw.

It was easier to get back to the car. They ran through the side streets. When they got back, Jose tried, in his limited English, to tell her that she had to keep on going north. North was *libertad.* North was safe.

Melinda explained as well as she could that her husband had told her to go to Cardona, to the west, and she was going to meet him there. Jose took her arms in both hands. *"Tye está muerto,"* he cried to her, and shook her. "You come with me, *Tye está muerto,"* but she kept shaking her head, almost numb. He was crying and she was quite calm. She watched Jose go slowly down through the meadow, cross into the road, and disappear.

Before they got into the car, the child made a motion and pointed to the rock wall behind them, but she, or he, would not let go, so Melinda went too, and helped take down the men's underpants, which were tied with thick rope. It was a girl. She squatted without any embarrassment, and the little stream of peepee made Melinda smile.

It was when they turned west that the people who had clamored to get into the car abandoned it, at the first crossroad beyond the city. They were like lemmings being herded in the wrong direction, and Melinda had to let them out.

Along the road to the west they passed fewer people, all going east and north. They looked at Melinda as if she were mad, but she had to do what Tye had told her. She knew she was following him and that he would be waiting for her at Besalú, where Diego Díaz had his cafe.

There was no clown sign on the doorjamb at the cafe, but when she went inside, Diego welcomed her with a slow hug that she couldn't break free of. He had had a letter from Tye, but it had been sent before he had disappeared beyond the Ebro in September. Melinda told Diego that Tye was coming after her, and didn't tell him any more. When he looked at the little girl, she said, "I don't know her. She won't let go."

There was little to eat, because the refugees going northeast had combed the town, but Diego found a glass of wine and some beans, and when Melinda drank the wine it made her so dizzy that she had to lay her head down on the thick wood table. When she woke up, the little girl was still clinging to her hand. She had already grown so used to it that she hardly registered the small pressure of the child's fingers.

She forgot where she was, and thought she might have been asleep in one of the caves. She was under a vaulted roof with iron-colored beams the size of tree trunks, and Diego was beaming at her from across the table.

"Stay here," he said. "You are exhausted, and you must sleep inside, where you are warm." He took her arm.

"No. I have to go." Melinda tried to pull away from him.

"Then think of the child," he said.

They slept together at Diego's, behind the bar, on a feather bed he brought from his house. He explained that he could not take them home because the house was completely full of his and his wife's families, who had come from the west, but they had tripled up so that one feather bed would be free.

The child did not let go of Melinda's hand, even after she drifted off and the rest of her body grew peaceful in its trusting abandonment. Melinda slept deeply, and when she woke, the child had either kept her hand clutched all night or had wakened first and clutched it again. They went to the toilet together, and Melinda smiled and made the signs of affection she had learned to make when she did not know enough Spanish, her own deaf-and-dumb language. The little girl pointed to her own ears to show that she could hear, and smiled back.

By the time Diego returned, it was getting dark

outside. They had slept for eighteen hours. Melinda could hear Tye calling her, but she couldn't say so. She got back into the car, which Diego's son had watched all night, and by six o'clock they were on the road west again, only the two of them. She had to drive with one hand. The little girl would not let go.

It was so early in the evening that the snow-capped Pyrenees gleamed almost red in the twilight. There was not a sound except the crunch of their tires on the road. The moon rose, full and almost as bright as day. When she got to Olot, she looked for the caryatids. "Remember," Tye had said, "the caryatids that Tandy made me see when he gave me an interminable lecture on Catalán modernism."

She found the house, with its wonderful swirls below the balcony, its stately, silly caryatids watching the refugees sleeping in the square and in the doorways. She knew there would be a sign from Tye there. She was convinced of it. But there was no little clown face. So she made one on the right buttock of the right-hand caryatid.

The little girl slept as if there were no trouble in the world, all the way across the mountains under the moon, the bomber's moon that meant Melinda did not have to turn on her lights. Her hand was still tight in Melinda's.

There was nobody on the road. Melinda could see campfires in the meadows, some near the road, where the faces of people trying to stay warm were pink in the light. Most of them held children in their laps and massaged their feet, as she had seen the man do at Figueres.

She drove all night through the silent mountains under the moon. If she prayed—and she was hardly aware of that—it was that the car would not break down, that her last two cans of gasoline would get her to Cardona, where she was certain there would be a message from Tye. She could see ahead the warmth of Señora Zuda's fire and hear the people singing as they had at her wedding. Her head felt light and her body floated in the night, and she concentrated on the white road ahead, over a high pass, down into a valley with a lake which was already beginning to show the faint echo of the mountains on its dark surface. The mountains, veil behind veil, grew lighter and lighter, and she didn't know where she was except that she was going west, and she was sure that if she made a mistake on the road, Tye would tell her. He had explained that the road between the old cities had been used for many centuries. Phoenicians, Roman legionnaires, Saracens, Christians, all of them. She could almost hear them tramping in the night. She did not dare to let herself be afraid. But the world was indifferent, with silence and mountains and still water, and not a living soul passed.

He had said to go southwest after Olot, and to follow the river flow. She carefully stopped the car when the little girl was asleep and had let go of her hand at last. She bent down and touched the freezing water and let it flow through her fingers to be sure she wasn't going in the wrong direction, and when she got back into the car, the little girl was awake again and grabbed for her hand, her eyes dead with fear. The physical connection seemed to be all she cared about. There were no tears, just the dignity of a still face.

At dawn the planes began to fly over them again, on the way east and north. She drove along under them, too tired to look up. They interrupted the peace of the morning. Then, to the south, ahead of her, she saw the glittering salt hill, and she tried to remember who it was who turned back in the Bible. But she was too tired, and she knew that Tye was waiting for her at Señora Zuda's house, and that if she could only get there she would be safe and warm.

She drove into the empty plaza of Cardona, with its windows with their green blinds drawn against the winter and the snow that had drifted around the trees. She parked the car. Then, after looking all the way around the plaza and then along the road through the town archway, she lifted the hood, took off the distributor cap, took the rotor out and put it in her pocket, and replaced the distributor cap.

The little girl took all of this for granted. Melinda had begun talking to her, partly to hear a voice, partly to have someone to talk to, even though the child couldn't have understood a word.

"Look, a fairy castle." She pointed up to the heights where the *jóvenes* and the prisoners had been, but even from such a distance, it too looked empty. There was nobody on sentry duty against the morning sky.

Together they walked through the arch by the

church and along the street Melinda knew so well. The shops were all shut, the morning hardly begun. There were only little sounds—a child being called, a goat bleating to be milked, a donkey whickering.

Señora Zuda opened the door and looked horrified to see her. She took her and the little girl into her big arms and led them into the house. She spoke to the child in Spanish and then in Catalán. The child said nothing, but did politely put out her other hand for the lady to shake.

"Tye?" Melinda couldn't remember the word for "here," the word for anything. She was afraid she was going to faint. Señora Zuda called deep into the house after she had led Melinda and the little girl to the fire and helped them shed their clothes. She looked appalled at the sores on Melinda's arms, and Melinda apologized in English—"We all have scabies. They don't heal very quickly"—and fell dead asleep. The last thing she heard was Señora Zuda calling deep into the back of the house, "Miguel, Miguel!"

The child slept beside her, still holding her hand. When they woke, Señora Zuda watched both of them eat, and long before they had had enough, she took the plates away and said something to Miguel, the youngest son, who was standing there waiting for her to tell him what to say. He had learned his English, starting when he was twelve, by helping his older brothers guide the International Brigades across the mountains.

It was late in the morning. The sun was threading its way through the plants that Señora

Zuda kept in the window to remind her of summer.

"She say you have car?" Miguel asked.

"Yes, I have a car. Where is Tye?"

"She have letter in what month I forget English name, maybe three months ago, say when if you get here first you fuck off to France at Puigcerdà. She say you go right away."

"Where is everybody? Where are the soldiers?"

"Everybody fuck off. She say I go with you, show you the way. The shit rebel army is at the Segre and they are only two, three mountains away. She say you fuck off right now and I go with you and show you the way, and then I will join the *guerrilleros.*" He looked happy about this.

"Will she come with us?" Melinda remembered the words for "come" and "please" and "darling." She said them all, and took Señora Zuda's arm, and Señora Zuda smiled at her, that wonderful sunlit smile that transformed her square hard face. She said something.

"She wait for sons," Miguel said.

But she did follow them to the car and stuffed the back with blankets, a large sausage as hard as rock and smelling so that it threatened to make Melinda sick, bread she had baked while Melinda slept, and a large goatskin of wine. She watched Melinda put the rotor back, and she watched them all the way through the town gate, and walked out beyond it to keep on watching until Melinda couldn't see her any longer in the rear-view mirror.

They drove to the north, and the brilliant sun warmed them in the car and made the sausage smell even more. In the night they slept in the car outside of La Molina, so deep in the mountains that they could no longer see the veils of mountain ranges, only the heart of the mountains, the Cadí, the tiny valley, the evergreens, the towering slides of rock and snow.

On the day they got to La Molina, they crawled along, so high that the road was slick again from ice, which the sun was melting. They were going north again and they had rejoined the refugees, who stepped aside when the car pushed through them. By the time they arrived at the plaza, the car was so full that they had to turn people away. It hardly mattered to Melinda. She was beyond the luxury of grieving over those she couldn't take. She was simply going north. She clung to the little girl's hand. The pressure had changed. Her own hand pressed the child's for warmth.

Melinda found the cafe that Tye had told her to go to. There was bad news. The proprietor, Monsieur Rodin, was very sorry, but he had to tell her that when he had received Tye's letter in September, he had had no way to tell him that the Collada de Tosses was closed to cars for the winter.

"Madame, my dear," he said, "it is the worst pass in the Pyrenees, even in summer. The Collada de Tosses. It is so bad that they say here that if you want to get rid of an enemy, throw him over the side of the Collada and he will never be found. But there is a footpath that has been made by the refugees. Oh, madame darling, you are so tired. I cannot let Monsieur Tye's wife start the walk to Puigcerdà without a good day and night of sleep and food. No. No. I will not let you go yet. Perhaps Monsieur Tye will come tonight. Perhaps he is following you." He persuaded her as if she were a child, and it comforted her.

She and the little girl slept in a bed. "Are you sure this won't get you into trouble?" was the last question she needed to ask before she could succumb.

"Cierto!" He laughed. "I am an innkeeper, not a *político*. Everybody likes me. I am also the mayor of the town, because nobody else knows the skiers as I do. Anyway, I am a French citizen as well as a Spanish citizen, but neither country knows about the other. Now you sleep and sleep and I feed you carefully, and the little girl, and I will prepare a document to get her across the border with you."

When his wife brought them breakfast the next morning, she said, "Eat slowly, will make you sick if you eat fast, madame darling. Here is the document that my husband has prepared for you."

It was beautiful. It had ribbons and seals with crests, and a large mayoral seal and several others she was sure he had made up. One of them, thrust into the soft red wax, said "1 liter."

"It is worth damn nothing," he told her later in the morning, "but it says in French and in Spanish and in English that the little girl has been adopted by you and Monsieur Tye. But who reads English and French at the border, and who cares? I wish this war would be over soon.

My business is terrible. You know my nephew taught the nephew of General Franco to ski."

Two mornings later Tye had not come. Melinda was beginning to know that he wouldn't, but she thrust that thought aside as too heavy to bear. Miguel was still waiting when they came down to breakfast. He had gone to his cousins, who taught skiing, and had slept well, and had packed a backpack of food. He had brought blankets from the car, which they slung over their shoulders. The last thing she saw when she turned on the path above the town was the Ford shooting brake, with bullet holes she hadn't noticed in the scarred wooden sides, parked in front of Monsieur Rodin's *posada.* She had given it to him.

They climbed up the winding path made by the feet of animals and people, who stretched away, a straggling black line in the snow. When they reached the top of the pass, they could see the black line for miles, across the mountains and down into the gorge below them. They passed people curled up beside the path in the snow, just dark bundles, and Melinda assured the little girl that they were only asleep, to keep her from being afraid.

They walked eleven miles along the pass, and when they stopped to rest, the world below them was a terrifying chasm of white snow and jagged rocks, black lines of people, more bundles asleep by the path. Once the child fell, and Melinda and Miguel grabbed her. There was no danger, with the mounds of snow on both sides of the path, but it made Melinda shiver with horror and cold as they went on through the last mountain pass. Miguel was carrying the little girl on his back. She slept on his shoulder, but she still held Melinda's hand. Every time Melinda tried to take it away, she woke up.

The border crossing was a bottleneck of thousands of figures. It was a huge black field that moved and breathed in the valley of Puigcerdà. Senegalese soldiers and border guards were patting down Spaniard after Spaniard in the long lines that had formed. Miguel put the child down. "I leave you here," he told Melinda. "I go another way. I have a cousin." He smiled and was gone before she could thank or hug him.

They waited for four hours in the long queue. At the border, her passport and the child's document got them waved through by the overwhelmed guards. A pile of personal belongings—a camera, some guns, one ancient hunting rifle, half a doll—lay in a head-high pile by the road on the French side.

It was almost evening when they finally walked, free, into the street beyond the flowing mass of people. Melinda heard a voice in English. "Are we in France, madame?" It was the little girl. She stood there stiff with politeness. She had let go of Melinda's hand. While people still swirled and pushed around them, she said, "My father told me not to say anything until we got to France, and not to release your hand."

"You come here." Melinda hugged her, and they walked down the road away from the crowd. She found a bare rock to sit on and pulled the little girl down beside her. "Now, who are you, darling?"

"My name is María Dolores, María for my mother and Dolores for my father's mother. I was born in 1932. I am six years old. I'll be seven in December. I speak English and French. My father taught my mother and me. He said we would be useful to the Front Populaire. He is the English teacher at the boys' school in Madrid."

Once she had started, she couldn't stop. She nestled next to Melinda and prattled on as if they were not sitting on a cold bare rock, and all in the same voice she told about horror and family and home. "I know I have an accent," she apologized, "but my father said we would go to England someday and it would be better to learn there."

"How did you find me?" Melinda managed to stop the flow long enough to ask.

"We saw you at Figueres. My mother and my brother died at your hospital in Albastro. You gave me soup. My father saw you standing by the automobile, and he recognized you. He found some paper on the side of a building, a wall that had been bombed, and half a sign warning about venereal disease was flapping and he tore it off and wrote a letter to you. Here is the letter."

She felt deep in her pocket and took out a crumpled piece of a brightly colored wall poster. On the back her father had written,

Dear madame,

You were kind to us at Albastro when my wife was hurt. I am relying on your kindness to take my child into France with you. I beg you. I will try to find you on the French side. If you will leave your address where I can find you at the École des Beaux Arts in Paris, where there is my friend Monsieur Borgan, I will be in your debt forever. María is all that is left of my family. Thank you. God bless you. *Viva la República.*

The words trailed off, wet with his tears, so that Melinda could not read the name. Then the writing started again.

María my dearest, you know that there is more than one mother. There was your own beloved birth mother, and then there is always the Mother of God, who looks after us. Now this is your new *madre.* Not for always; I will find you. Be good, and remember that you are Spanish. My love and prayers, Papá.

María hid her head in Melinda's coat and cried, but not for long. She seemed to remember something that made her stop. "My father says," she said, "that we must face the truth always. I think you should know that you made a mistake about the people who were lying beside the path over the mountain. They were not asleep. They were dead. I'm sorry I must tell you this, but it is best."

They could hear the planes coming closer, across the border beyond Puigcerdà. The planes wheeled over the town, and explosion and smoke and snow filled the air on the Spanish side of the border. Then they were gone, and the snow began to fall again on the clotted crowd of refugees waiting in line, on their heads and on their coats, on the newly dead, and in the trees around them. Snow and fog, the blessings of war, protectors of the innocent moving targets from the hostile air, began to blot out their terrible distant voices, some crying, some cursing, all of them huddled together as if they were trying to bring Spain across the border with them.

Along the road, under the snow-laden trees, Melinda could hear the rattle of some sort of car with chains. She stood, ready to wave down a lorry, anything that might take her on to the last stop, to Tye.

It was a Jaguar touring car, long and elegant and gleaming. It was full of skiers, two young men and two young women. Melinda stepped back. They were so sleek and so warm that she felt like a beggar on the side of the road. But they stopped.

The young woman who was driving called, "*Aller?* Oh, Christ, I'm sure I got it wrong." She had an earth-owning, West End of London accent that cut the air, and Melinda had never been so glad to hear anything.

All Melinda could say was, "Château des Filles."

"*Entrez.* How the devil do I say we're going there, too?"

Melinda and María huddled together in the back seat of the car, trying to keep as far as they could from the bright clean ski clothes of the couple sitting next to them.

"My God, darling, they hardly look like they are going to the Château!" The skiers talked to each other, taking for granted that Melinda knew no English. "Well, anyway, that's what she said."

Melinda and María passed into a new land, where even the country was different, at peace.

Snowplows had opened the resort towns; the tops of evergreen trees stuck up above the drifts. They drove along a road that in places was almost a tunnel through the snow. They were half unconscious when they drew up to the front of the hotel.

It rose five stories high above the crest of a hill behind the small town of Fille Marie. It had a façade of curled fronds and caryatids, and in the distance a fountain, with a dryad or a goddess that in the summer would have been protecting her genitals with her delicate hand from a shower of water but in the winter seemed to cringe from the snow that had filled the large basin below her. There was such silence after the young woman turned off the engine that Melinda was almost afraid to move. They waited. She waited.

Then she made herself get out of the car, and María crawled after her. Melinda said, "Thank you very much. Your Jaguar is beautiful. But your sparks want cleaning."

"I say!" One of the young men left his mouth open after he spoke, and María said seriously to the young lady who was driving, "You should say *Ou voulez-vous aller?*, not just *aller.* I like your hair. It is very chic."

They walked into the marble lobby, which was as clean as a dream, and they wanted to cringe away from their own smell. Women walked around them as if they were not there, through the lobby and down into a glassed-in room filled with winter sun, where there were small rococo tables and a light murmur of conversation—no words, just murmur. The receptionist was ready to come around the desk and usher them out when Melinda found the words.

"I am Mrs.. . . *Je m'appelle Madame Dunston.*"

The young man changed from ogre to fairy in front of her eyes. He was arch, he was apologetic, he was professionally ecstatic. "Welcome, madame. Your mother is waiting for you. Let me call her. You stay here."

She thought for a terrible minute that her mother was indeed there, out of place and time, but it was not her mother. It was a stranger who came toward her.

She was a small woman, not much taller than Melinda. She wore an old felt hat pulled down around her ears, a large sweater, and a kilt, lisle stockings, and ghillies. Her hair stuck out from under the hat as if she had forgotten a long time ago that it existed.

"Now isn't that just like men?" she exclaimed. "Tye didn't tell you what I looked like. Come, my dearest child." She took Melinda by one hand and María by the other and called to the still bowing and scraping receptionist, "Which room? You have saved the room beside me as I told you to?"

"Yes, Lady Dunston, of course. It has been ready for a month."

She prattled on to cover the shock and the silence on the way up in the mirrored elevator. "Darlings"—she included María—"oh, this is a miracle. I got a letter from Tye in late September, and he gave me instructions about what to do. He said that one or both of you would meet me here—of course I thought he meant himself, too—and if you did not arrive by spring I was to go home. Really! So I brought money for you, and I would have brought you some clothes but my idiot child didn't tell me what you looked like, except that you were dirty, which God knows is more than true. Never mind, darlings, I'll pop you in a bath, both of you, and put lots of Floris in it, and you can soak and steam and be safe. By the way, the family call me Missus, left over from when my mother-in-law was Lady Doodah."

She unlocked a door and ushered them into the most luxurious room Melinda had ever seen. It was 1910 pink. The carvings at the corners of the ceiling looked like they belonged on a cake, curved woodwork ran down the door sides, and the large bed was piled so high with pillows that Melinda couldn't see the headboard. The carpet was soft and thick and dusty pink, pink and ivory, everything. Someone had run ahead of them with flowers, pink roses in winter, pink roses without any scent. The stalks still moved a little from having been carried so fast.

Lady Dunston told María she should come with her and have a bath in her room. María obeyed, but she kept looking back at Melinda until Melinda said, "It's all right, dear one, I will be right here."

She lay in the bath with the Floris bubbles around her chin. The bath was too long for her, so she had to brace her feet to keep from slipping underwater. She was afraid of that. She was so nearly asleep. She hadn't paid much attention to the sores on her body. They were ugly, and they stung when she lowered herself into the water. She wondered vaguely what day it was and where Tye was in the hotel. She was sure she remembered that Lady Dunston had said Tye was there. When she got out of the tub and wrapped herself in the huge warm bathtowel, she sat down for a minute on the bath stool, and that was all she remembered.

When she woke, it was still light or light again, and María was sitting beside her bed, dressed in a red ski suit. "Missus gave me this," she said. "Isn't it pretty? You have pneumonia and scabies, and the doctor has been here and he is silly and says everything comes from the liver, and you have to stay in your bed."

The smell was not of Floris but of Friar's Balsam in an electric kettle that steamed beside her bed, and of the sulfurous salve she was familiar with for disinfecting body sores. She lay quite still, and when she tried to speak, she found that her voice was only a croak.

"You have a temperature of one hundred and three Fahrenheit," María told her. She was cheerful about it. "This place is beautiful, like a fairy palace." She seemed to have forgotten anything that had gone before, but when a door slammed down the hall, she jumped and started to tremble.

"No, dear one, that's over," Melinda managed to croak.

They could hear a trolley outside the door, and Missus came in, followed by a waiter rolling a table with a gleaming white cloth and places for three. The smell of meat, sauces, wine, some kind of sweet thing mingled with the Friar's Balsam, obliterated it, and Melinda was caught in the overpowering smell of food. It made her gorge begin to rise. She tried to run to the bathroom in time, but she had to be helped by the waiter on one side and Missus on the other.

Missus closed the door, helped her kneel in front of the toilet. She retched and retched and couldn't bring anything up. "The dry heaves," Missus said over her head. "Oh my sweet child, I should have known better than to bring rich food anywhere near you."

The voice went on quite calmly over her head as Missus held it steady. "Now let your head go forward and out, lengthen, darling, lengthen, that's it, now let it go. It was the same with the women who were on forced feeding in the suffragette movement. We waited outside Holloway Prison for them. We had been warned that after a month their stomachs would have shrunk and they must have nothing but gruel and soup and dry crackers."

She chatted gently on as Melinda heaved and gagged and thought it was over and heaved again. "You know, those were brave women. I guess we all were. I would have gone to prison with them, but I had those two small children, Tye and his brother."

She could feel Melinda stiffen at Tye's name. "No, darling, he has not come yet, but he will. I'm sure he will. Tye is very good at that sort of thing." Melinda could not see the tears in her eyes or hear them in her voice. "As I said, we knew not to give them rich food. Never mind, darling, let it go, let your head go forward and your back lengthen." She massaged Melinda's back until the dry heaves stopped at last.

When they came back, María was finishing her lunch. "I could not wait," she said. "I was very hungry."

Melinda was in bed for two weeks. The doctor let her get up and even dress, but he insisted that she stay in her room. María and Missus bought her some clothes—white silk underwear with lace, a pleated skirt, a blouse, some slippers she could poke her feet into. She hardly noticed them. All of the clothes were a little too big, but María said quite sensibly that she would gain weight.

She was tired of pink, and tired of bed, and tired of her own pale face and her cough. She was certain she was being left alone so that she could face the fact that Tye was never coming back. She grew to love Missus and María more and more every day. They had played together, and María had become sturdy, almost pert. She talked all the time, about everything—her new clothes, the town. She noticed everything and she brought it all home, prattling to Melinda. But she never mentioned Spain.

One night late, when Melinda had had so much sleep she couldn't sleep anymore, she knew that an angel had sent María to keep away despair when she finally admitted that she would not see Tye again. In this world, she added to herself, because it was late at night, not the kind of thing she usually thought. She tried to read the mystery novel Missus had brought her, and she finally laid it down and stared at the carved ceiling until the room was pink again with the morning.

It was afternoon, she was sitting with a day-old Paris *Herald-Tribune*, trying to do the crossword, when someone knocked on her door. She had thought that Missus and María were going down into the town. They always went in the afternoon for tea. She thought, They must have forgotten something, or it is later than I think.

A man stood at the door. He had a white beard. He was ragged. He swayed against the doorjamb. His cheeks were creased and gray with dirt, his eyes red. There were sores on his face. Then she looked beyond them to his face again.

"Don't touch me," he said. "Just run me a bath, like an angel. I really must have a bath."

As she knelt beside the bath to test the water and wait for it to be deep enough, Tye spoke behind her. "I've been in prison, darling. A lot of us were shot, but I was one of a hundred men who were exchanged for Italian prisoners."

She couldn't speak.

"It was dreadfully uncomfortable," he muttered, and when she turned around he had taken off his clothes and put them in the covered bin so they would not contaminate the pink and the marble and the Floris and the bubbles and his clean wife. "They just let us loose on the road. We came through Figueres," he said. "No, don't touch the sores. Not yet.

"The Nationalists came north, and the refugees came ahead of them. I walked with the others from Girona. I think it was Girona—it's vague." He sat there in the bubble bath and tried to shave with Melinda's little razor and her hand mirror, and she gathered the white hair and held it in her hand. "We were strafed all the way. I tried to help, but after a while we just walked." He concentrated on his shaving.

"Just outside Figueres there is a big field." He shaved slowly, because his hand was trembling. "The planes stopped coming. There was dead silence. Then the rumble of lorries in the distance took the place of the noise of the planes—a long line of lorries, as far as you could see, with people clinging to the sides of them for safety as they came slowly up the road to Figueres. There were twenty, thirty, sixty of them, a whole convoy, just moving silently, with the people clinging to them and no strafing and no planes. We stood beside the road to watch them pass.

"Do you know what they were? They were all the paintings from the Prado that had been hidden at Montserrat, and the planes were under orders not to bomb them. There had been an art truce. The only chance that human beings had to be safe was to go along beside them. We joined the rest, walking along beside them all the way to the border, and I could almost see the arrogant aristocrats of Velázquez, and the holy El Grecos, and the comic kings of Goya with their ugly wives and daughters, and those terrible scenes of war that Goya painted and that finally drove him into the darkness. We went along together, *infantas* and dwarves and humans, all the way to the border. It was opened by then. The Senegalese soldiers dragged people away from the lorries, and some of them were screaming. I was dragged away and they grabbed my papers from my pocket, but when the soldier saw my British passport and my visa to France, he called an officer, who actually apologized, while all around us the soldiers were manhandling people. He gave me a few francs and saw that I had a ride to Perpignan, and from there, would you believe it, I took a country bus. Just a simple country bus, a normal country bus."

The door to the bedroom opened, and María ran ahead of Missus. "We found a pullover for you. A beautiful pullover with a skirt to match."

When she saw the strange man in the tub she stopped, and Missus blundered past her, crying, "Oh, darling, I knew you would come. You always have," and she hugged him, soap, sores, and all, in the tub.

He was finally able to look over her shoulder. "Hello, who are you?" he asked, as politely as a man can with two women covering him.

"I am María Dolores López García," she said. "I speak three languages. How do you do?"

"She followed me home. Can I keep her?" They were the first words Melinda had said. She started to giggle and couldn't stop, and then to cry and couldn't stop.

Book Four

England • 1939–1960

24 St. Michael's Square

At ten o'clock on Sunday morning, September 3, 1939, in their kitchen in St. Michael's Square, London, Tye's beautiful brother Ewen, Missus, Maria, and Melinda sat around the table drinking coffee. A proper English breakfast—bacon, eggs, kidneys, fried tomatoes, marmalade, and thin dry toast, the way Tye and the others liked it—would always be, for Melinda, the scent of prewar England in the morning. They were all trying not to look at the round black mouth of the radio that sat on the kitchen counter, spewing out sonorous music for hours. Ewen said, "For God's sake, get on with it," to nobody.

Melinda, still half asleep, so that dreams were near the surface of her mind, could almost see through all the walls to all the kitchens to all the radios that people had been moving closer to all weekend, radios that had become atavistic centers of life, like hoboes' campfires. She shook herself awake. How domestic the English make their wars, she thought, but didn't say. Missus was warming herself by placing her wrists on her mug of hot coffee—a way she had. Maria was eating oatmeal. Her cheeks were pink, and she had gained weight a little too quickly, so that she looked pudgy. Tye said the fat would go away, not to worry. He was already in the garden in the sun, hunched like a praying mantis over the roses he had been nursing all summer, as if he were trying to finish them somehow before they were destroyed.

Missus had come up from Wiltshire on Friday, when the Germans had marched into Poland. She said she was damned if she would stay alone if they were all going to be killed. She brought with her a large bolt of black heavy cloth, which she could hardly carry. It had been in her attic for twenty-five years. Lady Dunston, her mother-in-law, whom she called the Leviathan, had bought it during the World War so the parlor-maids would have fresh uniforms in the winter, in case there was a shortage.

Missus had dragged a sewing machine from the box room in the basement and started lining the long thick draperies in Tye and Melinda's bed-sitter and Ewen's drawing room with blackout cloth. The new blackout curtains she had made for the French doors of the kitchen hung like sentinels. Black radio, black curtains: England ready to plunge into mourning.

Missus and Ewen and Maria were excited by the idea of war. Ewen said if they didn't go to war, he would resign his commission. Tye and Melinda clung to domestic chores like spars. That was the difference between them.

Missus was watching Tye with the roses. "Why is he scratching around them like that?" She smiled at Melinda.

"I think he examines them leaf by leaf. He does it every morning." Melinda stretched and then laid her arms along the table and yawned. Everybody had had too little sleep. Maria stuck her own arms out when she finished eating, imitating Melinda, and caught the yawn.

"Is it war yet?" She asked the question as if it didn't matter very much.

"No, darling, not yet." Missus went on watching Tye.

Tye and Melinda had planned to look for a house as soon as they came back from France, but Tye had gone back to medical school almost at once, and Melinda knew so little of London that when Ewen let them have the ground-floor flat, they were relieved. It was partly because they still awoke almost as tired as when they went to sleep, at least at first, but gradually even that passed, and melted under the light of the new days of summer.

The flat had been abandoned in one evening by Ewen's friend Ron, who, he explained, had swanned off to better gold cufflinks than Ewen's. Ewen had stuffed into what had been the dining room all the abandoned furniture of the house when he had inherited it. Long elegant twenty-four-paned windows looked out onto the street. The room had inherited the library rug, a soft dark Persian with stains made by animals and children, the squashy sofa with its flowered cover, the two squashy chairs, which had been hollowed by years of comfortable bottoms, and the cat, a gray striped London prowler who still wandered where she pleased, ignoring any change. Her name was Brit. Nobody remembered why.

Behind the old dining room, what Missus still called the new kitchen, even though she had moved the kitchen up from the basement to what had been the garden room in 1927, had not been changed, but a long deal table and six chairs that had been in the servants' dining room had been refinished and moved into it. Off the kitchen, a larder with a window that looked into the garden had been made into a bedroom, and Ewen had put in a small bathroom between the bedroom and the kitchen. Tye and Melinda painted the little bedroom pink because that was Maria's favorite color, and they bought frilly curtains and put in a delicate, lacy brass bed from Missus's house in Wiltshire.

All summer Melinda and Tye and Maria had played house. They painted the kitchen chairs bright red and the kitchen walls lemon yellow, as if they were trying to capture the flirting, evasive sun of England. They bought blue-and-white Cornishware plates and cups, a teapot, some storage jars, and a coffee jug that Melinda was still trying to learn to use.

Tye and Melinda changed the main room into their own bed-sitter. It was so big, thirty feet long and twenty feet wide at the front windows, that they could move the sofa and the squashy chairs next to the carved marble fireplace and make a corner in front of the windows for the boat bed they had found at Missus's house. They read and lay back with their legs straight out along the green velvet counterpane.

Missus had given them carte blanche, she called it, to take whatever they wanted from the house in Wiltshire, and they had found treasures: the two beds, a Victorian birdcage that looked like the Albert Memorial, a large gilt mirror that was First Empire, a black papier-mâché table with mother-of-pearl flowers that Tye had loved when he was a child but that Missus had exiled to the haunted, turreted attic in her Heals Mod phase. It all came up in a pantechnicon. Melinda loved the word. It sounded like the Ark.

They made it all as cozy as they could. Tye said coziness was the one traditional gift that England had given to the world of interior design.

Ewen said, "Très chic, presque Victorian," and Tye said, "Chacun à son bloody camp." Melinda didn't know what they meant, and she had already grown tired of asking. They tended to argue. Ewen always ended with, "You may be right, my dear, but the working class vote Tory," and it made Tye furious.

Tomorrow was fragile in the summer of 1939, but nobody quite admitted it. They simply waited, Maria in the little bedroom, tucked in, read to, and listened for—she had nightmares that she didn't remember—Tye and Melinda close together on the sofa before they made it into bed for the night. They accepted together, for a little while, the illusion that nothing was going to happen.

Everything they did that summer took on a glow of luxury. They walked, at first around St. Michael's Square, then farther and farther, to Green Park, to the National Gallery. Tye showed

Melinda his London, from the great buildings to the East End, where he swore at the way people had to live.

Once they ran into a demonstration by Oswald Mosley's Fascists that had been attacked by Communists. It was a three-way fight, with police with billy clubs and mounted police on horses trained to break up crowds. The Communists and the Fascists threw marbles in front of the horses and they slid and neighed. Melinda and Tye hid in a doorway while the crowd scattered, leaving blood, marbles, and leaflets on the dirty street.

Upstairs the party went on and on.

Tye said they were postwar on the ground floor while prewar ran down upstairs. Late at night they could hear it, only faintly, because the house had been built at one of those times of thick-walled stability in the early 1830s—another postwar period, Tye said, when people were holing up after decades of fragile revolutionary and Napoleonic tomorrows.

Ewen had gutted the drawing room, which was the width of the house, and the library behind it, and made them into one black-and-white L-shaped room. He called it a Lady Mendl sweep. The old double doors had been taken down between the rooms. Melinda and Tye found them later in the basement, thick, solid, carved oak. In their place Ewen had put carved columns, white, made by a friend of his. The floor was covered with black-and-white tiles. Melinda was afraid to go in without taking off her shoes. The room was stark and grand, with square white chairs, square white lamps, and a slash of color in a huge abstract painting. Tye said it looked like the painting had bled on the wall, and Ewen called him a philistine Bolshie.

There had been a lot for Melinda to learn in the Chinese puzzle of the English world that was bound by Regent's Park on the north, the Savoy Hotel on the east, the river on the south, and the Borough of Kensington—"Well, most of it," Ewen had informed her—on the west.

Noise. The room upstairs was full of the bright effervescent noise of Ewen's friends. The women were younger than they looked that summer; they wore Chanel suits, Chanel pearls, Chanel No. 5, and little hats that tipped over one eye, and they were thin. They were the only people Melinda had ever seen who could lounge standing up. Sometimes she thought that the conversation was so brittle that if it were dropped, it would shatter with little tinkles.

Melinda's grandmother had taught her that you didn't say who you were kin to, everybody was supposed to know, but the English seemed to tell all whenever they could. Only it wasn't Confederate generals and Tidewater governors, it was peers and bishops and sometimes things like the Brides in the Bath murders or kings' mistresses. These were a bit more fun than Confederate generals, she had to admit. It was all restful and trivial after being at war.

But there was one major and wonderful difference that Melinda took to herself like a balm. She had never seen such a family for letting each other be. Ewen was outrageous at home but totally, conventionally Tory, dress and all, when he went to the City, where he had one of those ill-defined jobs the English had when they all knew each other. Missus went her own way, in and out of town, hair flying like the White Queen, in butt-sprung skirts and ghillies, with her Labour Party politics and Allinson's bread.

Tye went headfirst into the garden and into painting and nesting. He had regained—Missus said he had always had it—the talent of looking happy all by himself. He took to the growing of roses as if his life depended on it, and in a way it did. His face was still, in certain lights, transparent, but he was growing younger by the days. Melinda watched him sitting at the kitchen table, engrossed in some paper he had written on medical policy and wasn't ready to show her yet. It was for a Labour Party committee that he served on with Dr. Wimpy, to plan for National Health if they ever had a chance.

Tye had lost years. She could see a hint of the boy he had been, the damp, shining hair, the beautiful hands she wanted to touch, going back to school at twenty-eight as if a war hadn't molded him and thrust him out again.

They had already been too long at war to take anything—a chair, a meal, each other, the house—for granted. There was a delicacy, a recognition, a heightened noticing of small things. Its dark side, its night, was the sheer danger of being alive, the blank fear of the disappearance of all of it, the listening. They had no idea that the sense of ephemeral life would last them for the rest of their days.

When Melinda tried to find words for the joy of that sweet summer, only one survived. Inevitable. Happy was too light a word. Of course she was happy, but more than that, deeper than that, she was more at home than she had ever been in her life. During mornings in the kitchen, with the Aga murmuring and warm, the faint murmur of the city in the distance, she played and read with Maria. She remembered once sitting quite still in the kitchen watching Tye kneeling among his roses, with the seldom-seen sun brushing his hair and the French doors, and she was flushed suddenly with some light she couldn't name.

All around them in London people treated war as something new on the horizon, made trenches in Hyde Park and went to meetings, listened to announcements on the BBC, volunteered for the services, had uniforms tailored just in case, and tried to pretend that their lives weren't being tossed to and fro by a surge of distant decisions. Melinda found herself longing for someone of her own who was postwar. So she went to the office in Smith Square where she and Fig had reported, to find a connection again after being plunged into peace and the nightmares that came with it. She found Penny, who had guided her so long ago, and they kissed each other as if they were old friends. Penny had, of course, gone to nursery school with Tye.

Tye had taken Maria to his heart, and so had Missus and Ewen. There had not been one comment, one hint that she was any sort of burden. It was part of their view of themselves. When things happened and people turned up and life changed, you were decent about it. That was all.

They were at first in touch with M. Borgan every week to see whether he had heard from Maria's father. But the weeks and then the months passed, and there was no word, nothing. Of course they had talked to Maria about who she was and had even given her the letter in English, but she had danced away from what they were saying. They thought she was hiding something, and then they realized that she had wiped Spain from her mind. She remembered nothing. Tye said it had happened to a lot of people. It didn't last long, and they had to be prepared for when it ended. When a few of the children from Germany, Jewish children, had come to England alone, he said that their minds had been wiped clean for a little while. That was the way he said it. Wiped clean.

It was nearly eleven o'clock. Another hour had crawled by. Somewhere a church bell tolled for Sunday morning prayer.

There was an empty pause on the BBC, and they all turned to look at the mouth of the radio. The announcer introduced the prime minister, and they heard the reedy, high-pitched voice of Neville Chamberlain say, "Consequently, a state of war exists between—" The radio coughed and crackled. The church bell echoed among the buildings. Melinda never remembered hearing another church bell until the end of the war.

Missus's mouth was white around the edges. Ewen got up and stood almost to attention without knowing he was doing it. Melinda looked at Tye, who was trying to keep from laughing, and she knew as if he had said it, "It's about bloody time."

They were still digesting war and breakfast when the air-raid siren wailed over the city like some lost thing, up and down, up and down. It was the raid they had waited for all summer, when London was going to be destroyed like Guernica.

They trooped, embarrassed, down the steep basement stairs into the makeshift shelter. They sat, not looking at each other, and the sun struggled through the dusty barred windows of what had once been the kitchen in what Missus called the bad old days, when there really had been a below-stairs and all the servants had seen when they looked out had been the areaway and people's feet. The sun threw shadows of the bars across the dull floor. The old sink was stained with neglect and age.

They had cleared the old kitchen of the junk of years—piled newspapers, magazines, huge hatboxes that had belonged to the Leviathan, with hats that carried fruit and flowers like trays on Maria's head when she pranced around in them. They had put in cots and chairs, and food and coffee makings—just in case, Missus said.

They could hear the clatter of feet above them in the street, running to the public shelter that had been made in the square in the summer of '38, during the Munich crisis. Melinda and Maria had peeked into it once. It was full of the dank smells of urine, lovemaking, rain, and leaves.

Melinda tried not to look at the others. When she couldn't resist any longer, Ewen was examining his hands, turning them over as if he hadn't seen them for a long time. Missus was trying not to cry. Tye kept wandering over to the window and watching the running feet. A man ran down into the areaway and stared in through the bars like a frightened monkey in a cage. Maria had retreated into sleep in Melinda's lap.

Nothing happened. The all-clear sounded, the climbing single tone that, with the up-and-down wail of the air-raid siren, would stay in their minds forever, and that they would learn to bury below attention for the next five years. They trooped upstairs again. Melinda made more coffee. Tye said it was still too strong. Ewen said he liked it that way. They were facing at last the fact that what was going to happen was not dramatic, as all who had not been at war expected, but as different from life before eleven o'clock as two different countries.

After the first thrill and fear of the warning, which had been a mistake, causing a panic that had sent the whole city under chairs, into cupboards, under beds, underground, nothing happened. The state of war began. Melinda liked the phrase "state of war," a state that changed the temper of the days to cold, the color of the days to gray drab. There were no events, only a daily state they existed in, deeper into September.

While so much of England seemed to strain at a leash of action, Melinda learned to cook for fewer than a hundred people and to shop for food in London. She found a school for Maria that had not been evacuated. She had resisted Missus's offer to take Maria down to the country before anything happened. Every time Missus spoke of it in front of Maria, Maria grabbed Melinda's hand again and held it tight, but when she was asked if she wanted to, she shrugged and said, "I don't mind." She was learning more than slang at her school; she was learning sangfroid, the English bloody cold.

London drew Missus back every week. She brought vegetables. She brought fresh chickens. She brought Tye's childhood books for Maria, and read with her *Cautionary Tales for Bad Children, The Arabian Nights, The Knights of the Round Table, 1066 and All That,* and all the Father Brown stories. When Missus gave her *Wind in the Willows,* Maria gave it back to her. "Animals," she said, "don't talk."

Melinda knew that she was luckier than most wives, except for Ruth in the Bible. She loved her mother-in-law. Whenever Missus came up from the country, Melinda told her she had never been so glad to see anybody in her life, hearing herself use one of Boodie's favorite phrases.

One day in late September when she was coming back from taking Maria to Miss Puttick's Academy, she saw Missus sitting in St. Michael's Square on a wrought-iron bench, eating an ice-cream cone she called a cornet and staring into the air, which she was letting toss her hair. Melinda sat down beside her, and Missus said, "It won't be long now. The bad part. It's like a black stain that has been spreading nearer for ten years, like that awful black cloth of the Leviathan. God, what a tall beaky woman she was!" She said to herself, letting Melinda hear, "I'm too old for this," and when Melinda looked at her, she was crying at last, quite silently, eating her ice cream.

Ewen had been called up in the Irish Guards. Every time he came back on leave, the parties began again, with the same voices but new subjects. "God, darling, no more Tangiers, how can we bear it?" and "Will the royals go to Canada?" and "This is the total end of the diplomatic corps as we know it, my dear, the total end."

Ewen looked so handsome that the women flocked around him, even though they knew it was no use. The women all seemed to be in uniform, either in ATS officers' uniforms or RAF blue or WREN white stockings. They were all officers or they drove generals; Melinda could never quite get it straight. Ewen said they had wangled cushy jobs. He was already mixing the language of what he called the forces with his own mixture of affectation and Tory.

Some wore their air-raid warden blue, or what they called "the terribly chic" blue and red of the Fire Service. Some of them were still dressed in what Ewen called "prewar chic"; he made it sound as if they were dressed in their grandmothers' clothes. Two of his dearest friends—they were always dearest, not best—ran the canteen at the National Gallery, where they all went to hear concerts at noon.

Somebody said one of the times—she couldn't remember the parties separately—"Isn't it marvelous what the war has done, my dear? The great British unwashed are reading poetry and listening to good music." Ewen called across the babble, "Of course they are. The music is free, and they can't find any other books these days. All the lovely trash is gone."

Rumors were batted back and forth like balloons. The black-and-white room was scented with gin, single-malt whiskey, Pimms No. 1, and perfume brought back on leave from Paris.

When Melinda heard someone explain, "I'm not in Debrett's, but I am in Burke's," she asked Ewen what he meant.

"Oh, darling, he's afraid he *won't* be hanged from the nearest lamppost come the revolution."

The gray days passed; the waiting was like thirst. Melinda remembered long afterward, not important things to anyone else, no history, just flashes of where she was. She saw herself sitting with the *chicas*, her friends, on the bench at Albastro, watching the empty road. War to her was empty roads, waiting and watching, the same guilty hope that something, anything, would happen. Why was it always gray? In Melinda's memory, the mornings sagged into other gray mornings, so that she knew later that it was the gray of war itself that she remembered. Other things were clear, but they were always within the gray and the damp. She remembered, then or another time, looking up at the silver barrage balloons, the blimps, named after Colonel Blimp from the cartoon, and thinking, They are holding up London, and if the wires were cut, the city would sink in a gray bog of damp and stained sandbags.

There was the day in the early spring of 1940

when Tye came back and messed around making tea and scrumbling for sweet biscuits and complaining without any real passion about finally leaving medical school and becoming a resident, years later than all the others. He went on muttering about them, how they complained that they were going to have to do a year's residency before they could join up, saying that it was just bloody incompetence when they were going to need . . . Murmur, murmur, mutter, mutter, until Melinda said, "Come on. What's the matter?"

He sat down and started to speak very carefully. "Now, it isn't important," he said, convincing her that it was. "I still can't pass my medical."

"What do you mean, still?" She was getting angry.

"Well, darling, I didn't want to worry you. Wimp and I thought that it would pass and it will, but it hasn't yet. Franco's hotel left me with a heart murmur. Now don't say a word. It is usual when you have been badly starved. Don't *look* like that. When starved people die, they usually die of heart failure. If you survive the first few months, it passes. It's only a slight murmur. I have asked for a residency at St. Christopher's." He tried to change the subject. "It came through today."

She ran around the table and started to pound on his chest and then remembered that that was where his heart was, and she burst into sobs and let him put his arms around her. She muttered to his white coat, "Why didn't you tell me? Don't keep things away. It makes it worse. Don't keep things away from me anymore."

He stroked her hair as he always did and said, "Not to worry. It passes. It always does. One thing that is good," he said over her head, "I won't be useless. Wimp has appointed me to lecture to Medical Corps doctors on what we learned in Spain that was new—blood transfusion, abdominal wounds, and triage. Isn't it terrible that we only learn these things in crisis?" He went on stroking her hair.

Then there was the afternoon when she had come through the wind and the rain of the square, laden down with the inevitable drab wartime shopping bag which seemed to be the badge of women with families, her hair covered with a scarf rolled around it like a cap, which had become part of their uniform. She fumbled with the door key, dumped the groceries on the kitchen table, and heard mewing. She thought it was the cat, but it wasn't. It was Maria, lying like a newborn baby on her bed in her uniform from Miss Puttick's Academy, her blue serge skirt wrinkled around her little bottom. Her round blue felt hat with the school motto, "Integrity," on the front had fallen on the floor. Brit was curled up behind her back, but when Melinda sat down on the bed, she flowed to the floor and stalked away.

When Melinda held Maria's shoulders and asked what was the matter, she only turned her head back and forth on the pillow, as if she were trying to shake something loose and refused to tell. "I don't carry tales," she sobbed with some dignity.

"Maybe it isn't tales. Maybe I should know." Melinda reasoned with her until it finally came pouring out.

"They say I'm not English. I know I'm not English. They say—"

"Who, darling?"

"The girls at Miss Puttick's. They say I'm just a refugee and my English is like a foreigner's, and they don't want me there and I don't have a father. I told them my father was a soldier, and they said he was not, he was a Bolshie, and you and Tye just felt sorry for me and they don't want me there because I am not English and I am a Spanish Bolshieee . . ." The last word was elongated by a new sob. "I don't even know what that is."

Melinda realized for the first time that Maria remembered her father. "Sit up, young lady." She found her Grandmother Mason's voice. "You are a Republican Spaniard, and your father fought for democracy before any of these people knew what was happening or cared. Dammit, you should be proud of that, and I am American and I am proud of that, and you should tell them—" She almost said, "That you don't want to be English, and neither do I," but she thought that Maria might blurt it out when she was teased.

A fit of homesickness, not for her new home but for some old home—maybe Kregg's Crossing, someplace she had been before so much had happened—engulfed her for the first time in years, and she and Maria cried together and felt better, or at least they promised each other they felt better and found they could laugh at the way each of them looked, both snotty and tear-drenched. They made tea and made jokes about it, made the *English* way, and waited for Tye to come home. Melinda said over tea that Maria didn't have to go back to Miss Puttick's, that she wouldn't stand for one more day of that bloody place.

They found a school where she could take Maria on the bus. It was L'École, in Regent's Park, in a house in one of the terraces. They sat on the top front of the bus, Maria's favorite seat. Every day when they passed through Park Lane they could see the Home Guard marching back and forth in Hyde Park with broomsticks on their shoulders in the bright mornings. The men were all shapes and sizes. Some of them wore bowler hats, some caps, long coats, short British warms—civilian clothes that shouted who they were, what class, what job. Melinda thought, No wonder it is easy for them to go into uniform. They have been in uniform all their lives.

The French school was full of children who had come from France and from Germany, and even, some of them, from Spain. They were all refugees, from the war, from the English, but this was never mentioned. Maria bloomed again, like a plant that had been starved of water.

Ewen came home on leave from France and brought Melinda a lovely ostrich feather, which he said was "her." "I'm an ostrich feather," she told herself, and giggled. She sewed it to a little black tippy hat that she wore over one eye and met Penny at the Ritz for tea. They played at being ladies. Penny was off-duty as a trainee nurse at the hospital at Hyde Park Corner. She told Melinda that she could join the VAD at Hyde Park with her and work while Maria was at school. Penny added, "Don't tell them you were in Spain. I had a bloody awful time persuading them to take me."

The little tippy hat, the ostrich feather, Penny's giving her a way to start becoming part of it again, all tangled in Melinda's mind. So, when she had dropped Maria at her school, she came back on the same bus from Regent's Park, past the Home Guard, and knelt to scrub her way across new floors in a new phase of an old war.

Tye began his residency in April and came home from St. Christopher's aglow with righteous anger. "God," he said, slamming the teapot down on the table. "Eighteen-year-old girls from the East End with bodies like forty-year-old women, made of white bread, marge, and black tea from living on the dole!" He said that the war and the rationing was the best thing that had ever happened to them, and that goddamn he was going to see that after the war that sort of neglect of people never happened again.

The children who had been sent out of London to the charity of strangers, many of whom had been conscripted by compassion that soon wore off, had drifted back to London. Nothing was ever going to happen.

Ewen brought back pâte and cheese from Paris when he scrounged a lift on leave. Sometimes he scrounged, sometimes he wangled. Then, almost before they were aware of it except as headlines in the papers and announcements on the BBC,

Hitler had opened the blitzkrieg around the end of the Maginot Line. They went to the pictures and watched newsreels that showed people from Belgium, Holland, and France clogging the roads and being used, as the Germans had learned in Spain, as human buffers against the movements of troops. Melinda sat in the dark and cried and tried not to let herself be heard.

Once, in the night, Tye was off-duty and they were spooned together in the sweet warmth of each other. They had turned off the lamps and opened the blackout curtains, and the summer touched their backs in a light night breeze from the square. Melinda half woke to find herself pounding his back and calling, "Face down. Face down." He held her and waked her, and said, "You've been having a bad dream," but she couldn't remember any of it.

Then, for years, when she least expected it, there was a piercing recall. She never remembered what she had been doing, but she saw herself standing in the bed-sitter, and she heard a knock at the door and thought Tye had forgotten his key.

It was Ewen, who knocked at his own door like a stranger. He had a week's growth of beard. His uniform looked as if he had slept on the Embankment among the tramps. His eyes were glassy with the kind of fatigue she had not seen since Spain, hopeless, demoralized fatigue, where the body had taken over and sleep was all that mattered. She touched Ewen for the first time ever, put her arm around his waist and led him to the nearest bed, hers and Tye's. He smelled of dry seawater.

"Where on earth have you been?" she asked, and as he closed his eyes, he said, "Dunkirk. This morning. A destroyer picked me up and gave me some hot Bovril, and then they put me ashore at Deal, I think it was, and I wangled a lift to London." He was asleep.

He slept for fourteen hours, while Tye sat by his bed.

The air war began. Missus came up from Wiltshire, because the house was too near an airfield and London was safer. That was in August. In London, they could hear the guns all the way across the Channel in the night. People were taking up residence in the tube stations and the public shelters. Tye said it reminded him of the refugees in Spain, who seemed to know before anybody else what was going to happen. Maria had stopped sleeping well. Melinda could hear her turning and making small cat-whines in the night, but when she went to comfort her, Maria was still asleep. Once Melinda found the bit of paper that was what was left of her father's letter clutched tight in her hand. Melinda watched it in the dark, a little white fist, the moonlight touching it.

First the coastal towns were hit, and casualties were brought by train to London. Melinda went on full duty. Tye worked and slept at St. Christopher's. They got used to the growl of planes away in the distance, as if the clouds themselves were moaning.

Then one night in late August, the air-raid sirens woke London. Tye was at the hospital. Melinda ran to wake Maria and Missus. They gathered the gas masks and blankets they had brought back upstairs after the first alarms and trooped into the basement kitchen and drew the blackout curtains. Missus lit the Primus stove and put the kettle on. Maria huddled on her cot and dropped into a deep sleep.

When they heard the blasts, they turned out the lights and opened the blackout curtains to watch. There was a glow in the distance toward the east. Melinda, confused with sleep, thought for a minute that it must be dawn, and then the glow began to snake into the air: fire, not dawn. The black sky was lit with pencil lines of searchlights. Where they met there was one tiny black plane, caught like a moth in the flame. The lights moved away from it. "One of ours." Melinda said for the first time the chorus of the Blitz—"One of ours," "One of theirs," and later, "Ack-ack," "It's only ack-ack." They listened to the pulse and grunt of the distant explosions, and watched the drunken searchlight lines crisscross the sky and turn the few clouds pink.

The all-clear went, and Missus and Melinda decided to stay in the basement for the night so they wouldn't wake Maria again. When Melinda went to tuck her in, she whispered to Missus, "Come here. There's something wrong."

Maria's breathing was loud. Her skin was icy, and cold sweat shivered on her body. When

Melinda tried to wake her, she only muttered and cringed away.

"She's in deep shock. Get all the blankets," she whispered to Missus, who had already gathered them.

Melinda sat beside Maria on the cot until the early morning. When Maria woke, she was herself again, not a shivering little animal. She was surprised that they were in the shelter. "What did I miss?" she asked, disappointed.

"Darling, listen to me," Melinda said at breakfast. "You have to take Missus down to Wiltshire today. She is frightened. You look after her. You can come back soon."

Maria looked up from her oatmeal. "You aren't telling me the truth," she said, and went on eating.

"All right. You passed out last night, and you have to go."

"Will you go with me?"

"No. Not right now. I'm on duty. I'll come soon."

Maria looked at her. "No, you won't. You will get killed. I'll go. I don't mind." She shrugged her shoulders.

Getting ready to go to the country was the same flurry and argument it had always been, only the objects were different. There were the gas masks, the rabbits Tye had brought to Maria, the two baby chicks from Easter, which had grown into gangly pullets. When they tried to find Brit, she was gone. Missus explained to Maria, who had started to cry, that Brit was a

London cat and that she wanted to stay in London.

Melinda kept trying to get through to Tye to tell him she was only going to the station, in case he rang and was worried. She wanted to hear his voice. That was to last all through the war; the minute she heard his voice, even in a hurry, anytime, something within her that had knotted would release, and even at the worst times there would be that surge of peace.

They couldn't find a taxi, so they trudged to Sloane Square tube station, laden with the cages for the rabbits and the pullets and Maria's huggy bear, which she couldn't leave behind. Their gas masks hung from their shoulders and flopped against their hips. Along the platform at Sloane Square, people had set up their places to sleep at night, all kinds of blankets and mattresses and baskets.

It took an hour to get from Sloane Square to Paddington. Every platform was filled with people, belligerently cozy, some knitting, some calling to each other, some looking upward, as if they could see through the roofs of the tube stations to the sky. Little groups sang, being jolly, as if it were expected of them, "Roll Out the Barrel" and "Run Rabbit Run Rabbit Run Run Run."

Paddington was dark under the dirty glass of the high roof. A woman of about sixty in a WVS uniform stood beside a sign that read NO. 6 AND 7 PLATFORMS EVACUATION TRAINS. She was calling out in a voice that was used to being heard, "Evacuation trains, platforms six and seven. Go to the evacuation queue and you will be told which train. Please move along, move along, please."

They found a place to sit on the platform floor, behind a kiosk so that they could put down the animals, and the crowd surged over their heads like ghosts in the gloom. A child cried, all alone. One of the WVS women guided him along to the queue. There was a dusky quietness about the crowd. Where the Spanish had relied on dignity, Melinda thought, the English relied on calm. She tried to think of a better word and couldn't.

Maria sat on the top of the rabbit cage. She had forgotten any trouble in the night. She watched the children and said, "Do I have to go with them?," a new snobbery that Melinda thought she would talk to her about later. She said, "Of course not. You're going with Missus when there is a regular train."

They waited four hours. Over and over Melinda tried to ring Tye at the hospital, but the queues were a hundred feet long at every telephone kiosk, and when she got there, twice, he was on duty and they refused to put through a personal call.

Maria was getting tired; she slept a little, then started to grizzle, and Missus snapped, "Do be quiet, Maria, don't you see the other children?" Maria was so surprised that she didn't say another word.

The long queue of children stood, so patient that some of them seemed to be frozen, some holding the hands of their mothers, some each other's, some with fathers, trudging nearer and nearer the gates. That was it: beyond calm, that infinite, never-ceasing patience, the public behavior they expected of themselves.

Finally Melinda and Missus were balancing the cages, closed in by the crowd hoping to get on the train at platform one, where there was no queue, no gate. The train was open all along the platform. A mass of people, as patient as grass pushing through cracks in concrete, moved onto it. Children were handed over heads, the seats filled, the floor space in the carriages filled, the corridors filling.

At the last minute, Maria refused to let go of Melinda's hand. Her face had gone white and numb, and she had begun to shiver again, with a cold that went through her hand up Melinda's arm. So if there was a decision at all, it was made once again by that small hand. Melinda was pushed into the corridor of the train, and it started out, slowly, then faster, past the dirty tenements of Paddington, then through the suburbs. Melinda leaned against the window, pressed there by bodies, and tried to remember if she had left a note for Tye. She remembered writing it and saying that she was only going to the station and then on duty.

They were in the country, stopping over and over, and when they finally reached Chippenham, the bus to Linfield was full of airmen. Two of the airmen gave them seats. They sang too: "Roll me over in the clover, roll me over, lay me down and do it again." It was like Spain had been at first, when everybody sang.

Maria had shed war. At Missus's house she

ran up to the third-floor room she had long since picked as her own, because it made her feel like a princess in the tower. She asked Melinda shyly if she would mind sleeping in the bedroom next door. "You'll like it," she added. "It looks out over the garden and the dovecote."

In the afternoon the phone rang. It was Tye, and the first words he said were, "Thank God. You stay there, at least for a couple of weeks, until we know what is going to happen." She could hear people talking behind his voice. When she asked him what had been hit, he said carefully, "We've been very busy." Then he sounded so falsely amused that she was annoyed. "Do you remember old Milton?" he said, and laughed. "He got drunk last night and fell off his perch at last. You know what a prig he has always been—I've got to go. Stay there, just until we know what's going to happen." He hung up so quickly that Melinda called, "Love you" to an empty phone. What was going to happen was invasion, and neither of them said a word about it, but she leaned her head against the flowered wallpaper by the telephone in the hall, too tired to cry.

When Missus asked what Tye had said, Melinda told her. She admitted she couldn't make head nor tail of it, but Missus said, "Oh, that means the bombs fell on Cripplegate and hit St. Giles Church."

Two weeks later, a huge daylight raid on London was the beginning of the real Blitz. It was four months before Tye could get away from the hospital to come down to Wiltshire. When he did, he slept all weekend and said almost nothing about what was happening in London. He did say, "I want you here. I want you to stay here. Please God, stay here." He was asleep again before Melinda could say a word.

Ewen called the house in Wiltshire Castle Dreadful. He said it hadn't been built but had just grown, like a mushroom. From the sixteenth century on, every time anybody had any money they dabbed another bit on. It had started as a Tudor farmhouse. It had been a jail, and there were still iron rings on the basement walls. Its façade, which had been put on during the seventeenth century, was what Ewen called "mini-Blenheim red brick and pinnacles." Tye's great-grandfather had bought it when he became a baronet.

A month after Melinda had left London, a van pulled up in front of the house at teatime and two children, a boy and a girl, got out slowly. They stood quite still, and looked up at the high brick housefront with its glistening windows.

"Lumme," the boy muttered, and the girl slapped him and told him to belt up.

"We don't do that sort of thing in the country," the WVS woman, who was delivering them like parcels, said with icy kindness.

"Oo the fuck says so?" The girl, who looked about eight years old, put her arm around the boy to shelter him and looked up at the WVS woman, her chin stuck out. For the rest of the time Melinda was to know Nella, and that was all her life, the sticking-out of Nella's chin was a sign that she was not to be budged.

Missus herded them into the house. She was quiet. She didn't try to explain. She just sat them down and said, "Now. What are your names?"

Nella and her little brother, Terence, told their names.

Melinda, Missus, and the children had a silent tea with scones and butter and jam and cake until the children's eyes and mouths were finally full. Then Missus spoke like an oracle. It would put her in charge for the next four years.

"Now listen to me," she said, looking from one to the other, so that she seemed to be saying what she had to say directly to each one. "We're going to live here together for a long time. I'm glad, even if you are not. But maybe you will be. In the meantime, you will do what you are told. You will each be assigned a chore to do, and if you don't do it, I will bleedin do you, and I mean it. Don't I?" She said it to each of them, including Maria.

"Yes, mum," Nella and Terence said.

When Melinda later asked Missus how she had known what to say, she shrugged and said, "I ran a soup kitchen in the East End after the first World War."

Maria and Nella became friends in that way that Melinda remembered from childhood, when you either did or didn't and there wasn't any in-between. They sat together on the stone wall of the terrace. When Melinda went to the French door, she paused because she didn't want to disturb them.

"Oh, Melinda is not my mother. My mother was killed in the war," she heard Maria say.

"So was mine," Nella told her. They were both completely calm about this information.

Maria didn't want to be interrupted. "Melinda told Missus that when the bombing started, I nearly went mad. Really mad. Loony, gaga. I learned about that when I listened at the door when they didn't know I was there."

Melinda thought she ought to tell Maria that it wasn't nice to listen at doors, and then she realized that she was doing it herself.

Fall came, then the beginning of winter. War day after day became a pattern. The house grew colder as the fuel gave out, and the coke ration was too small to run the huge old furnace. They found a second-hand gas geyser to put over one of the bathtubs. It exploded into life when it was lit and provided two-inch hot baths which only Missus could get the children to strip and take. Missus and Melinda were better off than most. They knew that, but it didn't keep them from beginning to wake up as tired as they had been when they went to bed.

The house went back a hundred years, to being heated by logs in the fine stone fireplace of the great hall. When there wasn't enough wood for that, they retreated into the kitchen and the little housekeeper's room, which Missus renamed the Cozy. They lived there, except at night, when they braved the icy great hall, where the shrouded furniture was caught in the wavy shafts of their torchlight like ghosts, and they fled up the fine curved stairs to escape the cold and go to bed.

Missus brought down from the attic an armful of earthenware hot-water bottles shaped like loaves of bread. "Thank God the Leviathan never threw anything away," she told them. "Now, I'm going to fill these every evening with hot water and wrap them in blankets, and I want all of you—you too," she said to Melinda, "—to take them up to your beds and put them under the blankets to warm the sheets."

"What about you?" Melinda said, counting four bottles.

"I've decided to sleep in the Cozy and keep the fire going. I don't want all of you to be down with flu. Maria, you and Nella go and bring the cot down from my dressing room."

In later years, when the war came unbidden to her mind, Melinda expected herself to remember events that everybody thought happened in wars. She had been trying to crawl along the sidewalk in Regent Street when a buzz bomb with its motorcycle noise overhead stopped and the world became totally silent. When the buzz bomb exploded a hundred yards away, the pavement hit her in the chest and knocked the air out of her lungs for a second, and when she got up, she found a piece of shrapnel a foot from her head. It was hot. She took it back to the country to show the children, and then it got lost.

Then she remembered hitching a ride in a lorry when she missed the train into London, and she and the lorry driver, who had very dirty hands, which he licked from time to time, spent an hour in the lobby of the Cumberland Hotel drinking beer, hearing crumps in the distance, and trying to think of things to talk about.

But sometimes, always a surprise, when she saw a moving light in the dark or felt coldness in her bones, she was walking again in a line with the children in the dark of the great hall, the only light from the little fluttering blackout torches. Each of them was hugging one of the earthenware hot-water bottles wrapped in a blanket, and to keep the children from being afraid as they passed through the huge dark haunted room and up the stairs, they chanted, "How many miles to Babylon? Three score and ten. Can we get there by candlelight? Aye, and back again." Terence was always a little behind in the chant, his voice finishing with "cennelah back agin." Nella said, "You don never get it bleedin right." It was that recall that made Melinda's eyes sting.

Even the decision to transfer as a VAD to the hospital in Littleford was undramatic and domestic. Melinda cycled there for the first time along the deep country lanes with high hedges on both sides, completely alone, in the nurse's aide uniform she had been wearing to go on duty when she took Maria to Paddington Station.

The commandeered manor house of the Littleford hospital was familiar—the air of neglect in the gardens, the dull blackout curtains in windows that had once been clothed in brocade, the dim floors that had been scrubbed instead of polished. It brought back the convents, the houses in Spain. It was the way houses looked when they had been turned into things they were not meant to be—unlived in, unloved, even unhated.

She told the matron that her papers were in London, and when the matron called to see about the transfer, she hung up the phone and said, "You'll be pleased to know there's another Bolshie from Spain here, one of the nurses." It was Sister Lily, who had held the baby in her arms when they drove to Vilateresa. They fell on each other, and both cried.

One morning in the late fall, when Melinda said that it was her turn to feed the chickens, Missus hardly looked up from her cocoa. "You'll find some new feed in the barn," she said. "Mr. Naughton brought it yesterday." She fell back to reading the paper while Nella and Maria whispered and Terence had a little sleep on the kitchen table.

Melinda came running back into the kitchen. Her eyes were shining.

"My God, darling, you look as if you've fallen in love," Missus said.

Nella and Maria looked at each other. Nella had long since told Maria about falling in love and what came afterward.

All Melinda said was, "Whose is it?"

"Whose is what, darling?" Missus went back to the paper. "Bananas in Chippenham! Two each—"

"The SS100 Jaguar," Melinda almost whispered.

"Yours, if you want it, darling. It doesn't run. It belonged to Hartley. When he died we put it up on blocks. The boys couldn't use it, and I never got the hang of it." She had begun to dream at her cocoa. "Hartley adored sportscars. It was, alas, his only vice." Melinda already knew that when Missus talked about her husband, Hartley, she made little jokes to keep from being sad.

To Melinda, the SS100 began to mean the war too. There it was, put up on blocks in the old barn. Its headlights and its trim of chrome and the racing green of its body, put on coat after coat, so thin that it took nine coats at least to make the glorious patina, was dull, dusty. The leather seats had been sat on by chickens. The grilles, which should have caught the sun, were cobwebbed. It looked crippled, forlorn, orphaned.

She began at once to clean and shine it. Sometimes when she came back from the hospital she cycled straight down to the car for a quick look before she came into the kitchen for tea. Sometimes, when there had been an influx of patients from London in the overflow from the Blitz and she was so tired she couldn't talk, she would disappear into the barn. In a little while the purr of the motor would comfort her, and she knew that Maria and Nella and Terence and Missus would leave her alone for a while.

Sometimes she let Maria and Nella sit in the car and pretend to drive it while she worked. "Vroom, vroom," they would chant, pretending to steer. Once Maria asked Melinda why she loved it so much. "It's only a car."

"It rests me," she told them. "I lost a car once. It got burned." She launched into a story about that, but her head was under the left bonnet and

Maria and Nella didn't pay much attention. By the time she had her head up again, she was, as usual, connecting the story with something else.

She said, "I have an aunt, Boodie, and she made dollhouses when she was grown-up, because when she came to my house she saw my dollhouse and her mother said she couldn't have one, that they couldn't afford it." She laughed then and said, "When Boodie grew up, she made about ten dollhouses. Maybe she will let you play with one when I take you to America."

"Will you take Nella too?"

"Oh, I'll take everybody."

The children started going to the village school across the road. The others teased Nella until she whomped them and they didn't anymore.

Maria told Melinda years later that the best thing Nella ever did for her when she came to Missus's house was to put things into real words. Maria learned to speak then what Nella called proper English, not like a bleedin ponce. She said she would never forget the day after Nella and Terence got there from London, after Missus had washed and fed them, combed the nits out of their hair, and hugged them. Nella caught Terence down in the garden, wailing, with the snot running down his face and the tears streaking the dirt from where he had been playing in mud. Nella ran to get him. He wouldn't move. He just said, over and over, "I want to go back. I don't like this fuckin plice."

Nella put her hands on her hips like a grown-up woman and said, "You stupid nit, there ain't no bleedin back."

There wasn't no bleedin back for Maria either—she knew that, she told Melinda—but she said nothing at the time. Terence peed on the floor when they first came, and in the bed for a long time, but Missus wouldn't let them tease him and wouldn't let Nella beat him for it, as she wanted to. He got over it.

In the medieval dovecote, which had niches for eighty birds and was so old that Maria asked Melinda if lots of people had died in it, Nella and Maria used one of the niches to write secret letters to each other. They made the others members of the Order of the Rigid Digit, then giggled and wouldn't explain. It was RAF language. They learned it all. When there had been a crash, they learned to say that the pilots had pranged and gone for a Burton. The RAF buried them in the village churchyard, and some were in coffins far too little for whole bodies. Nella said that the RAF was either being mingy or saving wood.

They always knew when a funeral was coming. They could all hear the slow march coming from the distant station. Maria and Nella ran to the lych-gate to watch. They watched until the little band disappeared again toward the station, playing the quick march.

Tye, when he finally could come down a little more often, said that Maria was becoming as ignorant as a pup. He went to the RAF station and asked the Jesuit padre if he would tutor her. She said she wouldn't be tutored unless Nella was. So Father McKnight taught them both when he could get away, Latin and Greek. Tye said it would keep them out of mischief.

The war was far away after a while, and RAF Linfield became a training command station. The pilots were younger and younger. Once a plane swept overhead, low-flying, and hopped their hedge when Maria was looking for mushrooms. The pilot waved at her. She could see the shadow of the wing only about a foot from the ground as he turned. At first she was so terrified that she screamed and ran to find Melinda, but Melinda told her it was "ours." Maria said with some annoyance that she knew that; she was embarrassed over being afraid.

But when Tye came on Saturday, Melinda told him about the low flying and he said, "Those bloody fools. They're just bored. I don't blame them." He said that some of them were burned out from the Battle of Britain and had been posted to training command for the rest of the war and were about half crazy. He said they had had a terrible war already, but Maria said that it wasn't true. She and Nella had heard the pilots in the pub, and they had said it was a piece of cake. Melinda asked, "What on earth were you doing in the pub?"

Five months after Melinda had gone to the country, in January, on a bright clear cold day, she went back at last to London. Paddington station was full of sunlight, because all the dirty glass was gone from the roof and the skeleton of the station rose into a blue sky.

The flat was dead, the glass in the French doors broken, the garden covered with rubble and bricks from the house on the next street. Damp had seeped in and stained the floor. Everything was cold to the touch. Melinda lit the Aga with what coal she could find and set about cleaning. Brit sauntered in through the cat-hole in the door, looking healthy, and brushed against her leg and purred.

Melinda worked all day, until Tye found a way to get home, and while they lay on the bed together they could hear the murmur of Ewen's perpetual party. That hadn't changed. He had been seconded to a new airborne unit, but for a while he was stationed in London.

Melinda found herself years later dividing what they had learned to call the phony war from the Blitz by what Ewen's friends twittered at his parties. They talked then about who was alive and who was dead and who had sloped off to Canada and who had lost everything, and then there would be sudden gales of laughter. "My dear, stark naked and thrown into the street with her lover, and his wife who was a dim little thing but has the money is suing him for everything he has left, which isn't much, God knows, after the bombing."

"Oh, my dear, do understand," Ewen whispered once when he read her face after a particularly outrageous remark. "They are all right-wing, anti-Semitic, anti–working class, and brave as hell. Those people you see have been up night after night dragging bodies out of the wreckage." He thought he was explaining when he added, "Never forget, my darling, that camp is a form of courage. It's propping them up.

Solemnity is c-o-m-m-o-n." He spelled the word to avoid saying it. Then he sighed. She let herself think about that, after so many people who had been at Ewen's parties were dead and gone. She promised herself to try it. Camp. A form of courage. They had become what, in the circumstances, they expected of themselves.

It was such a different war from Spain; they were in it because they were patriots, not because they cared about Hitler or anything else. And there was, in the beginning, a terrible excitement. It was not Ewen's friends, though, but the older women of London, too old for the services, or those with small children, who she learned to love—unsung women who stood in the queues, which grew longer and longer, making do and eking out as their wartime duty. They looked grayer and grayer as the months passed into years.

Like so many married people, Melinda and Tye had fallen into a pattern. They could spend only their leaves together. Melinda went to London; Tye went to Wiltshire. Just before Christmas in 1944, Melinda went up to London to see what she could find for the children beyond the tinfoil strips the German pilots dropped to deflect the air-raid warning signals. The children had gathered them for years to trim the tree.

London was freezing. Ice glistened on the trees in the square. She never remembered quite what she found for the children. She knew that she went back to the house, dumped the loot on the kitchen table, and tried to get the Aga going so they wouldn't freeze when they came back from dinner and their treat, a revue. Melinda chose it.

She said that if she didn't laugh at something, she would shoot herself. Like everybody else, they had gotten used to the doodlebugs, and even the far worse V-2s.

They met at the White Tower for jugged hare and some wine. Tye said that rabbit and herring were the only unrationed food in England, that and mangelwurzels. "Whale and horse," Melinda added.

The blackout had lifted, partly, to a dim-out. At least they could see the street as they walked back fast through the snow that had begun to fall, to get to the house and keep each other warm. Melinda remembered that she and Tye were trying to sing the words to "The Borgia Orgy Tonight," and the song that the lovely girl in a top hat had sung, "I'm going to get lit up when the lights go on in London," which had made Melinda cry. They were humming, trying to get the tunes, shutting each other up and beginning again.

In the distance they saw the new searchlights that the rescue teams were finally being allowed to use. A V-2 had destroyed the backs of all of the houses on the west side of St. Michael's Square. From beyond the barricade set up by rescue workers, they could see the exposed bedrooms, the broken floors, half a table, Tye's bathrobe, broken glass. Long stalactites of icicles already hung from the shattered boards. Ewen's white columns were flung against the frames of the open front windows, where the snow poured in. Melinda could see what was left of the Christmas parcels under the fallen ceiling in the kitchen.

Tye said it looked like the barbarians had entered Rome. He said, "Well, at least Ewen didn't have to see this." Ewen had been killed at Arnhem. He had left them the house. They had played at night when they were together about how they would make it their own when the war was over, as if of all the houses in London, theirs would be safe.

Tye said, "Come on. Let's go." They walked away and left it to the wind and the snow. They went toward the sounds of the wounded. A shelter had been set up by the WVS, who were doling out tea and buns. The snow fell on army-issue blankets wrapped around the shocked people in the tea queue. It was quiet. Far away somebody said, "You bloody fool. Get down from there," and Melinda remembered hearing a voice calling over and over, "He's here. He's over here."

The crater where houses and shops had been was a large lake that a broken water main had already half filled. Where Melinda had stood in queues for fish, for the tea ration, or sugar, or marge, or the meat ration, the plumber, the greengrocer, the junk shop, the post office, the stationers, were all blotted out. A man wandered around the periphery of the crater, saying politely to anyone who would listen, "Have you by any chance seen my wife?"

The cold kept the smell away and muted the sound. Splashed blood turned the falling snowflakes pink.

Endurance. In durance vile. Melinda's mind played tricks. She watched as rescue workers climbed into the wreckage, so carefully they seemed to be walking on eggs. Another cliche. True. It was worse than anything she had seen in Spain. There were dead people, and pieces of dead people, which the rescue teams covered at once to keep survivors who were wandering back and forth in the dark from seeing their relatives or their neighbors. Sounds came from inside the wreckage, sounds like the moans of animals, and once in a while a faint "Please."

Melinda and Tye reported to the medics and were put to work. It was odd, Melinda drifted into thinking while she was bandaging a woman's arm, to get a rocket meant to be told off, and then meant death. She was afraid that after all she had seen, endured, become inured to, she was going to vomit. She couldn't get the words to "The Borgia Orgy Tonight" out of her mind.

The woman was saying, "I liked them doodlebugs better. You knew they was coming. We was used to them things. We was having our tea. Kippers and potatoes, and a bit of marge and toast and jam I found in the larder, strawberry jam." She went on about the tea, and then said, "Find my husband, the old fool. We never heard nuthin. You don't know you are going to be hit when the V-2s land. You only know you are still alive when you hear the noise."

That was the last thing she said. She just slumped over, and when Melinda yelled for Tye, she was dead. Dead of shock, he said, nothing but shock. She had had enough.

After the V-2 landed there were only three walls standing, but the house was so solid that it had not been condemned. On the day they were allowed back into it, Melinda let herself see it again as it had been when it was new to her, black and white and brittle with the gaiety of ghost people, instead of in the twilight under the tarpaulin that had been put over the shattered roof.

Everything that had ever been precious was soaked trash. The furniture of Ewen's sitting room had been crushed and tossed by what the Bible called a mighty wind against the shattered windows. Rain-sopped curtains had been flung by the same wind into a corner of the room, where the fine woodwork had shattered over the pile, all of it exposed. There was something shameful about it. Obscene. Their boat bed was crushed, Maria's brass bed contorted. Whenever, later, the V-2 crashed into Melinda's memory, she shivered. Her skin would grow cold, and when somebody asked her what the matter was, she would say, "Nothing. Somebody just walked over my grave."

Before the bomb, the oval-spiraled stairs that rose to the third floor, where the skylight cast prisms in summer, had been lined with Ewen's collection of etchings, Piranesi's *Prisons.* The banisters had been polished, the steps covered with long dark red stair carpet held to the risers with shining brass. The oval spiral of stairs had miraculously survived, its shape as elegant as ever, rising into empty space past the snaggled floors under a blank sky where the skylight had been. There was only the smell of mildew and rain and the silence of ruin.

"Watch out," Tye called back, "stay close to the wall." Then he said, that day, still on the stairs, "You know I'm going to practice here, right here, don't you? I knew it when we helped dig those people out, I think, but I didn't know it enough to tell you yet. When the National Health comes in, I'm going to be a GP."

"I knew that," Melinda told his back. He didn't realize how often he had dreamed of it.

When they told his mother, one evening in the kitchen in Wiltshire, which they still kept, by habit, as the center of the house, she raised Cain, which she seldom did. But she was suddenly old by then. The murderous discomfort of war, which sounded so unimportant but loomed so daily, had worn her down. She said Tye ought to become a specialist, a surgeon, as he had always planned. But he just went on with the business of making an omelet; he had taken up cooking.

"You are as stubborn as a mule," she said to his back, then grinned. "I picked that up from Melinda. It's Southern. She says so too."

"What?"

"That you are as stubborn as a mule."

The first thing he did when the war ended was to share a surgery with another doctor in Pimlico. He found a flat as near the wreck of the house as he could, so that Maria could go back to the autumn term at L'Ecole. She was nearly thirteen by then. She had flown through the school certificate with what Tye called Jesuit honors, but she was still sometimes like a small child, and didn't know it. Melinda refused to let her go to a boarding school. She said she distrusted the food, but what she really meant was that she wanted a nest at last and she knew Maria needed it as much as she did, even though she was already champing at the bit.

Once when Maria was sulking—and she had grown good at that—Melinda said, "I don't know what I'm supposed to do with you."

"I'm thirteen years old," Maria had said with great dignity. "Whatever you haven't taught me, it's already too late." Then she burst into tears and sobbed, "Can't you just *be* there? Be there and shut up." She flung herself out of the kitchen. It took Melinda several angry minutes to realize that she had been given some excellent advice on how to be the mother of an adolescent.

Late at night, when the house was still a dream, Tye walked back and forth in the anonymous flat full of furniture that nobody had chosen, that had just been bought and put there, all brown in one way or another. He made sketches on the anonymous table, talking not about patients but about plumbing. From time to time he said things that made her see as well as he could what the place would be like, the new place in the old walls. He clung to the planning as he had once clung to the garden, and when she was making dinner or reading, he would suddenly bring out a new thought. "Would you like the front bedroom on the third floor for us?" or, "I think the back for Maria, over the garden, but let's ask her. She has to choose for herself," or, "The other two bedrooms on that floor . . ." He existed in the brown flat, but he already lived in the house, which was slowly being dug out of its ruin. She would shift into his dream and see it with him, loving it and loving him.

"Listen. Listen!" he called from the table once. "We won't have to give up the garden kitchen! Listen!" She knew he could see his garden in perpetual bloom when it was still covered with the flotsam of war and rebuilding and when what ground they could see was as hard as stone.

"Listen!" He was excited, but then he was so often, rebuilding the world, as new as the plans, and she listened to Tye again while he said, "Don't you see, I can put my surgery where our bed-sitter was. We will use fifteen feet for the waiting room, then a wall, then ten feet for my office, then ten feet for an examining room at the back."

"That's five feet more than you have," she told him. "You remind me of a will Uncle Brandon made when he was drunk. He didn't have the proverbial pot, but he left half of nothing to his mother, half to Boodie, and a third to me."

Tye paid no attention. "You see, we can use that five-foot alcove of the old kitchen where the sink and the draining board were, so we can use the pipes, and we can use that plumbing outlet for both the kitchen and the examining room! That way"—he was drawing again with the ruler—"I'll be able to pop in and have a cuppa when I'm too bloody tired to climb the stairs, and I'll be able to hear you both and know when you are there." He came over to where she and Maria were reading, both of them in one ugly, overstuffed chair, and buried his face in her hair and then in Maria's.

"Goddammit, we're going to be married and a family, married like people are every day. We're going to be bored. Won't that be marvelous? Marriage. What an odd word," he said. "When have we had time, except for one summer? Christ, we've been lovers. That's all you can be in wartime, and that's not enough." He was lecturing to the tops of their heads. "Listen! The other word for peace is time, peacetime. Peace *time!*" he shouted.

Everybody seemed to be getting younger, Tye and Penny and herself, with the war over and the frail beginning of the acceptance of peace. They got sick and laughed and cried easily, like children. Tye got flu too often, but he wouldn't stay in bed. He lay fully clothed and read Proust in a foul temper. Once, coming into their bedroom, she heard him mutter, "Shut up. Shut up. Shut up."

"Who, me?" She handed him the inevitable tea.

"No. Proust," he grumbled. "Marcel and Saint-Loup are going on and on and on about military tactics. I'm getting out of this damned ugly room tomorrow."

"You are not." She went out and shut the door.

As soon as the basic work had begun, they spent every hour they could at the house, as it was gradually dug out of the rubble.

"Look! Look, Melinda," Tye would call whenever he had rescued something. He uncovered the Aga. It had been protected by the ceiling, which had fallen at an angle over it. The Christmas parcels, flattened, were still there. He found a drawing of Ewen's that had not been scratched, a pair of socks, several unbroken pieces of their Cornishware china, three or four of his books that had not been soaked by rain. He set them all in a row, and they carried their finds back to the flat, which became less anonymous as they dug and discovered and cleaned. Each unbroken cup, plate, table, soggy blanket, became a small triumph, cocking a snook.

Once in a while, though, the rigid happiness broke, and they would look at the retrieved pile and Tye would say, "Bloody pathetic." It was like climbing two steps up and one step back out of a deep pit, which no one called despair.

Then one day Melinda heard him call, "Oh my God, come here." He was crouched over a small space in the rubble of the garden, his hands cupped around one of his roses. It had been blown almost to the ground, but spring had come and it was putting out little pink bumps that were going to be leaves. He stayed that way for a long time and wouldn't let her see his face. He found some chicken wire and made a cage for the rose, and he painted a large sign that said, "Do NOT repeat NOT place anything over this."

Melinda never forgot the sound of London being remade all around them. She remembered the hammers, so slow that sometimes she wanted to shout, "Not bang pause bang pause bang.

Bang bang bang bang bang!" The English had been slow and patient, and it had made them survive. Now they were slowly and patiently rebuilding, and sometimes it drove her, as they would say, round the bleedin bend.

But when Melinda tried to find words for moving into real marriage, she couldn't. There was rest in it, no events, no excitement. Tye said they had had enough of that to last forever. There was an everyday joy, and friends—noisy, opinionated, lovely, lively, postwar friends, born again into uneasy peace. Their noise was not the frenetic noise of Ewen's friends, in the same place but not the same house. It had been instead arguments, great arguments. She could place the years by the arguments. During the Labour Party landslide in 1945, when people shouted in the streets, she and Tye and Penny and Penny's new husband, Cotty, a sculptor that her family disapproved of, got drunk on plonk and sang, "The people's flag is deepest pink, it's not as red as you might think, the middle class is now our goal, no income tax but birth control," and "That Trotskyite Mammy of Mine," until Maria called out, "I can't sleep."

Penny said her father and the other old Tories at the Junior Carlton Club had gotten drunk on the last of the prewar wine and held a high Anglican funeral service for the Conservative Party on the billiard table as the head of one cabinet minister after another fell. Churchill was no longer the head of the government. Tye explained, "It's really a question of casting. He's miscast for peacetime. All that Spenserian prose!" Cotty said Tye thought he invented the Labour Party and the National Health.

The new house was finally ready, the new shining paint, the kitchen that was the same and not the same. All of it was the same and not the same. They settled into it like birds in the nest. They made a world of their own, their own noise, their own peace, hardly realizing that they were part of a great sigh that was London around them, getting used to peace and small things. The garden was finally cleared of rubble. The rose that Tye had found bloomed.

They found more Victorian furniture in Missus's inexhaustible attic, a Persian rug, two marble-topped tables with ridiculous lions holding the tops up to the wall. They said they wanted the sitting room to look like Sherlock Holmes's rooms. They painted it dark green like the Jaguar, nine coats of thin carriage paint, which Tye said would last forever. "The word *forever.* What a luxury," he said, painting the wall.

They hunted the junk shops. They found a chinoiserie table with red and gold carving. They put it in the hall where Tye's patients came in. Melinda kept flowers there, and a silver tray to hold the mail. Missus said it "had been in the family." When their insurance company had insisted that they have everything valued, the appraiser had said it was fine late-seventeenth-century silver but that it had tired edges. Tye said, "Who doesn't?"

So at last the spiral staircase shone again. The windows were clean. The skylight glistened. The dark green living room was a night castle, an aerie. Finally the doors closed, making a fug sweet with tea and then drinks and the fire, and the closed curtains were no longer blackout curtains but an almost-gold that Melinda had found in Missus's attic and cut down, old and silk. The cloth came from Siam, Missus told her, when Tye's grandfather had been in the Foreign Office and brought back everything that wasn't nailed down. That was where the marble-topped tables with the crazy lions had come from too. Siam. Thailand. Melinda never could remember which it was called.

They had put a round table with a green baize cover in the part of the room that had been the library. Tye said he didn't like sitting at the head of anything. They had planned to use it sometimes for a dining table when they had what she still called company and Tye called guests. There had hardly been time for that in the slipping by of all those days piled on days, mostly alike, as if time didn't pass but repeated itself. A constant jigsaw puzzle, which replaced the guests they didn't bother with, was spread out on the green baize. The room was a place to come into when it was over, whatever "it" was.

They ate with their friends and argued in the warm kitchen. When the lamplighter came by at twilight to light the Victorian gas lamp in front of their house, they waved to him, and several times when it was pissing down with rain they asked him in. He was an art student from the Slade. He was a series of art students from the Slade. They all said it was the best job they could find, just twilight and dawn, when they didn't want to paint anyway.

When the war ended, Nella's aunt in the Isle of Dogs insisted that Nella and Terence go back to her. She wanted their ration books. But that hadn't stopped Nella. She went to secretarial school after her O-levels on a scholarship that she had uncovered, which had to do with war orphans. She went back to school at night and got six A-levels, with honors. She said the education was her ammunition when anybody tried to bugger her up. She said she could do bleedin Greek as well as Maria could—better, in fact. She had a job as secretary at a local Labour Party headquarters in the East End, where she said most of the voters were Communists.

Then one evening in 1949, when Melinda and Maria had finished packing for Maria to go to Cambridge and were having their tea in the living room in front of the fire, they heard Nella stomp up the stairs.

"I'm going. I'm going too!" Nella yelled ahead of herself.

She hugged Maria and Melinda and then Maria again. "I've wangled a scholarship to Cambridge through the Labour Party." She roared with laughter at herself when she said she had just marched up to Harold Laski's house with the six A-levels under her belt and knocked on his door as bold as brass. Everybody said he was the brains of the Labour Party.

She said she had told him she wanted to go to Cambridge even though he was at the London School of Economics, because she thought her political contacts would be wider in scope. She had thought of the phrase on the way in the tube.

He had said, "That is what we hope for." She said he had put his fingers together in front of his chin, and she could see her reflection in his glasses, and he had said, "We hope to have two thirds workers with the maind"—that was the way he said it, *maind*— "and one third workers with the hands." She said what he really meant was a lot of Labour Party professors pushing working people around for their own good and it didn't change a thing, not really. Nella imitated him when she told the story. She laughed and said, "Can you believe that?"

The winter of 1949 was the coldest winter in memory. There was not enough fuel, not enough food, not enough anything, and no war to give it all a reason. Melinda and Tye wore ex-issue Royal Navy duffel coats with prewar Irish sweaters underneath. When they could get petrol, Melinda covered the seats of the shining Jaguar with a tarp, drove it to Wiltshire, and piled it high with wood. Then they sat almost on top of the Aga, holding hot drinks against their wrists to get warm. The pipes froze and they gathered dirty snow to flush the loos.

Melinda stood, or sagged, with other women in the perpetual queues, which had not stopped with the end of the war. She could sense the dog-tiredness around her, and it made her stomach hurt in sympathy. If the soldiers and the airmen and the young had had a change from war, the women had had none. They were condemned still to eke out and make do with that patience that she had seen sometimes on the faces of the nearly dead, the trudgers—what she called, including herself, the dropped-womb set. They wore their medals in their lined faces. The Labour Party called it "austerity" and gave the street cleaners cavalier hats so they would feel more dignified in their jobs. For Tye, the women were like his lovers. He talked about them until their names were as familiar as the family's.

Desmond—dearest, dearest Desmond—turned up from Cambridge. He was twenty when he came to the door in slept-in gray flannels and a tweed jacket that looked as if it had held several volumes of the *Encyclopedia Britannica* for a long time in its pockets. He said that he was entering University College Hospital as a medical student and that Maria had told him at Cambridge that Melinda and Tye might have a room. He said that he could pay thirty shillings a week and he wanted to help Tye in surgery to make up the rest.

Several young doctors had wanted to be Tye's assistant, because the surgery was near Belgravia and Tye was, after all, a baronet, not one of the new Labour Party ones either. Nella called him Doctor Sir, which stuck, and added that they were all bleedin nobs. Too many of the young doctors could see themselves with fine private practices. Tye said he could tell them a mile off. So he waited until Desmond turned up, as if he had known that, sooner or later, he would.

The National Health was Tye's obsession, his

dream come true, what held him together. He accepted appointments over and over because he was a socialist, but Nella said he was asked because he was a baronet and the Labour Party were bleedin snobs. After the Tories came back into power, he went on as the minority member so they wouldn't dismantle the system, but he grew more and more depressed about it.

He said the National Health had begun like the volunteers in Spain, who fought for things they believed in. The conservative young doctors were like the conscripts who found the Second World War dead and gray—all but Desmond, who became like a younger brother to Tye, almost from the time he began.

Then there were all the friends, Maria's lot, and Desmond's. They gave Nella her wedding reception when she married Ludlow, who was a labor solicitor. He never said "solicitor," always "labor solicitor," as if it were a title. Terence gave her away. He was a sprog in the RAF, a conscript, and he hated it. Nella was in a safe Labour seat in the House of Commons, a worker, she said, with the maind, laughing that marvelous laugh every time.

Penny, Melinda's and Tye's ever-present help in time of trouble, came to run the surgery. At weekends and when Penny had babies, Melinda took her place.

Tye worked like a dog. Melinda could hear him dragging his steps through the years up from the surgery. He said that there was so much to catch up with: the men who had neglected their own health so that their wives and children could use what little money there was to go to the doctor, the neglected women who he had seen so often in the wartime emergency wards, where some of them had rested for the first time in months. The color had come back into their cheeks, and they hadn't wanted to leave. Tye seemed to want to help people be younger, and sometimes he succeeded, when the war had lifted from them and they got the attention they hadn't had before. He said the one asset of the war was the half-grown children. Their rations had included milk and orange juice. That had made a healthier generation, that and conscription, since so many of them had eaten better in the army than they had for the eighteen years before they were called up. He kept saying it, and then ending with "What a bloody shame" or "It had to take a war."

Sometimes he came upstairs after nine, sometimes even later. Some of the people who had signed on with him when the National Health came in were the surviving members of families who had been killed when the V-2 fell. It was odd how London divided itself into new little neighborhoods—bombed neighborhoods instead of the old divisions, as if the craters that were filled again were some sort of terrible fireside that they could sit around, not letting anybody else close: our bomb, our neighborhood.

They all came to Tye, and it wasn't just for the colds, the fatigue, the flus, the pains in the belly, it was to find out what to do—where to go for the eyes that had been blinded by flying glass, where to go for the silence some people couldn't come out of, where to go for teeth that had been neglected, youth that had been lost, a birth or a death or the National Health way of coping with the mountain of human debris left from the war, the never-ending postwar rationing, the drabness.

Tye would sit on the horsehair sofa that had once been in the morning room at Missus's, and he would think for a long time and then say, "Now, I'm going to write you . . ."—an address, an appointment, a drug, a panacea for dry fatigue. It was what he treated most, and people died of it. But like fire that had turned to embers, there were shoots of a new blaze, and he fed them with energy and whatever hope there was. Tye said when the *Times* published rafts of letters about the first cuckoo in spring that it was really over, whatever the postwar had been.

In 1953, for her coming-down from Cambridge, Maria asked Melinda and Tye to take her to Spain. Melinda was against it. She thought Maria wasn't old enough to face it, and Maria said Melinda thought she wasn't old enough to come in out of the rain. When she said it, she brought the sounds and scents of Kregg's Crossing back to Melinda and confused her so that she couldn't argue.

Tye said that Maria ought to go. He said that she had a whole new life to face, and that she ought to have her wishes honored because she had come down from Cambridge with a first, well, with two, whatever that was, they were. Melinda dropped out of the discussion, since she had little idea what they were talking about. Tye couldn't go because he was still *persona non grata* in Spain, and Melinda grumbled, "With what's going on in the States, I must be *persona non grata* there."

"So aren't you delighted you married me and McCarthy can't get at you?" Tye grinned and was about to say more.

"Oh, shut up," Melinda said. She agreed to take Maria to Spain if she could take the Jaguar and, as she put it, "let it out," as if it too had been caged in postwar England.

"It's a right-hand drive. You can't drive that on the continent," Tye fussed.

"Why not? I got out of Spain with a right-hand drive and I can get back in."

"Did you really? I didn't know that." Tye forgot what he was complaining about.

Melinda said, "We will go back and tilt again at windmills."

It is all the car's fault," Maria said. After what had seemed to Melinda to be years of silence between them—known, she supposed, as adolescence—Maria had hardly shut up since they had driven off the ferry five hours before, onto the continent of Europe for the first time since the war. They were cruising along a straight French road in the June sun, which skipped along the shiny racing-green grilles on the bonnet of the SS100 and flashed on the polished chrome of the huge headlights so that it was nearly hypnotic. They put down the windscreen and sped through France with the wind blowing their hair, like people in the flicks. They had had a wonderful unrationed lunch, and the car was perfect.

"I'm getting younger by the mile! It's the car. I grew up in it, watching you diddle with it. I was so old when I left Cambridge," Maria went on, not bothering with the fact that only a week had passed since then. They were getting nearer and nearer the barrier of mountains.

"I know," she said, surprising Melinda, "I know with my mind that I am Spanish. I know you and Tye worried that I couldn't remember. Well, I did. It was in my mind but not in my dreams—you know, deeper, realer. I hoped for that, but it never happened. So all I really know is medieval Spanish and the history of the Moorish wars in Spain. I tried to relearn modern Spanish, but it seemed to be the only language I couldn't quite grasp, think in.

I used to sleep with the scrap of paper from my father under my pillow, until it wore out. I used to hold it on my way to sleep and hope that it would give me back some blank space waiting for something, like those horror flicks where you expected somebody to walk out of the mist toward you. But nobody ever came. Nobody."

"Oh, my darling, I don't know what to say." Melinda slowed the car.

"Did you ever try to find the man in Paris? You never told me."

"He never heard from your father. I'm sorry. We tried for months. Then we were cut off from France by the war. As soon as peace came, we tried again, but M. Borgan was no longer at the Ecole des Beaux Arts. Nobody seemed to know what had happened to him. He was the only link we had. We hated trying to find out after so long." She touched Maria's hand. "But we thought you would blame us someday if we didn't try."

They were sharing the driving. It was Melinda's turn. She drove, intent and relaxed, downshifting, the way she had taught Maria, glancing right and left like a fighter pilot, then back to the front. They were somewhere beyond Carcassonne.

They drove for twenty miles before either of them spoke again. When Melinda broke the silence and the hum of the tires on the road, she said, "Spain broke our hearts." But she was talking to the mountains, not Maria.

"You've never talked like that before. It was always stories about when you met Tye and where you were married, and all that." Maria was surprised.

Melinda seemed to be driving into spaces in her memory. "The war in Spain was the worst thing that ever happened to us. Something died there. We just felt lost with people who hadn't been there, as if we knew something we couldn't tell and they would never understand."

They were high up in the mountains. Melinda stopped the car beside the road, in a wide place in front of a small shack in the shadow of the mountain pass. "Thank heavens, it's still here," she said. "This was the last place Fig and I had food before we went down the mountain into Spain."

The door was so low, the one window so small, that the room within was like a white cave. There were no angles in the place. They had all long since been worn away. The little wooden bar had been rounded by bodies leaning against it. The tables, covered with red oilcloth that was so old that the cloth showed through the corners, were without any sharpness.

When they went through the bead curtain that kept the flies out, no one was there. It was like the *Marie Celeste,* but clean. The Pernod waited in its bottle. The wine waited behind the bar. The glasses behind the bar were muted by the dim light.

The door behind the bar swung open, and a man who was so large that he filled it came through sideways, carrying a tray. There were glasses on it, and the sound of their shifting broke the silence with little music. One of the glasses was a quart wineglass.

He and Melinda stared at each other as if they were seeing ghosts.

"Do you know me, madame?" he said.

"It's been fifteen years."

The man smiled. "I was young then, and thin. Now I have raised a fine stomach and survived two wars. You look somehow familiar, but I don't know, madame, there are so many." He smiled his polite patron smile and showed them to a table.

Melinda told him that when she had been there before, they had sat at the table and drunk wine and toasted the Front Populaire.

"Madame," he said, "I don't remember any single one, but I remember you all. No, wait. Your friend had been here before, and you were driving an ambulance. Of course. Of course. I have had to keep quiet for so long I am afraid to remember." He bustled away, carrying his weight lightly, as some fat men do, and came back with plates and napkins and knives and forks, all jangling. He poured the wine and raised his quart glass. *"Salud. Viva la República."*

It was the first of several toasts, and they both had tears in their eyes. They had fallen into time past and left Maria stranded, watching them.

"And where is your friend now?" the patron asked. "I am usually afraid to ask that question."

"Il est mort," she said, and they raised their glasses again.

"So many, oh God, so many. You know, I have many relatives across the mountains. Families are older than borders here in the mountains. Many of them, and many Spaniards who were put in the camps here on the French side, fought with the Maquis when they got out. You see, they knew the passes."

The patron's wife, who was fat too and smiled a lot, brought omelets and salad and soft cheeses and bread. They had had nothing like it, the scent of it, the fresh eggs, all the cheese they wanted, in England. The room smelled of wine, cheese, vinegar, hot bread and butter.

The patron was a young man again, and he was in the mountain caves, hiding. He was learning to be stupid. He was throwing grenades. He mined bridges. He told jokes. Melinda was there with him, and the level of the wine bottles went down and down, and several times they laughed together. All the time he was pointing to places with his large arms. Then Maria suddenly interrupted.

She spoke without hope. "Did you know a man named Juan López García?"

"The professor! But of course. Of course. He taught me English when we were hiding in the mountains. He had to teach somebody, anybody. It was like food for him. We fought together, and we lived together like brothers in the caves for a long time—months, anyway. My wife, who has gone back into the kitchen because she doesn't understand English, ran the place when I disappeared. She told the French police and the Gestapo I was dead. She showed them my grave. It was my father's, but we had the same name. She used to send chickens and milk and cheese up to us in a basket. My nephew came up half the way on a bicycle and left the basket behind a rock. Oh, the professor! She always said, make the professor eat. He is too thin. This is the country of Gargantua and Pantagruel, and we believe, as you can see, in being strong and big." He raised the quart wineglass again.

Maria couldn't say a word, but Melinda looked at her and then asked for her, "Can you tell us what happened to him, where he is?"

"Ah, yes. He was a fine man. *Mort. Kaput.* It wasn't the Germans who caught him. It was the Franco soldiers."

Maria sprang up, and red wine snaked across the oilcloth and dripped to the floor. She ran outside.

"That was her father," Melinda said. "You must tell her everything you remember about him, and everything you don't. She remembers nothing."

"You are not her mother?"

"She is adopted."

He got up and left the table. Melinda never knew what happened outside in the car. She could see them through the little window, Maria's head bowed and her hair over her face and the patron leaning down with his hand on her back. They talked for a long time, and when he came back he said, "I think we should leave her alone. Wait." He disappeared through the small door behind the bar.

The patron carried a packed basket when he came back. "Here. My wife has made it just like she made for me and the others and for her father. No, madame, I do not take payment from my own. And you must come back, many times. I am lonely in peacetime. We all have grown apart again after the comradeship, the *fraternite.* People come by now and see a simple place and they hold me and my wife in contempt and ask if things are clean and go away without thanks. *Camarada,* the answer to that Fascist contempt is not good manners or equality beyond the door but *fraternite,* a glass of wine, a friend . . ."

He stood in front of the low door, waving his huge arm until they turned a curve of the mountain and Melinda could no longer glimpse him in the rearview mirror.

Maria had not said a word or lifted her head. She only swung her heavy hair to hide her face. Her shoulders heaved with sobs, and when she finally ran down, like someone tired after all the years, she looked at Melinda and said, "Damn you. You knew, didn't you?" But she said it like a blessing.

"I hoped," Melinda told her, watching the mountain road. "You see, people were close then. They had to be, and, well, after the letter he left, Tye and I looked for a long time at the map and we hoped. He would have tried to find you across the border in the mountain towns too."

They drew up to the same border post that Melinda had stopped at with Fig so long ago. The border guard said *señora* instead of *camarada,* and he said *adiós* when he gave them back their passports: *"Adiós,* Lady Dunston. *Adiós,* Señorita García."

While Melinda negotiated the curves of the Pyrenees as if she were riding a spirited horse, Maria laid her head back on the seat and looked at Spain for the first time that she could remember.

Figueres was as silent as the tomb it had been fourteen years before. But it was only the siesta. It was not yet three o'clock. Melinda said, "Whenever we were waiting, and the war was mostly waiting, the Spanish soldiers took their siesta—on the ground, in the snow, in the mud, anywhere."

Figueres had been rebuilt as the old city had been. Some of the stones had begun to weather, and the trees that lined the plaza were pollarded instead of torn by bombing. In June they had crowns of leaves which were beginning to shade the tile designs on the pavement.

Melinda and Maria found a small hotel, and when they went into the lobby, the men at the bar through the arch stared at them. A large sad woman dressed all in black was behind the small, freshly polished counter. *"Bienvenida, señora, señorita,"* she said. *"Una habitación con baño?"* and Maria spoke the first Spanish words Melinda had ever heard her speak. *"Con baño, sí,"* she said. *"Dos habitaciones."*

They had decided right at the beginning that since Spain was very cheap and they would be together all day, they should have separate rooms. Maria smiled at Melinda. Melinda had never seen her look so beautiful. Her face had the same poise that she had had as a child, a waiting calm that she had never lost. Her eyes were still huge, her hair a straight black silk mass which she let fall below her shoulders. Her clothes were straight and dreary in the 1953 student fashion of despairing existential black.

They walked along the street in the first darkness to join the *paseo.* The posters on the buildings advertised well-covered *señoritas* in *mantillas,* with red blossoms behind their ears, preferring this to that Spanish drink. Melinda was trying to control her tears and find some words to comfort herself. It was to her a limbo of lights and handsome people, moving like a dream, meaning nothing.

"Isn't it lovely?" Maria said, and she stopped at a shop window and went in and bought a ruffled Spanish shirt. They sat outside a cafe across from the plaza and drank *sangría.* Guardia Civil, in their patent-leather tricorns, marched along the plaza among the strollers. The young men walked two by two in one direction, the girls two by two in the other. They seemed not to be looking at each other. Maria was amused by the formal flirting. Girls threw ribbons down from the few balconies, but most of them landed in the street.

Melinda thought, Where are the pert girls with their caps and their *monos,* their free strides, their singing, their shining dirty faces?

They had dinner at ten o'clock in the dining room, with its modern medieval chairs and its blue chandeliers casting pretty light. A gilded angel on the wall stared at them. Tiles covered the walls and made mosaics of vines and flowers, an imitation past. Melinda and Maria were the only women in the room. They had two little flags on the table, Union Jacks, to show that they were tourists and not whores, dining alone.

It was on the road to Besalú that Melinda began to say what she had been thinking. It was rambling and unexplainable, but she tried as they drove over the mountains, past the *fincas* and the ruins of castles, which looked like rocks grown out of the hills, and rocks that looked like castles, past newly restored convents and ruins of isolated houses that were not old.

They passed gangs of prisoners working on the roads, watched by armed guards. "I have to stop," Melinda said, and Maria asked if she were feeling sick on the mountain curves, but she wasn't. "I can't keep my mind on the road. It's someplace else." Tears were running down her face and meeting under her chin.

The tears turned themselves into words. "There is a gulf to cross, and I can't cross it. I know the words, but I can't say them. Tye taught me the words, and so did Johnny. Poor Johnny. How he would have reveled in Spain and been heroic. Maybe everything you learn that takes, like a vaccination takes, is from people who love you, or who you love. It isn't always the same." She put her head down on the steering wheel. She was telling something new to herself.

"You can tell about blood, but you can't smell it. You can tell about fear, but you don't want to force it on anyone who doesn't know it. How do you tell about the first great love of your life? Because that's what it was, for all of us. Even if Tye said we were just visitors to somebody else's war, we were at home here in a way I don't think any of us have ever been again. We sang and we loved each other, and we groused and we wanted to go home, and we . . . glistened."

But she had not said a word. When she did speak again, to Maria, she only said, "I wonder if those of us who were here will ever get over the pain of this war's loss. I know that Tye won't. He still carries it. Sometimes at night . . ." And she let the rest of that drift out to the fields, and said nothing more, thought nothing or tried to think nothing.

Finally she started the car again, and the sunlight flashed on the bonnet, and the headlights, and she drove as if she owned the world and didn't intend to give it up. She was completely concentrated, racing with herself.

At Besalú they had their dinner out on a terrace overlooking the river. The ancient towered bridge was drenched in light from the moon, so huge that it cast the bridge's shadow onto the water. *Avión* moon. They sat honoring each other's silence, quiet together, as they had so often been through the years, like mother and daughter.

Melinda thought, How isolating this dark nostalgia is. She reached for Maria's hand, and Maria left it there, passive, touching hers, on the table by the nearly empty wine bottle and the plates of fruit and cheese.

Melinda told the moon-drenched river that things were like war and love and maybe God, but war and love and maybe God weren't like anything else. They couldn't be explained by metaphors, but they were metaphors for so much else. And she grinned at herself, because until Johnny and Tye had taught her to read, she hadn't even considered things like metaphors.

They started early in the morning along the mountain road to Cardona, and Maria was in one of her own silences for a long time. Finally she said, "Something is coming back, but it's like a dream that keeps being just beyond my mind."

Melinda said, "Don't grab for it and maybe it will stay."

They turned under the high arch into the plaza. North of them, the mountains they had crossed were still snow-laden. The salt hill glistened. The castle with its star pattern of a redoubt reached above them to the sky.

"A castle in Spain," Maria said, entranced. "The highest tower is second-century Roman, and much of it was built by Wilfred the Hairy. I looked it up."

"He is Tye's favorite king," Melinda told her.

They sat for a little while on one of the benches where the morning sun filtered through the new growth of the pollarded trees. The *posada* where Melinda and Tye had spent their wedding night had a new German name. Melinda got up and said, "You look around. I'll meet you right here again in half an hour and we will go and see the castle."

She drifted off along the narrow street, past the shops with meat and cheese—still, after eight years of peace, almost unknown in England—to the low, dark passage. She was afraid to take Maria, after seeing the Republican prisoners working on the roads, and the blank stares of the women in Figueres, and the strange man in the *posada* in Besalú.

Beyond the passage, in the sun again, she looked, and there of course was the house where they were married, and the red rose tree in front of it was in bloom. The balcony had been painted, and the brass nails on the door, as big as door-knobs, were polished to bright gold against the nearly black wood of the door. She stood there and took in all that she had forgotten or not noticed the last time she had seen it, and then she found the courage to knock.

Señora Zuda's hair was snow white. She seemed to have shrunk from the tall, strong woman who had made a wedding for her Tallo. Her face did not change, but Melinda knew she had recognized her. She looked along the street in both directions, glanced over her shoulder as she turned back toward the hallway, and then put out her hands and drew Melinda into the house. Inside, they held each other.

"We sit here," Señora Zuda commanded, and she sat Melinda down in front of a painted wooden cupboard. "Now, I am a little deaf," she said, in Spanish, and when Melinda did not understand the word *deaf,* she pointed to her ear. Then, in English she said, "You tell loud and you say in English. I understand but speak little."

So Melinda, as formally as if she were under questioning, told about Tye and how they had found each other, how Tye had finished medical school, and how he had become a National Health general practitioner. She was caught up in her story and forgot to speak simply while she explained that sometimes she thought Tye was wasted and other times she admired him, but he had too many patients and was working such long hours at his surgery that he came up to dinner sometimes as late as midnight.

When she had finished, Señora Zuda held up her hand and told her in Spanish that all her sons were dead. She said it without any passion at all, as if she had burned away her caring so long ago that she had forgotten it. "You must tell Tallo that we still have the cupboard and there is still room for two. Don't forget to tell him that. Still room for two." She spoke so low that Melinda had to lean forward to hear her. "He will be amused . . ." She used the word *complacerse.* "You say that word to him."

She got up and motioned Melinda toward the

door again. "You stay enough now. They see you." She struggled with the English long enough to make herself understood, then pushed Melinda out of the door, and called, *"No, señora, no es una pensión."*

Melinda felt watched as she went back along the passage. The door to the meeting place had been nailed shut. She was cold in the sun, and when she found Maria she said, "Do you mind if we walk up to the castle? I am cold."

"But it's warm. Look at that sky, it's so blue over the mountains and the tower, dark blue. I expected that blue." Maria didn't look at Melinda but strode on ahead up the old street toward the first stone entrance to the redoubt. "Where were you for so long?" she asked as they strolled around the high court and through huge arches toward the church. The whole place was deserted, a part of the silence of the new Spain.

"Noplace, I was just wandering," Melinda lied, afraid to tell her any more but not knowing why. "Do you know how you can tell you are in a dictatorship? People glance over their shoulders before they say anything."

As they drove along the road toward Cuenca three days later, Maria was glowing with pleasure. She was beautiful. She was being a tourist and practicing with the care of a foreigner the Spanish she had learned at Cambridge, not yet the words that were deep within her. She was so busy looking that Melinda had long since stopped telling her about the places they passed. The ruins had aged into sameness—the twelfth-century castle rocks, the fortress churches, the railroad stations of Villalba and Alfambra, where Melinda and Tye and Tandy had stopped among the men having their siesta. There was little difference between the ruins of war and time. She let Maria talk about the wars between the Christians and the Moors. While she explained the centuries, the wind played with her hair. The sun cast shadows of the pines on the grilles on the bonnet and the chrome headlights of the Jaguar.

Maria watched her. "You're driving differently, faster, more securely—you're not happy, exactly, but somehow all there, all driving, intent . . . I love the way you have your hair now, like a pageboy. It's darker than it was, but I like it.

"It's so odd," Maria said what Melinda had been thinking. "We're seeing two different Spains. You're seeing the twentieth century, and I'm seeing the twelfth." She lay her head back against the seat, reminding Melinda of Fig's favorite gesture. "I'm happy," she said. "I'm really happy."

They drove through the last of the pine woods, where the shade of the evergreens skipped along the car and their faces. Above them a small city rose, sun-gilded, above the high hill. It was Cuenca. They drove up the steep street and through the arch to the plaza. The houses had been newly painted, and the whole place, with its Renaissance fountain where on that long-lost night they had refilled the radiators of the convoy of *camiones*, was clean, for tourists and for pride. They parked beside the cathedral, where a large new cross to Jose Antonio, the Fascist martyr, had been hung against the wall. There were new wreaths under it; they looked municipal.

Maria said, ecstatic, "This was one of the first of the twelfth-century Christian fortress churches. God, look what they've done to it. It looks ghastly." Melinda thought she meant the cross to Jose Antonio, but she went on before Melinda could explain: "Eighteenth-century reconstruction. Ghastly!" Melinda had one of her little regrets that she couldn't say *ghastly* or *bastard* or *sorry* the way the English could—*ghastly,* an aesthetic judgment; *bastard,* as *bahstid,* a description of a friend, and *sorry,* meaning "piss off."

She followed Maria through one of the arches, staring down the almost straight drop of the high hill at the valley road that she had driven so long ago, it seemed, as long ago as the wars between the Christians and the Moors. The convent looked small in the gorge below.

Maria stood in the hilltop wind, her black hair thrown back and forth. Her stark black jumper, long black skirt, and black stockings made her look like a harsh virgin against the painted houses and the Spain-blue sky. But she had at least thrown off the English cloak of anger and sophistication that she had picked up at Cambridge.

She was like the child she had been when she first took Melinda's hand. But that child had been solemn and wise; this one was the child that Maria had not been allowed to be, except later, from time to time, in England. Melinda remembered the first time she had heard her laughing, no, giggling, in the garden at Missus's house, playing with Nella. Her eyes stung, and the valley below shimmered.

Maria turned and called, "Can we stop—oh, can we stop? Just for a while?"

They sat on a bench and ate a picnic, which Maria was proud of having bought in Spanish. She said she thought more might come back to her if she used the language. They were high over the road in the shade of a wall, looking down for miles at armies that were not there.

Then Maria touched Melinda's hand and said, "There is something I have always wanted to know," and Melinda waited and was patient.

"When did you find out what you ought to do? Do you know what I'm asking? It's hard to say."

Melinda had to wait for an entry into her mind where she could start, and then she said, "Well, the easy answer is that I learned a terrible lesson when my father killed himself." Then a total recall made her shiver, and it was as if Uncle Brandon, twenty years dead, sat down beside them on the stone bench. "There are things you just don't do," Melinda could hear him say inside her head, as if she were holding a shell to her ear and hearing the sea.

She knew she couldn't explain any more because she had been a part of it, of making it all happen. In her way she had, young and arrogant with certainty as she had been, and she had never solved it for herself except in nightmares. Here was this child, this beloved bald-faced truth seeker, asking her what she couldn't answer. All she could say was, "The people who got in the way of all of us were the real victims, not the people who chose. In a way, to choose is not to be a victim of war. Uncle Brandon didn't choose, for instance. His number came up. He was conscripted." She moved away from what she couldn't tell, and said, "Uncle Brandon died the year you were born," as if Maria had been born to her instead of found.

Maria was impatient. "Darling, that's just personal. You always retreat to your Uncle Brandon or Boodie when I ask you something that is too hard to answer." She only said "darling" when she wanted to argue. It was a Cambridge habit. "So you came over here. Why?"

"I don't know what it is you want to know," Melinda said, trying to lie. Maria still held on to her hand. "Maybe so people wouldn't get run over? Is that an answer?"

Maria laughed and told her she just didn't have the words, but Maria thought she understood anyway. "Anyway, it was a jolly good thing to do." The Spanish Cambridge girl patted Melinda on the shoulder and said, "The shops are open again. Do you want to come and watch me slaughter the Spanish language?"

"You go on," Melinda told her. She looked up at the lovely face and couldn't say what Maria wanted to know, but the words *jolly good* made her shiver.

Maria was gone. The words wouldn't leave her. Why did memory come back to break over her like waves, with silly words that she had taken for granted and used herself for over fifteen years? It was Tandy who had once said to her, "Jolly good, your coming all that way"—the first time she remembered hearing the phrase outside of the movies.

She finally answered Maria aloud, as if she were still sitting beside her. "At first I ran away. I was like the gingerbread man. I ran away from my father's death. Then I was running away from what was wrong, but I couldn't define, not sensibly, what it was. Then, without understanding the change, I was running toward something, something that was right, and for a few months, right at the beginning, in the convent at Albastro, I found it, but there weren't any words. Tye said *anyway.* You do it anyway."

Maria said behind her, "They did understand me, and they all said I looked Spanish and I told them I was but I hadn't been back in a long time, and then the woman who said it went all quiet and looked over her shoulder as if she expected the Guardia Civil, and she told me that the children said there had to be two of the Guardia Civil together because one could read and the other could write. She asked me if I were a widow and she asked it in Spanish and I understood without thinking about it, and said, 'No, why?' She said because I was wearing black. So I bought this. Look, isn't it lovely?"

She lay a long bright red-and-blue skirt carefully down on Melinda's lap. "Look, Melinda." She saw that Melinda was asleep; at least, her eyes were closed. "Come on!"

"I don't know what it was that made me think of all this. I just did. There are people who do and there are people who are forced to." Melinda tried to come back to Maria's insistence.

But Maria had forgotten it. "What on earth are you talking about? You've been asleep."

"Maybe I was still trying to answer your question."

"What question? Wake up. Don't be enigmatic." She sat down beside Melinda. "Look at my skirt."

"That's it. Why?"

"Why *what?*"

"That's the question. Why?"

"Oh, you are awful." Maria hugged her. "I'm hungry again."

"You're always hungry. I'm enigmatic. An inscrutable nit."

They walked together, arms linked, along the hilltop to the plaza. The sun threw their shadows, one tall and slim, one short. "I'm getting fat." Melinda pointed to her shadow, insulted.

"No, darling, just plump."

"We look like Don Quixote and Sancho Panza."

The road ahead was empty. They had crossed into La Mancha. The sky was huge, the sky Melinda remembered as if they were crossing a sea and not the land that waved toward the horizon, leaving shadows from the clouds that sailed across the ground and the rocks and made them seem to move. It was a peaceful afternoon.

Maria suddenly yelled, "Slow down, Mother, you're going too fast!" She grabbed Melinda's jacket pocket and held on as she had so long ago. When Melinda glanced at her, she was clinging to the seat.

"Darling, I'm slowing down. I'm only going forty. Now I'm going thirty." There was no one else on the road.

Maria said, in the careful English she had spoken so long ago, "I'm sorry. It is extremely cold this afternoon. I'm frightened." She leaned back against the seat and closed her eyes tight.

Melinda didn't say a word for the next few kilometers. She didn't dare. She hoped and feared for the break in Maria's mind that Maria had sought with such yearning for so long.

There was nothing on the peaceful road. They were drifting north, and the sun went with them along Maria's side of the car. She lifted up one hand to shield her face.

"This is the road we courted on," Melinda told Maria. "Tye and me. We courted and argued. Look, away up there is the ruin of one of your castles. We used to climb there, and some farmer had left hay, so we could lie and watch the stars sometimes. They were so bright, here in this space, that you could see up through them, layer behind layer, star behind star. At least you could then, when there was no light."

She kept on driving slowly, and her voice was quiet, and she brought the night into the car. She glanced over again, and Maria's hands were folded in her lap, not clenched anymore. She was asleep. Melinda went on driving around curves toward the faint hillock of Albastro in the distance. There they were, the same flowers at the same time in June, and she could still tell time by them. And the gorse bloomed, and here and there cows lay in the deep grass. Some of the fields were not yet planted, and their soil showed, as red as Virginia.

The abandoned convent on the hill beside the road had been hit since she had seen it. It was pocked with shell holes, and the roof had partly caved in. And always in the distance, coming nearer, was Albastro, with its clifflike fortress, its church spire, and, lower, the roof of the convent where Melinda sometimes felt she had been born—one of the times she had been born.

Maria waked as quietly as she had fallen asleep. "Did you say that you and Tye courted here? I love that Southern word. There is something that I've always wanted to know. Do you mind if I ask you something?"

"Of course not, darling. Anything." Melinda prepared herself to tell things about Spain she had never let herself put into words.

Maria said, a little shyly, "How did you know?"

"What?"

"Well." Maria sounded embarrassed. "You know, what happens. How did you know Tye was the one? Not in love, but something more than that. You know, darling, the *one.*" She was almost belligerent.

Melinda grinned. It was a twenty-one-year-old question from a twenty-one-year-old girl, instead of the usual Cambridge gloss of Kierkegaard, Sartre, William James, *Das Kapital,* and *The New Statesman.* It was what she and Toto used to call girl-talk, so long ago, giggling late at night with their faces in the pillows when Toto stayed all night. "He *kissed* you? He really *kissed* you—on the *mouth?*"

War was forgotten, or at least in retreat for a little while. She laughed, not at Maria but at the memory, and Maria knew that and smiled with her, and the road was easier to drive.

"Maybe what is different from all the times you fall in love when you are growing up is the certainty, the calmness, the, well, inevitability. It's so . . . that's it . . . inevitable, even if there has been a *coup de foudre.*"

"Ha ha." Maria spoke the words, not laughing. "*Coups de foudre* are two a penny. Glandular." She drew the word out, sounding wise.

"Well, I wouldn't say that." Melinda was remembering again.

She drove slowly up the hill toward the convent. The Moorish arch that had once been the entrance to a city that was no longer a city made Maria grasp her arm.

"I remember that. I know I do. Because of the lions, the funny lions. They are eating people. Look! Yuck! Stone sinners in the hands of angry stone lions."

They passed the place where the ruined thirteenth-century almshouse had been, where Melinda had had her auto repair shop. Only the gate door and the stone wall were left, nothing else but weeds where the shop had been. The door still had a padlock on it, which nobody had thought to take away when the place had been destroyed. Melinda kept herself from crying. It had been her place and she said so. "Dammit, that was my place, my own place I fixed." She could almost smell the grease, the oil, the tires, the rubber, and the rust, and see the lovely stars.

They drove up to the great door of the convent and sat there for a little, Melinda looking across the front courtyard, now empty, where the *camiones* had parked, Maria at the mixture of styles of the great oak door, with its age-blackened studs in the shape of large stars and the smaller door set in it.

"Look! A statue of St. Joseph holding the Christ Child." Maria pointed up to the niche between pointed columns so old they were nearly flush with the wall.

"It wasn't there. There was an empty space," Melinda said, as if she were annoyed. The tumble of ivy and weeds was gone, the trees had been cut down; the convent had become part of the town. All the space in between had been built on, new houses that looked much the same as the old ones. But there, across the little plaza, was the house where she and Concepción had sat, singing and reciting, she learning Spanish, Concepción learning English. The bench was still there, and a new door had been fitted into the primitive stone doorway. Nothing was right. It looked unused and over-cared-for. She knew, for a single freezing second, that Concepción was dead.

They simply sat there, waiting for something or nothing to happen.

"No," Melinda said, suddenly furious. "Don't believe any of this. Even our memories lie. They come in levels, shallow and then a little less shallow. But we don't tell. We don't ever tell. Spain," she said to Maria, almost politely, "was the high point of our lives, and it was terrible. It wasn't even our war. Tye said that we were visitors to war, and that we could leave—that was the difference."

A young woman came out of the small door to see what they wanted. Down the hill, along the rocky path, the inevitable two Guardia Civil were coming to see who they were. By the third day they were used to that. Every time the car stopped, every time they went into a shop to buy bread and wine, every time they asked for a direction, the Guardia Civil, in pairs, with those harsh patent-leather tricorns they wore so straight on their heads, would turn up, completely polite, and ask if they could help in a Spanish that Maria didn't understand but Melinda did, although after a few times she acted as though she didn't, and then she said, *"No comprende"* and, driving away, muttered "Buggers" to herself.

The young woman wore one of those starched fly-away headdresses that looked like a white bird perched on her head, and she looked at Melinda, and Melinda looked at her. Neither of them said anything for a minute, and then the young woman, who had dark eyes sunk a little into their sockets, said, *"Señora,* may I help you? We get so few cars here"—*coches,* she said, but the rest was in English.

"Thank you," Melinda said, as formally.

The nun was walking down toward the guards. Melinda couldn't hear what she was saying, but they turned away, and she came back and said,

"*Señora,* I told them you were an English *duquesa* who had come to spend the night in retreat. We do take guests who want to make a retreat."

"Yes, yes, of course, we would like that. That's what we came for." Melinda was talking as if she hardly knew what she was saying. Maria started to remind her that they were going on to Madrid, and then she saw Melinda's face.

Melinda and the nun helped each other over the loose pebbles and up the single step like blind old women. The door closed behind them.

Maria waited a minute and then got out of the car and followed them. Melinda and the nun had fallen into each other's arms, and they were sobbing as Maria had never heard people sob before. An old woman, another nun, stood there watching them. There was no sound at all but their terrible sobbing.

The old woman touched them both on the shoulders and said, in Spanish, "Come, no one must see you like this. Come, *señorita.*" She took Maria's arm and ushered them all into a small room off the gateway. There were only a cot and two straight chairs. The pale pattern of the large crucifix that Melinda had replaced with her charts had been re-covered by the crucifix.

Melinda and the young nun sank together on the cot, still holding each other, still making that awful moan. They didn't say anything. They just clung to each other, and Maria and the old woman waited until the sobbing had run down and Melinda even began to smile. "Oh, thank God," she said, her cheek against Concepción's so that their tears had mingled.

"They were friendlies, in the days of the war, and each of them thought the other was dead," the old woman said calmly. Then, to Melinda, "You do not know me, but I indeed am knowing you, my dear." She began to sing, " 'Naught in dei you air the wan, only you beneath the man and under the sone.' Sometime I have to stop myself humming it when the others might hear me. In charity they misunderstooding."

"They would inform on her," Concepción said.

"Charity, charity," the old woman murmured, a habit word.

"That was why we sat against the wall, so that my aunt could learn English while I learned English from you."

"This is your aunt? Oh Lord." Melinda tried, after so long, to remember what they might have said that would shock a nun.

"Not worry." The old woman smiled. "You cannot shock a nun, not I. I lie for two years on top of St. Joseph and the Christ Child under the bed. I hear everything. No persons, even the Reds or the *señoritos,* disturb an old woman and look under her bed."

"When they came into the house, we said she had been shocked by the fighting and couldn't speak. All the other nuns in the convent had left," Concepción explained to Maria. "I remember them, like big birds in white bird hats like mine, tossing in the wind as they rode away in the back of a *camión.* That was the day my father was shot, but Mother Benedicta refused to go. It was her brother, and she said she was not going with people who did that. So we hid her. She had been the teacher for all of the children in the village, and the whole village knew she was in the house. When the war was over and the shooting was over, she came out and went right back into the empty convent after the Republicans had left and picked up a broom. She worked alone for about fifteen minutes, and then one by one, all the women of the village came and helped. When the Fascists came and brought her nuns back, there was their mother superior, waiting to greet them. Some were spies, but we all expected that."

"Now I tell. I tell," the old woman interrupted. "I lay there and for so long I listened and I said to myself, You call yourself a teacher, and you don't know, what do you say, bugger all."

"That is a swear word," Maria told her, shocked.

Mother Benedicta lay back her head and shook her headdress with laughter. She said in Spanish, "Oh dear, child. You must not have been brought up a Catholic. You take the nuns too seriously." Then sternly to Melinda, in English, "Why did you not bring this child up a Catholic?"

Melinda had the impossible desire to say, "I don't know. I just forgot. There was so much happening," so she said instead, "How did you know she is Spanish?"

"I have seen her since before."

"She never forgets," interrupted Concepción proudly. "She remembers everybody, all the wounded. She lay there and prayed for everybody, no matter who they were."

"Prayed and swore." Mother Benedicta

nudged Maria. "Eh? So I make Concepción bring Melinda to the bench because I was behind it and I want to learn, and God forgive me, I learn many things that shock me and some make me laugh. You try to laugh without making any noise?" Then, to Melinda, "You marry Señor Tye, I am hoping so after all that?"

Nobody said a word. Melinda blushed scarlet, and Maria giggled. "I'm sorry," she said. "I've never seen Melinda blush before."

"I remember another song, too," Mother Benedicta said. "'Sometimes I wander where I spin the lonely house.' Now please to explain that line. I have tried many times to find the meaning. Perhaps it is the poetry?"

"It is sometimes, you see, but not this time." Maria touched the old woman's arm. "'I wonder, *admirar,* why I spend the lonely hours, *horas,*'" she explained, then held her hand. "Do you really remember me?"

"Oh, yes, child." Mother Benedicta asked in Spanish, "You are a teacher? You have the calm for it. How could I forget your eyes? Of course, you were very small, but you must remember. You came with your father and your mother and your little brother, and Melinda held your hand and took you to the dining room to eat. I saw you from my window. But they didn't save her or your little brother. You had been strafed on the road. No, no, child, you must not cry so soon." Maria had laid her head down in the mother superior's lap like a child come home.

Melinda told her, as quietly as she could, over Maria's head, "When we met again, it was outside Figueres. I didn't remember her. Her father told her to stay with me and not let go of my hand."

Maria burst into a torrent of sobbing and words, Spanish words, fast, too fast for Melinda to understand. But Mother Benedicta said nothing, and her face never changed. She just patted Maria's head and smoothed her hair.

"I will get something to calm her," Concepción said. "Come with me, Melinda. She is better off with Mother Benedicta."

Melinda was so shaken that she let herself be led like a child too. "I thought she was your aunt."

"We are both nuns. Now she is my mother superior."

After compline, Concepción and Melinda walked side by side in the courtyard as if they hardly knew each other. Other nuns passed with their eyes cast down, under the squatting imps on the Moorish harem columns. The tile floor shone. The shrubs and vines were in bloom, and it was as quiet as some midnight that never ceased.

It was already dark when they got back to London. Someone had parked in front of the house in St. Michael's Square. Melinda was frantic. That was what Tye said when he stood in the door and saw her grumbling across the pavement.

"Uh-oh, the frantics," he said and kissed them both. "Was it that bad?"

Melinda pointed a finger at the world, at that part of it that was the street. "It's unfair. It's *grossly* unfair."

"After six years in this school and you still speak of fairness?" Tye and Maria chanted together.

"What?" Melinda was too distracted to pay much attention.

" 'Stalky & Co.,' Kipling," Maria informed her.

"Goddammit, don't you two gang up on me." Melinda was beginning to unload the car without waiting for them.

"Oh, come on," Tye said, "take her in the house. She is like a small girl when she is this tired. She whinges. I'll get the gear."

"I am tired," Melinda said, not apologizing, but almost apologizing. She looked at Tye as if she hadn't seen him for some years instead of two weeks. "Oh, you put on my favorite sweater."

Tye looked pleasing, familiar, and disheveled. His hair was messed about by the wind in the street, and his Irish sweater made him look wider than he was. He had pulled on it so much that it reached nearly to his knees.

Melinda took his hand and looked at it. The hand, the lovely hand, was long-fingered, white, gentle-looking under the gaslight of the street. She looked over his shoulder. "Remember what you asked me?" she said to Maria, who was waiting patiently for them to do a dance that was to her as formal and as expected as the dance of certain monogamous animals. "It was his hands," Melinda told her. "His hands and his father's car. That did it." She had recovered some of her temper.

They crowded into the lower hall. "Oh, Tye, roses and lilies!" The flowers were in a blue bowl on the hall table, with its stacks of mail and the pile of old dishes that he insisted she keep there and break whenever her mother sent her a complaining letter, so she wouldn't get what he called swelly-belly. When she got it, Tye told Maria it was because of the war. The huge bouquet scented the hall, mixing with the smell of a fire in the living room up above them.

"You are quite lovely, you old thing. Roses and lilies and a fire. We're hungry." Melinda started to pick up the mail.

"No, you don't." He guided her to the kitchen. "First a drink, then some dinner. Then the mail, in that order."

He looked at them when they sat down to the dinner he had made, one of those ration casseroles that made what he called a sow's ear out of a sow's ear, but the bread was good, and he had found some cheese and some fruit and a bottle of good wine. They were like birds that were gradually settling back into a nest after a long flight, fussing their feathers, then going quiet.

"You both look pretty bloody. Was it that bad?" he asked again.

Maria didn't say a word. She concentrated on a piece of bread. Her face was lined, as if she had aged. Her hair was lank.

"Yes, pretty bad." Melinda's voice was almost too quiet for him to hear.

Maria at last dragged herself to bed. In front

of the fire in the sitting room, Melinda curled close to Tye and watched his face in the firelight. "Where did you get the coal?" She murmured the question to keep from telling him what she knew she would.

"Mum brought it up from the country. She thought it would be nice for you and Maria."

"Why did she have to go through it again, Tye? It was awful for her. That is what I have been asking myself all the way across France, and she sat there beside me as if she hardly knew me, and I could see . . . really, Tye, I could see her hair getting drab right in front of me, and there were white hairs in it. It all happened in a day, while we were still at Albastro."

Tye held her against him. She smelled the familiar, safe sweater and his body. "Now, you listen," he almost whispered. "She wanted to do this. If you hadn't taken her, she would have gone alone." His arm tightened around her and he drew her closer, feeling that she was cold. He kissed her hair, and then he tilted her face up so he could kiss her mouth, and he tasted the tears that she had started to let flow without making a sound.

"The hospital was a convent again. There was Concepción. She has taken vows. She told me in the night that she had no choice, that her aunt was hiding her as she had hidden her aunt, but this time not in bed behind a wall, but behind a vow. Concepción whispered to me in the night what had happened. Even inside the convent we had to be careful about what we said.

"She said that two of the other *chicas* had been

caught in the breakthrough along the Ebro. You remember the sassy girl who changed her name to Libertad and followed the soldiers? She was raped and killed by Moorish soldiers when she went down from a cave where they had sheltered from the strafing to get water from a well. Some of the *camilleros* were hidden in the cave with them, and they heard the laughter and saw some Spanish Fascist soldiers tossing Libertad back and forth, and then they heard the ullulating of some Moorish soldiers, and the officer in charge of the Spanish threw her to them as if she were a bag of rags. Those were the words that Concepción said the *chica* who found her way back to the village used—'a bag of rags.' They raped and killed her while the others watched and couldn't help her. One of the *camilleros* held his hand across the other girl's mouth so she wouldn't scream and give them away.

"The mother superior of the convent thinks Maria must have seen things like that. There was so much of it. She says that is probably why she couldn't remember anything. She obeyed her father about saying nothing. She has been living with his hand over her mouth ever since. Mother Benedicta unlocked something in her mind, and she became a child again in front of our eyes, and the Spanish of a child was released."

They watched the fire until she was able to go on. "Tye?" she said.

He kissed her.

"Tye, I'm glad you didn't come. You would have hated it. Remember the one Concepción thought would be her *novio*? He came home. He survived the war, and when the body of Jose Antonio was brought past the village, they took him out and shot him and left his body by the road where Jose Antonio's cortège had passed. All the way across Spain, from Tortosa to the Escorial, men were shot in the villages they passed, like some terrible pagan ceremony. Oh, Tye, it has been terrible there, and nobody knows and the foreigners go to the goddamn bullfights and say Franco is a benign dictator. They make excuses because it is cheap in Spain and their money goes further. One of the tourists that we met when we were sitting in the square in Figueres told us solemnly that Franco wasn't really a dictator but a royalist and that he had put down a Communist revolt. He said a Spaniard had told him that. There were *señoritas* in *mantillas* and snorting bulls, and posters of Cristo Rey, the same sign that you saved from Tandy's kitbag after he was killed. It looked like an advertisement. Why do they do that to Christ? All of it was expected and false, glossy and aggressive. Our Spain is being buried, the bodies, the past, the facts."

"Well, it's not. So long as we are alive it isn't." Tye waited for her to tell all she was ready to tell and willing to remember. They huddled closer, and the fire began to go red before dying.

"Señora Zuda acted as if she didn't know me when I went to the door, and then she did a strange thing. She sat me down close to a cupboard against the wall. She said that all her sons were dead, but she seemed either stalwart or tired of it all, or so used to death that it didn't make any difference anymore, like a woman in a Greek play. She said for me to tell her in English about Tallo—tell slowly, she said—and I said you did become a doctor and you worked too hard. Then she said to tell you that the old cupboard was still there and that it still had room for two. She said to use the word *complacerse*. What did she mean?"

"Thank God, she meant that the two youngest had survived and that they were hidden in the cupboard. But if I know them, they don't stay there. They are back and forth across the border, as free as birds, but at night, always at night." Tye was laughing. "She would tell you that way, all that play-acting of a mourning woman. What a right phony."

"She has to be phony. Everyone has to be phony in a dictatorship."

"I want to talk about Maria," he said suddenly. "You might not like what I say, but listen and don't interrupt. I think that Maria is a very brave person. It will take a little time and she will be like a person sobered up and broken for a while. I saw it in this war, traumatic shock, and we dealt with it the same way. We made them remember, and after a while they got well. The shot-down plane became real again and not a nightmare, the V-2, the darkness, the sheer goddamn shambles of it all . . ." He wandered off to someplace that was his own. She knew it was the place he hadn't told her about, the time in the Franco prison.

She just said, "You've got to eat. You never eat enough when I'm not here," and she thought how beautiful he was, the thin profile, the haunted eyes, the locks of auburn hair that were already streaked with gray. He was only forty, frail and forty, war-wounded too, and never saying a word. She held his slim hand to her mouth.

"Don't mother me," he said, by habit. "You are my wife and you are my lover and you are my what do you Americans call it, my helpmate, and now I will get your mail. Who do you know in Italy?"

"Nobody but my wicked Aunt Maymay, and I haven't seen her since I was little."

He put an official-looking letter, very thick, in her hands. When she opened it, she didn't say a word for so long that he nudged her. "Don't go to sleep. What does it say?"

Melinda started to laugh. "My wicked Aunt Maymay has left me an island called Santa Corsara off the coast of Italy and the money to run it and a long, long letter explaining why. The first paragraph says it is because I was kicked out of the Red Cross!"

She passed the letter on to him, page after page, and when they had finished, Melinda said, "She was wonderful. Why wasn't I allowed to know her? I knew I wasn't the only one to fly the coop. Oh, darling, we will go there as soon as you can leave. Desmond will take over for you, and we will go to Circe's island and you will lie in the sun and we will have a honeymoon at last. Aunt Maymay. I'll be damned." She had started to cry, but not with sorrow.

Tye lifted her up from the sofa. "Come to bed. We won't go to Circe's island until August."

"Can we go then? Can we really? Shouldn't I go now?"

"I always knew you were going to be rich. That's why I married you. All Americans are rich. Everybody knows that." He patted her bottom to shoo her up the stairs.

"Ha-ha. *You* say." She let him push her on up the stairs; she was suddenly exhausted.

In the sitting room the fire turned redder in a last flash of life, and then darkened and died.

The fireplace looked like a cold, empty mouth. The stove black they used on it in summer had faded to gray. Melinda wanted to sit down, but the sofa and the chairs were gone. The console tables with their lion's feet had left wounds where they had been unscrewed from the green wall. The floor was dead brown wood, after the old rug that had been there for nearly fifteen years had been rolled up and taken away. The glass in the windows was streaked by the dim sun of one of the cold days that came in August, unforgiving after a lovely June and July.

Now there was nothing, nothing but the ghost shapes of where things had been: a pub sign of a lion rampant framed in gold; a nineteenth-century painting of Caesar, a prize hog; the early Renaissance painting they had found in Italy in the mountains, with its pretty killer boys in their multicolored tights; the high corner plinth that had held Tye's pearl of great price, a fragment of a marble bust, brought up from the sea around Cyprus. They said it must have been Aphrodite.

He had bought it because he said that its chinline reminded him of Melinda's, its marble of the color of her flesh.

There were the other treasures gathered over the years, glass and wood and stone and marble and silk, all brought there to make the room for them, all taking so long to bring together, so short a time to dismantle, as if the show were over, the set struck, and the actors gone.

Twenty-one years had been thrown away, given away, shipped to Italy, shipped to New York State, where Maria taught. There was nothing to do but leave.

Melinda let herself sink down to the floor. She was so tired. She wasn't remembering anything, not like that. She simply was letting people and times come and stay a little while. She had always done that, a kind of floating. Tye had known when she had watched that way, had gone into a private place, and he had always said, "Where are you now?" She could still hear his voice, as strong as ever—"Where are you? Where are you now?"—and his laugh, which had always been like that of a child surprised by pleasure.

Even his voice within her, where it was safe, drifted and faded. She sat clutching an old Delman's shoebox in her lap to keep Maria from throwing it away. Most of the things in it were bits and pieces that nobody else would understand. Maria was one of those healthy-minded people who wanted to throw away everything and start over every day. How could you just pack it up and shift it away, the way Maria kept expecting her to do? But gradually she had done it, and now it was August again, the time they usually went to Italy to the house that Aunt Maymay had left her, where she could see Tye grow young again every year, after the first few days of worry about his patients.

She could hear Maria upstairs in her room, tearing and dropping things and walking and talking with Nella. Once one of them sat down on the bed they were leaving for Desmond. She could hear it creak, as she had in all the years when Maria had come home late and tried to climb the stairs without making a noise. The bed would betray her when she sat down to take off her shoes. Tye would reach for Melinda's hand and they would smile in the dark—well, not the dark, exactly. The streetlight made a pattern of leaves from the ginkgo tree in summer and bare branches in winter on the ceiling of their bedroom even in the darkest night.

She leaned her head against the wall. There was a mark there, a mark of time, darker than the deep green of the wall. Tye called the spot "hair muss." Desmond and Maria and Nella had had the habit for years of slamming a cushion against the wall and then leaning their heads back, letting their long legs stretch out across the rug when they were arguing or listening to music or just being there, quiet, which wasn't often—well, not with Maria and Nella, anyway. They were too full of life and plans.

So much life in a house that had nearly been destroyed by war was a miracle she needed to take with her, that and Ewen's camp, which he had said was a form of courage.

That night in late February there had been a coal fire in the fireplace, which lit the face of the wrought-iron woman on the Victorian fireback they had found in the Portobello Road. Melinda had kept dinner on the Aga because Tye had rung upstairs and said he wouldn't be up until late, there were still eighteen people waiting.

When she heard him finally climbing the stairs that night, his footsteps were so slow and so heavy that it frightened her, but she made a joke of it: "You're walking like Frankenstein." He wanted her to. They made jokes together.

When she saw his face, she had a moment of sheer panic. She ran to the door and led him to the sofa, and he didn't even pull away as he usually did. He hated to be cosseted. He just let himself be led like a lamb to the slaughter, and he dropped onto the sofa and laid his head back and closed his eyes. She went toward the stairs to the kitchen and called back, "I'm bringing your drink and some soup up here. Don't move." When she came back, he was asleep, and his forehead was burning with a temperature.

"Bed for you." She woke him.

But all he said was what he always said: "It's only a little bout of flu." He didn't argue, though, when she helped him to his feet and they got up the stairs together and she tucked him in.

"Flu, for God's sake, only flu. It's only flu," he kept saying, almost whispering, "I feel like shit," and he turned away from the soup she had brought and went to sleep again. She hadn't even got him to take off his clothes—the Irish sweater, the corduroys he had had since Cambridge. He wore those when the weather got so damp and cold that nothing else could keep him warm, even with the central heating they had put in. The surgery door was always being opened and shut.

She let him sleep and went into the back bedroom, where Maria's posters still covered the walls, even though she was nearly twenty-eight years old and long gone to America. Melinda remembered lying for a long time, longing for sleep and looking at a "Ban-the-Bomb" poster.

He was right. It was only flu, she kept telling herself—at least, she remembered that she had kept telling herself that, but what she had really done was to be slightly annoyed at Tye for not taking better care of himself.

Sleep wouldn't come. It kept flirting with her. There was only the sound of ragged breathing in the front bedroom, and Tye coughing in his sleep. She saw it as her failure to care for him, to make him—And then she laughed in the dark. Make him do anything!

"Dammit," she said aloud to the posters, "you ought to look after yourself instead of the whole damned world," and then, the unthinkable, because she knew she was not a selfish woman and that she was surrounded by his love and his comfort and always had been, a final whine in the night: "What about me?"

At four o'clock in the morning he came to the door and leaned against the wall. "Melinda." He had to whisper, but she was awake and up at once, and as she ran toward him he said, "I can't breathe. Call Desmond and tell him I don't want to go to hospital but to bring oxygen, and call Penny."

He slumped to the floor. He was so heavy that she couldn't lift him. She had to cover him with a blanket and put a pillow under his head before she called Desmond, who was asleep on the floor above.

From that minute it was different from any way it had ever been before. It's only a little cold, it's only a little flu, it's only a little pneumonia; he always said it that way. It's only a little dying. Damn overwork, damn February, damn demands.

She had only seen Tye cry twice in all the twenty-three years. He had cried when he heard that the British government had recognized Franco before the Spanish Civil War was over. They were in the hotel in France, and he had sores all over his body, and he yelled out at night when he was asleep and then swore he wasn't dreaming.

Then she had seen tears when he lay there looking out of their bedroom window. He looked for a long time, and she just sat there, holding his hand, and then he clutched her hand as if she weren't already holding his, and when he turned his head, there were tears but no sound. He said, "God, Melinda, I hate to leave."

It was the second time in the whole week that she had had that cold stopping of her heart, and she waited until it was over and stroked his head, still so hot, still so clammy with sweat. "You're not going anyplace," she told him and herself. She was sure it was just the fever talking; after all, he had told her it was only flu. "You're staying right here and Desmond is taking care of things. Not to worry."

Why did you speak to grown men that you loved as if they were children when you wanted to evade what they were going through?

"Read to me," he said, and he was docile, and that frightened her more than anger or despair. Tye was not a docile man. She opened *Paradise Lost.* Nothing calmed him more than that. He said that the words eased him when medicine just made him sick. All day and part of the night she had been reading to him. The words of *Paradise Lost* became cartoons to her, flat images around the walls of the bedroom, the huge archangels that spread up the walls and across the ceiling like the goddesses they had seen in the Egyptian tombs. Little Adam and little Eve, the prince of darkness sometimes huge, then man-size as he flew down and touched so lightly the edge of the world, then as tiny as a toad whispering in Eve's ear.

Once Tye had muttered, "Oh, God. *Paradise Lost* with a Southern accent. 'Masef am heyall.' "

"You shut up," she said, and went on reading.

A week later, at four o'clock on the morning of March 1, she had been sitting with him all night when she heard Penny coming up the stairs to take her place. Penny made her go downstairs and try to rest, but she had not left the breathing of Tye's body, like some huge engine running without mind. She sat in the cold living room trying to drink the coffee Penny had made for her and listening to the impersonal engine, no longer Tye, drawing air from the whole house. His breathing had followed her down the stairs and filled the house, as if Tye were the house and the house were breathing and dying.

Suddenly there was silence. Dead silence. What dead silence was: silence where the clock ticked in the distance, silence of pure terror. She upset the coffee and started to run up the stairs.

Desmond caught her. "No suffering—listen to me!" He used the words that she had not heard since the war, when she had said them to grieving people. "He just passed away. It was peaceful. In his sleep." He held her so she would stop before she walked, slowly, to the room, and Tye did look asleep, all tension gone, all struggling, all memory. She looked at the lovely body that had contained Tye, stone dead, stone cold—not peaceful, that was a lie, dead, the bastard, she was bereft of him.

There was a time when she didn't remember much, except the lowering of Tye's body into the churchyard at Missus's house, the churchyard where the pilots were buried, and she thought, That is only right, that all the casualties of the perpetual war lie together, and then she couldn't remember any more.

Her nearest and dearest—Maria, Desmond, Penny, Nella—kept sneaking little peeks at her through the late spring and summer to see if she'd started crying yet, as if she were pregnant with her sorrow and had to give birth to it.

Then one day, in the sun, in the morning, she heard Tye again, and his laugh. After the first stunned brutal emptiness, his voice never left her. She had made herself reject the voice, and then she thought, Why should I? It isn't dotty. It's private, so long as I don't say it aloud so that they all look at each other over my head.

She hadn't been able to leave the house, not until Tye told her it was all right. But she couldn't tell that to a soul. At first it had been empty, even if it was full of everything they had made and used together for so long, and after that, when she was alone, or asleep, there he was, not gone at all. She could go into a room and let a hint that he had just left it brush the corner of her eyes; she could see the sleeve of his Irish pullover, which he wouldn't let her even patch, and then it would be gone; or she could go into the kitchen in the morning and there would be, not Tye, but a glimpse of Tye, down below in the garden, squatting by the lavender, pruning it into a graceful mound the way they had seen in France in the lavender fields.

But sometimes in the night, sometimes when there was no voice and no dream and no hint, she was back in those first empty days. She relived them, facing the emptiness, the nothing, not that stupid "nothing to live for," just empty, a vacuum, nothing, no wind in the void, no objects, no voices, no hope, a nothing that she sometimes tried to break into, at least whisper in. It was what she knew she would finally have to face, after she had put it off by memory and reliving and dreams.

"It is generally supposed," she told the empty room, "that you can be surrounded by those who love you, but when your other self is gone, you are alone. It's a deep inner circle and only you are there. And there is no way to tell Maria or Desmond or Penny or Missus, but Missus already knows. She always does, so there's no need to tell her."

"Darling," Missus had said, when Melinda thought it was too soon to face what she was going to do, "I think you ought to go home." They were having tea, as they always did. It was still March, in the windows the sudden sun, then shadow, then sun of March. "Now, we will see each other as much as we ever did. I will come to Italy when you are there, and in the winter you should go and live near Maria in America."

Melinda suddenly found that she was telling Missus that she wished they had had children, how they had tried and tried. She had never spoken of this before. You didn't; she had found that out early in England. You just had wordless thoughts.

"Darling child, you have Maria. Isn't that enough?" Missus had reached forward and touched her hand.

"That is the kindest thing anyone ever said to me," Melinda said.

Missus was right. She had never quite got used to England. It was, she told herself, all stepped on so much. She had found herself through the years longing to walk in woods where nobody had ever been, only animals.

"I don't think I can stand this," she said aloud. Then, for the first time, she knew she could. She had to. She was ready at last to leave all the make-work, the busyness, the acts that filled the days, the wandering up and down the stairs in the night trying not to disturb Desmond, who had so much to do with Tye gone.

She was leaving him the house, the surgery, the dark green walls, but not the papier-mâché occasional table that they had rescued from the wrack and ruin, or the round table with the green baize cover they had worked the jigsaw puzzles on. She had insisted on taking that, with the rest of the room, bag and baggage and jigsaw puzzles.

"But the sofa is nearly worn out," Maria had said, and she had not said a word back. Maria had always known not to argue when she went absolutely still like that. She found herself grinning, and it weakened her face, and she tried not to cry over a silly thing like that when there was so much to wail for, like one of Desmond's banshees. But they weren't banshees, they were live people, and now one of them was dead, and the sprung sofa was on its way to New York State, where she had never lived, never even been.

There had been so much to do. The cleaning up after death took so long. She had made promises, and she clung to them to keep from having to leave until she was ready.

One of the promises had been to Boodie. In her late thirties, Boodie had surprised herself and Mr. Percival by having John Randolph Kregg Percival. She said that since she had sold the land, the least she could do was keep the names going. She had written Melinda a series of letters begging her to let the boy come over. He was in trouble, she wrote, when he had never been in trouble in his whole life. She underlined "whole life."

So Jakey had come when Melinda needed somebody to demand that she be there and alive—dear Jakey, four-eyed Jakey, an angel in the form of Jakey. Maria always teased her about her angels. "You don't even go to church," she had said once.

"Oh, dear Lord, you don't have to sit in some church to know about angels!" She had laughed at Maria for being so naive.

So Melinda had written to invite Jakey to spend June and July with her before she moved back to the States. She had gone to Heathrow to meet him. It was his seventeenth birthday. There he was, small, bespectacled, blinking in the light as if he had been deeply asleep—a blinky boy. She thrilled in her chest because she knew him and had always known him, even before they spoke. He was Johnny. He was Tandy. He was the wimp, the drip, the questioner, the commando, the Nobel Prize winner, the boy left out when the gangs were made, the kind of boy she had learned to love. It was the first time since Tye had died that she felt some surge of life.

His suitcase was a Gladstone bag that had been their grandfather's. He carried a portable typewriter, and a raincoat over his arm. He was her responsibility when she needed one so much. She felt selfish, thinking like that, but it was true, and her reward had been so surprising that she thought of that small figure, blinking at the gray morning, exhausted from the thirteen-hour flight, as an act of God.

She had driven to Heathrow in the Jaguar as a special treat, but Jakey didn't even notice the car. He didn't say much at first, he just kept looking at England as they drove back into London. When he finally did begin to talk, he didn't stop for the whole time he was in England, except when he shut himself in Maria's room, which Melinda had fixed for him, and then the typewriter talked and talked and talked as if it and he had been pent up all their lives.

He began on the way into Chelsea, as they crossed Battersea Bridge. First he told her what he planned to do while he was in England. "You know, I get so little time to work at home, with all that is going on, so I thought that if you don't mind I will spend my mornings writing. I am writing about Moral Certitude and the Art of Compromise. I have decided to go into politics, but don't tell my mother. She thinks I'm going to be a scientist. She has this innocent idea that people with brains are always scientists."

That was at the beginning of June, and they walked together through London. Melinda remembered it as a double image, images of Hyde Park and then Green Park and then St. James's Park, spring moving into summer, measured by the length of the shadows across the paths between the trees, and at the same time Jakey's voice bringing her the heat, the streets, the house with its verandas spread out like a nesting bird that was Boodie's house in Bonnevue, Louisiana, which he talked about as the center of all activity, as if he were still there. "You just don't know what is going on," he told her. "It's a real revolution."

She could see Bonnevue as he talked—the courthouse, the dusty lawn around it, the patch in the door where a drunk had put his fist through the glass, the long steps, the Confederate flag, the dusty Confederate soldier that someone local had made.

Jakey told her about climbing to the top step outside the courthouse. He said he had been scared to death somebody would shoot him. She could hear his voice growing stronger as he read his revolutionary manifesto to what at first was nobody in the hot wide street, and then a few people, and then the sheriff.

He told her that his voice was squeaky with fear as he began to read, squinting in the sun through his pebble-thick glasses: "We hold these truths to be self-evident." He went on, his voice getting stronger. "That all men are created equal; that they are endowed by their creator with certain unalienable rights; that among these are life, liberty, and the pursuit of happiness." It was then, he said, that his voice just took off. He said he had felt inspired. "Liberty and the pursuit of happiness. Way out!" he told the trees on the Mall.

Then the sheriff had torn the paper out of his hands, and he was sorry about that, because he had planned to nail it to the door of the courthouse, like Martin Luther had done. "Did you know," he said to Melinda, "that Luther said he could do no other? That's the way it was with me. I'm sorry I embarrassed my mother."

The sheriff had been nearly whining. He had said, "Now, Jakey, you know better than that. What did you up and go and do a thing like that for? On a nice morning like this?"

There had been some colored people Jakey knew, standing way at the back. He was sure that it was the first time they had ever heard the Declaration of Independence in their whole lives. They were just watching the show. They always did. They were too far away for him to see who they were, even though he knew everybody in town and knew everything that was going on, but he was as blind as a bat, and when the sheriff had grabbed him his glasses had fallen down on the courthouse steps, and they just lay there, and when he started to pick them up, the deputy, a big awkward oaf, Elmore Jones, who was older than he was but who he remembered in school, all the way back to the first grade, had stepped forward and put his big foot right on them, not meaning to.

Sheriff Goodfellow—he loved that name—said, "Now look what you've went and done. His mama is just going to kill me." Jakey told him not to worry, that he had another pair at home, and then, he said, he tried to explain to Sheriff Goodfellow what his name meant. He'd always wanted to do that, and it seemed the right time to get their minds off what was happening as Sheriff Goodfellow marched him through the dusty little crowd that had gathered, and he said it was the first time in his life he had heard somebody yell, "Nigger lover!" He had lived in

Bonnevue all his life and had never heard it before that day.

All the way around the parking lot to the jail he told Sheriff Goodfellow about his name, how *goodfellow* meant *elf,* as in Robin Goodfellow. He said he had read all about it, and sometimes it meant *woods colt,* like *bastard,* and Sheriff Goodfellow got mad then and told him not to talk like that. It was as Sheriff Goodfellow was closing the door to the only cell they had there that he thought to tell him about the etymology of the word *sheriff.* He said it was very interesting, but Sheriff Goodfellow didn't want to hear any more. "You call me a bastard one more time and you get this stick right upside your sissy little head," Sheriff Goodfellow said.

Jakey said that his mama had brought him a casserole and cried all over the jail bars, and then the next morning his daddy had come down and bailed him out and said, "What in the hell are you doing in there? They don't put anybody but niggers in jail in this town," which gave him the chance to say, "What are you doing out there?" and the only reason his daddy didn't whip him for being uppity was that his mama said if he laid a hand on that boy she would walk right out the front door. It was the first time, he told Melinda under the Admiralty Arch, that she had ever raised her voice in the house.

He got sent to his room like a little kid, when he was already sixteen years old. He confided to Melinda in front of the Rokeby Venus at the National Gallery that they had always called him a sissy—and pantywaist and four-eyes and teacher's pet. That was because he never took his nose out of a book. He was used to it. He said that if you were intelligent in the South, you had to expect that. He had a few friends. Who wanted any more?

His special friend was Aiken, and they had grown up together. His aunt worked for them, and Aiken cut the grass. Aiken's great-great-grandfather had been the governor of South Carolina, and his daddy and mama were dead and he lived with his grandmother, but a lot of the time Boodie let him live with them. Jakey said he was worried to death about Aiken.

Aiken was with Melinda and Jakey most of the time they wandered around London. Aiken and I, Aiken and me—it was a litany of Jakey's childhood.

"I spread my mind all over the walls of my bedroom," he said to Lord Nelson in Trafalgar Square. "There was a picture of the Reverend Martin Luther King, the only black face except Aiken's in that room. There was the Declaration of Independence, torn half in two and put up on the wall with the tear showing—that I was real proud of.

"Aiken and I looked at magazines together, like the necket women in the *National Geographic*, or went to the movies, and he sat in the balcony and I sat downstairs. He said he was invisible to everybody but me. He said it was like looking in a mirror and nobody looked back at you. You knew you were there but there wasn't anybody to tell, nobody but me. I said there was Mama and he said, You ain't got no idea. Well, I found out.

"Mama couldn't see him either. She came in the room when I put that picture of the Reverend Martin Luther King on the wall and she said, 'I declare, I don't know what in the world I'm going to do with you, Jakey, put that nigger trouble-maker right up on your wall. You just wait till your father sees that. He'll have a fit.' Then she turned around and saw that Aiken was there and she was embarrassed, and she said, 'I'm sorry, Aiken. I don't use that word often. It just slipped out. I'm truly sorry, but those preachers are just making people unhappy when we have always been so happy together. It just breaks my heart,' and she started to cry and ran out of the room. She really believed that."

Melinda thrust her pent-up love toward Jakey like something released from her heart. At first he was her excuse not to leave St. Michael's Square, then, in a strange way, the reason why she knew she was going back. She began to think of England as away instead of home. She had been away long enough. It was over, dead, gone, and all there were were the fragments she had shipped ahead of her, and Penny and Cotty and Missus and Nella and Desmond, and she would see them every year in Italy. They promised faithfully.

It was the South she missed, especially when Jakey talked, the language and accents of the South that were deep in her soul. When he said that the sheriff had said, "What did you up and go and do a thing like that for?" it was like a call home. Yet she knew she couldn't live there. She was as much an exile as the Spanish Republicans in Mexico. Maria had gone to Mexico for the summer to interview them for fieldwork. She said that the Republican factions still fought with each other like rats in a barrel.

Melinda was going to live in a place she didn't know, in a house she hadn't seen, and she couldn't summon up the spirit to move a muscle. She went on sitting against the wall, cradling her shoebox. How long she sat there, she didn't know.

Someone was coming up the stairs when she didn't want anybody to, but it was Penny, thank God. She could tell by her footsteps on the stairs, and then she blew in. Penny always blew in; she never wandered or trudged or sauntered. She blew.

"What in the world are you doing just sitting there on the floor, darling? I've got the van down below. It took Cotty all morning to clean out that trash he always carries in it. He wanted to drive us to Southampton, but I said, Good God, we have enough worries. You know the way he drives. Are you nearly ready?"

Melinda stretched out her legs in the dirty corduroys she had used to pack in and said, "No, I don't think I'll go." Then, the thought that had been at the back of all that thinking and remembering came out. "Penny, I can't do anything. I can fix my car, and bandage people and take temperatures and wash bodies, and I can cook herring thirty-five ways because of the rationing, and I can make Tye's house his castle when he is so tired, and I can dance, and I can, oh what . . . What am I going to do?"

"Well, darling, you can type."

"She can type!" It was one of the first things Penny had said to her so long ago in the office in Smith Square. They both remembered at the same time and they both laughed, and Melinda's laughter flooded over into the first tears she had shed. She struggled up from the floor and let Penny hold her tight until the storm was over.

"I'm glad," Melinda said finally, when she could speak again. "I'm glad that happened here, in this room, with you."

Penny let her go and talked to her as she did to her children. "Come on, darling—bath, clothes. I'll start putting things in the van. What the devil is this?" She picked up the Delman's shoebox.

"That's my box." Melinda grabbed it back. "I'm putting it in my suitcase. Nobody can have my box." She held it to her like a little girl.

"Nobody is going to take your box, darling. Now go and get dressed. Is Maria ready?"

Penny followed Melinda up the stairs. Maria came through her door. Nella was standing behind her. "All finished." Maria smiled. She is so beautiful when she smiles, Melinda thought to herself. She is the only truly beautiful woman I have ever known who doesn't give a damn.

"Nella's going with us to the boat. She doesn't want Penny to have to drive back alone anyway." Maria's arm went around Nella's waist, as if she didn't want to let go.

"I've never seen a boat—a ship, I mean," Nella said.

Melinda called from the bathroom, "Maria, you are an angel. You've left me the great big foozy thick towel all warm for my last bath in this house, in St. Michael's Square, London, England!"

Book Five

New York and Mississippi • 1964–1969

An Inlet of the Sea

New York State in the fall of 1960 was as alien to Melinda as her first sight of Spain had been. She couldn't believe that in the United States of America, her country, she had to guard her mouth. Maria said so. She said that people who had had anything to do with the International Brigades were being hounded out of job after job. Her own, she said, was shaky, because she was a Spanish Republican, even though she was six when she left. It was an election year, and there was hope; but, Maria said, if Nixon won, it could get worse. She told Melinda not to walk on the roads at night. There was a lot of feeling. But she didn't say what the feeling was.

Maria had a special reason to be careful. She was doing fieldwork in Albastro, searching for skulls on the battlegrounds of the twelfth-century Moorish wars, and she had to be able to get back into Spain. Of course, it was easier with the Spanish government since the United States had opened airfields there and made pacts with Franco. She said it was the CIA she worried about. She was doing something else too, which she only hinted about to Melinda, as if she were afraid for it even to leave her mind, that far away from Spain. So she went in disguise, and lived as a lodger in the house that had been Concepción's family's.

In the summer of 1961, Maria married, as a Catholic, in Spain, a Catalán named Manuelo Castels Saval. She had met him in Mexico. Melinda lent them Santa Corsara, the island off Italy, for their honeymoon. What it meant was that after one year, Melinda was left high and dry in the American North.

She was feeling something she had never before felt. Even in the high-gabled, barn-red house that she and Maria had found together, with her green room as nearly like the room at 24 St. Michael's Square as she could make it, she was lonely and, she had to admit it, bored. It wasn't that people hadn't been good to her. It was just that they were all new, new in every way. She had never been around academics, and she had never spent so much time with people who hadn't been through anything with her. Nobody spoke her language, a polyglot English, Southern, and war.

She found herself trying too hard, giving too many dinner parties like a Richmond widow, and even, out of loneliness, keeping her mouth shut around Republicans who liked her title. So, in the fall of 1962, she went to the president of the college and asked for a job. As she had said to Penny what seemed so long ago, she could type. She was aware that "Lady Dunston" would cut it with the trustees.

Charles Wesley College had been named in the mid-nineteenth century by its richest donor, a Methodist with an attitude of steel. If he had seen it in 1962, he would have whirled in his grave. Only the name was left. It was no longer Methodist. It was sometimes referred to as a hotbed of liberalism, sometimes as a nest of pinkos. Every spring the students protested with banners to change the name; some read TRUMAN, SOME READ FULBRIGHT, SOME READ CHE GUEVARA, and one read KARL MARX. Melinda grew to love it. She had finally found her place, she told herself, like Brer Rabbit in the briar patch.

By the fall of 1964, she had been made social dean. It said so on her door, and when she looked at it she was amused. It was the only job that all her experience fitted. She had been with the young at war. She had been with the young while Maria grew up. So she took to the young as if she had come from a far country to find them.

On the afternoon of September third, the day before the term started, she sat alone in her office and waited for a stranger. Not any stranger. That had been made clear to her. One of ours.

Boodie had written, as if Jakey hadn't told Melinda all of it back in London, explaining about Aiken, how he was just like one of the family. Aiken's aunt worked for them, and after his mama died, he hung around and mowed and raked the lawn and did chores so he could have some money to go to school and get his clothes. But he had gotten into some kind of trouble, like Jakey. "You know," Boodie wrote, "all that trouble down here. Jail, reformatory, so many of them, just *babies*. You have no idea. Honestly, I wish those Negro preachers would just preach the Word of God, like He intended."

Jakey's letter was different. He had learned a new language, but the old Southern devil reared its head underneath what he wrote. Melinda thought, Poor Aiken—Jakey is still looking after his own pickaninny. He said he thought that Aiken ought to live at Melinda's house, where he would feel more at home, as she was family, until he got used to the North. "He never has been north of Mississippi and Louisiana. Look after Aiken for me. You know they get lonesome away from their own people." Melinda cringed at that.

Then, as if he were writing about another Aiken, Jakey said, "Aiken is like my comrade-in-arms. He has had a terrible time; this has been a scary summer, but deeply exhilarating for all of us." Who "us" was, he didn't say. "Now he has been in jail *eight times!*" The words were underlined, as if they were a badge of courage. "He's been beaten up—we all risk that, of course." Then a divergence: "You should have been here this summer. There were so many came down to help with the registration for the vote. Remember, I told you the revolution would start here? Well, it has. It's like a brave new world." He added one of those innocent insults he gave as a habit: "If you know your Shakespeare. Aiken is burned out. He has been in the movement since he was fourteen. He has been given a scholarship for brothers who have served a long time and need to get out. He is extremely intelligent. He didn't know where to go, so I told him he ought to come up there where you are and go to school. He isn't very well prepared, because of being in jail so much, but I'm sure you could arrange some tutoring or something like that."

He told her how brave Aiken had been, how he had stood for the right things and it took more courage than she could ever believe. Then he added, echoing Boodie, that Melinda had no idea how bad it was.

He wrote that Aiken had never even been across the Mississippi River until he started out for Baton Rouge when they all decided to integrate the ferryboat right in the middle of the Mississippi River, and the ferryboat captain just turned the ferry around and took them back to the west shore, and the sheriff, who didn't know Jakey but seemed to know Aiken, put the others in jail and sent Jakey home and told him he ought to be ashamed of himself. He wrote, "Melinda, I was so ashamed, sent home like that when they went to jail." Jakey's words had fallen so fast on the page, as fast as tears, that there was a lot she couldn't read. But she got the idea.

Family, family, the same as forever in the South. No matter what they called it in 1964, you had duties to people. Aiken had been Jakey and Boodie's duty, and they were sending him on to Melinda like a parcel, and they didn't have any idea that it was insulting. Then the letter exploded into some kind of wild grace.

"Oh, Melinda, Melinda, I am at home at last and in my own place, in the South. I can live here now!" Jakey believed it. He really believed it, because he wanted to. "I feel like I haven't ever been so at home here before in my whole life. It is wondrous." Jakey would say *wondrous* instead of *wonderful.* She smiled, reading that.

There was a knock on her door. She called, "Come in."

She never forgot her first sight of Aiken. Even as he changed through the years, she still saw him sometimes standing in the door of her office, looking around it, judging it, weighing it, as slow to move as a hunter or a good quarterback. He was carrying Jakey's Gladstone bag.

Aiken was elegant and very slim. His face was what Maria would have called a Nilotic face, the kind from the Upper Kingdom of Egypt: long neck, sharp profile, large self-protecting eyes. They were the oldest eyes in a young face that Melinda had seen since Spain. She thought, My God, this child is eighteen going on eighty.

Instead of the uniform that most of the students in 1964 thought was so individual—a mixture of rags, ruffles, and Prince Valiant hair—he wore a collar and tie, a jacket, and blue jeans, obviously new, which he told her later he had bought at the Allied Department Store in Plaquemine, Louisiana, and kept until he got ready to meet her.

Neither of them said a word. Then he grinned, a private grin. He said, "I'm Aiken. How's your blood guilt, man? Jakey told me to say that."

"It's terrible. Jakey told me to say *that.*" Melinda smiled. "Welcome. Please sit down."

He sat down in the comfortable chair she privately called her confessional, and he didn't say another word. She finally lost, and broke the silence.

"How did you come up? Have you been to the registrar yet?"

His face and his eyes simply shut down. She knew she had said something wrong. She tried again.

"Here, let me see your papers, your scholarship. What did they give you to show up here? Has your scholarship committee been in touch?"

Without a word, he handed her a heavy envelope. Then he settled back into the chair and looked beyond her, out of the window, as if she didn't exist.

Melinda looked at the papers. Then she jumped up from the desk. "You wait here, Aiken." It was the first time she had used his name. "You hear me?" The language came back as easy as silk. "I have to go see a man about a dog." She muttered "For God's sake" to herself as she went out the door and closed it behind her, but what was for God's sake, she didn't say.

When she came back half an hour later, Aiken seemed not to have moved a muscle.

"Well, that's done," she said. She didn't even sit down. "Now I'm going to take you over to my house for a few days until we find a bed for you here. You can register tomorrow morning. Get your things."

He picked up the Gladstone bag. She looked at it and laughed.

"Lord, that used to belong to Boodie's father, my grandfather. Come on."

It was a beautiful car, a robin's-egg-blue Thunderbird. Melinda got into the car and waited. Aiken waited. She opened the front door on the passenger side and said, "Come on up here. Put your suitcase in the back."

She drove as if she had the devil on her tail, clean driving. She could sense Aiken's body beginning to relax beside her. He was letting himself enjoy the drive. The wind blew his hair.

When Melinda turned into the circular drive of the tall red house by the little graveyard, neither of them could have known in a million years that he was never to leave it, wherever he was—not in spirit, anyway. Wherever Melinda was after that, there was always a room that looked the same, enough the same so that they could walk into it together, taking it for granted, as they did that first evening, and feel that it was the center of something. Aiken always said it was love, or maybe safety. "God knows," he said once, "I needed it then. Maybe it was the kind of comfort you get when you know you can let what's behind your face come out of your mouth."

That first evening, Aiken wandered around before he sat down. He inspected her green living room as carefully as he had inspected her office and the house from outside—the dark green walls, the white woodwork, and a fireplace with a bright brass fender. He stood by the table with the big jigsaw puzzle on it. He inspected the books, all in white bookcases built into the walls, and in between them, a big painting of a lion that was faded but had a gold frame.

Her voice followed him from the big overstuffed chair she always sat in. "That's an old pub sign—you know, like a barroom. Maybe it's two hundred years old. We found it in England, where I used to live, and that's a lion rampant. He looks surprised to be so rampant, doesn't he? My husband, Tye, always said he looked like the unicorn had just goosed him. That's a fragment of a bust of Aphrodite that was found underwater off the coast of Cyprus, where she was supposed to rise up out of the sea. Have you ever seen a picture called *The Birth of Venus,* by Botticelli?"

"No, ma'am," he said. "The stone looks like flesh."

"That's because the iron in it got colored by the water. You don't need to say 'yes ma'am, no ma'am' to me, Aiken. There doesn't anybody up here say that."

He was studying a painting of a huge hog whose name was Caesar. A little man in old-fashioned clothes was holding it with a bridle. "Lord, that is some kind of hawg! I never saw a pig in harness before." He laughed. "What do they say up here?"

"Oh, I don't know, Miz whatever-your-name-is if you don't know them, and their first name if you do know them. You might as well get used to calling me Melinda. Everybody else does. But don't for Lord's sake call me Milly. I can't stand it. I bet you're just worn out, honey. I'm going to get you a beer and me a drink and then we are going to have something to eat and you're going to bed and get some sleep so you can think in the morning."

"Yes, ma'am," he said, and they both laughed, for the first time together.

It was after dinner when she finally got to what she had been waiting to ask. "Tell me, Aiken. What did I say wrong today—you know, when you shut your face so tight I wasn't even there?"

"I thought you were mockin me, that how-did-you-come-up stuff. You white folks say 'grow up,' we say 'come up.' I thought you were tryin to talk nigger, like some of those white kids did this summer. They were only bein friendly. They didn't know it hurt our feelings. Anyhow, I didn't know what language to use. I speak some!" He grinned a face-lighting grin.

"God, Aiken, I only wanted to know how you got here from Louisiana. Now let's get this straight right now. I don't want to have to feel like I'm crossing a minefield every time I talk to you. You got to tell me when I say something that bothers you. What do you mean, all those languages?"

"Well now, let me see. I talk low talk and high talk and Miss Ann talk, and proud talk—that's Mister Prince talk, and field tacky, my grandmam calls it."

"What is Miss Ann talk?"

"Yes-ma'am talk. Miss Ann is Mr. Charlie's sister."

"Well, how did you come up?" Melinda grinned with him.

Aiken laid his head back on the couch and

stared at the ceiling for a little while, waiting for himself to begin. When he did start, he talked for an hour by the clock, as if once he opened the door of that closed face, it all poured out, good Southern story-telling. The place changed. They were in the South, way deep in the South.

"Where I'm comin from, oh Lord God! Let me see, where I start? Where *do* I start. That's high talk. Let's you and me go down a road. A terrible road to a ferry. If you go across the ferry from Plaquemine, Louisiana, you get on the back road to Baton Rouge. Red Stick. Redneck Stick. Jakey always told me not to say that. He said it was pejorative. He sure is one for high words. Well, he never went down that road black. That's all I can say right now. That's the meanest road in the United States. There's a lot that Jakey don't know."

He switched to Melinda's office so suddenly that she could hardly follow him. "It came over me like a chill this afternoon, that I was sittin by myself in that room, all four walls mine, for one of the few times in my whole life. There had been so many people always, a cocoon of people, and I felt naked as a jaybird without them, and relieved at the same time. It was as if my mind"—he looked at her—"what was left of it, could just float right out all the way to the walls and there wouldn't be nobody to stop it.

"Did Jakey tell you about that day when he went to jail?" He didn't give her a chance to answer. "Swear to God, he was as proud as Mr. Peacock. I watched him, and I was proud too. That took plenty of spit and vinegar, let me tell you. Do a thing like that. When I saw that dumb honky step on Jakey's glasses, I waited until everybody had gone on down the road and wherever they sat on hot days and the courthouse went back to sleep. Then I went on up there and picked up the glasses. The only other time I been up those steps was when I ran up there and drank real quick out of the white drinkin fountain on a dare.

"I still got the old broken frames. They stand for somethin, and they were my souvenir for standin for somethin. Jakey's glasses stood up for what I stood up for.

"I sat there waitin for you and I thought to myself, Well, here I am, still bein handed from one white person to the other who don't know a thing. Even Jakey don't know who I am. If you asked me one more time where I was comin from, I was just goin to give you some sassy answer like I came on the bus all the way from Louisiana to Port Authority Bus Terminal, where nobody looked at anybody.

"I was sore from sittin all that way up from Baton Rouge and I had me a stretch, and then I went and sat at a counter and swear to God I was scared, but nobody even looked at me, much less told me to get out of there. I ordered a hamburger and it wasn't political, it was just a hamburger. I sat there eatin it and tellin myself there wasn't anybody goin to push me off the seat or arrest me or threaten me or jeer at me for eatin a hamburger. How could they when they couldn't even seem to see me? Don't these people up here ever *look* at nobody?

"My great-grandmam was borned into slavery. She told me white people in those days treated you like that, never looked at you. You were like a chair to them, and they didn't seem to know you had eyes and ears, you just weren't there, just a thing like a chair. She said they'd say anything in the world right in front of you and not seem to know you were listenin and takin it all in and storin it away. That's how she knew who she was. She was the daughter of one of the Aikens, real fine family, and they had sent her away like a package so his wife wouldn't be reminded. They seemed to think you just forgot who you were. Boy, she never did. Worse snob than Miss Boodie and neither one of them knew it."

Melinda didn't interrupt for fear of that closed face again. She let him take her from place to place, back and forth, and she followed as best she could. He went back to the Port Authority bus station.

"I went into the big men's room where I could get washed and change my clothes. I didn't want to come up here to Jakey's cousin all wrinkled and dirty. Well, anyhow, that was one way I came up. When we drove over here, you know that's the first time in my life I ever sat in the front seat?"

"Sure, I knew."

"I knew you did." Aiken got up and paced around the room as if he were caged. When he spoke again, he was in another place and another time.

"Then there was the long way. We got this new teacher, Sergeant Prince. He was the smartest man I had ever seen in all my born days. But we never called him Sergeant Prince in public, not in front of white people. That was his secret name. White people down there don't like black people been in the U.S. Army. Sergeant Prince walked into our little old one-room schoolhouse about to fall down on our heads on the first day in the fall when I was thirteen years old and the smartest boy in the sixth grade. They called it the sixth grade but they were all in the same room so I never moved into another room, just into another seat, nearer the back. If I'd of been white I would of been in the eighth grade, but there wasn't any eighth grade so I just stayed anyhow. My grandmam made me.

"Sergeant Prince was a great big man. He didn't look like a teacher at all. He looked like a sergeant. He never said one word. He just took and put a hammer and nails and some pictures and some signs on the teacher's desk, and he lit into nailin them up all around the blackboard. The pictures were all of black men and black ladies, and the signs were printed in great big letters.

"Then he turned around. He said, 'I'm your new teacher. My name is Mr. Prince, and you are to call me Mr. Prince. I speak English, and if I hear one word of field tacky in this room, I will tan your hide. I had to learn when I joined the United States Army when I was fifteen or get beat up. I lied about my age. I said I was eighteen. I stayed in the United States Army for thirty years and I came out a sergeant, and if you don't believe that, just talk one time in this school out of the wrong side of your mouth and you'll find out. When I came out I had the only two choices an intelligent black man has. I could be a preacher or I could be a teacher.

"'I have seen too many of you people try to learn when it is too late, so I decided to be a teacher, and I went to school and sat with all those youngsters in the normal school and they called me Papa.'" Somebody laughed. It wasn't me. 'And don't a one of you ever call me that. I am Mr. Prince. That is your first lesson on how to behave to a man.'

"He picked up a ruler. 'Now I am going to introduce you to your own people.' He tapped the ruler against the first picture. 'This is Mr. Douglass.' And the next, 'This is Mr. Garvey,' and the next, 'This is Mr. George Washington Carver. This is Miss Sojourner Truth.' It wasn't a real picture, it was some kind of drawin. 'And this, this is Miss Harriet Tubman.' That was a picture of a real old lady. She looked like a monkey. 'They are all Mr. and Miss to you, and don't you forget it. We are going to find out all about them. These are your people, and they were smart.' The ruler slapped his hand. 'And they were brave.' The ruler slapped again. 'And they *knew who they were.*' The ruler slapped his hand with every one of those words. "'Now, over here are three sayings. You are going to learn them by heart and you are going to say them with me in the morning after we say the pledge of allegiance and the Lord's Prayer.'" Aiken had begun to act it out. He was seeing Mr. Prince and he was being Mr. Prince.

" 'This.' Mr. Prince tapped every word of the top sign. 'Read it.' The whole school except for the little ones in the first grade read slowly, *I started with this idea in my head. There's two things I got a right to . . . death or liberty.* He had signed it in big writin like it was her signature, Harriet Tubman.

" 'All right, next.' He tapped another big sign he had made. *No man can put a chain about the ankle of his fellow man without at last finding the other end fastened around his neck.* He had signed that one Frederick Douglass.

"Then he went on to the third one. 'Read.' The whole class read slowly, a chant. *Straight is the gate and narrow the way, you want to walk on it, do what I say. Learn the way you want to be through ABC and three times three.* Signed Booker Allen Prince, Sergeant U.S. Army, retired. He turned around and snapped at us, like a sergeant in the movies, 'What is the difference between you and white people?'

"One little girl raised her hand, Miss Liddy's youngin. 'Them slap you upside the haid.'

" 'Next.' Mr. Prince pointed the ruler and Miss Leulie's little boy said, 'Them lick all the molasses off your hand and then call you nigger.'

"Then that ruler came round real slow and pointed right straight at me. I had somethin that was just like a revelation. I said education."

" 'Education. That's it. Education. Not color or money or background. Education. Now I have another saying for you.' We had already forgotten to be scared of Mr. Prince and the slappin ruler. We read, *Write how this young man squeezes the slave out of himself, drop by drop, and how, on waking one fine morning, he feels that the blood coursing through his veins is no longer that of a slave but that of a real human being.* The signature wasn't like anything any of us had ever seen. It was foreign.

"Mr. Prince said that was written by a Russian called Anton Chekhov. Anton Chekhov. He said Anton Chekhov was the grandson of a slave just like our grandmamas and grandpapas. They didn't have black slaves in Russia, they had white slaves. He turned to the sign and read it aloud again, almost to himself, and there was wonder in his voice.

"Then he turned around and pulled out his chair and sat down behind the teacher's desk, and he started ramblin like he wanted to be friends. He told us there wasn't much to do in the army for a lot of the time, and how he got to readin. He said he read everything he could get his hands on, and one day he found this book called *The Letters of Anton Chekhov.* He said he didn't know Anton Chekhov from a hole in the wall. He found that sayin in one of his letters. He told us it was like a sign unto him out of the Bible. After that he read everything Anton Chekhov wrote. He said Anton Chekhov might have been white but he saw like we do, from outside lookin in, and he had another thing about him that was like us, he had this kind of compassion for people who you would think would have been his enemies—poor silly ladies and men who had never had to have any get-up-and-get.

"Then Mr. Prince opened a book. He said,

'Sometimes, though, Anton Chekhov got mad, and when he got mad he turned it into a story. I'm going to read you a story like that first thing we do, and you will see just what I mean.' He opened the book, and he looked over his little-bitty glasses. 'How many of you ever been read to?'

"Some of us raised our hands. 'Well, you got to sit still and listen. I'm going to read a story to you every day.' His voice was quiet when he read, but it went all the way out to the bare board walls and seemed to float in the sunstreaks. It was a story about a coachman whose son had died and he tried to tell people who rode in his sleigh, but nobody listened because they didn't even see him or hear him, and finally he had to tell his horse about his grief. Mr. Prince read it to a bunch of kids who had never seen snow and never heard of Russia and didn't know what a sleigh was, not then, and the whole room was completely still, so still that when a bird sang way outside, it seemed to be right in the schoolroom with us.

"Then he snapped the book shut and said, 'This place is filthy. We are going to clean it up before we do one more thing.' " Aiken smiled at that. "Man, we scurried around like fleas. We already knew, right at once, we better not mess with Mr. Prince. He would tell us that. 'Don't mess with Mr. Prince,' he would say about himself, and everybody would look at the ruler, but I never saw him use it on one single person. It was just there, like the great mace that was the symbol of the House of Commons in England he told us about.

"When Mr. Prince tested us for readin, he told me I could read at high-school level. Then he asked me if I liked to read. I never heard such sweet words in my life. From that time on, Mr. Prince lent me books he got by mail out of the state library or someplace in the North.

"He taught us a lot. He taught us all to read and write and multiply and divide and talk high. When we were supposed to leave the school when we finished the sixth grade, he taught us until the school got too small, and then he taught us at his house, the ones whose parents would let him. He did a lot of arguin about that. Some of the parents were scared. Things were already happening. All of this had to be secret.

"Man, I had already learned that. Once when Mama was still alive, when I was in the fourth grade, I had this pretty girl I made friends with. She came from Alabama, and we liked each other, and we started walkin to school together. She didn't live far from the school. She would just wait at the gate of that shotgun house they lived in and we would walk on down the road together. I hadn't hardly noticed—well, sure I had noticed her color, because I thought she was so pretty, but it didn't seem to make all that much difference. Her mother was light brown and she, her name was Samantha after her grandmam, she was high yellow, almost white.

"One day we were just walkin along mindin our own business, and we had walked almost to my grandmam's house, and I said, 'You come on in and meet my grandmam.' I didn't say 'meet my mama' because I didn't know how she would be feelin that day, but I always knew how my grandmam would be feelin, as strong as a silo and about as big. So we went on up onto the porch and inside, and I was so proud of my friend and so proud in front of her that we didn't live in a shotgun house but in a house with six rooms and a veranda all the way around it, wide enough for a swing.

"Grandmam made Uncle Obe paint the house every year, not with paint, that was too costly, but with whitewash. We have fruit trees with whitewashed trunks out in the side yard, she says it keeps the bugs out, and a live oak that spreads its low branches so that it looks like it protects our piece of property. Uncle Obe, that's Obe for Obediah, he calls it a hangin tree. He says they ought to cut it down, what it stands for. Grandmam said, 'Over my dead body, Junior.' Mama had put two whitewashed tires, one on each side of the path, and they looked pretty that evenin with the last of the petunias and marigolds.

"Grandmam, and Mama too, were just as polite to my friend as they could be, made her right at home and gave us cake. I walked her back home because it was gettin dark." Aiken sighed. "I was just walkin on air when I got back home. Mama met me at the door and she didn't say one word. She just slapped me so hard she knocked me over.

"She stood over me so I couldn't even get up. The foot of the rocker was diggin into my hip, but the way she looked I didn't dare to move. She spoke real slow, every word separate. '*Let me tell you.* Don't you ever walk in public with that girl again. *Ever. Ever.'* She reached down and hit me every time she said *ever,* and the tears were just floodin down her face. 'They ain't goin to wait and ask for her parents' and grandparents' name if she white or colored. They just goin to see a white girl walkin with a colored boy. I done lost too much already for you to start somethin. *Ever.'* She said it again and hit me again and ran out of the livin room. I could hear the screech of the bed when she threw herself down on it.

"Grandmam said, 'Come here, son.' I started cryin too, a great big boy. 'You come here to me. She don't mean to hurt you feelins. She blue.' I crawled to where Grandmam sat in that chair, the only one she fitted in. I put my head down in her lap. Lord, I must of done that a thousand times since I was a little baby. I could feel that leg like a big tree branch under my cheek. I could feel her hand, her great big hand on my head, and she stroked and stroked. She seemed to tower above me, and when I looked up at her, her eyes were lookin someplace I didn't know, not till that day. She had cataracts, but there wasn't a thing they could do about it. Those eyes always reminded me of through a glass darkly and then face to face. I thought that if the cataracts were gone, I could see right through her eyes all the way to China.

"I was hopin she wouldn't say anything, just let me lay there, but she started in talkin anyhow. She said, 'Let me tell you somethin, son. We didn't never tell you because we didn't want you to grow up bitter. We wanted you to get your strength from home—that's where colored people have to get their strength. There ain't none out there for you.

" 'We always tole you your daddy was wounded in the war. Well, he wasn't, not the war you thought it was, nohow. Everybody knowed you cain't git off the train in the South after the war in your uniform, they was fellows waitin, but he didn't get the message like your two uncles did. They got it in New York City when they come home and they went and bought theirselves some clothes and wrapped up their uniforms they fought in in the Second World War and they both got the Purple Heart, and your Uncle Baron the Bronze Cross, fat lot of good that done. We always tole you, and so did your daddy, that he got wounded in the war too, but it wasn't the same war. It was this war, down here. He got off the train in Baton Rouge, and them poor white trash used to wait at the station to catch somebody colored in uniform and teach them a lesson they wasn't in England and Europe no more, runnin around with no white women, so they jumped him. Remember what a little fellow he was? You get your heighth from my side of the family. He wasn't even in England and Europe. He was a clerk in Camp Dillon.

" 'They broke both his legs and they kicked his kidneys so he never got over it, and he couldn't go to the Veterans because they said it wasn't no war-related injury. So he just come home to me and your mama and he sat on the porch with them twisted legs you thought he got in the war, and he just plain died of bitterness. He had brains—you get your brains from his side of the family.

" 'Your mama and him got married before he went to the army, and she wasn't no more than fifteen years old, but they wanted to, and they managed to have you after he come home, but that's all he ever done with his life, and then he just sat out there on the porch with them crutches leanin against the house wall and he stared into the distance or read the paper and then he died. He just took and shrunk to death. You remember that, you remember when he died, right there in the back bedroom. They said it was diabetes and meningitis, but it wasn't nuthin but he was bitter as he could be. The Lord give him bitter herbs to swallow and he couldn't do it.

"Your mama never been the same since he got off that train and she was waitin there for him and she seen the whole thing happen and she picked him up and he screamed because his legs was both broke. There ain't a one of us ain't got somebody in the family or we know hasn't had somethin like that happen to them. Not one. I don't know. I just don't know why the good Lord put us here. I ain't got no answers. I used to have a lot of answers and now I ain't got none.'

"Then she said my mama was scared to death I was goin to get out there with that bunch of fools and stir everything up like they was beginning to do other places, and git hurt like that. She said people ought to let well enough alone. She said the preachers were goin to get people hurt and killed, and I never thought in my whole life I would hear her say one word against a preacher,

her an elected mother of the church. She said they ought to take and preach the Word of God. She sounded like Miss Boodie but for different reasons.

"I didn't say one word then. I didn't want to lie, but when they thought I was goin to the picture show, I was baby-sittin while some of the women went to meetins in Baton Rouge, or I stood guard when they met in whatever church the preacher would let them have, acted like it was Wednesday night meetin. I just let her comfort me for a lot more than she could ever know about.

"She was way too fat to go outside anymore, so she didn't know how it already got ugly in the street. People went along and said 'Good mornin' and 'Nice day' like they always had, but that was about all they dared to say in public. Men in the street gathered like they did to do for a lynchin, or burn the fiery cross, but we didn't do anything because Mr. Prince had told us how to behave so nobody could have an excuse to mess with us. Once I heard one of the white men say 'over my dead body.' It wouldn't be over their dead body. It would be over our dead bodies. Every single one of us had seen the pictures of Emmet Till, the boy that came down from Chicago and got uppity with a white woman. He was only fourteen years old.

"They raised and lowered the Confederate flag every day in a little ceremony they made up at the courthouse. The men stood there fat and embarrassed in a row that was supposed to be military. They were funny-lookin all right, but they were killers all right, too.

"Mr. Prince said we didn't need to live in fear anymore, not at home, not in our souls, but we were not to be damn fools. He didn't swear much, which made *damn* all the stronger. He was a deacon in the church. He said the streets and the woods and the rivers were as dangerous as powderkegs. He said keep our heads down and don't look straight at a white man, and certainly not at a white woman. It wasn't time yet. It would be time, but it wasn't yet. That was all there was to it.

"Then in 1960, when I was fourteen years old and already as tall as I am now, Mr. Prince told me and some of the other brothers to come to his house after dark and we were goin to meet somebody. That was the night it began, the night Mr. Prince said we were called to the colors.

"There was a little frail-lookin fellow standin in the half-light from the porch, and he lined us up like soldiers. This little cat named Gabriel, Gabriel Ebersole, had led a march and had been beaten up, and he started talkin about Mahatma Gandhi. Mr. Prince had already told us about him a long time ago. That little cat's voice in the dark of Mr. Prince's back yard was talkin about how Mahatma—the mahatma, he called him—had brought down the British Empire without raisin a finger. He called it nonviolence.

"He had already led a strike at a school in Mississippi, the scariest state in the South. He told us how he learned to roll up in a ball so they wouldn't kick him in the head or the genitals. He called his balls 'genitals.' He talked like a black Jakey, and it made me smile in the dark.

"Then he said, 'Now everybody isn't ready for nonviolence. It takes a sight more guts than hittin back, and you got to learn it. It does not come easy. How many of you think you can learn it?' Of course we all raised our hands. Then Gabriel Ebersole, who just came up to my shoulders, stood there in front of me and all of a sudden he hauled off, slapped the breath out of me. I just stood there, tryin not to cry. But I never moved. Then he said some sweet words. 'Okay. You'll do,' Gabriel said. We got to be close friends later, not deep like Jakey and Mr. Prince, but close. He was the one made me come on up here."

Aiken laughed. "I never did tell him I didn't hit back because Gabriel was littler than I was. Anyhow, that was the way we got started."

They talked half the night about things he hadn't ever told and things that she had not told since Tye had died. They didn't know or question why they could do that. It was just comfortable, and too delicate to talk about why.

Eleven o'clock chimed in the black clock with the mother-of-pearl, which Melinda said was papier-mâché. Out of the silence, while they were both listening to the clock, she said, "What is it like to be a Negro?"

He thought for a long time. There was so much he could tell her, and so little. "Watchful," he finally said.

"What do you really think of white people? Do you hate us?"

"Naw, I don't hate you. Well, I hate the idea of you, but I can't hate you one by one, that's all. Sometimes you bother me and sometimes you tickle me."

Then he thought for a while. "Have you ever been scared to death?" he finally said.

"Oh Lord, yes." She was looking at the empty fireplace as if she wished it were winter and cozy. "I was in two wars, and the funny thing is, I wasn't scared, not at the time, except one time when we were under bombing and we were trying to crawl through the ground and the ground was coming up and hitting me in the stomach. I found a spoon. No, a knife. That was the only time while I was there, but afterward I was scared all the time. Scared of noises, scared of anything sudden. I still am, jump out of my skin."

She was surprised that he had asked her that. Since coming back, she had sat so often and let them talk, the tall boys, the tearful girls, but not one time had they ever asked her anything about herself. It wasn't their way. She had been the listener, not the teller. Wars and Italy and strikes and all the years kept silence in her memory. As far as the young were concerned, she might as well have been off robbing banks. She remembered being young like that and finding out one day that one of her teachers at school had had a lover, a real lover, and she was as surprised as if she had stumbled on her naked.

Aiken wasn't saying anything. He was waiting. Then he said, "Fear. You don't know. It's in my genes. Mr. Prince said that, and before he could explain, one of the boys laughed because he thought it was in your jeans like your ass and your uglies. Oh, you know with your mind and your nerves, but you don't know with your genes. You know what they do with uppity niggers where I come from?" He didn't wait for her to answer. "They torture them to death and they truss them up in chains and they throw them in the Mississippi River. That's what we come up knowin. 'You step off the goddamn sidewalk, nigger, or we will cut your uglies off and we will truss you up in chains and we will throw you in the Mississippi.' When those northern white boys got killed and put in the dam, they raised all that runkus, they dragged the river and they found ten, twenty bodies of black men half-eat by catfish. Nobody ever bothered to drag for them. They were just gone.

"You know what saved us this time? The reporters and the photographers. When the white northern kids come down there for the registration summer, they was big news, and we had to take care of them without they knowin it, they was so careless, and so proud of theirselves. Some of them didn't have sense enough to come in out of the rain. We had to teach them not to ride black and white woman and man in the same seat in a car, and we had to tell them, Don't stop, don't ever stop, keep you car in good repair, don't stop when they followin you, the sheriff, the deputies. They deputized every white trash in some of the counties.

"Yessir, you said it, man! The reporters and the photographers saved us, still savin us, but you just let what's happenin way down there not be news no more and it will all start again, man, the chains and the river."

He had gotten up and he was walking around the room, telling it to the books and the lion and the fragment of the bust of Aphrodite, not confessing, not mourning, just telling, flat. He touched the chin of the cold marble. It was as if Melinda had gone to bed and left him there, wandering around that pretty, innocent room, and he was cleansing it and himself with what he had to say. His voice wasn't aimed at her. He didn't seem to give a damn whether she listened or not.

"This one night, now you remember, all the churches, the black churches, they are out in the country, alongside the graveyards down there. My grandmam said it is to keep the dead company. This one church was out there in the country in the dark, by the graveyard, real old graveyard, back to slavery.

The dark, that was what you have to remember. Some of the preachers and their people didn't want us there, they say they just depend on God to get them out of their messes, but there was that one preacher, over in the next parish. He let us meet.

"God, I never will forget that church, because it wasn't quite dark that night. There was a moon. We told the reporters and we didn't tell anybody else, not the FBI who were still down there, because we didn't trust them, we just told the reporters we trusted because that meant we would be safe, but that night somebody told on us. We started the meetin with singin. We always started that way. Black people always like to start with some singin. It makes the soul feel good. We was singin some integration songs we all know, you know, 'We Shall Overcome' and that one I like the best, 'Eyes on the Prize,' and some others—I forget, people made them up, and they made up more verses too. We felt safe that night. The reporters come and they brought photographers, and I can still see the old kerosene lamps, you know, makin the nice patterns on the wall. You know them. Then every once in a while, a white flash from somebody's camera.

"Then we heard the horses. They come on horses. There was three steps up to the church door and they just flung it open and rode the horses right in with us. I've never been so scared in my life, the little ones was screamin and the women, and some of the horses stepped on people, and my first thought was where are the reporters and the photographers, and then I saw they took care of them first, smashed their cameras, hit press people in the face with whips, they was whippin us out of the church, way up there on those huge horses. You know how big a horse looks inside a room? It was only one room, a big room, and they was millin around, and we was tryin to sneak by them and hide behind the tombs in the graveyard. Then I saw they had masks on and masks on the horses—not masks like the KKK but masks for gas, and then they got to sprayin that tear gas, and people were vomitin on the floor and tryin to protect their own.

"I still don't know how I got out of the front

while they was millin around in there. I thought, Jesus Christ they're goin to hit the kerosene lamps and the whole place is goin to go up in flames. I grabbed the first people I could find, just felt for them and dragged them with me. It was a mother and her three children, hollerin and cryin, and I got them all sqwunched down behind a big tombstone. We's all shiverin with fear, and if ever I heard the voice of Jesus like my grandmam always said she did when she had somethin to tell us she wanted us to do and don't argue, I heard it then, with those little youngins and their mama. I didn't even know them. They come from someplace else. That was the minute the voice of Jesus, I swear to God, said, 'I am not goin to stand for this.'

"It was like new life came into me and into them, us cringin behind that tombstone and then nobody was cryin, we was just hidin from some of the horsemen who had ridden out of the church whoopin and hollerin and ridin around the graveyard, but we were back between a tree and an old tilted tombstone so nobody could get back there. We were still for a long time and then the woman sighed and she said, 'I ain't goin to stand for this no more,' like she had heard the same voice. Have you ever had downright fury replace fear?"

"That too," she said. "In Kentucky."

"It's like one kind of blood replaces another kind of blood. That's what happened. Every muscle I had wanted to kill them all, drag them from their horses, but then I knew right then that the Reverend King and Gabriel Ebersole were right. It wouldn't do one damn bit of good. We had our story—it was all over the newspapers, up North and everyplace, and the FBI said they would investigate. The orders came straight from Washington. We heard all that at the office the next mornin. We were a fine-lookin bunch, all punched up and eyes swelled up and somebody had a broken rib, and you know it was a miracle nobody was killed.

"You know something?" He turned and actually smiled at Melinda. "We met the next goddamn night in the same goddamn church as soon as the ladies cleaned up the vomit and the blood and the broken chairs. The place was full to the rafters. My friend and her kids was there. They was all sayin that Jesus wouldn't let the church burn down. Some He did, though, some of the churches. I'm so tired I can't stop walkin and talkin," he said, and wandered around the room and looked at the pictures he had already looked at on the walls.

Melinda had a whole line of little model cars across a table in the corner of the room that he hadn't seen yet. He stopped. He put out his hand and then drew it back, as if he were afraid to touch them. Melinda went over and stood beside him. "Go on," she told him, "pick one up." When he didn't move, she put one into his hand.

"That's the finest car ever made, a 1937 Jaguar SS100. Better than the '36. All these are cars I've had. They're gone, some in Spain, one burned in Kentucky. But this one I brought back here with me. It's right out there in the garage. It still runs perfectly. Maria said leave it, but I wasn't about to. It was Tye's—well, his daddy's. It's in perfect condition. I look after it myself. Some rich man in Chicago who collects cars is after it. He offered me eighty thousand dollars for it. He calls me about every month to see if I've changed my mind. Can you imagine?"

"Holy shit," Aiken said, forgetting or not caring where he was. She noticed that he already didn't bother to apologize, and she knew they had crossed over.

The phone rang. They both jumped, and then Melinda said, "That's my daughter. She is living in Spain, doing research. She always gets it wrong, figures five hours behind instead of five hours ahead."

He could hear her voice from the kitchen, and then pauses, and then her voice again. "Oh, darling that's wonderful. Congratulations!" And then another "Congratulations!" and the sound of a kiss and "God bless your darling soul, you are wonderful," and he heard her hang up. She came back into the green room, looking radiant, tired as she was, as if he hadn't told her the story at all.

"She has just found out she is pregnant, and she has found a whole pile in one place of pure something-cephalic skulls, which, according to her, shows that probably Seljuks did fight as mercenaries in Spain in the twelfth century." She laughed. "I don't know which she is most excited about, the baby or the skulls. Oh, I didn't tell you. She is what she calls a historical anthropologist. She says it's one of those disciplines where you can write a whole book explaining why you don't know something and can't find out. She and Manuelo have a house in a little town called Albastro—I used to know the house. A friend of mine lived there. Maria's husband is Spanish, but he grew up in Mexico. Now he is American, so they are safe in Spain—sort of, anyway. He teaches at Harvard. Maria used to teach here before she married. That's why I'm here. Now, that doesn't make a bit of sense, does it? You come on to bed, honey, so you'll be bright-eyed and bushy-tailed in the morning to sign on for classes."

Her voice was so cheerful it was almost hysterical. Then she suddenly changed, almost to tears. "Don't think I don't know. I do know."

Aiken was trembling with fatigue. She put her hand on his arm and guided him upstairs. She didn't say anything. She just guided him to the door of his bedroom and kissed him goodnight, and said, "Oh, you don't know how glad I am you're here."

Melinda sat back down in the green room and waited for Tye. It was her way of thinking about what Tye would do, what he would say, but she could hear it in his voice, and she waited for that. She didn't have to wait long.

When he was there, she asked, aloud but softly, so she wouldn't let Aiken hear and be disturbed, "Does it ever end?"

"Oh, knock it off, darling, of course it doesn't." Knock it off: that was Tye. "You've seen that all your grown-up life."

"What can I do?"

"Darling." She could hear him say it the way he used to say, "Darling, where the bloody hell is my brolly, it's pissing down out there," slightly annoyed, but not at her, she knew that. "Darling, you've known about this for several years, ever since you saw Jakey. Don't be silly. You'll know what to do. Just wait."

Wait. She had waited long enough, and she hadn't known she was waiting to know what to do. They had sent Aiken up to her without enough money to go to Charles Wesley. When she had gone to the registrar to see what could be done, she had been told they didn't have funds to fill out his scholarship. She had long since learned that that was academic language for no. The registrar had looked over her huge rhinestone glasses and said, "Too bad the boy isn't kin. You could have the employee discount." She had looked down at some papers on her desk then, dismissing the whole problem.

Melinda was tired of being caught between the rock of Southern arrogance and the hard place of northern cold-bloodedness, and she was bound, damned, and determined to do something about it, on both sides. She knew that if she took Aiken to raise, it wouldn't be for one year, it would be for at least seven, if Aiken was going to be a lawyer as he wanted to be.

She sat in the night and made herself figure, and wished she had an envelope like her daddy always used to figure on. In 1955 she had given the income from the trust her father had left her to Maria. It wasn't much, but it was enough money to give Maria some extras.

Extra money. Melinda needed extra money, and she needed it right away. The income she had not used had mounted up to about $70,000 after she had spent funds to go to Katie Gibbs, and to Spain, and of course to buy the ambulance. It wasn't enough, and she couldn't break the trust and leave Maria without extras, especially now that she was going to have a baby.

Melinda had been waiting for a sign for a long time, four years, while she didn't know what to do or where to do it, and now there he was, an eighteen-year-old, thin as a rail, with eyes that were so much older than hers would ever be that they scared her, and made her feel like a fool.

"All right." She heard herself, and realized that she was grinning. For God's sake, what about? "Of course. I was waiting for Aiken. A face, a person. Not an idea, not an anger when I saw the news or read the paper—that easy anger where you jerk off and don't do anything—but anger with a face and a name. Jakey and Aiken, who would have thought it? The same old fight. And I thought I had given up, what is it they call it? Been reconciled. Reconciled, hell," she said to the lion.

When she passed Aiken's door at seven in the morning, it was open, the bed was made, and she could not see any sign that he had ever been there. In the kitchen she started to put on coffee, then glanced out onto the back porch. He was sitting on the lowest step, with his legs splayed and his head in his hands. He was staring at one place on the soapstone paving she had put down as a path to the garden, as if he were trying to memorize it.

She called out, "Good morning, Aiken. Come on in."

"I'll be in in a minute." He answered like a sulky child, and he didn't turn his head to look at her when he answered. Then she noticed that the soapstone he was staring at was sopping wet. Aiken had been crying.

She stood in the doorway behind the screen, waiting for him to tell her.

"It's awful," he finally said. "For the first time since I was fourteen, since I was a little baby, I reckon, I can walk down a road without havin to be ready for somebody to throw a rock at me or worse, and my knees won't work and I can't stop cryin."

"Tye did that after he came home from being in prison in Spain. He did it for two months, and he always swore he didn't." Melinda leaned against the doorjamb and let the sun touch her. It was a conversation, a morning conversation about things they both took for granted.

"I don't have two months to spare."

"Oh yes, you do."

The sun shone on the water of the river away in the distance, and the flowers were still blooming and the leaves hadn't turned so the garden was in light and shadow. "You come on in here, son," she said. "I'll make us some breakfast and then I'll carry you over to the school."

The Southern words started him crying again, and she didn't pay any attention. "I can't stop," he wailed.

"Then don't, honey." She broke two eggs into a black iron skillet. "I've figured out what we ought to do," she called to the top of his head. He was holding it down so she wouldn't see the red eyes he was ashamed of. It made him seem to be pouting, but he wasn't pouting. He was embarrassed.

"Come in here right this minute." She knew that would jog him out of his trance. He unfolded very slowly and trudged in, his whole body letting her know he didn't want to. "Now you listen to me, Aiken," she said. "You may be as old as a stone, but you are also eighteen years old. I've decided what I want to do. You are part of the only family I have already, you and Jakey and Maria. God knows there aren't too many others from our part of the world, and we are all lonesome as hound dogs until they welcome us back to the South, which may not be in our lifetime the way things are going on there. So we have to make a little South, a little family, all by ourselves. I've seen it so much, in Spain and in England, that drawing together of Southerners, that making a family, all over the world. We have to do it. A Southerner without a family is like a loose marble."

He didn't say a word.

"Go ahead. Eat your ham and eggs," she ordered. "Now I've been thinking. You don't have enough money to go to Charles Wesley. But they have a cut rate for the families of employees.

So the sensible thing to do is to adopt you legally. I've thought it all out. You understand, it's only for the money. I've saved enough for you to go through here and then to law school, and it's money I wouldn't use. One day I'll tell you why, but there isn't time right now. We have to decide."

When he didn't answer or look at her, she tried again. "You haven't got another soul right now except your grandmam and Jakey and now me and some friends you've made in the movement. Most of them will disappear in time. You don't know it yet, but I've seen that too. Somehow we are like people who have been in prison or a shipwreck. We don't want to be reminded anymore. For a while you will make plans to meet, and then you won't anymore. That's only right. Tye would say it's a bloody waste of energy."

"That won't happen," he said to the eggs.

"Yes, it will." She sounded so annoyed, he looked up at her at last. "If I were down there, I could do something, but I'm not. I realized last night that I've done nothing for ten years, since I've known what was going on, except be proud of having dinner in public with Negroes and be suitably horrified at what other people are doing. A network-news liberal. I have kept my skirts very, very clean, and I didn't know it until last night. Do you want some more toast?"

He nodded, and she went over to the toaster. "Now, I want you to feel like a real member of our family, you and me and Maria and Jakey. I have thought about all this." She turned around.

"So that's why I think the most practical thing for both of us is for me to adopt you legally, so we won't waste any more time. I want to call my lawyer this morning and see what the laws are in New York State. It is, as you children say, no big deal. Call it an investment." She was trying to sound logical, and she was aware that she was lying; she didn't know quite how. "You have too much catching up to do to waste time taking a part-time job. If you want to go to law school, like you told me last night, you can't be worrying about working your way through. That takes too long, and you've got too much to do."

"Hey man, I'm *black!*" he finally said. "I can't be your baby boy!"

"And I'm white, and you're too old to be anybody's baby boy." She taught him the second lesson she was to teach him, after the lesson about the minefield. "Don't you be racist in this house, young man, not for one minute."

"Yes, ma'am," he said, not as he would have said to a white person but as he would have said to his grandmam.

She didn't tell him she had decided to sell the Jaguar.

Don't you dare. That's all I have to say to you." Melinda's mother was yelling over the telephone at seven o'clock in the morning. She didn't give Melinda a chance to get a word in edgeways. It was the voice she used when she had been reading James Jackson Kilpatrick. The calls came about once a week, every time he wrote about the civil rights movement in the *Richmond News Leader.*

Melinda said, "Mother, good morning."

"Don't you *dare* go down there. If you go down there, you needn't ever to come into this house again. You are going. I know you," her mother trumpeted, as if she didn't need the telephone, all the way from Richmond to New York, in an ecstasy of hysterical matriarchy.

Since Melinda's grandmother's death, at ninety, her mother had decided to inherit her mantle of authority. Thinking for herself for the first time in her life, at over seventy, was painful to her. There was nobody to hear her opinions, so nearly every week she either wrote to Melinda or telephoned her and pinned the sins of the world to her bosom. Melinda was used to it, but it did make her sad, and it kept her away from Richmond, where she would have done her bounden duty by the old woman more than she did if the old woman would just once in a while shut up.

"Mother, I have to hang up." She finally interrupted the flow, which seemed that morning to come from her mother through the *News Leader* via Ma Bell to her. The coffee was ready.

"Why in the world you have to work like that when you have money I don't know. I wish you would come on home where you belong and stop all this nonsense. Children are supposed to look after . . . You don't care what happens to me. I'm sick—"

"Mother, you have Imogene and Marshall.

Don't they look after you? You have your friends every afternoon, at your house or their houses."

"God knows they ought to do what I tell them. I pay them enough. But they've gotten full of a lot of fool ideas too." The voice of the Old South mourned on and on, and Melinda resolved once again to get a longer cord for the telephone so she could listen, or half listen, and reach the coffeemaker without hurting her mother's feelings.

"Mr. Coffee is at the door, Mother," she said. "He has something for me." She hung up.

She took a cup of coffee and sat on the back steps, where Aiken had sat in the fall. It was a beautiful day in late May. The roses were healthy and full of buds. The late red and yellow tulips were bright in the shaft of sun that came through the tree beside the porch. She had grown to love the time all to herself, with the new sun and the house, her own, the only one she had ever had in America. The Hudson flowed in the distance, and everything was all right.

She had been waking earlier and earlier in the mornings as the days got longer, as if she didn't want to miss daylight. She was so proud of Aiken, the way he had floated so gracefully into his life at Charles Wesley, the way he had learned, and even, although she laughed a little at herself for being proud of it, how popular he was. The children's crusade that was gathering all around the college had made him a hero, a CORE commando. She breathed a sigh of relief, there in the morning, thinking about it. He had been at war and the others had not, and they honored him for a little while. Then, gradually, through the first winter, they forgot, and he made friends for himself and not for his rarity.

Nobody except the administration and the president knew that he was legally her son. Neither of them wanted that. He wanted to be on his own, and she honored that by stressing that it was only a legal arrangement, after all. But to herself he was her son. She had a son at last. She prayed without knowing it. She did not use words to pray. She never had. She just sat there on the bottom step, thanking God for the sun and the garden and Aiken and the life that had come back to her after the four dark years. She had thought of the years as a mixture of reconciliation and patience and hiding all the sorrow in her soul, even from Maria. She loved Maria too much to bear to upset her and hear her healthy advice.

That was where Aiken found her. He didn't say any of the things he said, no good morning, nothing except "Something has happened. I know it has. Jakey made a solemn promise to write to me every week when I came up here. I wouldn't pay any attention, except he promised. He's such a damned fool, I didn't want him down there all by himself. He kept the promise until five weeks ago, just before the first Selma march. At first I thought he had gone to Selma. He would do something like that. But when I didn't hear after that, I knew something was wrong. I can't call Miss Boodie, but you can. I got to go down there."

She turned to look at him. She couldn't see

his face against the sun. She could only see his hair, which the sun shone through. He was so tall standing over her like that.

"You're not to do anything of the kind. You know Jakey wouldn't want you to." She climbed the steps into the kitchen again, walking slowly and wondering how many phone calls, how many blows, it took to get her to move. She sat down by the kitchen window that looked out on the garden. "You wouldn't last a day down there the way things are right now, but I would.

"You see," she told the coffee cup that was turning and turning in her hands, "I can go in disguise. I can go as a lady." She began to plan. "Well, now, let's see. I'll be a white lady with a white mind and white gloves in a black Buick. How do you like that? I know there's nothing to worry about, but I have to go see my mother anyway, and I might as well go on down. I'll call her tonight."

She was scared, frankly. There had been shooting at cars with northern license plates. A woman from Chicago had been killed. Why wasn't everybody there? She was ashamed of herself for saying it, even silently to herself, so late.

"Get yourself some coffee and stop beetling around and help me plan this thing. I'll have to get leave. I'll just say my mother is sick. That's easy. Now, wait a minute, let me get maps out of the car." She was in Spain again for a second. Know the safe routes, know the places to avoid.

He called after her, "I can't let you do this."

"Everybody is telling me what I can and cannot

do this morning. Don't you start." She came back with a fistful of road maps.

They spread the maps out on the table after they had pushed back the jigsaw pieces. *The Hay Wain* by Constable, or part of it, shared the surface with maps of Mississippi and Louisiana.

She talked to herself, letting him hear. "Now, let's see. It will be too hot down there to wear the Davidow suit I bought for the anti-Vietnam march down Fifth Avenue. I'll get a lighter one at Miller and Rhoads. Pink, I think."

"Man, that sounds disgusting." Aiken had started studying the map.

"It will work, though," she said, running a finger along the Natchez Trace. "Yes, I think I'll go to Miller and Rhoads. They'll have white gloves too. I never know where to find them in New York. I'll lease a Buick with a Virginia license from the people Daddy always bought his cars from. They are still there, still selling daddy-cars."

"You sound like you are going to a tea party."

"I am. The Boston Tea Party." They both laughed and then together knew what they had to do. They both knew that Aiken couldn't go and she could and she could be Lady Dunston and find out more in a day than he could find out in a year. That was a fact of life.

"But I don't know." Aiken tried again to argue.

"Look here." She put her hand on the map and leaned on it. "Do you want me to make a statement or do you want me to find Jakey?"

"You know I can't answer that," he sulked.

"Let me explain something to you. I'm going to tell you a story."

"You always explain with a story." He still sulked a bit.

"So do you. We're Southerners," she said. "Once when Tye and I went to our house in Italy, we met a lovely couple. We met them on the little beach on the island. I remember, we were all sitting on a steep rock and looking out to sea. Only the four of us, so we introduced ourselves. We saw them almost every day after that. He was a historian at the University of Uppsala, or some such place. I can't quite remember."

Aiken began to fidget.

"Stop that and listen to me," she ordered, hearing her grandmother. "They were Dutch. He was small and very elegant, and she was a Dutch aristocrat, a head taller than he was and very beautiful. One evening we were sitting on the terrace at our house after dinner, and we began to talk about—now, what started it?—oh, something had been in the papers about an experiment in fight adrenaline and flight adrenaline, that you weren't responsible when you reacted to stress. Something like that. 'You may not be responsible,' I remember the woman saying, a voice out of the darkness, 'but you can control it. But you have to pay.'

"Everybody was quiet. She went on. 'I remember that I did not show one reaction in health, I didn't even dream, when the war was on, but the very day that the Allies marched through Amsterdam, my knees buckled and I fainted. I was in bed for a month, they said, raving.' Her husband said, 'Dear one, you didn't rave, you have never raved in your life.' She said, 'Well, my cousin always said I did.'

"They both laughed. They laughed. Then they told the story. She was a member of one of Holland's leading families. All through the Nazi occupation she had posed as a collaborator. She had been spat on in the street by her relatives. She had hidden seventeen Jews in her Amsterdam house. One of them became her husband later. He interrupted then and said, 'I read a lot.' He had spent nearly four years in a closet, behind a row of evening dresses. He said he still couldn't stand the smell of silk. Every Sunday she had ridden her bicycle out into the country and put peroxide on his son's hair so he would pass as a nice little Aryan Dutch boy. She kept him with her old nurse. She saved seventeen people by living a lie. It won't hurt me for a few weeks, or however long it takes."

Aiken didn't say a word.

"The last night they were there, he proposed a toast. He said it was because of what he had learned in the closet. He raised his glass and said, 'To traveling light!' Traveling light, can you believe it?"

She leaned over the maps again. "Come on, son, tell me where on this map to go and where not to go."

They looked at the map of Louisiana. Melinda read the names. "Assumption, Lafitte. Do you think that is after Jean Lafitte? I hope so. A place named for a pirate, like our island."

“Man, you ought to see it.” Aiken kept his finger on the name. “I registered voters there last year. Mean place for me. All those black sharecroppers got themselves registered. That took more guts than any of us had to have. They could get kicked off land they had been on, and been cheated on, for years. One old man said, ‘Well, it’s wuth.’ He said he was ‘going to reddish to get respeck.’ He was about eighty.”

Melinda stared at the map, and it swam in front of her eyes. She controlled her voice. “You make the decisions of men and you are still boys. I never thought I would have to see it again in my lifetime.”

Aiken moved his finger. “Now look here. That’s the ferry we decided to desegregate.” He laughed. “That’s where all the brothers got put in jail and poor Jakey got sent home to his mama.” Melinda followed the forefinger of his long, delicate-looking hand as he spoke. “The school Jakey told me he was working at was in St. Francis de Sales, right over here, just a little old place. Not good. Not as bad as Mississippi, but not good. He wrote that they set up the school in a big broken-down plantation house. He said that it was like a castle of old, like places you showed him in England, what did he call them—follies. Are they really named follies?”

Suddenly Melinda felt a chill of horror. She had to get beyond it. She didn’t know why. Maybe it was talking of haunted places; maybe it was a memory of a ruined place that she had forgotten. She brushed it out of her mind.

“I’ll leave in the morning and drive to Albany

and take the plane to Richmond from there. Come on. I'll take you back to school."

The garage held only her Thunderbird. Aiken said, "Where's the Jaguar?"

"Oh, I'll tell you later—had to do something." She was mumbling and fumbling with the car key. "Damn," she said. "This car bores me."

On the way to school, she said, "Can you go with me in the morning and bring the car back? I don't like to leave it in Albany."

He had already gotten used to driving with a white woman in a car and not worrying about a thing. It was lifted from the shoulders of his mind already. He said, "I better stay over there at the house while you are gone."

"Don't have any loud parties." She grinned.

"Oh, come on, man."

They rode past the Hudson River bracketed houses, past the Gothic church, past the early-eighteenth-century stone house, past the entrance to one of the Hudson River estates, taking it for granted. The town was a place so safe for both of them that she breathed a sigh of relief every time she had to go to New York on the train and came back from Rhinecliff, Lily Bart's station, down the River Road to home.

Melinda had to go all the way through her childhood to get to Louisiana.

She flew to Richmond and took a taxi straight to Miller and Rhoads. It was the same as it had been all her life. She entered into an atmosphere that was deceptively secure, smelling slightly of perfume and wool. Something in her let go, as it always did when she went back, back all the way, so she was not fifty-four years old but eighteen, when she knew where the right suits were and the right gloves and the right underwear and the right best dresses. Some of the counters had been rearranged over time, but not enough to stop the ecstatic irony of her search.

It only took an hour. She packed the trousers and sweater that she had traveled in for comfort back into her bag, and she came out of the ladies' dressing room pristine in pink, with a white embroidered blouse with what she always called a country-club collar, a "good" leather handbag hanging from her arm. She was stepping through the aisle past cosmetics on the way to shoes when she heard the voice she had expected all the time.

"Why, honey, you look just wonderful." It was a friend of her mother's who had come out with her in 1908, straight-backed, wrinkled, and totally unchanged. She too wore a pink suit with a round collar, and she carried a leather handbag. She wore white gloves. Her hat sat high on a pillow of faintly blue hair. She still wore the sweet smile she used and had always used since her picture in the yearbook at Oakley Hall.

"Why, it's just lovely to see you, Melinda. How's your mother? We played bridge last week, but I haven't seen her since, just talked on the phone." The voice flowed over and around Melinda, a caul of a voice. Melinda said what she remembered as the right things, fine, just fine, flowed along with the words that slid over her between the counters in Miller and Rhoads, among the high imperious voices of the women of the West End of Richmond, voices that owned the world and all that was in it.

It was, of course, a small world. Melinda always forgot that. Its borders were the James River, the Capitol, the country club, and a little north of Cary Street—not too far, though. Of course there was only one country club in the world, one Commonwealth Club, one statue of Robert E. Lee, and one Cary Street.

She went to the Buick place. It had no name that she knew, it never had: it was the Buick place. She leased a black Buick from a man who called her Melinda and said she looked wonderful. She had known him all her life and she couldn't remember his name.

She had called her mother to tell her she was coming. The door almost crashed open when she parked the hired car. Her mother had been watching for her. She called out, "What in the world do you think you're doing? I *told* you not to go down there."

"It isn't what you think, Mother! I have to go to Baton Rouge to LSU on college business." Melinda lied easily, as she had to her mother all her life.

She hugged her mother to keep her from asking any more. It worked. Her mother had grown young again, and as flighty and flirty as a pigeon. She led Melinda into the hall, trailing Richmond gossip. "I called the paper," she said. "I knew you wouldn't mind if it's social things. That's all right."

She had renewed her virginity, copying Hera,

as Virginia women did when they had been released into age. She voiced opinions, thousands of them, at dinner, as if Melinda agreed with her. Melinda never said a word in argument. Girls don't, she thought. We girls don't. She watched her mother's mouth go on and on. And she thought, If I had stayed, I would have been so isolated I would have gone bananas or died of drink.

She planned her route in her old room, with the same flower prints on the walls, the same wallpaper, even the same lost, left things in the drawer of the bedside table: an invitation from 1931, a matchbox cover from a place she remembered going to in 1936, an old ribbon that had come off a corsage, a key to nothing, a smooth, thick visiting card that read MELINDA MASON KREGG, all stained with time. She found the extra car keys her father had had made for her and made her keep at home, her keys to the little Ford, and beside them, under all the flotsam of forgotten things, an unopened letter from her mother sent to Kentucky, a dusty black pompom from an old costume, a note with the word *no*, which made her smile, and the extra keys to her Stutz Bearcat. She put everything in her leather handbag, not questioning why. It was late at night and she was tired.

She wanted to go the way she had gone before, past Kregg's Crossing, through Cumberland Gap, even if it took a little longer. The comfort and the past and the mildness had half convinced her that she was on a wild goose chase anyway. She was in Virginia. She was going to Louisiana.

These were not places where people died without anybody ever knowing.

She escaped Richmond before anybody could blame her for not staying longer. Her mother had had her breakfast in bed. She said she didn't feel well. Imogene, grumbling, came down the stairs with the tray as Melinda was ready to leave. "I sure am glad you come back. There ain't nuthin wrong with her but relief her mama died, that's all," she said, and she went on past. She had grown heavy, and she stomped toward the kitchen.

Melinda thought of herself driving so long ago through the early morning, in uniform then too. This time the uniform was a wraparound denim skirt and a bleeding-madras blouse. She wore stockings and a garter belt, which felt funny around her hips. She was twenty again, crossing the James, and she began to like the drive, as she always had. The road was good, not like it had been in 1931.

The morning was lovely, the James ran smooth, and she followed along it, flowing like the water in a car that was like driving a sofa, with automatic gears, which she had never used—all so simple. Her disguise began to sink into her skin like a tattoo of comfort.

Then she got closer to Kregg's Crossing. The smell was terrible, and she remembered that Boodie had sold the land to a paper mill. She tried to remember a phrase of Shakespeare's. That part of her that had been homesick without her knowing it for so long was so at ease that she felt a twinge of fright, and then let that go, driving at an easy sixty-five, careful and efficient with her body and hoping she wouldn't get caught.

Melinda had forgotten something, and she couldn't think what it was. She slowed the car. She saw Imogene again, grumbling her way to the kitchen. Melinda hadn't said a word to show she was glad to see her, not "How's your health? What do you hear from your children?" Not a damn word.

Imogene and Marshall had raised four children over the garage, and Melinda couldn't remember their names. She hadn't thought about them for so long. Grown now, one in Detroit, she believed. She made herself remember—Eleanor and Isador, twins, Kregg and Mason, the boys. Her mother had said that her grandmother had said at the time that she thought it was so sweet of them to use family names, just like they were part of the family. Melinda had even let herself be godmother to Mason. They had gone to the Negro church, self-consciously dressed up, ushered to the front row, and she had been—oh, Christ—pleased with herself, pleased with them for being so close.

The flow of the drive, the flow of her mind, came together like a creek that grew into a torrent, and she remembered what she had tried to remember as the Shakespearean quote about the paper factory: "Oh, my offense is rank, it smells to heaven." It had been an English schoolboy joke about farting, and now it released a torrent of grief.

She pulled over to the roadside. She couldn't see to drive. What had triggered it she never quite knew—the fact that she hadn't asked Imogene about her children, the fact that they had been so pleased with themselves at the christening, the facts, the facts, the killer facts, the fact that she had gone halfway across the world to speak her mind when her voice had been silent on her own doorstep, the fact that she had kept silent when the racist stories were told, the black children hurt and frightened. She saw the polite arrogance of the country club as the genteel version of the gun rack on the pickup truck. It all came at once. They were all the same. Of course Imogene and Marshall had called their boys Kregg and Mason, because that was who they were, the secret Kreggs, the secret Masons, the secret Aikens, the names they had taken when they were finally allowed to have last names, not those of their masters but those of their blood brothers and sisters. All the knowledge flooded her at once. Her sobs were literally shaking the car, and the front of her blouse was soaked.

There was a knock on the window. A young man in uniform stood outside. She let down the window, which she had put up for the air conditioning.

He said, "Is anything wrong, ma'am? You out of gas?"

She managed to shake her head and find a handkerchief in her pocket and scrub at her face. "No," she finally said. "I just realized something, and then, you see, my husband died . . ." That hadn't been what she meant to say.

"Oh, ma'am, I am real sorry." He had a soft, sympathetic face, the kind of face that had learned to smile at everything a long time ago. "I'm the sheriff. If you want me to follow you?"

"No, thank you," she managed to say. "I'm all right now." He was a sweet man, a sheriff, and she wanted him to know that she was grateful.

Then he said, "Well, now, don't you stay here long. This is one of them roads the freedom-riding niggers and the white niggers use. That's why I'm here. It ain't no place for a lady. Where you going?"

She managed to say, "Knoxville." It was the only place she could think of. She dared not speak for fear of screaming at him or, worse, crying again, impotent and weak.

"Well, you ain't got far to go to get back to 81. You'll be safe there. Now, what you ought to do, ma'am, you ought to—" He had started waving his arm.

She interrupted to thank him, so angry that she felt choked, angry at his goddamned innocent evil, angry that she was who she was and he was who he was, and if he couldn't help it, she could. She drove off down the road toward Cumberland Gap, slowly enough so he couldn't pick her up for speeding, and she was relieved when he stopped following after a few miles and turned his car onto a county road.

She didn't recognize Cumberland Gap. There was no hotel, no Mrs. Hightower. The time leaped back again. She stopped the car and got out to stretch and find someplace where she could get a cup of coffee, but there was nothing, only the scent of mountain spring, the tumbling water, the valley. She drove the car near the creek and got out and took off her shoes and put her legs in the cold rushing water as if she had to keep on cleansing herself, the past, the tears, what she had been, what she still was, in the wild creek.

She sat there on a rock, as empty as she had ever been in her life. She couldn't even talk to Tye, and that was the worst isolation of all. She was completely on her own.

She let herself wait. The sun came through the treetops and caressed her head. The freezing water was a good pain on her skin. She sat until the sun changed toward evening and her legs were numb, as if she wanted to hurt herself into some new life.

By the time she got up, she knew what she was going to do. She drove to a motel outside Knoxville and called Boodie to ask if she could stay with her while she went to a meeting in Baton Rouge, and heard the formal delight: "Why, honey, I can't tell you how pleased I am. Elsworth will be, too. You get here in time for dinner, you hear? Why, this is just wonderful . . ." But there was something thin in her voice, and when Melinda hung up, she thought, How naked voices are on the telephone. Boodie sounded naked and afraid, but the words were the same. They were all the words she knew.

It was ten o'clock at night, and Melinda had followed the tunnel of her lights down the empty road between the great trees, on and on and on. She had been twelve hours and fifty-four years on the road, and she dropped on the motel bed like a tree trunk dislodged by a flood.

How beautiful it was in the South in May. Melinda drove around Birmingham, and Jackson, and along the Natchez Trace, a long trail of green stillness and peace, through to where the live oaks began to spread their shade across the road, through Port Gibson, a tomb town, downriver past the bluffs and the deep gashes of the old creekbeds, which looked so dark under the heavy green of the underbrush that they seemed to have no bottom, no source, as if the earth had been cut with a wild knife. They had been dredged out as part of the flood control of the river, but she thought of the creeks as entrances to some kind of wet Hades through the gashes of black water.

She crossed the river at Natchez, as she always had. She stopped only once, to have a sandwich at a motel and go to the bathroom, which was unlocked for her by a very polite young girl, a peach-colored girl with hair as blond as hers had been once. The girl apologized, "We got to keep it locked. You know . . ."

It was beautiful along the river and through the towns with their pretty white houses and live oaks that stretched May shadows over the beds of iris and late tulips. May and beautiful—she kept repeating it to herself, and she listened to a country music station where a singer was mourning the loss of his girl and his job and his truck, all on the same day.

Bonnevue was as slow, the streets as calm and shaded, the flowers as bright in the twilight of the heavy shade, the front porches as serene, as if time had stopped. On the street where Boodie lived, people lived their evening lives, swings creaking, women fanning, men just staring at the street and waiting for television time in the cool of the evening. They were already out, the ones who had their dinner at six o'clock, the ones who had their dinner late.

Boodie had explained years ago that you could tell who was an Episcopalian by whether they had a glass in their hand or not. It was a sweet little joke they all had together, the people in the slow-moving swings, the rocking chairs, on the white wooden porches in the early evening.

Boodie jumped up from her own swing and ran down the walk. Melinda only knew how exhausted she was when she got out of the car. Elsworth ambled behind Boodie and picked up Melinda's bag from the back seat. "Nice car," he said. The man she had known for so long as Mr. Percival never had said much. He had gotten fat. Boodie was like a stick, her face famine-thin, shocking, her smile a parody of itself, her voice wispy.

"I'll declare, this is the nicest thing that has ever happened to me." She held Melinda's arm, but the effusion was preoccupied. "We saved dinner for you."

"She's got to have a drink after all that way," Mr. Percival called from behind them.

Melinda walked among the few bits of furniture Boodie had saved from Kregg's Crossing—the spindle-legged table in the hall, a vase she remembered, flowers that she knew Boodie had picked that morning and so carefully arranged in the half-dark where the blinds kept the heat out in the daytime. It was just twilight. In the living room, she sank onto the sofa that she remembered had been in the family, and she wanted to burst into tears again, not for the new reasons but for the house, the people in it.

She waved Boodie back into her soft blue rose-flecked chair when she wanted to take her up to her room. "No, I want my drink." She told herself nothing was wrong. The furniture was the same, the scent, the voile curtains, the dark green blinds, the bowl of cosmos and bachelor's buttons. Melinda watched the lace-edged handkerchief that Boodie was crushing in her lap.

When she followed Boodie toward the stairs that led up to the guest room, Aiken's Aunt Elmira was standing at the door of the kitchen. She caught Melinda's arm and whispered, "Is Aiken all right?"

Melinda wanted to hug her, but she didn't dare. She was so self-conscious about every move. But she whispered back, "You would be so proud of him, Elmira. Cock of the walk." The door to the kitchen closed while Elmira was still smiling.

Melinda felt like the sameness would choke her, that and the talking. Jakey wasn't mentioned by either one of his parents. He simply did not exist at the table in the evening, while Elmira served the dinner and Mr. Percival held forth on what was wrong with the world.

"We were perfectly happy down here," he said to Melinda and Elmira while she was passing gravy for the roast. There had to be a roast, even if it was hot as hell in the dining room, even with the slow-moving ceiling fan. "Bunch of northern trash come down here, outside agitators," he grumbled at the meat. "They got white girls and niggers staying in the same house. I hear tell that they bring nigger doctors in from Atlanta, and you know what Atlanta's like, well, they come in here to abort the white niggers of their nigger babies."

Boodie said quietly, "You don't know that, Elsworth. That's just what people say."

"I know it for a fact," he said, and went on stabbing his meat.

Melinda was so relieved finally to get into the frilled, sweet guest room that she sank down on the bed without turning back the lace-trimmed cover. She had made her excuses when Mr. Percival started looking longingly at the television. She said she needed to get some sleep after her long drive, and he said, "Goodnight. We sure are glad you came to see us. It means a lot to Bood." He was already headed for the television set. Melinda could hear a babble of electric voices from downstairs as she shut her bedroom door.

Boodie could be as quiet as a mouse. She always had been. Her tap on the door was so faint that Melinda wasn't sure she had heard it, and then Boodie put her head, mouselike, around the door and said, "Honey, can I come in for just a minute? I know you're just dog tired, but . . ."

The noise of the television behind her engulfed the room, and then she shut it out. "Elsworth is a little deaf, and he doesn't know how loud it is." She wandered over to the dressing table. "Aren't these just lovely?" She picked up a mirror and a brush with initials and the deep, soft shine of very old silver. "I just love these. They were Mother's, you know." Her voice went even softer at the word *mother*.

Then she said, without turning around, "Jakey's dead." There was nothing but a flat fact in her voice. Then she looked at Melinda. "Oh honey, everything that was solid is quicksand." She started to sob. "I've never been mean to a colored person in my whole life."

Melinda drew her down onto the bed and held her. Her bones felt as frail as chicken bones. She was only five years older than Melinda, but she looked and felt like an old woman.

"Now, you better tell me what you know. I came down here to help you," Melinda whispered. "You knew that was why I came down here, didn't you?" The frail head, the white hair, nodded against her body.

"I don't know anything. We always used to meet in Jackson. I would drive all the way to Jackson."

"Start at the beginning. I need to know."

Boodie told it so softly that Melinda seemed to be taking the story in with her whole self instead of her ears. It was a murmur, a faint reverberation against her chest.

"I told Elsworth I was going up to Jackson every week to see about my teeth. He said why didn't I go on into Baton Rouge? I told him a lie. I said the man in Jackson was better for root canal. So every week I went up to Jackson. That's big enough so nobody paid any attention to us. At least I thought so. I didn't know. I just didn't know. We used to meet every Saturday, when Jakey's freedom school was out, and have a Co-cola, and I would take him some clean underwear and things he needed. Elmira helped me do that. Elsworth never knew a thing. I knew it was wrong. Was it wrong? Was it?" She didn't wait for Melinda to answer. "Elsworth told Jakey he wasn't to come to this house until he came to his senses, and you know Jakey was dedicated, absolutely dedicated. So I went every Saturday to Jackson and we had a Co-cola and I took him some clean underwear. Elmira was very proud of Jakey. She always was. She goes to the meetings, but of course Elsworth doesn't know that.

"Why has everything changed? All the lies and the watching and I've never been mean to a colored person in my whole life," she cried again, an echo that she must have told herself a thousand times. "We used to just love each other, didn't we?"

She was quiet while Melinda stroked her soft, silky white hair. It had gone white in the last year, since Melinda had seen her and Jakey when they went to Italy for their vacation. Elsworth never had gone with them. He said America was good enough for him. Elmira looked after him.

Boodie sat up straight on the bed and folded her hands in her lap. "Five weeks ago, I went up to Jackson on Saturday and Jakey didn't come. I didn't even know where his freedom school was. He said he couldn't tell me, but he told me all about it. He was so proud of his pupils. He said they went all the way from six to sixty. That's the way he said it, from six to sixty. He was teaching people to read, and black history he called it, and what their rights were, and all that."

Her fingers, on their own, made little pleats in her skirt. "Five weeks ago today I went up there and he didn't come, and nobody came. I thought he might be sick and he couldn't come, and he wouldn't have sent one of his pupils into the white drugstore where we always met. It was right in the middle of the nice part of town, so I didn't expect that. Usually we had a pimiento-cheese sandwich and a Co-cola."

The television noise had crept through the door, but there were no words, only the rumble.

"Elsworth is not a bad man, you have to understand that." Boodie straightened her hair and said, "Lord, I must look a sight. I went every Saturday for three weeks, and then I went to the police and they said they couldn't help me. They don't like what's going on any better than Elsworth does. They didn't know where his freedom school was and they didn't bother to try to find out. The man I talked to said Jakey was a Southerner and he thought it was being a traitor to the South, at least the ones from the North didn't know any better. I was so mad I nearly told him so, but instead I asked for the address of the FBI office. I thought they might be able to help me.

"The man there was polite, but he said they worked in cooperation with the local law enforcement, something like that. He said kids were running back and forth in and out of the state but he would ask around. There are a lot of FBI men in Mississippi since those boys from the North were killed. People around here could kill every colored boy and they wouldn't bother to send anybody, but when the northern boys . . . Jakey made me see how wrong that was. He said they found several bodies in the Tallahatchie River, one cut half in two and one without a head, and they had chains wrapped around them, and I said, Jakey, that couldn't be right, that just couldn't, and he said, Oh Mother, the way he always said it when he thought I was being dumb. Oh Mother.

"I went the next week and I sat there in the drugstore with a pile of clean underwear in my lap, and he didn't come, and so I went back to the FBI office, and they told me they had asked around and that Jakey's freedom school was in Sweetwater. That is near Port Jackson. They asked the sheriff there and he didn't know a thing, and they asked their contacts at the colored office for the vote registration, they call it COFU or something. They told me not to go there. They said not to go there, and then they said they had done all the investigating they could and they were sure Jakey had left the state. One of them said he had a radical record, you know, from that time on the courthouse steps when he was sixteen, and I said I never heard such nonsense in my whole life. They said he might be a Communist and might have gone to Cuba. Can you imagine Jakey just hightailing off to Cuba or someplace without letting me know?

"I hoped he had come up to you or Aiken. But you remember I called you one Sunday evening and we talked for a long time about just all sorts of things, what a good time we used to have and how Jakey liked going to Italy and maybe we could go this year. I said it that way because I knew you would say, Why, honey, Jakey's sitting right here in the living room, do you want to talk to him? I couldn't ask right out because Elsworth is a little bit deaf but just when you think he won't hear, he does. Now you won't believe this, but our phone is bugged. I know it. When I said, He hasn't called home, to the FBI man, he said, Yes, we know that. You don't know how bad it is down here. Jakey wouldn't go away without telling me, would he?"

Melinda said, "When Jakey came to me in London in 1960, he was like a person who had had to keep quiet too long. He never shut up. I remember all the walks we had, Regent's Park and Jakey's voice, Hyde Park and Jakey's voice, Hatfield and Jakey's voice. He was with me, but he never left Louisiana. Once he said, 'Melinda, I love my mother more than anybody in the world and she breaks my heart, but there's nothing I can do about it. I have to do what I have to do.' You know, it was Jakey who got me through that terrible summer after Tye died. He just wouldn't shut up and let me mourn."

Boodie got up and straightened her dress and her hair again. "I ought to be ashamed of myself, after all that driving you must be ready to drop. We go to the eleven o'clock service, and then we always go for drinks and lunch at the country club. It's a little-bitty place, not like Richmond, but it's nice."

"I'm sure it's nice," Melinda made herself say.

Boodie kissed her goodnight and said, "You have a good sleep now." She was almost gay; she had plunged back into the habits that had saved her for a lifetime. "I can't think of anything in the world that makes me happier than you being here, just like the good old days."

But at the door she sobbed again. "Why Jakey? Oh, Christ, Melinda, why him?"

Melinda pulled her back and shut the door again so Elsworth wouldn't hear her.

Elmira came in to work on Sunday morning because Boodie and Elsworth had company. She told Melinda, who came down the stairs first, "Listen, I got things to tell you they don't know. You come on in the kitchen while they getting dressed, you hear me?"

The house had cells of truth behind closed doors so Elsworth wouldn't hear. "Him," Elmira said. "He ain't a bad man." She leaned against the kitchen counter. "Now, listen, we know things. We know that Jakey got picked up outside of Port Jackson, we know that. Them youngins went for a picnic. It was the day before Miss Boodie went over there to Jackson to take him some underwear. She always fussed. You go to the COFU headquarters in Jackson. Them FBI folks won't tell you. You find out. If she don't know soon one way or another, it's goin to kill her."

They could hear the heavy trudge of Elsworth coming down the stairs. "Now, you go on in there. Don't pay no attention to what he says. He don't know what to do. Them White Citizen fellows come night-ridin by here night after night when Jakey was home. They was so many ugly phone calls they had to take their phone off the hook so they could get a night's sleep. They's more in this than meets the eye. Go on in there, honey."

After breakfast, Melinda got into Elsworth's Buick with the others, and they drove into a Sunday lull on the way to church, with the scent of clean clothes and laundered shirts, the slow march of the Buick. Elsworth was in good spirits. "Don't you pay any attention to what this preacher says. He's one of those young Episcopalians not dry behind the ears."

They drew up outside the church, where people walked slowly two by two, with their adolescents and their smaller children, all two by two, like animals going into the Ark for safety from the flood. The minister stood outside the door. When he saw Elsworth, he drew him aside. Melinda heard him murmur, "I have to talk to you."

Melinda and Boodie marched in. They knelt together on the prayer pillows the ladies had covered with needlepoint through the years. After they had said their prayers and were seated, Boodie opened a prayer book and handed it to Melinda, who sank into the lovely prose of the 1928 version of morning prayer.

"We insisted on the minister's using it for this

service," Boodie whispered behind her handkerchief. "It's so beautiful, and it's what we're used to." It could have been an epitaph on the tombstone of the South.

It was just before the first prayer that they slipped in. There were three of them—a white man in a clerical collar, a young white boy, and a black boy, who looked younger. There was silence in the church. Then the minister, who looked freshly washed and young and pink, said, "Let us pray," and there was the rustle of skirts and the creak of wood as they knelt down.

"Almighty and most merciful God, unto whom all hearts are open, all desires known . . ." Behind Melinda and Boodie, people were moving, as quietly as they could, so that the three strangers were isolated in the middle of an empty pew. Several people left the church. Two or three of the youngest moved over to the pews near the three young men and smiled, little tentative smiles.

Melinda started to move with them. It was the first time since the flood of her recognition on the road, not to Damascus but to Knoxville, that she had had to demand of herself that she stand up and be counted.

Boodie felt Melinda's body begin to move. "Oh, don't. Melinda, please don't," she whispered. "I can't stand this."

'Honey, I have to," Melinda whispered back. She sat beside the young man in the clerical collar.

The rote of morning prayer went on—the responses, the prayers, the lesson, read by

Elsworth, whose voice was shaking, either from nerves or anger, Melinda couldn't tell. The young minister climbed up into the pulpit as if he were too tired to speak. But he said, "I have changed the order of the Gospel this morning." His voice rang out the way he had been taught in seminary. " 'I was a stranger and ye took me in; naked, and ye clothed me; I was sick, and ye visited me; I was in prison and ye came unto me . . .' "

"I'm not going to preach this morning." His voice threatened to break. "I have only been in Bonnevue four months, as you know. I thought I could help. But my wife has been threatened, and nobody speaks to my children when they go to school. We are not invited anywhere. This may seem small revenge to you, but my family can no longer stand it. I am leaving this week, and my family has already gone, to ensure their safety. Nobody outside the South knows how bad it is. But we all know. We live in fear of each other and of our own feelings. If there is another text for today, it is that the sins of the fathers are visited onto the children unto the third and fourth generation. Now we have visitors in our church. We are Episcopalians, and we are supposed to be civilized, polite people. I want you, as my last request to you, to welcome them as Christ would have done. Let us pray."

Melinda walked with the three down toward their car. Nobody spoke to them. She saw Elsworth and Boodie sitting in their car, waiting for her. She said, "I have to find out where you-all came from. I have to find out what has happened to my cousin."

The young minister said, "Thank you for sitting with us. My name is Truescott, I'm from Connecticut. This is John Wilson, and this is Jeremy Smith." He drew the young black boy close.

"Man, I was scared. I shouldn't of been there. I'm Catholic," Jeremy said to her.

To the cars passing slowly, they might have been any huddle of well-dressed people leaving any Episcopal church. When Melinda turned, she saw that Elsworth had driven away.

"Oh dear, I've lost my ride."

"We better not take you." The young minister from Connecticut laughed.

"Oh, shit, man!" Jeremy, who had walked ahead to the car, said, "Excuse me, ma'am. They slashed our tires and broke the windows. They ran some kind of rasp all over the paint."

"Well, that's show business," Truescott said. "We walk too, and get the bus back to Luneville."

"No, you don't," Melinda told them. "Walk with me and I'll take you. I have a car with a Virginia license."

A Thunderbird convertible passed slowly in the ease of the hot Sunday noon. The shadows flicked over the face of a pretty blond girl riding with a boy with a crew cut. They looked as if they had been to church. Melinda thought, I was like that, riding along above the earth. The girl banged on the side of the car and yelled, "White niggers, do you sleep with niggers?" and the car speeded up and they raced away, leaving laughter trailing behind them.

"They're the nice ones," Truescott said.

"I can't call you Truescott. What is your name?"

Everybody laughed. "Oh, all right, it's Reginald. Reggie. I'm an Episcopal minister from Connecticut." He looked embarrassed. "I hate being ashamed of my church."

They strolled through the Sunday shade, where the trees met over the street. Walking slowly, they attracted less attention; at least, Jeremy said so. He walked about ten paces behind them.

"How do you stand it?" Melinda asked.

"We don't stand it. We live with it, and by now we're kind of numb," John Wilson, the other young man, answered. "I'm from up in Tennessee. I thought it was bad up there."

"What does your family think about your being here?"

"My daddy sent that car." He laughed. "He's an old New Deal rabble-rouser from way back. Union man. He fought in the Second World War, that one, you know—"

"I know." Melinda was lulled by the creak of the porch swings across the green lawns.

"I would rather go to a Baptist church than an Episcopal one when it's my turn next time," John went on. "At least even if they hate you, they can see you. Those people this morning just looked through us. We didn't exist."

"Oh, you existed all right," she told him. He was a handsome boy, but he had a livid scar across his cheek.

Nobody called, "Good morning, nice day," when they passed. Nobody said anything. They walked half a mile through the pretty tree-lined streets of the small-town Southern Coventry, with the white front porches and the green, green lawns and the totally silent people sitting on the porches, fanning in the Sunday heat. Elsworth had put Melinda's bags on the front porch, and when she knocked on the door there was no answer.

She looked up to see Boodie watching from behind the voile curtains of an upstairs window. Boodie tried to wave, an exhausted flutter of her hand.

"It's killing her. She's too old. There are people who are too old." Melinda grabbed Reggie Truescott's arm. "Cover her up and hide her face for shame," she whispered, not knowing where the words came from, but he knew.

"William Carlos Williams," he said seriously. "Do you like Williams? I do. *Paterson*, especially *Paterson.*" He went on talking about William Carlos Williams as he picked up one of her suitcases. John Wilson picked up the other one. Jeremy had disappeared. When they got to the car, he had laid himself down on the floor between the back seat and the front. It was a tight fit.

Nobody explained. Nobody said a word. Melinda backed the car out of the drive and they started down the tunnel of green, under the lacy shadows of the trees.

"I think we better take you to Jackson. They'll know your car here."

"I can't believe this." Melinda drove on. "Just tell me where to go."

"Listen, there are things you ought to know.

Our phones are bugged." Reggie lounged in the front seat, letting the breeze fan his face. "They know everything that goes on. The spying is like a big spider web over the southern part of Mississippi and this part of Louisiana. The KKK and the White Knights have divided the territory like they are at war. You better stay in someplace so expensive it's not suspect. Do you have enough money?"

They were in the country, and the fields were already heavy with cotton plants. Nothing moved but the car, sliding past silence. "I have money," Melinda said.

"If we get you to Jackson, somebody will give us a ride."

"We're strung all over hell's half-acre," Jeremy called from the floor. "I'm gettin up. They ain't nobody out these roads. They all eatin their Sunday dinner." He pulled himself up on the seat and stretched and started to look out of the window.

"I'll stay wherever you tell me," Melinda said. She realized that they didn't know her. "I'm a friend of Aiken Armistead's. Do you know him?"

"Hey, hey man, Aiken, he is some cat. A cool, cool cat. That's where it's at." Jeremy thrummed the seat in rhythm. "How you know him?"

Melinda said, "He came to the school I work in." That was enough.

"All riiight!" came from the back seat.

"My God, excuse me, I never say that," Reggie said all in one breath, and loosened his holy collar and laid it in his lap. "Then you know Jakey

Percival." He let the breeze from the open window cool his neck.

"I'm Jakey's cousin."

"Melinda? The one who lived in England?" John Wilson jumped up out of a half-sleep. "Oh, man, do we know you. Jakey told us all about his visit to England, and when we wouldn't listen anymore he told us about the time he spent in Italy. He wore that shirt he got in Italy. He was so proud of it he washed it at night and put it on in the morning. It had the Leaning Tower of Pisa on it, and he wore that little silver cross his mother gave him."

Then, suddenly, nobody said a word. She waited, driving along. Finally she said, "You're speaking of Jakey in the past. Where is Jakey? Don't fool with me, tell me."

"We don't know."

Reggie had assumed a kind of command, as if he had told stories to people, broken news so often before that he knew almost by rote what to do. "Up ahead here is a roadstand that will serve us. May I drive from there? I know the way."

The roadstand was in front of a greasy spoon that had a large sign, GENTLMEN'S CLUB, WHITES ONLY, in red letters on the front door. Outside on the road, a woman stood behind a stand, fanning herself with a big bandanna.

"Jesus, ain't it hot? Hi, y'all. How you git along in Bonnevue?" She wasn't very interested. She just knew. Reggie brought back cold Cokes in bottles, with straws. Jeremy stood outside the car. "You don't have to do that," the woman called out. "It's too damn hot. They ain't nobody here."

She leaned both large arms on the counter and went on fanning and staring beyond the car at nothing as they drove off.

"We've been trying to find out about Jakey for five weeks." The others let Reggie talk first. "You came down here to find Jakey, didn't you?"

Melinda could only nod.

"We think he's dead," said a voice in the back seat. Between the Tennessee and the Mississippi accents, she couldn't tell which one had spoken.

"I think so too, but I have to find out. It's the not knowing . . ."

"One of the Saturdays his mother came over and met him in Jackson—she always did that—she brought a picnic Elmira Owens had made for us. We went where we had been lots of times before, way up the Yazoo where one of the brothers has a farm. He moved his family into town in case they tried to burn them out, so there wasn't anybody out there. We thought it was entirely deserted. The nearest neighbor was about five miles away. We knew that farm belonged to some people called LeClaire. We didn't know them. So we went up there. The man that owned it gave us the key so we could go in and leave the food in the icebox while we went swimming, and so we could change. He said he been out that week hoeing his cotton with his boy every day and he never saw a soul there. It was way up the Yazoo."

One of the boys in the back finished his Coke and made the straw whistle.

"We went up there, all of us." Reggie drove and talked, looking straight ahead. "There wasn't anything we had to do. The kids only came to the freedom school until twelve o'clock. Some of them hung around in the afternoon. They liked to read in the library. That day we told them we were going to shut down and go for a picnic, and they all wanted to go, so we drew lots. We said only three of them could go. Everybody was a good sport about it. So we went off in that car we came to church in this morning, John's daddy's car."

"My daddy saw that it had good windows. That didn't stop somebody taking a wrench to them this morning. Damned Episcopalians, let other folks do their dirty work. Oh, sorry, Reggie. I'm a Presbyterian myself."

"You know what the priests told us you Prots were? People who changed churches because the king of England wanted a divorce."

The two in the back seat started to bicker. "You black mack snatcher!" "You Prot honky heathen." They started to pound each other on the arms, laughing.

"Shut up," Reggie turned and told them. "We went on out there. There were the four of us, John and me and Jeremy and Jakey. Three of the girls from the North came, and one more . . . who was it?"

From the back seat: "Joe Edwards. He was over from Sweetwater."

Reggie went on. "So there were three white girls and three white boys and two black boys and three black children and we all rode out to the farm up the Yazoo on the back road he swore nobody ever used."

"Who?"

Reggie sounded annoyed. "The man who owned the farm." He was growing tense. "We got there and we put on our bathing suits and went into the river. There was a little wharf the owner had built for his kids. We were having a fine time. You see, we don't get much chance to just be out where nobody can find us and be just free to have a good time for a little while.

"Then they drove up. They were just as polite as they could be. Four grown men and one half-grown boy who looked like he didn't have good sense. He just stared at the girls. I told them to go inside and take the children.

"One of the men, who did the talking, said, 'I own the next property. We got kind of worried about our neighbor's house. We thought you were trespassing on his property.' He was dressed up in gaiters and britches and he wore an old hacking jacket with leather patches on the elbows.

"One of the other men lifted a shotgun out of the truck they were driving. It was an old towtruck they'd put a flat bed on on the back, and the first man turned around and said, 'Put that back. You hear me?' The man laid it back on the gun rack and lifted out a towing chain.

" 'Nice car you got there,' one of the other men told us. 'Now, we don't want no trouble, boys. You out here white and nigger together.' They were still as polite as they could be. 'We gentlemen live up the river and we got to protect our property, you understand that, even if you are outside agitating Yankee nigger-loving nigger-fucking trash.' That man never did change the politeness in his voice. But we could tell that the first man, the well-dressed one, didn't like what he said.

"Jakey spoke up then and said, 'You oughtn't to talk that way in front of these girls and these children.'

" 'Niggers and nigger fuckers,' the man said in the same polite voice. 'They can't hear. They inside waiting to get fucked. Now you go tell them ladies to git their clothes on and git the hell out of here.'

"Just then another truck drove up, and three more men jumped out. 'Leroy, we got here as soon as we could.' There must have been four or five men. The man who said he owned the property said, 'Oh. I forgot to introduce myself. I'm Leroy LeClaire, and this is my brother, Herbert Stanfield LeClaire. My daddy named him after Herbert Hoover and my mother's side of the family. He just loved Herbert Hoover.' Leroy LeClaire had leaned up against the hood of his truck. He could have been passing the time of day.

"I heard Jakey say to the kids, who had crept back out on the lean-to porch to listen, 'Get in the house.'

"One of the men looked around at him. 'You ain't no Yankee nigger fucker,' he said. 'You got a Southern voice.'

" 'I'm from Bonnevue,' Jakey said. He wasn't even scared. He just took the conversation for granted.

" 'Well, that's a mighty nice town. Maybe you ought to go back there.' Something had changed in the group of men. They hadn't moved, they were still lounging around, but there was the kind of tension you find when animals go still. Then I noticed that they all had chains. I can't think why I didn't notice it before. I was too busy looking at Leroy LeClaire, Mr. Leroy LeClaire.

" 'Now, Leroy, I would say that there is a traitor to the South and the flower of Southern womanhood!' One of the men laughed.

"It scared Leroy. You could see that. The young boy spoke up for the first time. He was kind of simple. 'He got a real pretty shirt on. I wish I had me a shirt like that.' He sounded sad.

" 'My little brother likes your shirt. Why don't you give it to him?' I really do think LeClaire was trying to defuse the atmosphere that was building up.

"Now, you know Jakey. Proud as he was of that shirt, he just took it off and handed it over. 'Here. You're welcome to it. Now, why don't you folks just let these people go? We know you don't like what we are doing, but that's because you don't understand.' He had launched into it before I could shut him up. Well, you know Jakey. He just sailed on. 'Don't you see, we're all in this together, poor and black and rich and white.'

" 'You calling us poor whites?' one of the men said, quietly. 'Let me tell you, our family owned all this side of the river. We owned everything, they come along and tuken it.' Who 'they' was, he didn't say. I couldn't understand why LeClaire never raised his voice. They could have been having any kind of conversation, just hanging around talking, like Southerners do.

"Jakey said, 'I didn't call you anything, sir. I have a deep respect for the way you feel. I would just like to talk to you about this.' He was like Galahad, or a fool. He didn't seem to catch the strain that was growing.

"One of the men slowly pulled himself up from the hood of his truck as if he was tired of the whole thing, and he called out, 'Now, you other nigger fuckers git them women and them kids and get in the car and get out of here. We going to have a little talk about the way we feel with this here Southern boy.'

"The women got in the car, with the kids on their laps. I went back and said to Mr. LeClaire, 'Can't you stop this?' and he said, 'Son, you ever tried? Get them out of here.' I got in the driver's seat. We were all wet, still in our bathing suits. The two black guys and John hadn't quite made it to the car and I saw the chains start to flail, and somebody yelled, 'Git in! Git in!' One of the girls screamed, and all three of them managed to tumble in. They were spraying blood all over the back of the car. That's where John got his scar.

"We waited for Jakey and he called out, 'I'll be all right. We Southerners understand each other.' He always said that. 'Go on!' His voice did rise then. 'You got to get the girls out of here.' I saw him in the rearview mirror as we rattled over those deep ruts down the road. He was as quiet as he could be, standing there with his shirt off. I could see the cross on his chest, and he waved. He actually waved, and then they went on talking to each other, leaning all over the car hoods.

"We waited all night for him, and the next day was Sunday. Monday morning we went down to the FBI office in Jackson and reported him missing. They didn't want to do anything. They said they had so many reports they couldn't handle them all. I remember one of them, a man I knew from some other times we had to call them. 'You fellows are always coming back and forth, leave the country and don't tell anybody.' He laughed. 'We know about this guy,' he said. 'Maybe he went to Cuba. He was a Communist, wasn't he?' I said Jakey Percival was about as Communist as he was, and he said, 'Well, he sure as hell acts like one.' "

"I'm staying with you until I find out," Melinda said.

Reggie took the warm Coke she hadn't touched out of her hand. "No, you're not," he told her. "If you want to help, you go in your nice clothes in your nice car over to Jackson. You stay at a place called Magnolia House, and you be as Southern as warm molasses. We pass the turnoff for it on the way."

Magnolia House had the finest in Southern cuisine. It was one of the most authentic historic mansions in the South. The sign at the turnoff said so. It quoted the *Atlanta Constitution.*

Reggie drove them toward Jackson to show Melinda the FBI headquarters, so she wouldn't get lost. He said, "You'll have to stay away from us. If they see you with any of us, they won't help you."

"Yeah, man." Jeremy's voice came from the back seat. "A white cat they take trouble with."

"Not a Southern one. They work with the sheriff and his deputies, and they hate Southern whites who work with us worse than they hate black men." John started to argue again.

"They don't hate us, massa," Jeremy said. "They just ain't goin let us cross over, no how no way. That Mr. J. Edgah Hoovah, he don't like black meat."

"Shut up and get down," Reggie told him.

"This here lady goin pass for white." Jeremy hid himself on the floor of the back seat. "Man!"

"You got a lot of mouth, you know that?" John told him.

They insisted on being left on a street corner at the edge of Jackson. The last thing she saw of them was in her rearview mirror. They were walking slowly through the heat of the day.

Magnolia House flirted with her through the live oaks long before she drew up in front of it on the oyster-shell circular drive. The *Atlanta Constitution* had been right. It was a pure, white, huge, authentic, columned, 1845, new-rich, cotton-boom, Mississippi plantation house. Wings had been added to it, in keeping. She was sure they said "in keeping" when they described the new sections. They had copied the windows, the woodwork, the French doors, the slatted shutters. The paint looked like white icing. She would have laughed if she had been with someone to laugh with, or it had been another time.

She rested against the steering wheel for a few minutes before she braved the three-story-high complex with Corinthian columns that was the front porch. There was a scent of lavender in the wide hall, and the rose Axminster carpet went almost to the walls. There were anonymous portraits. Two long American sideboards circa 1850 stood opposite each other. The chandelier was brass. The stairs curved up in a graceful flying arc toward the second floor.

Melinda found a bell on one of the sideboards. A black girl in a bandanna and a calico dress came out from somewhere in back of the stairwell and curtsied. She said, "My name is Tabitha and I am here to serve you."

Melinda grinned. "I bet your mama calls you Tabby."

"Yes'm." She smiled. "You just register right here and I'll show you to your room."

When Melinda had registered, she followed Tabby up the stairs. The woodwork of the banisters had been painted so often it was soft to the touch. The whole place was an expensive stage set for a play that was supposed to have happened long ago and far away, when people had plenty of money, the houses smelled of lavender, and everybody was happy, as Boodie had said, and got along with each other. Even the air in the place felt soft.

"Dinner's six to eight," Tabby said, and curtsied again.

Melinda's room looked out on the new old garden of roses and formal hedges. In the center of a fountain a marble girl hid her genitals. Melinda had last seen the statue at the hotel in France in 1939; it was a regulation garden virgin, only instead of snow there was a veil of water surrounding her. It was the same. It wasn't the same. She watched it for a long time out of the window, past the frilled curtains, and then she pulled herself up to sit on the high tester bed to rest a minute before she unpacked. She woke up when it was already nearly dark and wondered where she was. She lay under a tent-roof of lace. She had retreated into mourning sleep. Jakey was dead. She was furious with herself for thinking it.

For the next two weeks Melinda skated across the tourist surface of Mississippi, looking for a shirt with the Leaning Tower of Pisa on it.

She went to the FBI office on Monday morning, dressed up with her white gloves, and wondered why they didn't know she was a parody, but the man who talked to her didn't. He was polite. He had a New York accent, but he seemed to have caught slowness from the place. The big fan overhead groaned and complained a little as it moved the almost solid heat.

"The air conditioner is broken," he apologized.

"My cousin"—she could hear herself simpering—"you see, his mama is real worried about him, and I said I would just come on by and see if you found out anything."

"You wait right here, ma'am. I'll see if we have a file on him. What's his name?"

"John Kregg Percival."

"Oh, him." The man smiled. "I don't need to look. We know all about him. They tell me that kid has been in trouble since he was sixteen. His poor mother comes in here all the time. We don't have anything more to tell her. She probably sent you because she thought we were keeping something from her. You know how mothers are. We have investigated thoroughly—I did some of it myself. We followed every lead we could. We went out to the LeClaire farm and asked them. The last real lead we had was that he was standing having a friendly conversation with some of the men who work for Mr. LeClaire. They said he went on down the road and they never saw him again. We even looked around. They're nice people."

He seemed to be enjoying himself, telling her about it while the fan groaned. "I wish somebody would oil that thing or fix the air conditioning. God, it's hard to get anything done around here." He took out a handkerchief and wiped his neck. "Now, where were we?"

"At a farm, LeClaire Farm. Where is that?"

He sat up in his chair. "Now, don't you go out there bothering those people. It's not safe to go wandering around this county on your own, even for a lady like you. You get on some of those back roads and there are mean blacks and poor whites."

"About the farm," she interrupted.

"It's a nice place. About ten years ago, the old house burned down. The youngest brother—he's not right bright, as they say down here—says the Yankees burned it, and with the way the vines and the weeds grow down here it already looks like it. They didn't try to rebuild it—too expensive. They built a nice ranch-type house near it where the big garden was. They have a lot of property out there. They run a pig farm, but it's hidden, real pretty. They raise mostly peanuts and pigs, feed the pigs peanuts and make famous hams and sell them up North. They got a good little business. One of the brothers, the oldest, is a graduate of Ole Miss. He runs the place for his mother. What do you want to know about them for?" He was suddenly suspicious. "They didn't have anything to do with your cousin. Just a friendly talk, Mr. LeClaire told me." He fanned himself with a report that he picked up from the table.

"Well, anyway, can I see the report on John Percival?"

"Oh, no, ma'am." He was very kind. "That's confidential. We're down here to investigate, and we're satisfied he left the country. A lot of those kids do. Communists, or Communist-led. It's the black Communist professors and preachers who are behind all this trouble. We know that for a fact. His mother wouldn't want to know that. No, we'll be in touch with her if we hear any more. You know how those kids run off."

She looked around the office. She wondered if all the offices of the FBI, the CIA, the MI5, the GPU, whatever they were called in whatever country, were like it: impersonal, with the sound of typewriters, people cradling phones, leftover coffee cups, all so simple, all so ordinary. She knew, shivering, that the very triteness of it was evil itself.

He got up. "I hope we've helped. That's what we're here for. You come back any time."

"Where did you say the farm was?" She tried a last time.

He changed his face like she would change clothes. "I did not say. Now, we"—the imperial *we*— "don't want you out there bothering those people. Mr. LeClaire is well thought of and a deputy sheriff for that part of the county and he has every right to check on people trespassing on the next-door farm."

So they knew about the swimming party, and the men, and, she was sure, the chains. He was less friendly when he showed her to the door.

She made friends at Magnolia House, where every day, just as in the magic Old Days, everybody on the plantation dressed up, hoping for company. The whole white staff of ladies went into hoop skirts and explained to visitors that the chairs with no arms were designed for women to sit in with hoops.

She went through Natchez and listened to the lady docents tell about before the war and what the South was like, and how their grandfather's uncle had brought the chair, the table, the tester bed back from Paris or Philadelphia during the time when cotton was king. Melinda crowded with other visitors in the doorways against the velvet ropes, there so they wouldn't scratch the wide board floors or pocket little ormolu boxes and Staffordshire dogs.

What she saw was the cotton boom. Every house, every piece of furniture, would have been called Victorian anywhere else. It had lasted, according to the lovely old things, for about ten years before the war—the war, never anything but the war, until she could sense tourists from the North turning away, feeling guilty and satisfied. Black faces peeped through the doorways, and in some of the houses the tours were taken to the old kitchens, where mammys in bandannas acted as if they were cooking or cleaning and answered questions, as polite as the ladies in their hoop skirts.

She thought of the boom and bust of coal, like the boom and bust of cotton, and wondered when there would be tours of the coal-baron Gothic mansions that she had seen in Kentucky. She walked in such preoccupied anger on the thin surface of silk and velvet and polished floors and furniture and lies that she was almost taken in from time to time, when she was tired.

It took so long, so many miles, so much politeness. Her hostess—there were no proprietors—said to her, "My goodness, Lady Dunston, you sure are running around. I just bet you're writing a book about us. I hope you tell our side instead of all those lies in the northern papers these days."

She heard over and over how happy everybody had been until the outside agitators came in. They were Communist-led, and of course the youngsters were from the North, just down for the summer, but she didn't need to pay them any attention. Everything would go right back to normalcy as soon as they left.

But some of the hostesses looked as preoccupied as Boodie had looked at the dinner table, and when Melinda went to bed at night, she lay sometimes in a kind of restful horror at her love and hate for the place and the people, black and white, liars and truth-tellers, flora and fauna, and the slow deep flow of the rivers and the live oaks and the niceness of everybody, the real niceness, not puttin on, as Imogene would have said.

They were like people caught in waking from a dream that had protected them for too long. She drifted to sleep at last, into a sense as deep as hell for her that if she told or even faced the truth, she was betraying people she had loved all her life.

So she drove around the back roads in her black Buick daddy-car, the 1965 version of her father's tomb, and she watched and waited to see the Leaning Tower of Pisa across somebody's chest, and mourned for Jakey and the South.

On the second Saturday, when she came back to Magnolia House she found Boodie sitting there in an apple-green voile dress. She looked like she had faded after spending too long a time in the sun. She had put on her Panama hat and made a corona of fake flowers, as if she were going to a party. She wore white gloves. She got up and hugged Melinda and said, "Lord, isn't it hot, honey?" as if nothing had happened. Melinda recognized the preoccupied warmth and extreme politeness for what they were: the deepest expression Boodie could have of regret or loss or hatred.

She said Elmira had told her where Melinda was staying. She almost giggled—"They know everything, you know that." So she thought they would go have a Co-cola where she and Jakey met on Saturdays. She had gone there every week on Saturday at the same time since she had stopped hearing from him, but, she explained, she didn't bring clean underwear anymore.

So they sat at a marble ice-cream table that had been in the drugstore, the druggist said, for Lord knows how long. "It was here when I came, and that was 1938. Now, what can I do for you ladies? How's that nice boy of yours?" he said to Boodie when he brought the colas and the pimiento-cheese sandwiches.

"Why, he's just fine. He's away right now." Boodie's face had gone back to being as bland as it had been years ago when she had wandered around the ruins in Kregg's Crossing and said into the air, "This was my bedroom and this was the parlor," and Melinda was as gentle with her as Uncle Brandon had been.

"How would you like to go for a ride, honey?" Melinda asked. "We'll go out to Longwood. I think I've seen every house that they show around Natchez, but that one they told me you just go to and sometimes they let you in for a quarter and sometimes they don't."

"Now, that's the nicest treat." Boodie smoothed her dress. "I just love riding around and seeing things. Those poor people at Longwood. It was going to be the finest house around Natchez, but they only got the bottom built before the war came, and they had to live down there for years. They couldn't finish it. The Nutts still live there, the descendants." Her voice went up in a question that wasn't a question. She giggled. "They call the place Nutts' Folly around here."

They drove for an hour along roads where kudzu vines had made green monsters of the houses under them, the broken silos, the tumbled barns, lost along the roads. Behind them the fields and fields of cotton stretched as far as they could see.

Boodie prattled on until her voice found some kind of calm and her hands stopped shaking and she let herself be quiet and watch the road. "Nutts' Folly is the one I like best. I feel just like I'm discovering it for myself and nobody else knows, like the sleeping princess," she said. "I'm sure we have time before I have to get back." Her gloved hands were still in her apple-green lap. She sighed with pleasure. "I have to get home before dark. Elsworth doesn't like for me to be out in the car after dark." She didn't say anything for a while, and then she covered what they were both thinking by saying, "He worries about my eyes at night."

Longwood was more beautiful unfinished than it ever would have been finished. It was like a great tree dominating the long drive through the woods, a tree stripped of its leaves so that its skeleton showed. It rose, tier on tier of balconies, broken stone lace, tipped columns, and at the top a cupola, a lookout looking out on nothing.

"You go ask." Boodie giggled. "I'm scared to. Sometimes they are drunk. Oh, isn't this the most fun?"

Nobody was drunk, but the place was so neglected that Melinda had to find her footing around garbage and old tires and bits of broken and forgotten garden hoes and rakes. A hound bitch that looked half starved, with her dugs hanging down from nursing a litter, sniffed at Melinda's skirt and wandered off.

The man who came to the basement door was as neglected as the yard, but sometime, a long time ago, the jacket he wore had been good tweed. Its cut was turn-of-the-century. He waved them through for two quarters and said, "The place is yours."

They went politely through rooms that even on the ground level were spacious. Dust, papers, dirty plates, cups, tobacco pipes, had gathered on fine furniture where the veneer had dried and cracked. The old man followed them. "Now, you ladies can go up and see the structure of the rest of the house if you want to. The stairs are right steep, and there's nothing up there, but if you want to . . . your own risk." His voice faded as he went out of the front door, forgetting them already.

"Let's, oh, let's!" Boodie was as excited as a child. "I never have done that."

They climbed the stairs and opened the bare-wood door into a vaulted cathedral structure. The exposed wooden frame had been built of hand-finished virgin trees; the rafters were a foot in diameter. It was like the inner structure of a ship built lovingly by shipwrights. The heavy beams, the spaces in the shape of walls between defining uprights, grown dark with age, the glassless windows, cast shadows across the floors of rooms that were not there. Where the windows would have been were spaces within spaces, and they looked out onto what might sometime have been a lawn.

"My," Boodie said, "wouldn't it have been just lovely?"

"It is the most beautiful of all, I think. It has been allowed to grow old." Melinda was about to say something more when she saw the shirt with the Leaning Tower of Pisa. A young man was wearing it. He was getting into the passenger seat of a blue Ford. It was too far away for her to see the license, and she was afraid that Boodie would see the shirt, but Boodie was too intent on the ghost of the garden that stretched below them.

"Isn't it a shame," she said, "all those unpruned English boxwoods. They must be over a hundred years old."

Melinda stumbled against a wooden upright, blinded by fury at the surface of things at the apple-green dress, at the constant soft refusal to face all the dying. Maybe one day, one day there would be a stripping-down of legends and ways and the South could breathe, but it wasn't yet, not in 1965. She almost fell against the frame of the nonexistent window.

"Why, honey, what on earth is the matter? You're white as a sheet." Boodie asked.

"I don't know, I guess I'm just tired." Melinda, a Southerner too, made her polite little lie.

On Sunday morning she drove along the side roads of the Yazoo north of Jackson, as near the river as she could. At last she had something to look for—a blue Ford. She thought of all the hours she had looked so long ago for her father's railroad crossing, and she drove slowly.

It was after two o'clock when she saw the blue Ford, parked away in the distance in front of a ranch-type house. It was a quarter of a mile beyond a magnificent ruin covered with vines. She parked the car and rolled under a wire fence topped with barbed wire, and started to pick her way through the tall grass. The head of a stone goddess fell away from her foot, and the body lay almost undefined as woman by the rain and time. She realized that she was walking up what had once been a shrub-lined brick walk, but she couldn't see the bricks, only feel them under the matted undergrowth. She was careful and slow, afraid of snakes.

It had been a brick house with great stone columns, but the columns, except for one, had long been taken away. It lay broken in the grass near the porch, where the grass was shorter, so she could see its shape.

"At least this place is not nurtured," she said aloud.

Somebody in the distance called, "Can I help you, ma'am? Heel, Beau." She turned around. A slim young man was coming across the matted grass. He had the kind of grace and command she had trusted all her life. He had called back to a setter, and it followed at his heels, its head down.

Melinda said, "Why, I just wanted to see this lovely place. I'm from Virginia, I'm just visiting down here. I'm staying at Magnolia House."

"Well, ma'am, you're welcome to look around." He stood in the old hacking jacket that Reggie had described, with his shotgun broken and sloped over his elbow. "I just thought I'd get me some crows." He saw her looking at the gun. "You go right ahead and look around all you want to. We just have to be careful with what kind of people . . ." He was gracious. "This was our place for over a hundred years. It burned down ten years ago." He smiled; he looked engaging when he said, "Look there. A whole tree has grown right inside the living room."

"Good heavens," Melinda said, being polite.

He pointed off through acres of cultivated fields, across the flat river bottom to the ranch house. "That's the place my daddy built. He said this was too old and too big anyhow. When she had to live in a one-story house, it just about broke my mother's heart. I think she thought we were going to be drummed out of the Presbyterian Church." He laughed. "You know how they are."

"Yes, I know." Melinda made herself smile and smooth her denim skirt.

"All the family furniture that had come from Philadelphia was lost. Philadelphia was the nice place to buy things then. Did you-all do that in Virginia?"

"Yes, we did that in Virginia." Melinda had

to say something. He was watching her mouth and then her eyes.

"It looks kind of Gothic, doesn't it? Southern Gothic, like those damned lies people write about us down here. Think we all live on Tobacco Road, inbred and integrated." He laughed at his joke. He had thrown his head back so he couldn't see her face. She turned away from him to hide it anyway.

"Oh, I'm sorry, I forgot to introduce myself. I'm Leroy LeClaire. Now, isn't that an awful name? Sounds nigger but it was my French great-grandfather's name, and we have to keep him alive. I sure got kidded about it at Ole Miss. You know how it is."

"I know how it is." She finally was able to turn around and face him and smile and put out her hand, and even touch him to shake hands. "Why, I've heard about you. I think I know friends of yours. Now, let me see. Oh, I'm so silly, I can't remember. I've met so many people."

He started to walk away. "Now, you just take your time and look around, and come on up to the house and meet my mother when you finish. There's a good path right along there." He pointed the way he had come. "There comes my little brother. He loves to show people around. He'll answer any questions you want him to. Oh, he's kind of sensitive. Don't pay any attention."

The Leaning Tower of Pisa came nearer and nearer, larger and larger in her eyes.

Melinda and the boy walked together around the roofless rooms. Somebody had been smoking inside. There was a little pile of carefully smashed butts. She teased, "I bet you come out here with your friends and smoke where your mama can't find you."

"Oh, no, ma'am, I don't smoke. My brother says it will stunt my growth." He was over six feet tall, and his face looked like a child had drawn it.

"That sure is a pretty shirt," she said offhand, looking up at the trash tree that had grown up beyond the roof level of the living room. "I've seen the Leaning Tower of Pisa, the real one."

"You have? I wish I had. A fellah give this to me. My mama says I ought to wear something else once in a while. She's tired of it, but I like it best."

"Well, now, wasn't that nice?" Melinda sat down on the doorsill. "Let me smoke a cigarette anyway. I got the habit, cigarettes and Co-colas. I don't know how I would live without them. Doesn't this shade feel good, and the breeze?"

He didn't sit down with her, but he leaned in an imitation of his brother and bragged softly, "We used to live here. I mean, we lived here when I was little. My grandfather was a Confederate colonel. He was almost governor of Mississippi. We been on this land a long time. Mama always says we was somebody, and my brother always says we still are somebody, and don't you forget it." He was so tall that he hovered over her, putting out the sun. He pulled at the shirt. "Yeah, somebody give me this."

"Oh." Lightly. "Who was that?"

"Some fellah."

"Didn't you know him?"

"Naw, he was an outside agitator. He was real friendly. They was all swimming down at the next place. That place was owned by somebody used to be a good nigger, then they come and he turned bad nigger on us. But my brother says my mama said to leave him alone. She knew his mother. His mother worked for us in the big house until she got too old. My mama says we got to be nice. It ain't, isn't, my brother says don't say *ain't,* it's field tacky, and my mama said that wasn't true. She said gentlemen wouldn't be caught dead saying *isn't* instead of *ain't* when she was a girl. They thought *isn't* was prissy. I thought he was real nice." The boy's mind jumped and slipped from one thought to another.

"Fellahs work for my brother, they call themselves White Knights. I am not supposed to know they are White Knights. White Knights is protecting our way of life. I wish I was a White Knight, but my brother says I'm not old enough. Nice folks are White Citizens' Council and they don't do anything but talk and influence."

Melinda felt as if she were stealing the story from his terrible innocence. They both looked the same way, out beyond the overgrown path toward the road.

"Is that your car?" he asked.

"It's my daddy's car," she lied, not knowing it. "Would you like to go for a ride in it?"

"No, I'd like to but my brother won't let me. He makes me stay on the property. But I went to school. I went for a long time, but they teased me." She thought the big hulking boy was going to dissolve in tears.

"They teased that fellah gave me the shirt too. He was my friend, wasn't he? Didn't he give me this shirt?" He was getting excited, and Melinda told him yes, she was sure the fellah was his friend.

"The men took my friend over to the pig farm. That's real far away from our house because my mama says she might not be living in the big house anymore but she sure isn't going to live next door to five hundred squealing pigs. So it's real far away. All out there"—he waved his arm around, bragging again—"all over as far as you can see, that's peanuts. We feed them with peanuts, but they'll eat anything. I hate pigs. You have to watch when the sow births so she won't eat her little babies, some of the sows. We know which ones. We feed them peanuts and some meat and bone meal we grind up for them. Lord, you ought to see that big machine. Put in anything—cow's head, bones, anything. My brother gets scraps from the slaughterhouse. We don't feed them much meat, though. It makes them too mean. We don't like to slaughter the pigs here. It upsets Mama. You heard tell of people squeal like a stuck pig, well, that's the way they sound." He wasn't talking to her anymore.

"It was mean. The men had that fellah with them, but my brother didn't go with them. He said he did his job, it wasn't any of his business, he got those folks off the neighbor property. That's what he was supposed to do." He turned to argue with Melinda, but she had said nothing.

"My brother wouldn't do nuthin to nobody. He went in the house and shut the door and he wouldn't let me go with them and talk to the fellah. He was so nice. He tole me about how peanuts were better for land than cotton, something like that. They let me walk a little way with them before my brother caught up with me and took me in the house. The fellah had blood coming out of his mouth and I gave him my handkerchief my mama makes me carry to wipe it off, but there was too much.

"Them White Knights sure don't look like no knights in the book my mama reads me. My brother didn't go with them." He was accusing her. "Don't you think he did. My brother made me go in the house. They wouldn't give me back my handkerchief and I said my mama would tan my hide, and my brother said don't you worry, I'll tell her I borrowed it."

He was quiet for a long time.

"So they took the fellah who gave you the shirt . . ." She had to say it quietly, a little conversation in the shade.

"They didn't mean nuthin. They don't like white niggers. They told my brother that fellah was a special traitor to the Southern way of life, because he was a Southerner too and ought to know better. My brother argued and then he took me in the house. He wouldn't even let me look out the window. He looked out the window, but he wouldn't let me. Later one of the men came by, one I didn't know, and I heard him tell my brother swear to God all they meant to do was larn him who he was. My brother didn't say anything. The man said, You needn't to worry about a thing, and I thought my brother was going to hit the man. He just closed the door, real soft like he does when he is mad about something, and when I asked him, he said, You shut your damn mouth."

His big blank face trembled. "He never spoke to me before like that in his whole life. Then he said he was sorry and he took me by the shoulders and he said he saw that fellah walking down this road from the pig farm all the way to the main road. He swore to God he watched him go all the way to the main road. Don't you say he told a lie. I believe my brother."

Melinda got up and stretched as if she had had a little nap. She smiled at the boy. "Well, you sure have been nice to show me around." She took a deep breath and said, "Now you tell your brother and your mama I couldn't stay any longer. I have to get back to Magnolia House. Do you know it? It sure is a pretty place."

"I had supper there twice," he sulked at the ground. "Mama told me it used to look like Nutts' Folly until some people come had money and fixed it up. I like Nutts' Folly. My mama goes there to see if the boys are all right and take them things. They ain't boys, though, she just calls them that. Their sister was a real good friend of ours. She lets me go with her. Their hound got pups. My brother says the boys are both over sixty and they never done a lick of work and they ain't worth a hill of beans, and my mama says, Don't you talk like that, Leroy. They're our cousins twice removed."

"Where do you think he went? The fellah," she tried for a last time.

"Oh, he didn't go noplace, did he?" There were tears in the boy's blank eyes. "He went down the road. My brother saw him go down the road and my brother don't tell lies. Don't you forget it." He looked like he wanted to hit her. "If you wasn't a lady," he muttered. "Think that about my brother."

"Now, honey, I wouldn't think anything bad about your brother. You know that. Now." She was cold with fear at turning her back on him, but she managed to walk slowly up the overgrown walk the way she had come, even to wave back at him. He had forgotten everything but friendship in the afternoon, and he waved back. She rolled under the barbed wire and made it to the other side of her car before she began to vomit.

I told him you was sick as a dog, ate something." Tabby stood in the doorway. She was mad. "I told him I brought you some breakfast up to you, you was so sick and tired, and he said you got to get dressed and come on down to the parlor anyhow. Men." She went away, disgusted.

Melinda made herself dress. It was too late to pretend, too late for anything but the trousers and shirts she had traveled to Richmond in. She had stuffed all the costumes, wrinkled, into her suitcase the night before.

She got up slowly. Her legs hardly held her. She had had diarrhea all night, wave after wave of it. Her face was glossy white when she tried to wash it and brush her teeth. She didn't ask or care who was waiting for her. She had already done everything she had to the night before, between bouts of sickness. She had called Boodie's house, and when Elsworth answered she said, "Now, you get Boodie to the phone for me, Elsworth, or I'm coming down there." He didn't say a word. She could hear his footsteps, but not a word.

"Boodie, you come up here tomorrow," she said.

"I don't have any excuse—" Boodie started to say, and Melinda cut her off.

"You don't need an excuse. Just get the hell in your car and get the hell up here."

Now Melinda leaned against the wall for a minute to let a surge of fury and diarrhea roll through her, and then she was ready to go downstairs and get rid of whoever it was who was being so insistent.

They were all as still as statues. Elsworth had lit a cigarette and then put it out, not all the way, because a tiny ribbon of smoke was rising in the dead air. She didn't question why he was there, and she didn't know or care why the other men were with him. One of them was the man she had spoken to in the FBI office.

He said—and his voice was soft, as if he didn't want to disturb the smoke and the stillness—"I called your family last night to come up here. I wanted them to hear this."

"No. I called them," she heard herself say, but she was only somebody in the room, somebody they were treating as if she were sick or very young or had done something wrong and was sorry about it, that kind of uneasy gentleness. Even Boodie.

"Why, honey, you look just awful. Have you caught something?" She hugged Melinda.

Melinda managed to shake her head. She took out her handkerchief and wiped her hairline, even though it was cool in the room from the air conditioning, which hummed between their voices.

There was another sound, faint, faraway. Tabby had started the vacuum cleaner upstairs. Melinda concentrated on the vacuum cleaner. She didn't know why. She had meant to be strong with Boodie, but the men were there and she didn't know how to start.

The FBI man said, "Lady Dunston . . ." He knew that name. "Lady Dunston, we have had a complaint about you from Mr. LeClaire. Now, you shouldn't have gone out there, you know that, don't you?"

She was as still as the smoke.

"He said you upset his young brother. He said the boy is very nervous and they have to be careful with him. They don't even let him go to school. He said the boy makes up things, and he called us and told us he wanted you to answer for why you came out there."

"You know why I went out there." It was all too late.

"Now, I want you to listen. That poor woman, Mrs. LeClaire, has had enough heartache with that boy without you going out there and upsetting him."

The man was getting angry. She didn't know why. Nobody else was. They were all poised in the stillness, trying not to disturb it, trying not to face the next minute, ever.

"I ran a check on you. We"—the imperial *we* again—"know all about you." He actually ticked her life off on his young, smooth fingers. "We know you went to Spain in the Communist war there." She watched the second finger. "We know you were married to a radical member of the Labour Party in England who was one of the planners of the National Health. We know that you took part in politics in England. We still can't find out why you didn't lose your citizenship when you went to Spain. The law specifically says you should. All we know is that it was so-called humanitarian, and a lot of people hid behind that. We don't have any evidence that you were a member of the Communist Party, but we know you were a fellow traveler and a premature anti-Fascist."

He actually used the words. She hadn't heard them in years, since the McCarthy hearings had turned them into a sick joke. She wanted to laugh, but she was afraid it would turn into hysterics, and besides, she didn't want to disturb the tiny ribbon of smoke.

"We want to know if you have connections down here with the people who are causing this trouble."

He had gone through the fingers of his left hand, so she supposed that as far as he was concerned, that was the end of her life.

"Now, we made a thorough search of Mr. LeClaire's property, with his help. He hid nothing from us. He is a law-abiding man, a member of the White Citizens' Council, of course. Most of the community leaders are down here. Now get this straight. The FBI is down here to uphold the law, and that is the law of trespass, along with the rest. We watch troublemakers on both sides of this mess. We sent our findings about your cousin to Washington to see if they considered it a federal case. We do that with every complaint, including yours. There is no reason for an indictment. There is no evidence. There is no name."

Finally Melinda spoke. "Why don't you shut the hell up?" It was, she remembered for years, one of the proudest moments of her life.

But he hardly listened. He had turned and was concentrating on Boodie. His voice softened. "We really have tried, Mrs. Percival, but the boy had a bad record. I wanted you all together here to tell you that we know he is dead. That's all we know. A little silver cross that belonged to him was found lying in the road." He held her hand and dropped the cross into it and then, very gently, closed it. "I'm so sorry," he added.

"What road?" Melinda demanded.

"That is none of your business. Somebody brought it in and told us the boy was dead. He wouldn't say what happened, and he swore he had nothing to do with it. We have tried. We dropped the case. There are so many. We can't prosecute them all."

Boodie's face sank in as if she had died, and then filled out again, and she said, calmer than Melinda had ever heard her, "Oh yes, I knew he was dead. But I didn't know what to do." She turned to Melinda and smiled. The cross was still gripped in her fist.

Melinda said to Elsworth, "Crush that cigarette. It's making me sick again."

She went over to Boodie and held her in her arms. "Listen, Boodie, you listen to me," she said, so that the others could hear. "Jakey was the kind of lonesome, intelligent boy who would have made a fine man. Don't ever forget that. He died for what he knew was right, just as surely as anybody dies in a war. You put a gold star in your window and you be proud of him. If you can't agree with what he stood for, at least be proud."

They stood for a long time, caught together in the stillness. None of the men moved.

The FBI man—she never remembered that he had a name—said, "Mrs. Percival, I want to convey our deepest sympathy."

Boodie looked at them as if they were strangers, all of them. "I think," she said, "we can have a memorial service for Jakey like they had for the man that drowned in the Mississippi River and they never found his body. Don't you think that would be appropriate, Melinda? You stay down here, and we'll do that."

"I'm sorry, ma'am," the man interrupted, "she can't stay here. We've heard of threats because she has been barging in where she wasn't welcome." He looked at Melinda. "You know what happened to that woman from Chicago who went to Selma, where she wasn't welcome. I'm going to wait right here until you are packed, and then I have been ordered to escort you to the road to Atlanta. It's a main road, and it's safe."

Melinda was sure that the stillness could be felt, like rain or sunlight.

Then Boodie said, "I'm sorry," and Elsworth didn't say a word. But he looked as though he had lost his blood.

The FBI man did follow her, for nearly a hundred miles out of Jackson. She didn't stop until she got to Richmond at four-thirty in the morning and she went to a motel to wait for her flight. Her only thought was to turn in the Buick and get to Albany, where Aiken would meet her, and they could drive on the safe road, the River Road, to her safe house, where she and Aiken could mourn.

Whenever Melinda thought of the house in New York State, she could feel again the sweet relief of going home, when she had turned into the River Road, which went past the fine barns and the leftover mansions glimpsed through the trees. In the fall of 1968, the leaves along the road were brighter—red and yellow and colors that reminded her of melons and terra-cotta—than she had ever seen them. They floated down on the little graveyard by the church beyond her house, and the world was all its colors and her house barn red.

She ought to have seen clouds gathering. She thought they must have begun in the room in Magnolia House, when the man had counted out her life on his fingertips.

There were some things that belonged together, as if all through the years, they had happened at the same time, in the green room in 1964, on the night that Aiken had told her about the church, and, in August 1968, when she watched Italian television in the green room in Italy. A Czech boy ran out and kicked a Russian tank, a gesture so impotent in the short run, so powerful in the long run. Children were beaten by police in Chicago at the Democratic convention. All the same day, all the same news broadcast. These images and so many others met in her own mind, all through the years.

In the weeks before the 1968 election, students at Charles Wesley were warned not to go along the roads at night, because several of them had been hit with rocks thrown from passing cars. Strangers drove cars around her parking circle and honked at three in the morning. She reported it. When somebody came from the state police, he grinned at her with a "little lady" grin and said it must have been kids. There had been anonymous telephone calls, which made her feel naked and exposed. A man at a party who was acting drunk said he belonged to a club of state cops who liked to beat people who liked to be beaten and did she like to be beaten? The only thing she could think to say was, "Not really, thank you."

She had refused to be warned. She didn't put the incidents together until the man came to the door, and then she knew, and there was not a soul in the winter of 1968 who she could tell who would believe her, except the children, who had already been there. They had marched. They had been jailed. They had marched again.

Had that been the destruction of her house? For four years Aiken and his friends had been happy there. It became a haven for them all. She remembered going to the door and seeing one of her children—she called them that to herself—standing there swollen up like a poisoned pup, and she said, as stern as her grandmother, shaking her finger the same way, "If I've told you once, I've told you a thousand times not to go to demonstrations. You *know* you're allergic to tear gas." She had put the child, a little round-faced poet of a girl, to bed, and kept her there until the swelling went down.

It had been a safe house for them all, for the times they had to hide, for the times they had to rest, for the sacred hour on Sunday evening when they came in droves to watch *Mission Impossible.* She must have made a cotton field of popcorn on those evenings.

It had been a happy house, but happiness was so fragile by the fall of '68. It was the time of the first hate election she had known in her lifetime. It was a year of hatred, the year that Johnson was hated out of the White House by both sides—he who had done so much more for the South than anyone before him—hatred of "liberals," a pejorative term that was beginning to replace "Communists," hatred of the antiwar protesters, hatred of the soldiers who had had no choice, but above all hatred of the man who was elected in November. Melinda remembered crying with shame.

On a Sunday afternoon in December, the snow was a blanket of new clean whiteness as it fell and the wind blew it into drifts. She hadn't heard a car. The doorbell rang when she wasn't expecting anybody, and a nice-looking man, a young man with good manners who was going to be fat later, was standing there bundled to his eyes against the cold. He stomped snow onto the hall rug and beat his arms around his chest to show how cold he was, and said, "I had to come and meet you. I've heard so much about you, Lady Dunston. I was visiting friends and decided just to drop by. I hope you don't mind."

He walked into the green room and shed his coat and put his hands to the fire. She followed him. He was still smiling. "I'm in the embassy in Rome. I thought I would come and offer you any help when you are in Italy." He didn't tell her his name.

"That is kind," she said. "Would you like a drink?"

"Now that is nice of you. Scotch." He sat down in the green room, in the place where Aiken always sat. He had spread himself in a parody of Sunday afternoon coziness when she came back with the drink. She knew when she handed it to him that he was going to say, "That hits the spot." He did, and went on, "You know, people like you, who are well known and who live abroad so much, are like ambassadors." It made her laugh.

"I'm not an ambassador to anything," she said. "I just have a house on an island—"

He couldn't stop smiling. "Oh, we know all

about that." The imperial *we* made her shiver. "We keep tabs on all our distinguished Americans. For their own protection."

She laughed again. "I'm not distinguished, I just live there in the summer."

"Well, now." He didn't need to use his fingers, as the FBI man had. He was urbane. He smiled most of the way through the interrogation, which he called conversation.

"For instance, if you went to a dinner party in Rome, and somebody asked you what you thought about the Vietnam War, what would you say?"

She looked beyond him at the graveyard. The penny, as Tye would have said, had dropped.

"Well, now, let me see. I would say what I say here—that it is the murder of young men for political reasons that are invalid, that it is destroying a country, that it destroyed a good president and replaced him with a . . ." She didn't know the man well enough to use her favorite words for Nixon.

She got up with the Southern politeness of pure anger and said, "Will you excuse me? I have an appointment." Her elaborate politeness was crushing. "I'm so afraid I will have to ask you to leave." Tye had said that when she sounded that way it was time to batten down the hatches, but the man was oblivious. He didn't even move.

"Not many Americans," he settled deeper into the sofa and his drink, as if she hadn't said a word, "have Swiss bank accounts."

She stood with her fists by her sides, looking down at the fire, which was making the room so beautiful in winter. She thought that she was going to be sick, right in front of him. She thought that if she was, she would barf right over his highly polished black shoes and his nasty clocked black socks. There was no sound but the hiss of the fire. She hoped it was hissing at him.

She heard him get up behind her. "Well, I see you don't want much help from the embassy. Sorry I bothered you."

She was freezing, standing so close to her fire. She wanted to protect it from him. They couldn't hurt her house in Italy. There was a "they"—yes, Virginia, there is a "they," yes, Virginia, she told the fire. It brought out fury like vomit.

"My aunt left the money to me in a Swiss account because she said the world was going to hell in a handcart and that if brutes could take over in Italy and Germany and Spain and Russia, they could take over anyplace else but in Switzerland, because the Swiss loved money too much to let it happen. She did not get the money from drugs or Communists or what you people call 'flaming liberals.' She got it, as she said, honestly on her back by marrying three very nice American aristocrats, Lord Sewing Machine, Lord Baking Soda, and Lord Plastic Wrap."

"Oh, yes." He sat down again; his voice hadn't even changed. "I believe you made deeds of gift to your adopted son and your adopted daughter." He made the word *adopted* sound like it was in quotes. "At least, that's what they tell me. That was a nice thing to do. After all, your adopted son was only adopted when he was fully grown. I gather he spends a lot of time here."

"I adopted Aiken Armistead so that he could go to school without working and so if I died before he finished Yale Law School he wouldn't be hounded by my family—my blood family, not my real family. As you no doubt know"—anger was flooding her words—"they are Southerners, and Aiken is black, and Southerners love money so much they don't mention it in polite conversation, like the name of God in some religions. That money was the trust my father left me." She started to cry, but she hardly knew it. "I never used the money except to pay for a motor mechanics course and learn to type and buy half an ambulance for Spain, but then, you know all about that, I'm sure. And like Pudd'nhead Wilson's dog, my half got blown up."

She did turn toward him then. "I gave the deeds of gift to my children because my father killed himself to leave the money to me and my mother, and when she died last year I didn't want to touch it. To me it was blood money. But Aiken was a victim of where he was born and what color he was, and Maria was a victim of the same kind of people in Spain. They killed her father. She has been my daughter since she was seven." She was sobbing.

The man looked young and embarrassed. She could see that through her tears. He got up and set his glass down carefully, so it wouldn't make any noise. "I'm sorry, ma'am," he said at the door. He had been brought up politely too. "It's my job."

"Well, get another goddamn job." She heard

him shut the door quietly, as if he were leaving a sickroom.

She went around the room, feeling under the bookshelves, behind the sofa, under the table behind it for any bug he might have planted, and she sobbed all the time, saying, "I'm not doing this. This isn't happening. I'm American. This doesn't happen to Americans."

She heard the roar of his engine in the driveway. He was stuck in the snow. She locked her front and back doors and went slowly upstairs, ignoring the doorbell. She lay on her bed and listened to the wheels grind and the engine grumble and die and grumble again. Winter made a farce of the whole thing. She drifted off to sleep, and when she woke up in the early evening, when it was already dark, the fire was dead and the car had gone.

She called Aiken and Maria and reminded them that she had said once that if Nixon were elected she was going to leave the country, and she had decided to do it. Maria was in Spain and couldn't hear her very well.

"I'm finishing the term here, and then I am selling this house and coming over at Christmas," Melinda yelled across the turbulent Atlantic.

Maria caught some of it. "That's wonderful," she said. She sounded joyful. "You're coming for Christmas!" She also sounded sleepy. When Melinda hung up, she realized that it was one o'clock in the morning in Albastro.

When she called Aiken, she said, "I think my phone is bugged. It sounds funny."

He laughed. "So you just found out there wasn't no Sandy Claws."

"Don't be smart-aleck. I'm going to spend Christmas with Maria and then I'm going to stay in Italy. Nobody wants this silly house anymore, so I'm putting it on the market."

"You are?" He was surprised. "Why?"

"I don't want to stay here while Nixon is president and these things are going on in my own country." Aiken was laughing so hard that she interrupted: "Look, I'm telling it like it is," a phrase she had picked up from the children and didn't know she was using. She told him about the man and about going around the room looking for bugs. He took it all for granted.

"That's fine, man," he told her. "Now I can tell you what I am going to do. I am going to finish Yale Law School come hell or high water, and then I'm going to take it all back home and do a year at LSU so I can pass the Louisiana bar and set up as a civil rights lawyer. We left all those folks down there at the mercy of every white trash when they registered to vote. You remember *reddish* and *speck?* Well, I'm going back and stay with them and see that they get the speck."

"Oh, my God, Aiken, it's dangerous."

He was quiet for a minute, and then he said, "You haven't seen it for a while. Some way, some decency has begun to creep back. You know that? The decent people who were always there are getting less afraid to speak up. There is still hate there, but that is everyplace. You've just had a large dose of the cold-blooded kind. Down there the hate is passionate. At least they know your goddamn name and who your mama was!" He was suddenly furious. "Melinda, I don't like it up here. Everybody wants a little piece of me. I'm going to stick it out and then I'm going to go home and do the work of the Lord. I'm doing what Jakey wants me to do."

But laughter and joy were never far from him. She thought he might be in love. He could actually laugh, because none of what she had told him about the man was new to him.

"That's the man," he said. "That's Mr. Charlie. Did he come with one of those silent partners?"

"No, I wondered about that."

"Then he's CIA, not FBI. The FBI always come in pairs, like dice. I've been hearing that the CIA is trampling on the FBI's turf these days and they're all fighting with each other, dogs in a pit. You get on out of there."

The conversation was getting so calm that they could have been talking about plans for the week.

"You want to come to Spain for Christmas with me?"

"No, I think I'll go down and see my grandmam. She's getting mighty old and tired."

Melinda stood on the dock at Civitavecchia on the tenth of January in 1969 and let the wind and rain tug and buffet her. It felt good, a cleansing. The storm was so bad she couldn't see the faint hint of her island, the way she could in summer.

It was just out there. The lines were down on Isola Santa Corsara, so she couldn't even tell Pietro she was there.

She knew the storms. Three hours, they said, or three days. This one had already been two days and she had huddled in her favorite *albergo*, where they knew her and where it was warm, and read all the detective novels she had brought with her.

She knew she ought to be sad, but she wasn't. She was just there. She had made up her mind, looking not forward or back. The rain rushed at her face. She didn't even talk to Tye.

When she finally got to the island, it looked as if the whole village were waiting on the dock. The house was warm; the refectory–living room was suffused with the light of the fire. The kerosene lamps had been lit for her coming, and they made lovely patterns. Marcella said that the electricity had been out for a week. She filled the kitchen with the scents of good things to feed Melinda, as if she were home on leave from something.

When she told them about what had happened, Pietro said he wasn't surprised. It had been like that once in Italy—the listening, the prying. But it had been much worse in Italy; they had punished people by feeding them castor oil.

But when Melinda's friends came from England and she tried to tell them, even Cotty, who always looked for conspiracy everywhere, said, "Oh, you must be joking! In America!"

Years later, she remembered that there was a blank beyond sorrow or happiness, a waiting, and she had been in it on the dock in Civitavecchia, all that time ago, in 1969, nearly a third of her life ago. She hadn't intended to stay so long. But then, she hadn't intended much of anything at the time.

Book Six

Italy • April 9, 1993

Santa Corsara

When the sound of the car receded into the distance, Melinda sneaked out of bed. She always did, as soon as she was alone. She was so used to the time it would take Pietro that she could tick it off on her fingers: ten minutes to the dock, an hour in the boat from Isola Santa Corsara to the mainland, a minimum of half an hour for fidgets and flutters and missed connections, an hour back to the dock, and ten minutes back to the house.

She felt like she had been let out of a cage instead of just sneaking out of bed. Sneaking out of her own bed! No wonder people who hadn't been there and didn't know any better called it a second childhood. It wasn't yourself. It was the way you were treated, with the best disgusting will in the world. She remembered to put her feet down gently.

It was eleven o'clock on the morning of April 9, and Maria and Aiken were coming, and she had a lot to do. She had until noon, when Marcella would come to give her lunch, or begin those noises, *slam bang tinkle burble;* she knew them all, like clock chimes in the kitchen. It usually took Marcella a while, too, a real *pranzo! Mangia, mangia!*

Melinda had a strong sense that if she didn't go through the rooms she loved and touch everything and look at it, not just glance past it, taking it for granted, it would all die from not being noticed, not being laughed with, not being cared for anymore, as if it had all been deserted of affection and human breathing. She didn't want the rooms to be old-people rooms, the way they smelled and looked: too many things lying around and forgotten, too many prescription bottles, a mixture of English Friar's Balsam, which she never could get out of the house until the doors and windows could be opened in the spring, and her body, her old tired winter body, the smell of old strong pee, which Marcella swore she couldn't smell but Melinda could.

She and Marcella had argued for several years about when spring actually came to the island. Marcella said it came later for old people. She loved the way Marcella said "old people"—*anziani*, ancient, like the stones of Roman walls, instead of senior citizen, gray panther, all that crap. It was mid-April, and Marcella said the weather wasn't good for old bones. Marcella was the one who was too old. She was all of sixty-five. Melinda grinned.

"Old old old old old!" she told her funny feet.

She knew that if she didn't spray and squirt and look and put away, the rooms would upset Maria and Aiken when they arrived. They had insisted on coming all that way, right in the middle of terms and cases and children and their whole world flowing forward, when hers tended, if she didn't watch herself, to flop backward. She wanted joy.

She slipped into a soft woolly running suit that she had found at Bloomingdale's on her last visit. She liked the red color and the feel so much that when it had to be washed, she stayed in bed until it was dry, the way the seventeenth-century cavaliers in England had done when the one fancy shirt they could afford had had to be stripped off, once or twice a year, and taken to the river.

Maria had brought her a caftan from Istanbul, a beautiful fall of dark rose silk and gold embroidery, but she thought she would wait until they were almost there to put it on. It was so long that she was afraid of stumbling and not being able to get up, or breaking something, like the stupid hip she broke when she fell on the terrace and had to lie there for half an hour until Pietro came up from the garden, and then she was taken to the hospital, where the nuns hovered. At first she hadn't known whether they were shadows or nuns, and then they had begun to have faces and names. She swore then that she would always carry a detective novel in her pocket so that if she fell again, she would have something to read until she was found.

She rested for a minute on the side of her single Napoleon bed in the green room. She had moved out of the big bedroom when Roger died. She didn't want to stay rattling around with—what was it he always said?—nobody to nudge, and she wanted to be where the television was, and she certainly didn't want to seem "bedridden" half the time. She could see her bed, which tipped up at both ends, riding her like a cowboy. She hauled off the bedclothes and put them in the bottom of the cupboard under the niche where the marble bust was, lit up in the evening as beautifully as only Roger could do it. She always had to strip the bed herself because she had a running battle with Marcella over staying in it. The bed's silky wood shone in the sunlight that sparkled off the surface of the sea; its velvet surface was as dark a green as the walls.

The bed really did pass as a sofa when it was not made and she sat on it, or reclined, like Madame Recamier, to watch the television. The sofa—bed, whatever it was at whatever time of day—and the television were the only two new things that she had put in her green room. For the rest—the books, the marble head, the goosed lion, the painting of the hog named Caesar, all the bits and pieces that had gone from England to New York State and then to Italy—her cozy was the way it had always been. Even the silly lions that held up the tables against the wall and the soft chair she couldn't use any longer were there.

She stood for a minute at the medieval window, waiting until her feet were used to holding her. She watched the olive trees and her garden and, beyond the sloping hillside, which was evergreen, the wine-dark water of what Roger had called the Tyrrhenian Sea and everybody else called the Med. The flowers in the boxes that lined the terrace wall were already in bloom.

She let her cane help her into her bathroom. She was annoyed that her hair stood up on end, and she washed her face and combed her hair and put a little bit of pencil on her eyebrows. She told herself it wasn't vanity, not really; it was to see the things, for God's sake. They had gone from brown to white and made her look surprised when she had long since stopped being surprised at almost anything.

She stood back and looked at herself critically. "What am I doing in this ridiculous old body?" she asked aloud. Her ridiculous body that her doctor said—what was the stupid phrase?—didn't have long, as if she had rented it and the lease was up. She often saw through that old woman to what she was and had always been inside herself, but what she saw in the bathroom mirror was a little round withered apple of a face, her disguise and the container for her soul—a distinction sometimes, as when she was a child, when she and Toto called themselves "me, myself, and I." *Me* was the box, the container, grown old and worn; *myself* was the image *I* could see if *I* looked beyond *me* into the mirror, and it flickered and changed, but there was no use letting it do that when she hadn't much time, so *I*, the dependable, the never-changing, had to take over and stop her lollygagging, and she spoke aloud to the image in the mirror.

"I, dearie, am eighty-two years old, and I am a little old lady, or at least I live in a little old lady's body, and I am soon going to die, yes, die, and shed all this, they tell me, and then me and myself will be gone, and really God only knows what will happen to I." She wasn't talking to herself, like gaga people did. It was *I* talking to *myself* and *me,* a conversation.

It didn't scare her, except in moments when, like a train rushing full-speed through the house, she knew that she was being flung toward being dead. But then, she shrugged to herself in the mirror, she always had been flying toward it, but it was only as she got older that she had known that, and not even then, except when the rushing caught her unawares. What she knew then was not easy depression or sadness or even fear. It was way beyond that, something vital, vital as in having a life of its own, and in it she was totally alone—what was it?—on the edge of the wide world.

She wandered into the refectory–living room, which needed the most looking at, because she used it only when friends and family were there. It was too big, too grand. It had been designed for lots of people—the long sofa, the lamps, the piano, the great fireplace which Marcella kept so spotless, the flowers she put on the refectory table every day. The room, as it always had, waited for company. It had been the large side of a cloister or a great court; nobody could decide which. Roger had said it was earlier than that. He always said things were earlier than that, but she had stopped asking earlier than what a long time ago. Roger could read walls like other people read the newspaper, as Tandy had once done.

Tandy. Melinda smiled again, and thanked God that at least if she had lost her body, she hadn't lost her marbles, as so many did. Memory had grown stronger with the years, bright and sure and polished, almost too much memory. Sometimes it kept her awake at night, delayed before sleep in places she thought she had long since forgotten.

Tandy was as real to her as if he stood in the room running his hand along the stone frames of the floor-to-ceiling windows, which had been arches when Aunt Maymay and the last husband had found the house in 1927. It had been a ruin, and the people on the island had been nearly forgotten, half starved in the winter. There had not even been a Fascist headquarters on Santa Corsara, and only one picture of Il Duce, above the mailbox outside the only shop, and one policeman, who had long since been seduced by a widow in the town and had almost forgotten why he had been exiled there, accused of "anti-Fascist attitudes." He had helped load Aunt Maymay's yacht when she took her friends to Corsica. The mailboat had come once a week.

All of that was in Aunt Maymay's long, dashing, rambling letter to her, which waited in the small desk in the green room. Pietro said that Aunt Maymay had died right there on the Napoleon bed. Marcella said that she could see her sometimes out of the corner of her eye, and hear the swishing of the silk robes she had worn for years, and Melinda told Marcella not to be silly, but sometimes she had to tell herself that the slight movement was caused by the wind from the sea.

The letter had told Melinda exactly why she had been left the house and the money to run it—things, Aunt Maymay wrote, that couldn't be put in a legal will. It had obviously taken days to write. It was twenty pages long, starting neatly with each day and then getting more and more scrawled and illegible as Aunt Maymay got tired and had to stop. It was a history of the island, a history of Aunt Maymay, with instructions that hadn't been necessary until Melinda too got old, and—what was it Maymay had written?—"decreput." Much of the letter was misspelled, both in English and in Italian.

> My dear child,
> I haven't seen you since you were little, but I know, from family disapproval, what you have been doing. I am a very old woman now. I can't believe it, because I feel as young or as alive, neither young nor old, as ever. But I am going to die, here in *mi paradiso terrestre,* so near to *mi paradiso a dispetto dei santi,* at least that is where they tell me I will go, but they don't know any better than I do, which is not at all. You are the only one in my blood family that I have any respect for. Everybody needs a castle where they can draw up the drawbridge and rest, even if it is only one room. So I want you to have it, and the money to run it. I don't trust your mother with money. She is mean, she always has been. I bet she was the kind of child who could eat candy without rattling the bag.

Melinda and Tye had laughed at that, the first time they had read it, in front of the fire in London so long ago. Aunt Maymay was still a Southerner, from what Tye called the land of metaphors.

So this comes to you with two strings. Pietro's grandfather and father, and now Pietro and Marcella, have looked after me and the house for over twenty years. They have all had their children and their grandchildren in the farmhouse that is on the property. I want you to keep them always. People here are tied to the land as we are in the South. I think it is the one thing I miss in the South, the land, and a core of decent people. Which brings me to the second. When you are ready to die . . .

Melinda had grown to love the phrase "ready to die," as she most certainly was, except in those moments of icy cold that passed so quickly. Aunt Maymay, long gone and knowing the rushing train too, had reached out from that edge and touched her, and used the only word that could be used when you got there and all the metaphors seemed trivial.

. . . please let it go to decent liberal people. I don't mean liberal only as political. I mean it as *l'arte del gesto,* openhanded open arms open heart

and after that there were tears on the page, long dried. "You, my dear, are the only person in my family who is not *senza fegato.*" Melinda and Tye had translated that as "gutless." "When I heard that you had gone to Spain, I said to Clint, that girl is a chip off my block, and I bet her mother loathes it." Clint was the last millionaire she had married, the one she really liked best, she said.

Melinda treasured the letter more and more as the years passed. She treasured too what Pietro told her in those times when Aunt Maymay's life came out bit by bit as they worked together in the garden. She honored the fact that Aunt Maymay hadn't mentioned any of it in the letter.

Pietro's father had been the skipper of her yacht in the thirties. She had entertained like a madwoman. Nobody knew why except Pietro's father and Pietro and the policeman and the rest of the crew, who were all Pietro's cousins. She had given house parties over and over, always with a dashing Fascist officer who she bragged was "close to Il Duce," who she let the others think was her lover. During the house parties, filled always with enough famous people to be safe from Mussolini and anyone else who might interfere, she would suggest lightly that they go on the small yacht to Corsica overnight and have dinner in her favorite restaurant in Bonifacio. Going to Corsica had been part of her fame as a hostess. Her guests drank and flirted and slept with each other on the crossing. They invaded the quiet restaurant on the waterfront like barbarians from the sea. While they drank and ate and talked, Pietro said, the men and women in the hold were smuggled ashore for the next lap of their underground railroad journey out of Fascist Italy.

Nobody ever knew, not the ones who were cavorting on the upper decks, not the inevitable Fascist officer.

The last part of the letter had always made Melinda laugh. "The money I am leaving you is clean money. I made it on my back, with three lovely husbands. Two of them died and one of them went off someplace. We lost our taste for each other. But I have been happy here. Be happy and keep this house happy. It has been a safe house for a long time."

When Tye read the letter, he said Aunt Maymay made the island of the pirates sound like the island of Iona, where love and faith were kept alive through the dark times.

Melinda and Tye had walked into the house, so long ago, and yesterday. They had stood together looking out to sea through an arched window, holding hands, forty years ago. Sometimes she thought of it as a day. The house was a place where time didn't pass anyway.

They had left it almost the way they had found it. The ceiling of the room was vaulted, and the walls, which Roger said had once been stone, ecclesiastic and cold where the monks murmured at their prayers before their food, had been covered with plaster, a pure white that made the dark beams stand out like the ribs of some ancient animal. That had always reminded her of Spain.

One whole wall, which looked out to sea, was made of the glassed-in cloister arches, so that at eleven o'clock the sun lifted the room and made the colors of the thick Turkey carpet glow. That day so long ago, Marcella had put a great bouquet of flowers to scent the room on the black refectory table at the end by the kitchen. She had put flowers there again for Maria and Aiken, early lilac that Melinda and Roger had planted in a cup of the hills, away from the sea wind.

It had been an old woman's room then, with too many books, half-finished embroidery, a half-read detective novel, too many photographs on the piano—Aunt Maymay with Noel Coward, Aunt Maymay with Coco Chanel, Aunt Maymay with King Alfonso of Spain, Aunt Maymay with Cecil Beaton, Aunt Maymay getting older and thinner with people they ought to have recognized and didn't, all of them, or most of them, on the terrace, squinting at the sun, grinning, smiling, holiday people who had been swept away by war and time. How fragile it had all been.

They had found Aunt Maymay, years of Aunt Maymay, in a long closet the size of a small room. They counted three hundred dresses, all the way back to a glorious presentation gown, ivory satin with pearls, labeled "1899, Worth." Even Melinda, as small as she was, couldn't fasten the waist. The last dress Aunt Maymay must have bought, a New Look Christian Dior with a huge skirt, had never been worn. It had been too late.

Aunt Maymay had thrown nothing away. She had not neglected a single garment, not even the boxes of hats and underwear, some of it like the lacy silk step-ins that Melinda remembered Essie prancing around in over her clothes in Kentucky. Tye and Melinda had taken the whole collection back to London and given it to the Victoria and Albert Museum in Aunt Maymay's name.

Melinda had kept one picture of her, taken in England during her first marriage. She looked almost childlike, and she never had been that; at least, that was what Boodie always said. Melinda hung it in the place of honor on the wall behind the piano. The picture was faintly tinted: Aunt Maymay young, Aunt Maymay alluring, as she had been taught, glancing over her shoulder, smiling a little, as if she had a secret she was running away with, a great mass of auburn hair floating above her head. It had been taken in the days when women were famous beauties.

Where Aunt Maymay's frenetic life had been spread across the piano, Melinda had put, through the years, her own life, her own rogues gallery, so that when the wind blew and the rain tried to crash through the great windows in winter, she was never alone. She walked over and leaned on the piano to look at the family she had made, to bring the photographs alive again for Maria and Aiken. She lifted them one by one, breathing on them and polishing the glass. There was Maria as a serious child, with Nella grinning beside her; Maria as a Ph.D. in that wonderful drag from Cambridge, not the one in England but the one in Boston; Maria as a beautiful woman ten years later, on the day her first book, the book about the something-cephalic heads, was published; Maria with the last book, the one that had taken thirty-five patient, silent years, the history of a town under Franco, the hidden people, the informers, the defeated and the waiting.

There she was with her first baby, her second

baby, her husband, Manuelo. Concepción, who had become the mother superior of the convent, stood in front of the house in Albastro that she had been born in. Concepción's face still looked young, as nuns' faces did, young and worn and frighteningly calm with all that was behind it. She stood beside Maria's daughter, who looked like a replica of Maria at seven. They had named her Melinda. Another Melinda. There was eight-year-old Federico cavorting in front of the convent door. His pointed ears and grinning face made him look like a handsome imp, one of the imps that had looked down on Melinda in the convent at Albastro so long ago.

Melinda ran her hand over the picture to feel beyond it, the stones, the vines, the tiles that she had once cleaned in the convent, and said to Tye, "Oh, my dear, if you had lived to see people in Spain who are no longer afraid, old men who have finally won, after all the years of Franco. They have seen their grandchildren swinging along together, as untrammeled as we were. When I went back the last time, I passed a *posada* and I heard the old men laughing. Things have gotten better everywhere, Tye." And then she argued, "They have! They have!" She sounded like a child in the dark.

She talked to Tye more and more as they got closer to meeting—or not meeting; she wouldn't ever fool herself about that. Maybe what you did was live in somebody's mind after you were dead, like Tye did in hers. Maybe you didn't meet in heaven, as they said you did, or in hell. She knew several people who she was sure would go there, and she tried to repent of anything she could remember, even little things, so she wouldn't have to be with them. They bored and angered her. She had no intention of spending eternity with people she wouldn't have in her house.

The thought made her laughter ring out into the tendrils of sunlight that slipped across the floor and lit the room from within. Her grandmother had said that if you had to meet all your relatives in heaven, she was damned if she wanted to go there. They had bored her in life and she didn't want them to bore her in the great beyond.

Melinda turned to Aiken's photographs. There was Aiken as she had first seen him, tall, as slim as a reed, hiding whatever fear he carried in himself, a proud boy turning into a proud man. There was Aiken graduating from Yale Law School; Aiken after he had passed his bar exam in Louisiana; Aiken with Luella and the children, first one, then two, then three; Aiken growing, not fat, but into more of a man, growing solid, fifty pounds more of Aiken than the scared proud boy who had turned up at her door.

She had gone through the years of changes in the South with Aiken and his family. There was still so much to do. They had learned to take for granted the fact that they could have dinner together in Atlanta's best restaurant, but sometimes young black men still looked at the ground when they passed her, even though she was walking with her grandchildren, and the gesture broke her heart. But she put the last picture of them back after she had dusted it with her handkerchief. It was not heartbreak, it was reality, and the day her heart refused to creak and break a little was the day she wanted to be dead.

She picked up the picture of Jakey looking myopic and lost in the freedom-school room, his glasses making him look as if he had just waked up and was surprised at what he saw. But then, he always had looked like that, and been like that—surprised. Aiken had given it to her a long time ago.

There were Missus and Grace in 1954, the year Grace died. They were laughing. She picked up her favorite picture of Roger—dear Roger on a camel in front of the Great Pyramid of Giza. Penny and Cotty leaned on the balustrade of the terrace. Melinda could still hear Cotty raging up and down in the summer, remaking the world in some image of his hopeful boyhood; he was so young. Even now, shaggy and with his white hair flying, he was so young.

Melinda had searched for years for the picture of Johnny Bradford she knew she had somewhere, but she had never found it. She tried and failed to remember what he looked like.

She had saved Tye for last, Tye of course in the Irish fisherman's sweater she couldn't steal away from him even to have cleaned; Tye in Italy, stark naked in the pool, eating a *gelato;* Tye asleep on the chaise longue she had kept on the terrace, which had been Aunt Maymay's; Tye in Africa, looking ten years younger than he was, full of joy, smiling when he didn't know she was taking the picture. They were on safari in a lorry, and he was watching some animal. She picked up Tye with Desmond in front of the house in St.

Michael's Square. Tye was so deep within her that she needed none of the pictures.

On the wall above a huge inlaid marble table that Aunt Maymay had left she had hung what Roger called his life's work. It hadn't been, but he had always been amused at himself. Most people thought it was an abstract drawing in blue and red and black, but it wasn't. It was the product of years of what Roger called his poking and prying.

The black lines were the house as it was still: the living room, the library, the kitchen, the terrace, the stretch of rooms all around the inner courtyard, all in scale, all so clear that Melinda sometimes felt that she could walk through the map. For the walls that still existed of the monastery and the earliest building he had found, he had used lines; for the hints and fragments, dots. The blue lines were the lines of the monastery he had uncovered, followed, reconstructed, so that it was much bigger than the house. He had found below what had been for years a barn, the outbuildings, and the ruins of a chapel. These were scattered lines, as if he had seen the monastery exploding with time. Then, sometimes following the monastery walls, sometimes veering away, almost in a star pattern, were the red lines and dots, larger than both the others, the dents in the ground, the fallen stones, the faint hillocks that the sun brought out in shadow at twilight, all the ghost lines of the Phoenician stronghold that Roger swore was there before even the Greeks. He said he had seen stones like them, perfectly cut, so fitted that they made even the walls of Troy and Mycenae and the Hittite city walls look crude.

The red dots were scattered all around the house and the monastery; they looked like they had fallen there in a pattern of their own. All that was left of what he had identified was a stone bench and part of the retaining wall, where the courtyard was set against the hillside. The bench was, for her, a better reminder of Roger than all the memories of what he had said; how he had sat, lounged rather, with his long, easy Southern body draped over whatever he landed on, a thin, graceful man.

At last the pictures were all alive again for herself and Aiken and Maria, and she was tired. She lay on the velvet sofa, which was so long that her feet only reached to the center of it. She picked up a pillow with a needlepoint unicorn from the Bayeux tapestry on it and hugged it to the running suit and stared out of the great windows at the sea.

She looked at her watch and thought she must have dozed a little. It was almost noon. She scurried as fast as an eighty-two-year-old woman could into her rose caftan and back to her Napoleon boat bed so that she would be pretty and apple-cheeked, the way they liked to see her, when Aiken and Maria got there sometime in the afternoon.

Maria ran to the bed and held Melinda in her arms. Aiken stood and tried to grin, but he couldn't. He looked worried. He had turned into a serious man, but when he smiled with her, the old Aiken came out and danced.

Melinda gently pushed Maria away. "Come here, son. Give me my hug. Now you two go take a nap and get over jet lag. I have promised Marcella that I will stay in bed all day, and if everything is all right—I have ups and downs—I can get up and we can make dinner together."

"We don't need to rest. We met in Rome yesterday and came up together," Aiken told her, and he and Maria looked at each other.

"You've been conferring about me, haven't you?" Melinda smiled. "I knew you would. Don't look so stricken, darling." She held out her hand to Aiken so he would lean over and kiss her. She thought of what Tye would say—it's only dying—but that was not her language, so she said instead, "I just guv out."

It was the way it had always been at night on the terrace, where she had put the round table; she didn't like hierarchy at dinner. Through the years the original table had been replaced by bigger and bigger ones until there was room for at least twelve people, fourteen if they scrunched up. But there were only Melinda, Aiken, and Maria, and they argued as they always had, going to and fro, Aiken lighting the outdoor fire under the ancient grill in the fireplace, which cast a light over them when the night came. When the wind touched the flames, they seemed to make the table float and then settle again.

The three finally decided to sit where they could all see the fire and the night and the moonlight that flecked the sea beyond the trees. They could see it through the large stone arch that had been part of the cloister. Melinda loved it. She always had: the beeswax candles in their windbreak glass protectors, two feet high so people could see under and around them, glowing against the dark of night; the smell of the grilled meat that Marcella had marinated in herbs and wine; the cheese; the warm bread; the great majolica platter in the shape of a bright painted fish, piled with peaches and tiny melons that only Marcella knew how to ripen so early; honeydew and tomatoes from Capri; and the sound and scent of red wine pouring into glasses.

"Oh, Lord." Melinda sat back and sighed. "Three days ago, if anybody had told me I would feel this wonderful, I would have called them a liar. I'm thirty. No. I'm forty. I liked being forty. It was a wonderful time, wasn't it, Maria, in London with Tye then?" She was enjoying the evening as if she instead of Maria and Aiken had been away for a long time.

"I haven't done this since you were here last," she explained. "Trays in front of the television. Marcella won't let me come out here often at night this early in the year. Of course, as soon as she goes home I do what I want to."

She set her glass down. "Let me talk some more. I have a lot to say. I asked you to come by yourselves because I can't stand too many people around, for the first time in my life. I'm so sorry. Besides, I needed to talk to you alone. For some reason, part of which I knew and part I didn't, my bucket has come up full from the well several times. I've distributed all the rest except this house and the money to run it. I've left the house in London to Desmond and his family—after all, they've been there over thirty years. Maria, I've remembered Nella with some money I kept in England. You both have enough money so that if you are ill or anything else happens, you won't have to be beholden. That is the worst thing that can happen to a person. No, I guess having nobody to be beholden to is worse.

"Roger organized the co-op that most of the farmers on the island are part of. They make a decent living from the olive oil and the goat cheese. Roger took it to several fancy places, Fortnum's in London and some other places, so it is famous, which a cheese has to be, no matter how bad it smells. He put this island together, bless him, as what he called a 'paying proposition.' I get a share of the co-op profits because so much of the land is mine."

They were too still. They were being patient with her. She knew that there was little more to be said, but she insisted on hearing it herself, to get it straight in her own mind and let them hear.

"Anyway, when I divided most of the money between you when my mother died, it was because you both came from the receiving end of the whip and I came from the wielding end. The money my father left came from an obscene sacrifice to something that wasn't worth it. It has haunted my life. He thought it was love. That money came off the coal face. It isn't blood money to you, but it is to me. It always has been. I know I've told you this before, but I wanted to hear it again. Be sure . . ."

She was still for so long they both thought she had finished talking, but they all sat watching the candlelight, and the reflection of the fire in the red wine, and the tiny lights of fishing boats which were so far away they seemed to mingle with the low stars.

Then she said, "I always thought Tye was arrogant about money. He scorned it. I don't think that's right. I told him so. It isn't that you have it, it's what you do with it.

"I am so proud of you both. You have been such a worthy investment. That's what you were. An investment in time and life and love. No, I'm not being soppy. I'm telling the truth. I'm too old to mind being sentimental. Now, this is the only thing you don't already know. Nothing in my papers will surprise you except maybe this. I did it all by myself." She watched the tops of the olive trees, black against the moonlight.

"I never want anybody to argue about this house—it has been too precious. It was here at the time when I needed it most, and now, when the world is heaving and groaning and getting ready to be alive again after these awful frozen years, I'm old and decrepit and passe and redundant and I don't give a damn." She laughed, the easy laugh she had always had.

"Oh, what have I done with this house? I have made a foundation of the money in Switzerland.

I was never able to touch anything but the income, and Aunt Maymay left it in trust even to my heirs. She said she did it so that Pietro's family, who have been here so long, would never have to leave. I deeded the farm to them a long time ago. So I went to Switzerland, and I made a foundation. Each of you have the house for a month every year. That is all the time you have ever spent here anyway, all the time you could. For the rest of the time, I have left it in charge of the United Negro College Fund, which will make a committee, with both of you as members, so that young scholars and young writers and young painters can come here and live for a few months. Marcella and Pietro know about this. They will keep on running the house. I want you on the board of advisers so they won't send too many academics. I couldn't bear the thought of all that gloom."

She laughed at them and with them. "And I leave you Aunt Maymay's letter as a testament. She said it better than I ever could. *Arte del gesto,* openhanded, open arms, open heart."

And then, after looking out at the sea for a long, easy time, she said, "On such a night stood Dido with a willow in her hand and waft her love to Carthage." She was still again, holding Maria's hand. They were letting her have the night, she knew that, and she was patient with them and with herself in it.

"Oh, Lord," she finally said. "I've learned everything I know from the people I loved. You do that, whether you know it or not. Tye had a passion for Shakespeare, and he quoted him so often he gave me the habit. We read aloud." She patted Maria's hand. "You remember that." Their hands clasped again. "Now bear up, darlings. I want to go swimming."

"You can't do that!" Maria ordered.

"Let me tell you a secret. Every night since the first of March, after Marcella has taken care of me until I'm ready to scream, I have been slipping out of bed as soon as their lights are out, and I tiptoe down to the pool and I swim. Then I pour a glass of wine and try to catch the stars in it. It has kept me alive for a lot longer than medicine and care. So we will do it together tonight."

They took her hands, and nobody said anything. She could see Aiken's eyes glittering in the candlelight, and she squeezed his hand. "Oh, one thing more. I've cleared up all the papers I could. There's only that one box left. Mummy's box, you always called it, Maria. I just haven't had time to go through it. So much else had piled up. The legal papers are in the desk, in the drawer with Aunt Maymay's letter. Anyway, you both have copies of my will, and the deed for the foundation is in there, and the address of the bank in Switzerland."

Melinda was quiet for a minute and held her glass up to the candlelight again. "I love doing that. It's like a jewel," she said. She went on looking at the wineglass. They sat close together in the moonlight, quiet and drenched in the scents of wine and meat and night flowers.

Then they cleared the table. When there was really nothing left to do and it was time for bed, they all went swimming in the moonlight. Melinda swam smack into a frog in the pool, and the waves she made getting out shredded the light of the moon and threw it dancing across the water.

About the Author

Mary Lee Settle grew up in West Virginia and attended Sweet Briar College, which she left in the early years of World War II to enlist in the British Royal Air Force. Her was experiences formed the background for a memoir titled *All the Brave Promises.* After the war she stayed in England and masqueraded for a year as Mrs. Charles Palmer, "etiquette expert" for *Woman's Day.* Since that time she has traveled the world, always bringing far corners deeply into her fiction. She is the author of eleven previous novels, including the highly acclaimed five-novel series known collectively as *The Beulah Quintet* and *Blood Tie,* winner of the 1978 National Book Award for Fiction. She now lives with her husband in Charlottesville, Virginia.

About the Author

IF YOU HAVE ENJOYED READING THIS LARGE PRINT BOOK AND YOU WOULD LIKE MORE INFORMATION ON HOW TO ORDER A WHEELER LARGE PRINT BOOK, PLEASE WRITE TO: